CLINICAL
TRIAL

APRIL CHRISTOFFERSON

A TOM DOHERTY ASSOCIATES BOOK
NEW YORK

This is a work of fiction. All the characters and events portrayed in this novel are either fictitious or are used fictitiously.

CLINICAL TRIAL

This book is printed on acid-free paper.

A Forge Book
Published by Tom Doherty Associates, LLC
175 Fifth Avenue
New York, NY 10010

www.tor.com

Forge® is a registered trademark of Tom Doherty Associates, LLC.

Library of Congress Cataloging-in-Publication Data

Christofferson, April.
      Clinical trial / April Christofferson—1st ed.
         p. cm.
      "A Tom Doherty Associates book."
      ISBN 0-312-86899-5 (alk. paper)
         1. Women physicians—Fiction.   2. Viruses—Fiction.
3. Siksika Indians—Fiction.   4. Blackfeet Indian Reservation
(Mont.)—Fiction.   5. Montana—Fiction.   I. Title.
PS3553.H749 C57 2000
813'.54—dc21   00-031712

First Edition: October 2000

Printed in the United States of America

0   9   8   7   6   5   4   3   2   1

This book is dedicated to
Isabel, Jane, and Ruth,
for their courage, grace, and compassion,
And, of course,
Dad.

ACKNOWLEDGMENTS

Recently, I was standing, holding my horse while two veterinarians—my longstanding vet and another specialist he called in—examined her. After about ten minutes, the new vet turned to my regular vet and said (about me), "Does she always ask this many questions?" I realized then how many doctors, veterinarians, professional friends, and colleagues have patiently, thoughtfully, answered the never-ending questions I have plied them with over the years. Many of their answers have worked their way into my books, this one in particular. I'd like to thank Dr. Bill Schneble, Nancy Scheble, Dr. John Giesen, Dr. Dan Kennedy, Sally Teeters, Dr. Tina Ellenbogen, Dr. George Ihrke, Dr. Robert Lewis, and Joe Skovron.

A special thanks to Dr. Kit Bowerman, Susan Dos Pasos Fontaine, and Dr. Art Fontaine, who read my manuscript and provided valuable suggestions.

In Natalia Aponte, I have a terrific editor, whose vision is imprinted on every page of this book. The people at Forge are simply the best. And to my friend and agent Julie Castiglia, thank you.

Finally, to Steve, Mike, Crystal, and Ashley. You are my lifeblood. None of this would be possible without you. With you, everything is.

You must speak straight
so that your words may go as sunlight into our hearts

—Cochise, Chiracahua Apache (1812–1874)

CLINICAL
TRIAL

PROLOGUE

ASI ASKGYZ CONSIDERED herself blessed. She had been born in the same modest two-room shack that now served as home to her, her beloved husband, Gorik, and their three-week-old son. The house sat near the shores of Lake Issyk-Kul, in the central Asian nation of Kyrgyzstan, and each morning Asi walked the short distance to the lake, where she drew water for tea.

This morning was especially lovely. Inside the house, her family still slept, and the spring sun made Asi feel younger than she had in months— since before she'd become pregnant and awkward in movement. She'd decided to forego the babushka that she wore daily out of respect for her Russian heritage, allowing her dark hair to fall free on her shoulders, and giving her a sense of freedom and exhilaration.

The air was so crisp and clear that the peaks of the Tyen-Shan mountains on the other side of the lake looked near enough for Asi to reach out and touch, though in reality more than thirty miles separated them.

The only thing that kept the moment from being absolutely perfect was a strange scent in the air. Asi had noticed it as soon as she stepped outside. It was light and bitter; it reminded Asi of almonds. It wasn't really unpleasant, she decided quickly, just unusual.

Soon, Asi thought, Issyk-Kul would live up to its name—"Hot Lake"—and she would bring the baby down to begin teaching him to swim. But today she simply waded in to her knees, gathering her long skirt in one hand to keep it dry.

Because of its alpine origin and considerable depth, Issyk-Kul's waters were among the cleanest natural waters in the world, and Asi had grown to love their slightly salty taste. Switching the bucket into the hand still clutching her skirt, she cupped the other hand and scooped into the coolness, drinking greedily.

After filling the bucket and gazing appreciatively out across Issyk-Kul's brilliant aquamarine expanse, Asi lifted the bucket to her lips and took another long sip. Then she turned, eager to return to her sleeping baby.

The first muscle tremors hit before she'd reached the front gate. Alarmed, Asi dropped the bucket and began to run, but her breathing had become so labored and rapid that the added effort left her clinging to the handle of the house's front door, gasping for air. She tried calling for Gorik, but her voice had deserted her.

She made it through the door, then collapsed on the floor.

As if sensing his mother's distress, the baby awoke from his sleep and began crying. At first short, birdlike bursts, the infant's sobs quickly grew to one continuous wail as Asi lay there, unable to respond.

Didn't Gorik hear their son? Frantic, Asi called upon all her strength to roll slowly over. She had to get to her baby. Rising onto her knees, she tried to lift her head. As the wailing grew louder, she managed to lift her forehead an inch or two off the floor.

Finally, just before the convulsions took hold of Asi and carried her away, she heard the shuffle of Gorik's feet. The baby quieted some for several seconds, but then his cries reached a new height.

He was hungry now. Asi recognized the cry.

But she was helpless to go to him.

JON LECOQUE, the fifty-seven-year-old CEO of World Resources, Inc., stood at the head of the enormous mahogany conference table, white-knuckled and trembling with rage.

"Do you mean to tell me that our truck spilled two thousand kilograms of cyanide into the Barskoon River and you actually reported it to the local authorities?"

"I wasn't even aware of the spill until yesterday afternoon. I'd been in Guyana, at the Essiquibo mine."

"One of the drivers reported it?"

"No, no sir." Pedor Oliver's frightened voice came through the speaker at the center of the conference table. "Some of the townspeople. The accident was witnessed by several fishermen."

LeCoque pounded his fist on the table, making it tremble.

"This is a disaster," said Pierre Sabin, the portly company attorney sitting to LeCoque's right.

There was a collective moan from the group assembled in Vancouver.

Jon LeCoque surveyed those assembled around him.

"It gets worse," LeCoque said. "Continue, Pedor."

"Well, people have been getting sick. One of the fishermen who was standing in the water. And now a young woman has died. They say it's because she drank from Issyk-Kul."

"The lake?" Sabin asked.

"Yes. The Barskoon runs into it."

"Is that possible, Eleanor?" Sabin turned to the stone-faced Asian woman sitting at the end of the table opposite LeCoque.

"No," Eleanor Nguyen said. Nguyen headed up WRI's environmental compliance department. "Lake Issyk-Kul is several miles downstream from the accident. By the time the cyanide reached the lake, it would have been so diluted that . . ."

"You're wrong, Eleanor. It's definitely possible," Tony Wilderman spoke up. Wilderman served as WRI's top exploratory geologist. The wild, rusty curls that formed a semicircle around his balding head and the only blue jeans in the room set him apart from the rest gathered there, who, despite the fact that it was Sunday morning, looked to have spent every bit as much time grooming themselves to come into the office this morning as they did every other day. "It's just what happened in Guyana. As soon as the cyanide hit the water, it formed a poisonous mass that would have moved downstream. The town of Barskoon gets its drinking water from the river. Those slugs tend to stay intact for a while. Eventually it would have reached the lake. Plenty of time to poison people."

Eleanor Nguyen shot Wilderman a look of contempt.

"Did the fisherman drink out of the river?" Sabin wanted to know from Pedor.

"Didn't have to," Wilderman cut in. "Cyanide enters the body through inhalation of the gas, absorption through the skin, or ingestion. If he was standing in the water that close to the spill, chances are the fisherman both inhaled *and* absorbed it. What's his condition? Do we know?"

"I talked to a doctor at the hospital," Pedor said. "He's severely ill. Has an enlarged liver. But the doctor thinks he'll pull through."

There was a moment of silence as all present began to process the ramifications of the information presented by Pedor.

"Anything in the papers?" Mike Lane, vice president of public relations, asked Pedor.

"Front page. Headlines."

"Thank you, Pedor," said LeCoque disgustedly. "We'll get back to you once we formulate a plan. Stand by."

Impatiently, he punched a button on the phone's panel, ending the call.

"This spill has the potential to be devastating to WRI, people. Damage control is essential. Let's hear suggestions."

Eleanor Nguyen, hoping to redeem herself after being contradicted by Wilderman, spoke up.

"We could send a team over there. Check for cyanide in the lake and soil. By the time we get there, it's likely the readings will have dropped to a level that's insignificant."

"What else?" LeCoque said.

"I think we need to get on the phone with the chief of police," Mike Lane said. "Tell him we regret the actions of the drivers, their failure to report the accident. Tell him we've fired the men involved and we're initiating an internal investigation."

"That's a dangerous route. It can be tantamount to an admission of guilt," Pierre Sabin said. "If people are getting sick, even dying, the last thing we want to do is start expressing regret."

The room fell silent.

"Okay," LeCoque said. "Eleanor, you get over there and conduct those tests. Mike, once Eleanor has readings for you, call the local paper. Tell them there's no chance the spill caused that woman's death. That WRI accepts full responsibility for the accident itself, but that what's happened since is a result of hysteria. Tell them that we will consider taking legal action if their irresponsible reporting does not stop. And that WRI may have to reassess its presence in Kyrgyzstan."

"The Kamton is our richest deposit," Tony Wilderman said, scowling.

"Exactly," LeCoque agreed. "That's why we can't afford to let one accident screw things up for us."

No one in the room dared mention the fact that this accident made two, in two years.

"That mine contributes almost twenty-five percent to Kyrgyzstan's gross domestic product," LeCoque continued. "They're not about to let us leave over something this trivial. We just need to let a little time pass. This whole thing will blow over."

Suddenly, the shrill ring of the phone in the middle of the table pierced the air.

LeCoque signaled Mike Lane to pick it up.

Lane answered. He pressed the hold button and turned to his boss.

"It's the Vancouver *Herald*. They've picked up a story on the wire service about the spill. Are we prepared to comment?"

ONE

ARLO IRON HEART wasn't exactly living up to his name. This would be Dr. Isabel McLain's second attempt to draw the blood required for a blood sugar test. In the three months that Isabel had been running the Blackfeet reservation clinic in Browning, Montana, Arlo had made, then failed to show up for, no fewer than three appointments. Finally, today, he'd arrived at the clinic without one.

His timing was rotten—Isabel was already running behind—but, as he'd been instructed to do when he made the earlier appointments, upon his arrival this morning Arlo had proudly announced that he'd fasted for the previous twelve hours. Knowing that if she sent him away she might never see him again, Isabel worked him in.

Arlo presented classic diabetes symptoms: unexplained weight loss, frequent urination, and increased thirst.

"Mr. Iron Heart, every time you look at the needle, you jerk your arm away and I have to start over. I'd suggest you either close your eyes or focus on something besides what I'm trying to do here."

"Can't help it," the old, braided Indian groused through a puckered mouth that drew down at either end. "Shoulda never come here in the first place."

When she first came to the reservation clinic, Isabel had tried an approach intended to soothe and calm patients like Arlo, offering condescendingly simplified explanations for what she was doing. When that only seemed to create more distrust, and her patience grew thin, she'd dropped any attempt at a bedside manner.

"Do you want me to help you or not? Because I can do that, help you feel better. But I can't do it until I'm sure what the problem is, and I'm not about to fight you for the ridiculously small amount of blood I need for this test."

She pushed back, ready to go on to her next patient.

The bluff worked. Iron Heart held his arm in front of him and closed his eyes.

"Be quick about it," he ordered.

With a sigh, Isabel inserted the needle. Iron Heart's blood had almost filled the tube when the door opened and her assistant, Suzanne Featherhart, appeared.

At the sound of the door opening, Iron Heart startled and jerked his arm away, spraying blood across the front of Isabel's white lab coat.

Reflexively, Isabel reached for the old man's elbow, pressing her gloved forefinger against the entry site. By now, Iron Heart looked easily as pale as the fair-skinned Isabel.

Exasperated, Isabel looked up at Suzanne.

"What is it?"

"I have to leave early for lunch," Suzanne said. Suzanne had a wild head of black, spiked hair and enormous, dark eyes, but sometimes all Isabel saw when she looked at her assistant was the cherry-red lipstick she wore day in and out. "And I won't be back 'til later."

"How much later?"

Suzanne shrugged her rounded shoulders.

"Don't really know. Depends on how long the meeting takes."

"What kind of meeting?"

"Tribal business. My Aunt Mary wants me to go with her."

"And you just found out about it now? You know how busy today's going to be."

Suzanne pushed the door farther open, enabling Isabel to see someone standing behind her in the poorly lit hallway.

"That's why I asked Joe to come."

Joe Winged Foot stepped forward, out of Suzanne's shadow.

Shaking her head wearily, Isabel looked down at the tube of blood she'd withdrawn from Arlo.

"That should be enough for the test." She nodded at Suzanne. "Take over here, will you? Clean him up before you leave. And be sure to pull the charts for this afternoon."

"Already did."

Clutching his arm dramatically, Arlo Iron Heart eyed Isabel's lab coat in disgust.

"Mr. Iron Heart, these tests should be done by Friday. Please make another appointment to see me then."

Finally, Isabel turned to Joe Winged Foot and smiled. She was always glad to see Joe.

"Come with me," she told him. "I need to change into a clean lab coat."

AS JOE FOLLOWED her into her office, Isabel glanced at her watch. Eleven forty-five.

"How'd you manage to get out of school so early?"

"Suzanne wrote me a note." Joe grinned, sliding his lanky form through the door and flopping like a rag doll into the chair next to Isabel's desk. "Besides, graduation's only a coupla weeks off. No one's payin' attention anymore. Mrs. Andrews, she likes that I come to visit you so much. She says I can learn a lot here."

As he spoke, Joe's basketball sneakers drummed a staccato beat on the linoleum flooring. Despite his height—just five feet nine inches—Joe served as the point guard and star of the Blackfeet high school team that had lost in overtime to a Missoula team in the state championship. He took great pride in his basketball skills and his team's successful season, frequently, like today, wearing his championship jersey layered over another T-shirt. Isabel thought all the Blackfeet youngsters a pleasure to look at, but Joe's lively brown eyes, perfectly etched nose, and ready grin made him unusually appealing.

Isabel crossed the cramped room to the closet and grabbed a white lab coat fresh from the dry cleaner.

"You and Suzanne set me up, didn't you?" she said, turning to eye Joe good-naturedly.

Despite her chagrin at her assistant, Isabel found Joe's broad smile infectious. Still, today it seemed just a tad less blinding than usual.

"You feeling okay?"

"Sure. Just a little tired from a late pickup game last night. You gonna let me give some shots today?"

Isabel slipped into the fresh lab coat as she ushered Joe back out into the hallway.

" 'Fraid not. But I might let you take a temperature or two."

Grinning, Joe continued down the hall to the reception area to find Isabel's next patient. Watching Joe, Isabel could not dispell the impression that he seemed somehow subdued. She made a mental note to question him further.

Joe reappeared moments later with Eli Walker.

"Jason Little Turtle just showed up without an appointment," Joe told Isabel. "Thinks he's got the flu."

"There you go." Isabel smiled. "Why don't you take Jason into the other exam room and get his temperature?"

When Joe hesitated, Isabel added, "The thermometer's in a glass container on the counter, but you need to put a disposable shield over it first. They're in the drawer next to the sink. Think you can handle that?"

" 'Course," he answered none too certainly, turning back toward the waiting room.

Isabel ushered Eli into the exam room.

"How's that leg doing, Eli?" she asked.

Eli had recently been hospitalized for a deep venous thrombosis—a large blood clot in his right femoral vein.

"Still sore some," Eli answered, eyes glued to the floor. "But I don't see why I gotta come in here so much."

"I told you," Isabel said. "The anticoagulant the doctors in Cutbank put you on will keep you from getting more clots, but we have to monitor it. We don't want your blood getting too thin."

Isabel pricked the tip of Eli's index finger and directed two drops of falling blood onto the protime monitor. Within seconds, a number indicating the time it took his blood to clot flashed on a small screen.

"Eleven. That's high." Isabel had been standing in front of a seated Eli, but now she lowered herself to his eye level.

"You look like crap, Eli. Have you been drinking?"

The stale odor of alcohol wafted to her nostrils from Eli's person and clothing.

Eli did not raise his gaze to meet hers.

"Mebbe a little," he mumbled to the floor.

Isabel straightened up and placed her hand on her right hip.

"What am I going to do with you? Don't you realize that alcohol plays havoc with the anticoagulant you're taking? We need to get you within the acceptable protime range and keep it there. Right now, you could bleed to death over something as insignificant as a bump on the head. Just how much did you have to drink?"

Eli shrugged his shoulders.

Isabel felt like shaking some sense into him, but instead she reached out and touched Eli under the chin.

"Look at me, Eli." When he finally raised heavily lidded eyes to hers, she continued. "Be honest with me. Is there a chance in hell that you can stop drinking for the six months you'll be on the anticoagulant?"

A blank stare gave her her answer, but Eli also managed a weak, "Not really."

"Okay, then. How about this? You keep it to two drinks a day. Understand? But you have to be consistent. You have to drink those two drinks *every single day.*"

For the first time, Eli perked up.

"Ya mean you *want* me to drink every day?"

"No, that's not what I said. But I can't get your coagulation levels steady if you can only manage to abstain a couple days before going on another binge. It would be better to have you drink a moderate amount consistently. At least that way I have half a chance of adjusting your medication to keep you within an acceptable range."

"What about three drinks?" Eli said hopefully. "Or four?"

"Two. That's the deal. Take it or leave it."

Eli fell silent for a moment as he appeared to study the floor.

"Didja mean that? That I could bleed to death?"

"We've already been over this, Eli. Yes, I do mean it. Right now your blood's about as thin as the chicken soup they serve down at Sandy's Diner. Blood that's too thin is almost as dangerous as blood that can throw a clot. In some ways, more. But I can fix that. If you'll just cooperate with me. What do you say?"

" 'Spose two drinks a day's better than none," he finally muttered. "Or bleedin' to death . . ."

"You bet it is. Now listen to me closely. I want you to skip your regular dose of anticoagulant for the next two days. Then come back in here for another reading. Do you have any questions? Two days without your medicine, two drinks a day, then come back in and we'll see if your protime's back where we want it."

After getting a mumbled acknowledgment from Eli, Isabel moved on to the next room, where Jason Little Turtle sat on the exam table with a thermometer sticking out of his tightly clenched mouth.

Jason and Arlo turned out to be the first of four unscheduled patients that afternoon. Isabel and Joe moved quickly from one room to another, with Joe ushering patients in, then cleaning up the rooms between visits. There was little time for small talk.

FINALLY, AROUND THREE-THIRTY, just as Isabel finished her exam of a four-year-old girl who'd suffered an asthma attack the night before, Suzanne reappeared.

"I'm back," she announced, crossing the room to help the wide-eyed child down from the exam table while the young mother bounced her wailing two-year-old brother on her knee.

"Good," Isabel answered. "Did you let Joe know that he can leave when he wants?"

"He's already gone."

"Oh."

The rest of the afternoon proved even more chaotic than the morning had been—too chaotic to worry about Joe. Late in the day, when she went into the storage closet and opened a supply cupboard, Isabel almost had a heart attack when a furry projectile shot straight out, as if aimed squarely at her face.

A mouse.

Luckily it fell short.

She sent Suzanne down to Standing Bear Hardware for traps, then raced off from her last patient to her quarterly meeting with the tribal council, leaving Suzanne to bait the traps with peanut butter, as instructed by Dan Standing Bear.

It was much later—almost midnight—before Isabel had time to give serious consideration to the fact that Joe had left the clinic without saying goodbye. When she dropped into bed, completely and utterly exhausted, it was the first thing to come to mind.

It was so unlike Joe to leave today without saying goodbye.

She would make a point of taking time to visit with him tomorrow—surely he'd drop by after school—to make sure that everything was all right.

She was so fond of Joe, had such great hopes for him, as did everyone else in the town. Joe Winged Foot was the Blackfeets' shining light—college bound, intelligent, determined to make something of himself. He had recently told Isabel he might become a doctor, come back to the reservation and take care of his people. After he "got done playing in the NBA."

Nagged with a vague, unsettling worry about Joe, Isabel had difficulty getting to sleep. But finally exhaustion set in and she fell into a deep, profound slumber.

THE TRIBAL HEADQUARTERS business offices were located within a three-square-block area on the north side of Browning, half a mile from the clinic.

Suzanne and her Aunt Mary lived together in a trailer just off Highway 2, seven miles southeast of town. Mary had arranged for a neighbor to pick her up and drop her off at the Blackfeet Health and Safety Corps building, where the meeting was taking place. As Suzanne approached the dark brown, U-shaped log structure, she could see her frail aunt huddled outside on a bench next to a colorful sign that featured a large turquoise circle around a white, block-style cross. Overlaid upon the cross were an American flag, a turquoise star, and, in bold black letters, BHSC.

"Why are you sitting out here?" Suzanne scolded as she walked across the wet grass from the parking lot. "It's cold and wet."

"I was just waiting for you," Mary Talking Horse answered quietly. It had stopped raining but her thin powder blue sweatshirt offered little protection from the wind and fifty-degree temperature.

"But you could have waited inside."

With Suzanne holding one arm, Mary used her other hand to cling tightly to the iron railing as the two women climbed half a dozen cement steps to the building's front door. Inside, several familiar faces lingered in the hallway. Suzanne nodded at Sumner Willow and his daughter, Ann. A large hand-lettered cardboard sign read TRUST AFFAIRS MEETING and pointed down the hallway.

As they approached an open door two-thirds of the way down the corridor, Suzanne heard voices. She steered Mary inside, where at least a dozen tribal members sat on folding chairs arranged in four rows.

"Here's Mary Talking Horse now," a strong, resonant baritone announced from the front of the room. "And Suzanne."

Both Suzanne and Mary turned toward the speaker. In three long strides, Monty Four Bear crossed the room to greet them.

When Suzanne heard that Monty would be chairing today's meeting, her aunt's request that she accompany her became all the more palatable. She'd known the handsome lawyer since they were children.

"Thanks for coming," Monty said. He placed a hand on Mary's bony shoulder and nodded to Suzanne over Mary's gray head of hair.

"Hey."

"Hey," Suzanne replied.

As Suzanne directed her aunt to a chair, both she and Mary nodded respectfully at Sky Thomas, who was seated dead center in the front row.

Sky was the oldest living member of the Blackfeet tribe. She lived in a two-room wood frame house just off Main Street and, at ninety-three, still walked to tribal functions and meetings in town—even those, like the one today, that did not pertain directly to her. Sky was widely believed to have visionary powers. Age had not dulled her good mind, and she enjoyed great respect from her Blackfeet family.

As Monty returned to the front of the room, Sumner and Ann Willow slipped into the room, coffee cups in hand.

"I think everyone's here now," Monty said, grabbing an empty chair. "We might as well get started."

Turning the chair backward, he eased himself, saddle-style, onto it. Six feet tall and lean, Suzanne couldn't help but notice that Monty still moved with the grace of the track star he'd once been. In faded blue jeans and well-scuffed cowboy boots, his long black hair parted neatly in the middle and pushed behind both ears, the sight of him stirred memories of the girlhood crush she'd had on him when she was twelve and he was eighteen.

"I think I've had one-on-one conversations with just about everyone in this room before today," Monty began. "Lester Wolf Spirit first came to me about the problems he was having getting information on his trust account over two years ago. After I looked into it for Lester, I guess word got out, and pretty soon more of you started coming to me. Before long, I kind of became a poster boy for this thing. Unfortunately, I haven't had much success—for Lester, or the rest of you."

"At least them people at the Bureau, they listen more to you than they do to us," Wolf Spirit called from the last row. "After you started callin' 'em, they sent me a letter. There wasn't no money with it, but it's the first time I got anything on paper from them in the forty years since my father died and passed that land on to me."

"I get statements a couple times a year, but I don't trust what they put on there anyway," Sumner Willow huffed from where he and Ann had settled. "I know damn well that the B and N is payin' somebody to run trains across my property. But I haven't seen a penny of it."

Suzanne felt her aunt's body stiffen. Usually quiet and much too shy to talk in public, Mary surprised her by standing.

"I get a check here and there from the Bureau," she said, slowly straightening into her usual erect posture. "Most of you know of my great-grandfather Black Bull. When the government divided the land up, Black Bull and his brother got a hundred-sixty acres. That's been passed down to me. I know that land is producing money 'cause every once and again I get a little check from the Bureau. It's never much. Usually just enough for me and Suzanne to splurge a little, buy some groceries so we can get a break from commodity food. Or maybe take a trip into Kalispell."

When she paused, the group remained silent and attentive.

"Back a couple years ago," she continued, "when my husband Charlie got so sick and I needed money to go back and forth to Cutbank for dialysis, I figured if I could find this land of Black Bull's, I could see for myself what was goin' on on it. Far as I know they could be pumpin' oil out of the ground. I heard stories like that, Indians living with their windows all boarded up 'cause they can't afford to fix them, while just outside—if they had glass in there, they'd be able to see it—trucks are hauling oil off their property by the barrel. Same thing could be happening to any one of us here. My family hasn't actually lived on Black Bull's land for generations. My mama forgot just where it was. So I tried calling the Bureau to get some information on it. 'Course we all know how that is, trying to get someone to talk to you on the phone. They got this thing they call . . ." She turned to Suzanne, a scowl creasing her already deeply lined brow, and Suzanne whispered, "Voice mail."

"Voice mail. They call it voice mail. Well, it made me half glad I couldn't afford a phone back then 'cause if that's what you get when you call for help, I don't need it. I got dizzy tryin' to figure out what they were tellin' me, which button to press and so on. Anyway, I never did talk to a real live person and I never heard from anyone after I left a message.

"You all know Charlie finally died. Suzanne here, she moved in to help me out and now at least the bills get paid and we got a phone. But it's no life for a young girl like Suzanne. If I got a little more money from that land, on a regular basis, she could move out and have a life of her own."

Suzanne stared at the old woman. She had no idea Mary considered herself a burden. It was the Blackfeet way for family to take care of family. Mary was Suzanne's deceased mother's only sister, and when Uncle Charlie died there had never been any question in Suzanne's mind that she would move in with Mary. She would have preferred Mary to come live with her in her apartment in town, but Mary refused to leave the trailer she'd called home for four decades. And so Suzanne had moved to the trailer, where she slept in the living room, a curtain hung between it and the kitchen for privacy.

After that one time, the situation was never discussed again.

Suzanne grabbed her aunt's hand to help her back into her seat. It was cold, and it shook.

"What I wanna know is what're we gonna do about it," Wolf Spirit said. "Can you help us, Monty? 'Cause you're about the only one of us who knows how to deal with this kind of stuff."

Heads nodded around the room.

"We can always count on Monty," Mary Talking Horse murmured.

Monty had remained silent, monitoring the mood in the room.

"It's obviously not an easy situation to correct," he finally offered. "Everyone knows how long this has been going on. For over a century. And while it's become politically correct to voice concern about how our people have been treated, no one's really stepped up to the plate to make any kind of changes. At least none that really make a difference. And even if they were to make them now, even if they correct things from here on out, there's still the matter of the money that was rightly due all of you in the past. There's only one way I know to recover that." His eyes measured each of the room's occupants. "And that's sue."

"We can do that? We can sue them?" Ann Willow asked.

"There's been talk for a while now among many tribes about a class action suit, for mismanagement of Indian assets. Maybe even fraud. I think we've taken this long enough. It's time to make them listen. I believe a class action suit will do that."

"Let's sue," Wolf Spirit grunted.

"You bet," Sumner Willow called out. "Sue them bastards."

Excited chatter broke out across the room, but when Sky Thomas lifted her thick cane and brought it down hard on the wood floor, not once, but twice, the room grew completely still.

" 'Course we deserve what we got comin' to us," she said in a croak of a voice. "Monty here, he does a good job of looking out for us, and if he thinks we should sue, most the time I'd be right behind him." She'd twisted her aged body to get a look at the others. "But trouble's coming."

Next to Suzanne, Mary Talking Horse drew in a short, sharp breath and pressed a hand to her heart. Sky's pronouncement caused a number of raised eyebrows as well, even among the usually stoic men.

"What kind of trouble, Sky?" Monty asked. There was no hint of skepticism or disrespect in his tone.

"I can't tell you that," the old woman answered grumpily. "I just know it's comin'. And I've seen what happens when our people try to fight too many battles at once. You gotta choose your battles. That's all I'm tryin' to say."

She turned back around to face the front of the room.

The room fell silent again as Monty studied the faces turned toward him, looking for answers.

"A lot of preparation goes into a lawsuit," he finally said. "Especially a class action. There's no need to rush the actual filing. I can get started with some of the groundwork, and then we can meet again, let's say in six months, to re-evaluate. How does that sound?"

"That sounds like a good plan," Suzanne said.

"We better just wait 'til we see what the heck Sky's talkin' about," Sumner agreed hesitantly.

CHAPTER

TWO

WHAT DO YOU mean you cayn't find it?"

A product of Louisiana's Cajun country, Alistair Bott's carefully honed Northwestern accent sometimes slipped when he was caught off guard.

Bott had been so engrossed in the discussion taking place in the on-line chat room that he'd ignored the phone the first two times it rang. But when it became apparent the caller would not give up, he'd finally picked up.

The sound of fear in Mary Pelandini's voice was most unwelcome.

"I expected it to be in that stack of faxes you took from your office at home," she explained. "But I've been through those papers a dozen times. It's not there."

"You mean to tell me you still haven't shredded all of those documents?"

"I didn't want to shred them until I rounded up all the originals and matched them up to be sure both the originals and any copies were destroyed. You said you didn't want any mix-ups, any loose documents out there that could come back to haunt us."

"And that's taken three months?"

"What took time was purging all the files at the clinic. That was a huge job—we're talking hundreds of boxes full of files. I had to go through every word on every page of every file, tear out pages, remove charts, you name it." Alistair could hear Mary's anxiety turning to exasperation. "Without one bit of help from you or anybody else, I might add."

"And you did a wonderful job, darlin'," Alistair cooed. "I hope you know how much I 'preciate it. Listen, I've been meaning to tell you something. It's very good news. Remember I said I have a friend who works for the FDA? Well, he's been keeping his eyes and ears open, and he says the word so far is that they didn't find anything in the audit. Which is exactly what I told you would happen. Isn't it? Hell, those files had already passed the scrutiny of dozens of monitors."

On the other end, Mary let out a short, caustic laugh.

"You doctors really do live in la-la land, don't you? So incredibly out of touch with what goes on in the world of us mere mortals." She took a deep breath, signaling her impatience. "Monitors only look at data, you know that. They don't look any deeper. They're not gonna find a damn thing. These auditors, they're another story."

Alistair swallowed hard, biting back his impulse to take Mary to task. How dare she speak to him with such disrespect? His employees always, always treated him with the utmost deference. Or they simply did not remain employees for long. But right now he needed Mary. He could not afford to alienate her.

"That may be the case, darlin', but still, from what I heard from my contact, we're in fine shape. However, according to my friend, the investigation won't be formally concluded for a while yet. Maybe even another month or two. We just have to hang tight 'til then."

"Did your friend tell you that an investigator's been snooping around Harborview?" Mary asked.

Reluctant to miss out on the chatroom give-and-take, Alistair's eyes had begun straying back to the computer screen, but with these words, they snapped back to attention. His grip on the phone tightened.

"What do you mean they're snooping around Harborview?"

"Just what I said. Ariana called to say they'd been over there, talking to people. She's getting real nervous."

"What did they ask her?"

"They haven't talked to her yet. She was off on the day the guy came around."

This was not good news at all.

"Can Ariana be trusted?"

"Definitely," Mary answered. "She gave me her file with all the information she's given us. She wanted it out of there. Ariana's raising four kids alone. No way she can afford to lose her job."

"The list was there, in her file?"

"The original was there. And I found a copy of it in my files, too."

"Then that's probably all there ever was," Alistair said emphatically. "We've had this conversation too many times now, Mary. I know Ariana told you she remembered faxing it to me, but I also told you, I never got it. She must have given the list directly to you. I must say, dear girl, you are startin' to exhibit signs of paranoia, and it's not especially attractive."

His grip had relaxed a bit. The only weak link, as he now saw it, was Ariana. If she was cooperating, they would be okay.

"Maybe it's not so much that I'm paranoid as it is you thinking you're goddamned invincible. All you doctors are the same. Think you're omnipotent. For your information, there's a problem with your safe little assumption that Ariana never faxed the list to you."

"What kind of problem?"

"There was another sheet attached to that original."

"Jesus H. Christ, Mary. Will you just get to the point? What're you tryin' to say?"

"It was a transmission report. It indicated the transmission had been successful. The number the fax was sent to," she hesitated, perhaps for effect, "is *yours*. It's the fax number at your house."

Alistair's free hand closed around the phone cord and balled into a tight fist.

"Then you better keep looking," he ordered. "It has to be there somewhere."

"Unless *she* took it."

"If she took it, she'd have turned it over to that bull dyke attorney of hers and the authorities would've been swarming over us like gnats on roadkill by now. She can't possibly have it. It has to be somewhere. *Find it.*"

He hung up the phone, his interest in the goings-on online extinguished.

This was not good news at all. After his last conversation with Robin Getty—his med school roommate who'd turned to the bureaucracy of the FDA when he couldn't hack it in private practice—Alistair had congratulated himself.

Nobody was going to bring Alistair Bott down, least of all his estranged wife.

Not after all he'd been through to get where he was today.

The only son of a mean-spirited alcoholic from the backwoods of Louisiana. Lazy, temperamental son of a bitch unable to stay sober long enough to hold down a job for more than a few months at a time, which meant that after Alistair's mother died—her income as a housekeeper was meager, but steady—Stanley Bott would take off for days, sometimes weeks at a time, telling his young son he was looking for work, leaving Alistair alone, from the age of ten on, to fend for himself and, at times, literally forage for food to fuel him through the school day.

School. It had been Alistair's salvation. His safe haven, where, by working hard and playing upon the sympathy of his teachers, he learned what it took to garner attention and praise. He vowed as a young child to leave Louisiana the first opportunity that presented itself, and when he graduated from high school at the top of his class—a feat aided considerably by the copies he'd stolen of his calculus and chemistry final exams—that opportunity finally came, in the form of a scholarship to Gonzaga University in Spokane, Washington.

With each success, each move, Alistair managed to put a little more distance—not just geographical—between himself and his backwoods past, cultivating a gentleman's demeanor, an intellect, a mystique. He became something of a chameleon, able to adapt quickly. His charm and golden-haired good looks earned him instant popularity with the girls, but he was never as successful with the male population, who regarded him with suspicion—as something of a freak, with his silky southern accent, lack of interest in sports or beer, and his courtly demeanor with the coeds. Determined to overcome the frail, sickly image he had as a child, the long hours that Alistair spent in front of a mirror in the gym did nothing to further his popularity with his male colleagues, but his cover boy physique made a big impression on coeds.

With a 4.0 grade point and biology degree in hand, Alistair made the move across the Cascades to Seattle, to attend med school at the University of Washington, where he met Isabel McLain, the exotic loner in his first-year anatomy class.

In med school, study groups were just an analogue for small, tight-knit cliques. They formed instantly, like drops of oil hitting water, and had just as strong a tendency to cling together. Like him, Isabel was one of the few students who studied alone, who didn't really fit in. The difference, however, was clear to Alistair from the start—something about Isabel made her *choose* to be on the outside, while Alistair's need to be looked up to, admired, and envied, had tugged at every fiber of his being for so very long that he would have sold his soul to fit in.

Leggy, with long, thick black hair—usually tied back, which accentuated a face all angles and lips and eyes—all the guys in med school had a thing for Isabel. Alistair watched for two years, sat back with amusement, as Isabel politely but unequivocally rejected one after another, which, of course, only increased her allure, the entire male population's fascination with her. And only upped Alistair's determination to have her.

From the start, Isabel represented triumph to Alistair—triumph over his father's predictions that his son would end up just like the old man. Triumph over the poverty and hopelessness of the redneck hill country he'd grown up in. Triumph over all those arrogant sons of bitches who thought they were better than Alistair Bott.

And—the icing on the cake—Isabel also happened to turn him on like no other woman he'd ever known. Ever *had*. And he'd had plenty.

Isabel McLain would have nothing to do with the other guys, but eventually—perhaps out of pity for his outsider status, for he was not above using that to his advantage—she agreed to go out with him. He'd observed her, studied her for two years by that time, and he knew all the buttons to push. Environmentalist, openly disdainful of social status and wealth—yet still eager to please a father she clearly adored.

On their first date, he took her to a Sierra Club fund-raiser, feigning ignorance of the fact that her father was on the board of directors. Alistair had spent years hiding his past, but something told him that with Isabel, it could prove useful. For the first time since creating a new life for himself, he disclosed the hardships he'd endured as a child. He shared with her the fears and insecurities. The hunger and loneliness.

This took place at her apartment, as they shared a bottle of wine. That night, drawn into those eyes that were like deep, warm pools, he'd actually fallen in love with Isabel McLain.

Amazingly, she'd made love to him that very night, and he'd discovered that under that cool-as-cucumber facade that kept everyone at arm's length resided a woman of incredible appetite and passion.

Once she trusted him—which, with some additional "confessions" regarding his childhood, took only a few more dates—there was little Isabel would not do, would not allow him to do to her. Making love to her was like riding the highest and wildest of roller coasters—the anticipation building time and again, with one exhilarating ride, one wildly frightening climax after another.

In all their years together, there was only one place that Isabel drew the line, and that was when he suggested videotaping their love sessions. Alistair already knew by then that when Isabel said no, she meant it, and no amount of pleading or cajoling could succeed in budging her. And so he did the only thing he could do. He installed a video camera in the ceiling fan above their bed.

And in the light fixture in the Jacuzzi room.

WHEN SHE LEFT him, those tapes became his salvation. He played and replayed them, night after night. And then he'd decided to share them.

She deserved it, after all.

She'd betrayed him, tried to take him down. But there was no way, no way he would allow Isabel McLain to take him down. Not after all the muck, all the maggot-infested shit, he'd crawled through to get where he was.

Which is why Robin Getty's recent news had been so welcome.

This—Mary's news that investigators were still digging around—was not good. And what about that fucking fax she kept insisting he'd received?

It had been a long time now since Alistair had had any contact with Isabel. A long time since he'd laid eyes on her. Maybe it was time to instill a little fear, a little respect, in her.

The thought turned him on—just as everything about Isabel had always turned him on. Even now, after all she'd done to him, he could get an erection simply thinking about her.

And so, with all his other problems pushed temporarily out of mind, Alistair Bott turned back to the Internet.

"THIS THING HAS become a public relations nightmare," Mike Lane told the group of WRI execs assembled around him. "Four thousand have fled Barskoon. It's virtually a ghost town. Pedor tells me that families have grouped together. They send one of the men back for two days at a time to guard their homes, then rotate every other day because they don't want to endanger anyone by allowing them to stay for more than forty-eight hours."

"That's *bullshit*," Jon LeCoque answered, slamming his fist on the table. "Total bullshit. Our scientists checked for cyanide in the lake and river, even in the soil around Barskoon. It's safe there now."

Eleanor Nguyen nodded her bobbed hair in agreement. "Even Health Canada agrees. In fact, they've backed our contention that the level of cyanide received was never high enough to account for the problems they're alleging."

Her eyes made sure to seek out Tony Wilderman when she delivered this last bit of information.

"Still," LeCoque warned, "we can't be too careful about this. WRI's future is heavily dependent upon that mine. When's that lease up for renewal?" He turned to the company attorney. "Pierre?"

Pierre Sabin opened a file sitting in front of him and rifled through a half-inch thick document.

"Two-thousand-two," Sabin said. "Same year as the Essiquibo site."

"We can't let this incident become another Essiquibo," LeCoque said.

Heads around the table nodded.

Two years earlier, a dam holding toxic millings from WRI's Essiquibo mine in Guyana had ruptured, spilling 3.2 billion liters of cyanide-laced water into the Essiquibo River, which runs almost the length of the country of Guyana and happens to be one of its busiest waterways. The river had since been dubbed the "Cyanide River" and WRI was now drowning in a quagmire of lawsuits, especially after an independent engineer from the United States had reported that the dam, as designed and constructed, was "bound to fail." Fishermen had sued for loss of income. Loggers, miners, and those living or working on or around the river had soon joined in. Environmental groups, three at last count, had also sued. WRI had once been a popular presence in Guyana, but the public tide had turned, and there was little doubt among those in the room that the lease allowing WRI to continue its gold mining operations would not be renewed in 2002.

"I'm not ready to make any grand gestures at this point," LeCoque said. "But we can't afford more publicity or litigation. Pierre, I expect you to stay on top of this."

"Will do."

Tony Wilderman cleared his throat.

"Listen," he said, his voice coming out in a deep rattle, "this company has too much riding on those two mines. Especially if we're in danger of losing the Kyrgyzstan lease."

"What did you have in mind?" LeCoque asked.

"We should step up exploratory efforts," he said.

LeCoque lifted one of his bushy, gray eyebrows.

"Exploration's costly."

"Damn straight," Wilderman replied. "That's why we've had it on hold these past couple years. But we lose either of those two mines and we're in trouble."

"Those fucking foreigners," LeCoque fumed. "They're going to ruin this company."

Wilderman reached into the back pocket of his blue jeans and pulled out a flat, round can of Copenhagen. He lifted the lid, extracted a pinch of pungent, brown tobacco leaves, and then, to Eleanor Nguyen's chagrin, held it in front of him as he ran his tongue along his upper teeth.

"That's just what *I've* been thinking," the geologist said, opening his mouth and pressing the wad inside. "But what I have in mind this time is a little closer to home."

CHAPTER

THREE

WE GOT TWO more," Suzanne called out, holding the door open while Isabel made the dash from her Jeep to the clinic.

A gale force wind sent the heavy spring rain flying sideways, rendering the visor of the Mariners hat that Isabel pulled low over her eyes nearly useless.

For the past three mornings, Suzanne had begun each day with a report on their project to rid the clinic of deer mice. So far they were batting a thousand—each morning both traps held lifeless victims.

"There might still be more," Isabel said, shaking the rain off her parka and ball cap as she stepped inside the waiting room. She shrugged out of the parka, revealing her usual attire—blue jeans, long-sleeved T-shirt, and hiking boots—and threw both the parka and hat onto the rickety coat tree that stood in the corner of the newly wallpapered waiting room.

"Could be."

"Guess we better set them again tonight."

"Guess so," Suzanne echoed.

Isabel returned to the front door, her eyes scanning outside.

"No dogs this morning," she said.

When she first came to the reservation, Isabel had been struck by the sight of packs of dogs roaming Browning's streets, scavenging for food. So skilled were they that an odd metal contraption adorned the streets in front of each of Browning's small, mostly dilapidated houses: a post—once shiny aluminum but rusted now by years of exposure to the relentless elements—with a horizontal platform that held garbage cans three feet off the ground.

Isabel had taken to feeding the dogs that hung around the clinic. Most mornings now a group waited for her to arrive.

"Even those dogs're smart enough to stay outta this weather."

Isabel had turned and started down the hallway to her office when Suzanne's next words brought her to a complete standstill.

"You know some guy with a Southern accent?"

She twirled to face Suzanne.

"Why do you ask?"

Suzanne shrugged. She was always shrugging.

"Some guy was waiting outside last night. In this nice car. When I came out from puttin' the traps out."

"What did he want?"

"He asked for you. Wanted to know where you lived."

"Did he give his name?"

"Nope."

"What did he look like?"

"I dunno. White. Slick. Lucy picked me up last night. She got a better look at him than I did. She thought he was pretty good lookin', but Lucy likes white guys. The only white guy does anything for me is that actor, Vince Vaughn. Did you see that movie *Clay Pigeons*? He's so hot it's hard to believe he's . . ."

"*Suzanne*, describe the man to me, will you?"

"I wasn't payin' that much attention. He was sittin' in his car. Skinny. Kinda curly hair."

It couldn't be.

Only one person Isabel knew fit Suzanne's description—the person Isabel least wanted to find her.

"What did you tell him?"

"Nothin'. The guy gave me the creeps. I didn't tell him a thing."

"But you said he asked where I lived."

"Yeah. He wanted to know how to find your cabin."

"He said that? He called it a cabin?"

"That's what he called it. I told him I didn't know where you lived. And . . ."

"And what?"

"And I lied to him. I told him you were out of town. I told you, the guy creeped me out. I hope that's okay."

Isabel stared at Suzanne, lost momentarily in her past.

"Yes. It is."

The rest of the day, Isabel felt troubled and distracted by Suzanne's news. Driving home that night, after helping Suzanne set out the mouse traps again, Isabel went back over everything Suzanne told her. After asking to see her, her unnamed visitor had apparently asked Suzanne how to find Isabel's cabin. Thank God Suzanne had kept her mouth shut, had even lied and told him Isabel was out of town.

He must have believed her since he did not show up again today. Still, that was little comfort. Just a short reprieve, at best.

How did Alistair find out that Isabel had moved to Browning? And who told him that she lived in a cabin? Someone had been loose-lipped with information that was supposed to have been kept secret.

The first thing Isabel would do when she got home was make a telephone call.

Because she had a hunch just who that someone might be.

"MOTHER, PICK UP the phone. Please."

Isabel paced back and forth across the wood planked floor in the kitchen of her log cabin as she waited for Nada McLain to come on the line. Normally Isabel started a fire in the wood stove the moment she got home from work. Even now, in late spring, the evening temperatures could plummet below freezing. But tonight she'd gone directly to the phone.

"This is important, Mother. I need to talk to you."

She knew from experience that she had to continue talking or her mother's answering machine would cut her off.

"It's six o'clock. I'll be up for several hours. Please call me, it's very impor—"

"Hello, dear."

Despite her seventy-two years and fragile health, Nada McLain still had the deep, silky voice of the stage actress she had once been.

"I hate it when you screen calls like that."

"I don't screen calls, Isabel. I was simply engrossed in the news. You know how much I enjoy Tom Brokaw."

Tom Brokaw was one of the few things they agreed upon.

"Mother, I need to know something. Have you seen or talked to Alistair?"

The pause on the other end of the line gave Isabel her answer.

"So it was you who told him?"

"Told him what, dear?"

"Where I work. Where I live."

"I did not tell him where you live."

"But you told him I moved to the reservation. You told him about the clinic. And that I live in a cabin."

"You were married to the man for three years. Now you don't even want him to know where you live?"

"I asked you to keep that information secret. My lawyer won't even give him that information. How could you have betrayed me?"

"Betrayed you?" Nada's voice rose in indignation. "I'm your mother. I would never betray you."

"Then what do you call it?"

"I don't understand you, Isabel. You were crazy about Alistair once."

"That was long ago, Mother. A different lifetime. A different Alistair."

"What's so wrong with him now? He's a successful doctor. And so handsome. And he *loved* you. He still does, dear."

"Where in the hell did you get that?"

"There's no need to swear, Isabel. He just about came out and said so."

"You still can't see through him, can you?"

Nada chose to ignore Isabel's comment.

"You could still come back, dear. I just know Alistair would take you back. You could get off that godforsaken reservation and move back in to your lovely home . . ."

"Mother, stop. That's not going to happen. Ever. How many times have I told you? I like my life here. I feel I'm making a difference." Then, without thinking, she added, "Just like Dad did."

The bitterness of Nada McLain's laughter should not have stung Isabel so. After all, around Nada the family had *always* avoided the subject of Tom McLain's year on the Flathead reservation, just one hundred and thirty miles southwest of the Blackfeet nation's home. Burdened by med school loans at a time when he and Nada were newlyweds planning to start a family, Tom had jumped at the government's offer to forgive his debt in exchange for a year of service on one of many North American reservations desperately in need of medical personnel. The Flathead reservation had been the closest to home. Despite the fact that Nada chose to stay behind to perform in the Seattle Repertory Theatre, her mother's resentment of Tom's service in Montana never dimmed over the years. When Isabel was a child, it was only when she and her father were alone

that her father talked to her, with great fondness, telling Isabel stories
about the Salish and Kootenai who shared the vast reservation, about their
gentle spirit and way of life, their tragedy.

Those stories had planted a seed of fascination—even envy—within
Isabel's heart, her soul. A sense of longing that ran beneath the surface,
impossible to identify. Later, as Isabel grew up and began asking more
probing questions, even Tom seemed uncomfortable discussing that time.
Eventually it seemed that everyone wanted to forget it, put it out of their
minds. Everyone, that is, but Isabel.

"Just like your father," Nada huffed now. "Out to save the world. At
the expense of those you claim to love."

"Let's not do this to each other, Mother," Isabel said, hands shaking
with anger. "I'm going to hang up now. I'll call you again soon."

A sense of unnamed dread washed over Isabel as she replaced the
phone.

Maybe she should have been more honest with her mother when she
left Alistair. But despite the bitterness that had at times strained her parents' marriage, even after the passage of two years, Nada continued to
reel from Tom McLain's death. And despite Isabel and Nada's own dif-
ferences, Isabel felt a protectiveness toward her irksome mother. A mother
who placed undue emphasis on good looks and social status.

Nada McLain had always cherished her position in Seattle society as
a prominent surgeon's wife. Had she known the truth about Alistair, her
shame would have been tenfold what Isabel felt. Isabel had wanted to
spare Nada that. And she could only thank God that her father—her pure
of heart, generous-spirited father—hadn't lived to see this day.

Chilled inside and out, Isabel headed out to the porch for an armload
of the tamarack Gus had split for her weeks earlier and stacked neatly
under the overhang.

She should have known Alistair would eventually find her. Nothing
stopped him once he'd made up his mind. If her mother hadn't handed
him the information on a silver platter, he would have found another way
to get it.

But the question is, why had he come looking for her?

As Isabel balanced several lengths of firewood in her arms, her eyes
involuntarily swept the gravel road leading to her driveway. Then they
turned to the open meadow that began at the cabin's front door and flowed
to the road, where it picked back up on the other side until it reached a
stand of white birch and poplar.

Her cabin was remote. It would be impossible for Alistair to find it
without help. And no one, besides Suzanne and Gus, her landlord, knew
exactly where she lived.

Still, the simple knowledge that Alistair had been there, on the reservation, that he'd seen the clinic where she worked, made Isabel feel violated.

Instead of starting the wood stove up, she decided to use the tamarack for a fire in the fireplace. Sleep would not come easy tonight. A fire might help her relax.

Half an hour later, after checking all the locks on the cabin's doors and windows and eating a peanut butter and jelly sandwich, she sat staring into the fire, propped against a pillow in front of the hearth, sipping wine from one of the canning jars she'd found in the empty cupboard when she'd first moved in. She pushed her feet against the rusted metal firescreen, savoring the heat that burned through her heavy gray wool stockings.

Alistair had told her she would pay for what she'd done.

She'd passed along those words to K. T. Seinberg, her feisty attorney, who'd promptly headed to court for a restraining order. But the judge had decided that Alistair's threat, if it could be called that, was too vague for the court to act upon.

What difference would a restraining order make anyway?

As Isabel watched and listened to the flames spewing and spitting cinders skyward into the thin-aired Montana night, she knew better than to think that a piece of paper would protect her from her estranged husband.

CHAPTER

FOUR

J OE'S HERE . . ."

Phone pressed to ear as she listened to the Browning pharmacist's explanation for not being able to fill the prescription she'd just sent over with a patient, Isabel held up an index finger signaling Suzanne to wait.

"He don't look so good," Suzanne persisted.

Isabel's head jerked up, her eyes zeroing in on Suzanne.

"What do you mean?"

"I mean Joe's sick. Bad, I think."

Dropping the phone on her desk, Isabel rose immediately and followed Suzanne down the hallway.

If she hadn't been looking specifically for him, Isabel might not even have recognized Joe in the waiting room. The boy that sat hunched over, one arm clutching his chest while the other held the hand of a frantic-looking woman Isabel assumed to be his mother, might have been a stranger, had Isabel not known better. A stranger in deep distress.

"What is it, Joe?" Isabel asked, dropping to her knees in front of him.

His black eyes came up to meet hers.

"I can't breathe."

Isabel turned to the woman at Joe's side.

"Does he have asthma?"

"Don't think so."

"Anything like this ever happen before?"

The woman shook her head.

There was always the first time. Isabel reached out and touched Joe's forehead. Warm. A fever indicated they were dealing with an infection, not asthma.

"Come with me," she said, standing and grabbing one of Joe's elbows while his mother latched on to the other.

Suzanne had already displaced the patient who'd been waiting in the second exam room. Isabel went to help Joe up on the exam table, but he pushed her hand away gently and climbed up unassisted.

"When did this begin?" Isabel asked as she inserted a thermometer into Joe's mouth.

"Two or three days ago," his mother answered, her eyes glued nervously to her boy. "He started complaining about his shoulders aching. Then he got a fever. And he can't keep any food down. I thought it was the flu. But today he started this, like he can't get enough air."

Isabel took Joe's blood pressure. 122/83. Pulse 114. High—probably twice what it usually was. Respiratory rate was also elevated, to 27.

Joe's temperature—101.8—indicated an infection. Most likely pneumonia.

She lifted the stethoscope that hung from her neck to listen to Joe's lungs. She did not like what she heard. Bilateral rhonchi with coarse crackles indicated the presence of fluid.

"I want X rays," she said to Suzanne, who hovered nearby. "And let's draw blood."

A white cell count and an oxygen saturation test would be helpful in making the diagnosis, but the clinic was not equipped to do either. She would have to send blood out and wait for results. Meanwhile, it was clear that Joe needed immediate treatment.

MINUTES LATER, ISABEL held the X ray films to the wall-mounted light. Bright white patches confirmed that Joe's lungs were filling with fluids. But why?

"Let's get him started on IV. He needs antibiotics, and he's dehydrated, probably from the vomiting."

The IV catheter went in easily. Intravenous fluids would ward off shock and help prevent Joe's blood pressure from dropping. Not knowing what she was dealing with—if it was pneumonia, she hoped it would turn out to be bacterial—she chose a broad spectrum antibiotic and also piggybacked IV droperidol, for nausea.

"I'd like to give your lungs a little help here, Joe. That means putting you on oxygen."

Joe managed a half smile.

"I'll take . . . any help . . . I can get."

His voice was little more than a whisper.

She administered oxygen for several minutes. But with every passing minute, the sense that something was wrong—that her efforts were futile—grew stronger. Joe's condition seemed to be deteriorating before her eyes. His chest heaved with each breath and he looked more and more frightened, as his mother stood by, stroking his back and telling him he would be okay.

"Check his blood pressure again," she told Suzanne as she returned to the X ray films for another look.

"Ninety-four over sixty."

A drop of almost thirty points. Isabel looked at the clock on the wall. *In less than an hour.*

At the same time, Joe's breathing had grown more labored and rapid. A second respiratory reading showed his rate had increased to 39.

What the hell was she dealing with here?

Joe had been coughing intermittently, but suddenly, his entire being convulsed with his efforts to rid himself of the fluid accumulating in his lungs. As Joe's mother patted him futilely on the back, Isabel saw a drop of fluid fall from the hand he held to his mouth.

"Let me see, Joe," she said gently, pulling his hand down. A straw colored fluid coated his palm.

Serum.

Hantavirus. Adult respiratory distress syndrome—known in medical circles as ARDS—caused by exposure to aerosolized urine or feces from infected deer mice. The deadly disease had first surfaced in 1993, in the Four Corners region. It had claimed eleven lives that spring, most of them Native American.

Its victims drowned *in the serum* from their own blood.

Could Joe have contracted the deadly disease? Panic filled Isabel's every pore—a panic she had to keep hidden from Joe and his poor mother.

The coughing spasm had now passed and Isabel wrapped an arm around Joe's shoulders.

"I'll be right back. You hang in there, okay? We're going to take care of you."

Closing the door firmly behind her, Isabel ran at full speed to her office. En route, she debated about whether to call Harborview—which was a better equipped and staffed hospital, but was also five hundred miles away—or Missoula General. When she reached her office, she dialed Missoula General.

Immediately proclaiming the call an emergency, Isabel asked to be connected to the hospital's resident pulmonary specialist.

"I need a Life Flight. *Stat*," she blurted into the phone when Dr. Lehman Morris, Missoula General's acute respiratory distress syndrome specialist, came on the line. "I have an eighteen-year-old male with ARDS. I suspect I'm dealing with hantavirus. What can you tell me?"

"Have you done chest films?"

"Yes. They indicate extensive interstitial and alveolar infiltrates. His respiratory rate has jumped from 27 to 39 in just one hour. I've drawn blood but don't have the facilities to run a WBC or O-two. I've initiated IV fluids, antibiotics, and oxygen—two liters per minute. What else should I be doing?"

"Sounds like you're doing everything right. If your diagnosis is correct, at this point, treatment is mainly supportive. You have a mechanical ventilator, don't you?"

The two things Isabel had ensured after accepting the job at the clinic were that she would have a portable X ray and ventilator. She'd had to raise the funds herself for the X ray, but the clinic already had an old ventilator that was in decent working condition.

"Yes."

"I suggest you be prepared for prophylactic intubation. This disease can progress at alarming speed. Let's hope you're wrong and it won't be necessary, but you may need to ventilate him until the medevac arrives. I'm dispatching a helicopter as we speak. I'll be on it."

FOR THE NEXT hour, Joe seemed to stabilize.

Isabel did not want to intubate him unless or until it became absolutely necessary, for intubation would require sedation. While she did not allow the thought to actually take form in her mind, deep down, there was the knowledge that, if her diagnosis was correct, these could be Joe's last hours with his mother. As long as he remained calm and was able to bear the discomfort, she didn't want to do anything to diminish the quality of their time together.

Guilt had already begun snaking its way into Isabel's subconscious.

She'd been worried about Joe earlier in the week when he stopped by. Why hadn't she probed further that day, or gone looking for him when he failed to show up at the clinic the past few days?

She'd been so busy. It had been easy to assume Joe was busy as well, with final exams, or graduation parties.

But why hadn't she checked in on him?

If she had, maybe they would have caught this earlier.

"'Copter's coming!"

Suzanne had been standing at the window, her eyes glued to the skies, which, ironically, after months of rain (which Isabel would later learn had brought about an increase in the vegetation that led to a surge in the deer mice population), were a brilliant blue.

After a quick assessment that Joe was still stable, Isabel hurried outside and stood in front of the clinic, buffeted by the winds and dust as the helicopter settled nicely in the empty lot next door. Before the blades had stopped turning, the door flew open and a man jumped down, wearing a blue uniform with the Life Flight logo on the pockets. Immediately behind him a tall, dark-skinned man dressed in a physician's coat followed suit. He was so tall that he had to stay hunched over until he'd cleared the helicopter's blades.

"Dr. McLain?" he yelled over their din.

"Yes."

"I'm Dr. Morris."

"Thank you so much for coming," Isabel said, relieved to have the specialist there.

At a run, Isabel led them to the exam room where she'd left Joe. But in the mere minutes she'd been absent, Joe's condition had changed.

He clutched frantically at his chest and then the horrible spasms overtook him again.

"We'll need to intubate here," Morris said.

The medic administered a sedative via the IV catheter. In another minute, a second medic appeared with a wheeled cart. Slowly, as the sedative kicked in, Joe stopped thrashing. With a medic positioning Joe's head, Isabel used a laryngoscope to pass the endotracheal tube into Joe's airway while Dr. Morris placed him on the ventilator, using positive and expiratory pressure to maximize oxygenation.

"Blood pressure's down to 60 over 40," one of the medics suddenly called.

At this, Mrs. Winged Foot began to wail. Isabel nodded at Suzanne to move the distraught mother into the corridor.

She heard Suzanne say, "Do it for Joey, Anna."

It was the first time Isabel had heard the woman's name and it brought a lump to her throat.

As she turned the IV wide open to stem the rapidly falling blood pressure, one of the medics hooked Joe up to a heart monitor.

"We obviously can't transport him now," Isabel said softly, though by now Joe appeared to be unconscious. Then, the dreaded words she'd never expected to say, "Do you have paddles in there?" She nodded toward the cart the second medic had wheeled in.

At that very instant, as if her words were prescient, an alarm pierced the air. All faces turned toward the heart monitor.

Joe's heart had stopped.

Isabel began CPR, pounding on Joe's breastbone, but with each push, a column of blood-tinged fluid rose from his lungs through the tubing coming from his mouth. Just as the article had described, Joe Winged Foot was drowning, before all their eyes, in his own serum.

"Ready to defib?" Dr. Morris called out.

"*Ready.*"

Isabel moved aside, as Dr. Morris applied the defibrillator paddles to Joe's chest. A sickening *zzzzt* filled the room as Joe's legs flew into the air, then dropped heavily back to the table.

When Joe remained unresponsive, they defibrillated him again.

"Let's try some atropine," Morris said without looking up.

Isabel injected atropine directly into the pericardium, then epinephrine, then more atropine. But Joe did not respond, and soon the EKG appeared agonal.

"I think he's gone," one of the medics—Isabel couldn't tell which, since her eyes were glued to Joe—said.

"*No,*" Isabel responded defiantly, angrily. "One more time."

Dr. Morris complied, but Joe was gone now, and even Isabel knew it.

Resuscitation efforts ended at 3:15. Barely four hours after Joe had entered the clinic.

Isabel thanked Dr. Morris and the medics for their efforts, and, after crossing Joe's arms over his chest, pulled a sheet up to cover the burns left by the defibrillator. She could not break down now, for she had to go out and face Anna Winged Foot.

She had to give her the news.

NOTHING ISABEL COULD say would keep Anna Winged Foot away from her son. Wild-eyed in disbelief, clutching her grief like a pillow to her chest, Anna insisted on being alone with Joe in the examination room.

Anna's wails filled the clinic. Isabel did not try to shut them out. She wanted—more than she'd ever wanted anything in her entire life—to join Anna. She, too, wanted to hold that lifeless body and scream her anguish and anger. Instead, as she waited for the coroner's office to arrive with the sealed, leakproof body bag that would carry Joe to the morgue, Isabel sat, numb, in the clinic's empty waiting room.

It did not take long for other family members to arrive, each stone-faced as they approached the front door of the clinic, each pleading to be allowed inside with Anna and Joe. When Isabel turned them away, warning them of the danger, they would join the growing group of tribal members who had gathered outside, and the wailing would begin anew.

Isabel did not realize at first that Suzanne was gone, that she had joined the other Blackfeet gathered to show their support for the Winged Foot family. Instinctively, the tribe had come together, to draw strength from one another and suffer through the incomprehensible pain together.

As afternoon shadows inched their way across the waiting room floor, the rhythmic chanting from outside grew louder. Isabel sat, silent and alone, listening to the grief pouring out around her, her terror building with each passing second.

It would take several days to get the official results of Joe's autopsy, yet deep within her heart, she had little doubt regarding its outcome. She tried, in vain, to deny the similarities between the initial outbreak of hantavirus in 1993, where one of the first lives claimed was that of a healthy, young Indian male—that time, a Navajo—and an exceptional athlete.

Just like Joe.

That outbreak went on to claim thirteen members of the Navajo nation.

If, indeed, the autopsy results confirmed Isabel's worst fears—that Joe had died of the deadly hantavirus—what was in store for the Blackfeet, for Isabel's patients, in the coming weeks?

Despite the fact that it was growing too dark to read, Isabel's eyes strayed to the sheet of paper she'd held, clutched in her hands, ever since scrawling on it as she began her wait for the coroner. It was a list. Isabel had already read it so many times that she no longer needed light to make out the names on it.

Eli Walker

Jason Little Turtle

Sally Hawkeye and her two children, *Sam and Laurie*

It went on. Over a dozen names in total. Isabel had them all memorized now.

They were the names of the patients she'd seen earlier in the week. The day Joe filled in for Suzanne.

Names that until today held no more meaning for Isabel than those of hundreds of other patients. But now they were etched in her mind, along with each face.

For if the coroner confirmed Isabel's worst fear—that Joe's death had been caused by hantavirus—*would one of those names be its next victim?*

FIVE

Tony Wilderman's passion for his work could be traced to his childhood in Butte, Montana. His Dutch father, Henry, worked in the dangerously deep Anaconda mines until the 1950s, when his employer, the world's biggest producer of copper, moved from labor-intensive underground mining to open pit mining.

Tony could still remember the small yellow frame house on Butte's east side where he was born. He still remembered the day it was leveled, bulldozed flat as a pancake along with hundreds of other homes, to make way for the Berkely Pit—an ugly, mile-long blight on the land that eventually grew to a depth of over 1,800 feet. By the time the company switched to truck-operated open mining, the years spent underground had taken their toll on Henry's health; however, as a proven employee, Henry earned a coveted position driving one of dozens of trucks that hauled tons of sedimentary rock from the bottom of the vast pit to the mounds growing on its perimeter. On occasion, Henry would bring his son to work with him, entertaining a young and impressionable Tony with stories of mining catastrophes and terror half a mile below the earth's surface, explaining the mining process to him.

To many of Tony's classmates, "The Pit" symbolized everything they hated about Butte. Most left town as soon as they graduated from high school, some even sooner. But Tony loved The Pit and the time he spent there with his father. He loved the camaraderie of the mining community. Tony's carrot-colored hair and freckled skin, inherited from his mother, who had immigrated from Dublin the same year she met and married Henry Wilderman, made him a favorite of the droves of Irish who flocked to Butte in the 1930s and '40s to work in the mine. St. Patrick's Day celebrations were raucous and the highlight of the year for Tony.

Tony would gladly have remained in Butte and followed in his father's footsteps, but Henry Wilderman refused to entertain the possibility. He insisted that Tony get an education. At the University of Montana, Tony found a way to both placate his father and indulge his fascination with mining. He studied geology, earning first a B.S., then his master's and doctorate.

In the last three decades, Tony's keen mind and passion for his work had earned him a reputation as one of the mining industry's top exploratory geologists and one of the few WRI employees frequently consulted by its CEO. Like LeCoque, Tony considered the development of mineral resources essential; to Canada's, and the world's, future economic health. Also like LeCoque, he had little empathy or patience for the environmentalists that so often complicated their mission and their lives.

"I hear you've been back to your old stomping grounds." LeCoque had called this meeting the first day Wilderman returned from his most recent exploratory trip. "You still have family in Butte?"

"No," Tony answered, shaking a halo of rust colored curls. "After my father died, my mother moved to Los Angeles to live with my sister. I still like to swing through there once in a while, though it's a damn depressing sight anymore. But I didn't make it quite that far east this trip."

"Tell me about this trip."

Wilderman pushed back, elbows braced on either arm of his chair. When he lowered his jaw, his chin blended into fleshy jowls.

"Hell, Jon. You know I've always thought we oughta explore closer to home. Between the cost of doing business overseas and the growth of these goddamn environmental groups over there, watchdoggin' our every move, we can't win. I had a couple sites I'd been wanting to check out, one in particular. It—the one I'm referring to—could just solve a lot of our problems."

"Go on."

"Well, I visited four states in the Northwest. Idaho, Oregon, Washington, in that order, then finished up in Montana. Had some interesting meetings with folks from the USGS, and did extensive field evaluations in all four."

"And?"

"A couple interesting possibilities. The Owyhee region in southeastern Oregon for one. A team consisting of USGS scientists, university people, and Oregon state geologists has been evaluating the area. Geologic mapping shows a major gold deposit at Grassy Mountain."

"Volcanism?"

"Volcanism and basin development. The region has a bilateral symmetry along the Idaho-Oregon border, with older Miocene volcanic rock on the east and west of younger Miocene volcanic and volcaniclastic rocks."

"How big's the deposit?"

Wilderman shook his head. "Don't know. But we may be too late on this one anyway. Apparently Hudson Bay is close to tying up rights."

"How close?"

"I'd say it's pretty much a done deal. We'd have to jump in there pretty damn quick if we're serious. No time for us to do our own exploration. It'd be a wild card."

"We can't afford any wild cards."

"That's what I figured."

"What about Washington?" LeCoque pressed. "Find anything there?"

Wilderman's brows came together in reflection.

"It would take quite a bit more exploring to come up with anything definitive. Cannon Mine at Wenatchee's still the biggest producer in the state. It's possible there are other veins in that area. And granitic bodies scattered along the eastern Cascades indicate the possibility of copper and molybdenum. The deposit at Holden's pretty much depleted. But maybe it's worth a closer look."

"Hell, Tony, I expected to hear something more promising than *maybe it's worth a closer look.*"

Wilderman's thin lips disappeared in a smile. "Hold your horses, will you?" He leaned forward, his green Irish eyes flickering with excitement. "There is something more promising. In Montana, along the eastern slope of the Rockies. This may be the find of my lifetime."

Wilderman knew words like these tended to do powerful things to LeCoque. He could feel the CEO watching closely as he withdrew a folded sheet of paper from his briefcase.

Holding up a map, Wilderman's finger traced over a short yellow line he'd drawn earlier with a magic marker. It started at a point about a hundred miles east of the Montana-Idaho border and just below the Canadian border.

"This K-Spar zone cuts downsection and to the southeast. I'm convinced that it's gold-bearing. It consists of siltite beds. Fine-grained Middle Proterozoic metasedimentary rocks between twelve hundred and fifteen hundred years old. The gold should be widely distributed."

"What did your samples show?"

"Values ranging from point-fifteen ppm in disseminated sites to forty-one in veinlets."

Excitement flickered in LeCoque's usually steely gaze.

"Go on."

"The deposits shallow upward from basin plain to subtidal. Episodic submarine volcanism mixed with sediment during transport away from eruptive centers and resulted in turbidite hosted deposits along this entire region. Your classic basin growth faults."

"What's the land use now? Ranching?"

"Not really. There are a couple small operations, nothing of consequence. We're basically looking at a couple hundred thousand acres of bluffs, plateaus, and ragged mountains."

"State?" LeCoque asked. "Or federal?"

Wilderman's smile broadened, exposing a row of teeth that were perfectly shaped, but stained by years of chewing tobacco and a pot-a-day coffee habit.

"Indian. The deposit's on a reservation. That's the kicker."

A slow grin spread across LeCoque's face.

"What tribe?"

"Blackfeet."

"How bad off are they?"

"Plenty bad off."

LeCoque stared at Wilderman's map, momentarily lost in thought.

"EPA doesn't have jurisdiction over Indian lands, does it?"

Wilderman shook his head.

"No, sir."

"Tell me about the Blackfeet."

"They're one of the United States's poorest tribes. A couple other tribes with more resources have set up their own EPA-type agency, which, as far as I'm concerned, could end up a bigger pain in the ass than the EPA. But there's nothing like that there. There's nothing there at all. Just a pencil factory. Unemployment's close to sixty percent.

"But I gotta warn you," Wilderman went on. "I wasn't exactly a welcome figure down there. Got chased away half a dozen times when I was scoutin' around. One time I thought I was a goner. Didn't know I'd stumbled upon a sacred site until I found human bones. At a place called Ghost Ridge Lake. I guess hundreds of Blackfeet starved and froze to death there when the government didn't get supplies to them, so they're a little touchy about strangers up there. Fella ran me off with a shotgun. And that was just one of the problems I had to deal with. Never seen anything like it."

"What else?"

"I'll tell you what else. Nothing on that damn reservation is mapped. I mean rivers and lakes aren't named or even marked on maps. Half the roads that *are* mapped peter out into impassable tracks up a butte. And with the exception of one old timer I ran into at the gas station, I met with nothing but hostility when I tried to get any answers in town. So what I'm tryin' to say is, we may not be dealin' with the United States government and their fuckin' EPA, but this won't be any picnic either."

"But you felt you were on to something there? Something with the potential to be big?"

"There's gold there. Plenty of it. I can feel it."

LeCoque stared at the yellow slash on the map, which Wilderman had placed face-up on his desk.

"We could practically reach out and touch that land," he murmured.

Wilderman beamed.

"You got that right."

SIX

R EMEMBER, LYDIA," ISABEL said, as she walked her elderly heart patient back to the waiting room, where the woman's husband sat, stiff as a board and staring straight ahead, "you mustn't forget to take your Lasix. Twice a day. That's the only way you're going to get rid of that swelling in your . . ."

A loud thud from the front of the clinic drew Isabel's attention. In the next instant, a young Blackfeet woman stumbled through the door, her cough deep and violent, her eyes filled with terror—a terror Isabel recognized immediately. She had seen it just two days earlier.

"Get Dr. Morris on the phone," she yelled at Suzanne, who simply stared wide-eyed, paralyzed with fear. "Have them send the Life Flight."

One step inside the clinic, the woman froze, hunched over, one hand covering her eyes, the other pressed against her chest. All eyes in the waiting room fixed on her in horror. Isabel ran to her, grabbing hold of her elbow and supporting her, trying to hurry her through.

As she passed Suzanne, Isabel lowered her voice.

"Clear this place out. *Now.*"

Halfway down the hallway to the exam room, the woman doubled over, her body spasming with ugly, wrenching coughs. Isabel's heart sank. Fluid in the lungs. Was she dealing with end-stage hantavirus, like Joe's? Stiffening her arm to support the young woman, Isabel turned her head away, toward the wall, as the frail frame convulsed with the young woman's attempts to clear her lungs.

In its early stages, hantavirus—at least the strain known to the United States—had not been found to be contagious. But near the end, as the disease progressed, the virus could aerosolize, making it deadly to simply share the same air. Isabel's first priority was getting the woman back to an exam room, away from the other patients.

Behind her, she could hear Suzanne ushering the patients who had been waiting to see Isabel outside. Though the fear in the air was palpable, the evacuation took place in near silence.

"In here," Isabel said, half lifting the woman's limp form, as she directed her to the exam room that had just been vacated.

With no time to spare, Isabel began her questions before they reached the table.

"When did you start feeling sick?"

"Last week," the young woman answered, expelling precious air.

Isabel wanted to scream at her, to ask her why she'd waited this long to come to the clinic.

Perhaps she didn't know about Joe. At this point Isabel hoped that she did not. The fear in the eyes of the poor child—she couldn't be more than twenty years old—told Isabel that she knew very well how serious her condition was.

"Up here," Isabel said, helping her on to the examination table. "Can you tell me your name?"

"Dolores . . ." The breaths were shallow and painful. ". . . Birdsong."

"Okay, Dolores. I'm going to hook you up to an IV and start you on an antibiotic. Do you understand?"

Pressing her eyes closed, Dolores nodded and swallowed against the liquid drowning her.

Isabel stepped away momentarily to slip on a mask and rubber gloves. The full protective gear she'd ordered for both her and Suzanne the day after Joe's death had not yet arrived. However, just that morning something precious had. A shipment of ribavirin had been delivered, courtesy of Dr. Morris. The antiviral drug was extremely difficult to obtain. Its therapeutic value in the treatment of hantavirus was still in question, but Morris was convinced of its efficacy. He'd confessed to having stockpiled some of it and offered to send some to Isabel.

After inserting the IV into Dolores's arm, Isabel drew the ribavirin into a syringe. Lehman Morris's words came back to her.

"Let's just pray you don't need it."

Isabel was reaching for the IV tubing, the syringe full of ribavirin poised in the air, when Dolores Birdsong went into another convulsion of coughing. This time she could not stop. The same pinkish sputum that Isabel had seen on Joe Winged Foot's hands dribbled from the corners of Dolores's mouth as she sucked the room's air, desperately trying to inflate her compromised lungs.

Standard procedure would have been for Isabel to take an X ray, draw blood for a CBC and blood chemistry, but there was no time for that now.

When the spasms had passed and Dolores had grown still, Isabel hurriedly injected the ribavirin into the IV tubing. As she did so, a slender hand grabbed hold of her forearm and, with what little strength remained, squeezed. Dolores's eyes came up to Isabel's and held them, pleading.

Isabel recognized that the situation was becoming more critical by the minute.

"Listen to me, Dolores," she said, forcing a smile, willing herself to remain calm. "I would like to help you breathe. I think you need that. I want to put you on a mechanical ventilator. It will breathe for you, help you get oxygen."

Dolores's huge eyes never strayed from Isabel's, never blinked.

"But in order to do that, I'm going to have to give you something to put you to sleep."

The eyes grew even larger.

"Do you understand?"

A nod of the head. Talking was simply too difficult.

"A team of specialists from Missoula is on its way *right this minute* to help us out," Isabel continued, praying her words were true. "I will be by your side all the way. Do you understand? I will be here with you." She absolutely could not bear to see the terror in those innocent young eyes a moment longer and so she did the one thing she'd always vowed she would never do to a patient. She lied. "You're going to be just fine."

A flicker of relief flowed, wavelike, across Dolores's face.

"I'm not gonna . . . die?" she whispered. "Like . . . Joe?"

Isabel's eyes widened. Dolores knew about Joe.

"Not if I have anything to do with it," she said.

Isabel had hoped to avoid bringing Suzanne into the room, hoped to avoid exposing her assistant to the hantavirus again. After Joe's death, she had advised Suzanne that if another hantavirus patient arrived, Suzanne was to keep her distance. But she needed help to insert the inch-wide endotracheal tube that would allow the machine to breath for Dolores until the helicopter arrived.

Isabel squeezed Dolores's hand, then turned toward the door to call Suzanne.

She did not see that Dolores's eyes flickered open one last time.

All Isabel heard, all that she would remember, was Dolores's voice, no bigger than a shaky whisper.

"Please save me."

EARLY MORNING SUN reflected blindingly off the waters of the Willamette River in southwest Portland, but instead of appreciating the rare treat, Ken MacStirling, senior scientist at ImmuVac, rose and lowered the blinds in his office to eliminate the glare on his computer screen. On a clear day like this one, MacStirling usually took time to stand and gaze appreciatively at the splendor of snow-covered Mount Hood in the distance. As a child in Glasgow, hours of watching American Westerns had instilled in him an awe of the West's mountains, and he usually relished the days when the almost mystical Mount Hood was not obscured by Portland's dismal weather.

But today, Ken eagerly hurried back to the medical article he'd just happened onto while scanning the Web sites he'd bookmarked.

He reached for his telephone and punched a four-digit extension.

"Chris?" he said, a note of urgency lacing his Scottish tongue. "I've got to talk to Dr. Lyons. Is he in yet?"

Chris Finch, administrative assistant to James Lyons, founder and CEO of ImmuVac, announced that her boss was, indeed, in the office and placed MacStirling on hold.

The next instant, Lyons's characteristically abrupt voice came on the line.

"Ken. What's up?"

"Say, James," MacStirling began. "Are you aware of the hantavirus outbreak over there in Montana?"

Lyons's pause was not a good sign.

"No."

"It's on an Indian reservation," MacStirling continued. "Northwest Montana. Three confirmed deaths so far. In less than one week."

"Three deaths doesn't change the situation, Ken. You know that."

MacStirling swallowed against the disappointment rising in his throat.

"This disease is not going to just disappear, James. I implore you. Let me proceed with my vaccine."

"I thought we agreed that you were to focus on your AIDS research," Lyons snapped.

"My AIDS work is progressing quite nicely. Blount can attest to that. I assure you I have not been ignoring it. But when you hired me, James, you promised to support my work on the HantaVac."

"Dammit, Ken, when I hired you, we had big hopes pinned on HV 4230. If the Phase III trials had gone as we expected, there would have been plenty of money to fund HantaVac trials. But you know as well as I do that that's not how things panned out. How do you think this company can afford to sink a million bucks into a clinical trial for a product that's unlikely to ever break even when we had to scrub our public offering just two months ago?"

"I shouldn't think it would run so high as a million, James. Maybe half that."

Lyons issued a snort of frustration.

"You're missing the point. This company has to focus where we can attract funding. That means AIDS and cancer. Can't you get that into your head?"

Without waiting for a response, Lyons hung up.

"Arsehole," MacStirling muttered angrily as he replaced the phone.

He pushed back from his desk and returned to the window. Raising the blinds he'd closed just minutes earlier, his eyes finally surveyed the view from his office window, but in his disappointment, the magnificence of the morning escaped him.

My vaccine could have saved those people's lives.

Lyons thought MacStirling didn't understand the situation, but that wasn't true. The biotech industry was one big crap shoot. Companies like ImmuVac often staked their entire future—hundreds of millions of dollars—on one or two products. Disastrous clinical trial results, like their recent Phase III on a cancer treatment for which they'd already invested upwards of fifty million, could easily take a whole company down, and all its promising products with it. MacStirling didn't want that to happen any more than Lyons did. They had some promising therapies in R&D, drugs that MacStirling had to admit would save many more lives than a vaccine for the hantavirus. The AIDS vaccine ImmuVac had in development was one of them.

But it made MacStirling bloody crazy to think that corporate profit more often than not dictated what disease was worth eradicating, what human life worth saving.

Isn't there anything in this industry, this entire country, that matters more than money?

CHAPTER

SEVEN

ISABEL DROVE SO fast that on the final curve of the dusty one-lane road her balding tires sent her skidding off into the scrubweed that ran along the side.

Suzanne's aunt Mary had warned her about that curve. She'd told Isabel to look for the trailer immediately after rounding it.

There, ahead, she saw it. Blue. With Suzanne's champagne-colored Dynasty sitting outside.

Unlike many of the mobile homes populating Browning, this one was freshly painted, with a perfectly maintained white picket fence surrounding its tiny yard.

As Isabel hurried up the stone path to the front door, she noticed a small garden, with handwritten tags—peas, strawberries, carrots—clipped with clothespins to sticks protruding from the fresh dirt at the head of each row.

A frail, gray-haired woman met her at the door.

"Mary?" Isabel asked.

The woman nodded.

"Thank you for coming. Please, come in."

"I'm just glad you called," Isabel answered.

Isabel stepped inside. To her left was a well-scrubbed kitchen. Beyond that, through a short hallway, she could see a room with a bed. It was empty.

A brightly colored floral shower curtain obscured most of the room to her right, but when Mary pushed it aside, Isabel saw that it was a living room.

On the couch lay Suzanne.

"You shouldna come all the way out here," Suzanne said. "I'm just comin' down with a little cold."

Isabel crossed to the couch and pressed her hand to Suzanne's forehead.

It felt warm.

As Isabel removed a thermometer and stethoscope from her brown leather bag, her eyes surveyed her assistant head to toe.

"Any headache?" she asked.

"Just a little bit, but I always get them with a cold."

"Cough?"

"Some."

"Shortness of breath? Dizziness?"

Suzanne did not answer.

"She's been complainin that it's hard to breathe," Mary said.

Then the elderly woman turned to Suzanne.

"You tell her everything, you hear?" she scolded, her eyes filled with concern.

Isabel sat down on the couch, hip pushed up against Suzanne's. She laid the thermometer and the stethoscope in her lap.

"Please," she said, her eyes grabbing hold of Suzanne's. "Your aunt's right. You know better than to take chances. Tell me everything."

Suzanne took a deep breath before answering.

"I dunno . . . ," she said hesitantly. "Sometimes I feel like I'm havin' a hard time taking a deep breath. And I've had some dizzy spells."

"What else? Muscle pain?"

Suzanne nodded. As she did, her eyes welled with tears.

"In my shoulders."

Isabel reached up and brushed Suzanne's bangs off her face.

"You're going to be all right," she said, fighting back her own tears.

"That's what you told Dolores."

"You heard that?"

Suzanne nodded.

"Listen to me," Isabel said. "I lied to Dolores. I knew when I said it that it would probably end up being a lie. But I had to give her hope. I had to ease her fear. Please forgive me for that."

Suzanne's eyes were a mixture of suspicion, fear, and an intense need to reach out for help.

"But if this is hantavirus," Isabel went on, "we're catching it early. Very early. Much earlier than with Joe or Dolores. And I never even got to see Will Echohawk before he died."

"Do you think that will make a difference?" Suzanne asked weakly.

"It does make a difference. I know that. That's what I've been trying to tell you and everybody else. You have to come in early—the moment the first symptoms show up. Now, let me listen to your lungs."

Isabel's hands trembled as she helped Suzanne sit up. She lifted the yellow flannel nightgown and placed the stethoscope over her ribcage, instructing her to take a deep breath. She listened intently, then moved to Suzanne's back.

Just the slightest crackle. If indeed this was hantavirus, it was early stage.

They had a chance. Finally.

Isabel looked at Mary, who hovered nearby, her hands clutching the sides of her thin, blue-floral housedress. Red Converse hightops stuck out from underneath its hem.

"I'd like you to get together a few things for Suzanne," she said. "A small overnight bag."

Suzanne had fallen back to the pillow, but at this, she bolted upright.

"Wait a minute. I'm not going anywhere."

"Yes, you are," Isabel said. "You're going to the hospital in Missoula. I'm driving you myself. Right now."

"Hell you are."

Suzanne jumped to her feet, but immediately reached for the back of a chair for support.

"Take it easy, Suzanne. Please. Sit back down."

But Suzanne shook her head and remained standing.

"Treat me *here*," she said. "Right here. If I'm going to die, I'm doing it here, in my own house. My own bed."

"You are not going to die." Isabel practically shouted. "I won't let you."

Suzanne studied her, a glint of surprise in her eyes.

"Then make me well here. Save me here. In my home."

"Why? *Why are you willing to take such a chance?*" Isabel hadn't even realized that tears had sprung to her eyes. "I haven't been able to save *anyone*."

Suzanne turned her eyes downward, seemingly embarrassed by Isabel's tears. Then she lowered herself back to the couch and reached for the thermometer that Isabel had placed on the table.

Before inserting it in her mouth, Suzanne looked back up, into Isabel's eyes.

"Then save *me*."

"IT'S BEEN FORTY-EIGHT hours now," Isabel said into the phone. "The most recent radiographs show interstitial edema but no bibasilar or peri-hilar airspace. Surely that's a good sign."

Isabel's conversations with Lehman Morris had become her lifeline the past ten days, especially since Suzanne came down sick. As luck would have it—just when she'd begun believing there was no such thing as luck—the first person she'd called for help when Joe fell ill turned out to be the Northwest's most revered expert on HPS—hantavirus pulmonary syndrome. With Suzanne's life hanging in the balance, Isabel did not make a move now without consulting Morris.

"It's definitely a good sign," Morris answered. There was a pause before he continued. "But it's not conclusive. Why don't you overnight me those films so I can take a look at them? Meanwhile, don't get your hopes too high."

"She's going to make it, dammit," Isabel declared. "She has to. We started her on the ribavirin early. You said that could make a big difference."

"Yes. I told you. Ribavirin didn't seem to reduce fatality in the ninety-three outbreak, but it's been my theory all along that that was because the patients were too far along in their disease course for the antiviral to turn them around. You got Suzanne started early, and that may well make the difference. I suspect it already has. Typically, two thirds of the patients show extensive bibasilar or perihilar involvement within forty-eight hours of onset. The fact that Suzanne doesn't is definitely encouraging."

"Think there's any chance we're not dealing with hantavirus this time?"

"No. I'm convinced it's hantavirus. The interstitial changes in those first X rays you sent to me are classic indicators of early hantavirus."

"Also the Kerley B lines," Isabel added. She had done little but study this hideous disease—its symptoms, progression, treatment—ever since that day Joe Winged Foot walked into her office. Kerley B lines—the short linear opacities running perpendicular to the pleural surfaces in lung radiographs of patients with HPS—were not part of her vocabulary just two weeks ago. But they were now. As were Kerley A lines, longer lines radiating from the lung hilum.

"That's right. Now the question is, how did each of these victims contract it?"

Isabel rubbed her tired eyes. That was the sixty-four-thousand-dollar question that had haunted her night and day. Sleep was a thing of the past.

"The CDC investigator is due in town today," she said, "but I've been doing some investigating on my own in the meantime. Anna Winged Foot can't think of anything that might have exposed Joe. They haven't had any rodent infestation in the house, nor, from what I've been able to determine, at school. Joe'd been spending most of his evenings outside, playing basketball with his friends. Right now it's anyone's guess how he contracted the virus."

"That might explain it."

"What?"

"Playing ball outside. If those courts are anything like the ones I played on as a kid, and I suspect they are, the surface is like one big field of popcorn. A bad hop could send the ball flying into the weeds and dirt. Hantavirus isn't easy to catch outdoors, but say it's a still night, no wind. Joe bends over, stirs up the weeds and dirt trying to pick the ball up, gets a good whiff. It's possible. Not likely, but definitely possible."

"Why aren't I surprised to hear you played basketball?" Isabel asked, suddenly overcome by a desperate need to be distracted from this awful disease that had taken over her life, her very being. The image of Lehman Morris bending his six-foot-five frame to stay clear of the Life Flight copter's blades came back to her.

Morris chuckled.

"How else do you think a kid from the projects in Chicago ended up in Montana? Back in my day, someone my size could actually play center. That was my position here, at the university. These days, a center's gotta be seven feet. I tell you, I was really looking forward to watching that Winged Foot boy play for the Grizzlies."

"You knew Joe played basketball?"

"I saw him in the state championship. Hell of a player. Scrappy, and fast. It's such a shame, that boy dying like that. He had a chance. A chance to get out. To make something of himself."

The empathy in Morris's voice was as thick and clear as the Midwestern accent he'd yet to lose, even after two decades in the West.

It was no wonder. For the first time Isabel realized the strong similarities between Joe Winged Foot and Lehman Morris. Both talented young men for whom basketball had represented a way out of the poverty and despair that would eventually swallow most of their peers. But it was clear that Morris had long ago learned there was nothing to be gained by dwelling upon the inequities of being born poor and black.

"What about the others?" Morris asked. "What have you come up with for them?"

"About two weeks before she died Dolores Birdsong cleaned out an old pickup truck that had been sitting behind her house for years. She needed some cash and hoped to sell it now that the weather's turned nice."

"Classic scenario. The deer mice found a hole in the truck and have been wintering there, maybe for years, and she gets in there and starts stirring up dust containing dried feces and urine. What about Suzanne?"

"I think Suzanne was exposed here, at the clinic. She'd been complaining about mice. I asked her to set out traps. She found dead mice in them several days in a row." There was a hitch in Isabel's voice as she continued. "She picked them up. Threw them away, in the Dumpster outside. It never even occurred to me to warn her . . ."

"Listen to me, young lady . . ."

As far as Isabel could tell, Lehman Morris was no more than five or six years her senior, yet he often spoke to her as if generations separated them. Many of Isabel's male colleagues over the years had demonstrated condescenscion toward her and other women doctors. With them, Isabel simply refused to tolerate it. But intuitively, she knew that arrogance was not in Lehman Morris's makeup. His words were a genuine reflection of his concern.

"We've not had a single case of hantavirus in Montana prior to these," he went on. "You had no reason to think that extra precautions were necessary. You cannot blame yourself."

Isabel did not respond.

"Now tell me," Morris continued. "What was your exposure to these mice? Please say you didn't handle them too."

A brief silence ensued before Isabel answered.

"I had an encounter with one in the supply cabinet. Afterward, I cleaned up pellets."

"You may very well have exposed yourself."

"I've been thinking that's a possibility."

"How long ago was that?"

"Exactly thirteen days."

"Then you're not out of the woods yet. And neither is your patient. I'd feel much better if Suzanne would let us send the helicopter to pick her up. Any chance she'll change her mind?"

"Not for now. Suzanne's adamant about staying home."

"You've got her isolated? It's unlikely she'd be able to transmit the disease now, but if the virus progresses . . ."

"Aside from coming into the clinic twice now for X rays, she's stayed out at her trailer. There's no one out there but Suzanne and her aunt, and the aunt is as stubborn as Suzanne. But I did finally worm a promise out of Suzanne. That if her condition worsens, she'll reconsider going to Missoula General. That—the risk of infecting her aunt—was the only way I got that promise, by the way. That assistant of mine is so damn stubborn . . ." Isabel's voice rose in anger, then began to crack. She was furious with Suzanne for taking such a chance, insisting on staying home. And, if the truth be known, Isabel was terrified. She visited her newest patient each day, sometimes twice, to check in and make sure Suzanne and Mary were adhering strictly to the instructions Isabel gave them.

"Hey, you okay?"

Isabel swallowed against the flood of emotion threatening to choke her.

"I'm fine," she said. "Just tired."

"I imagine the clinic's keeping you busy," Morris said. "Usually one case of hantavirus sends everyone within fifty miles running to the doctor with the slightest ache or sniffle. It can create a real paranoia."

For the first time in days, Isabel let out a laugh.

"Well, that's certainly not a problem here," she said. "This place is like a morgue." She laughed again, a humorless laugh. "Forgive my choice of words. What I'm trying to say is either the residents of Browning have suddenly all acquired perfect health, or they've decided I, personally, am killing my patients."

"That bad, huh?"

"That bad. Hell, can you blame them? Joe, Dolores Birdsong, Will Echohawk. All dead."

"You never even saw Will Echohawk, did you?"

"No. When he came down with the same symptoms Joe had, his mother refused to bring him here. She said I hadn't been able to save Joe. Instead of bringing him in to the clinic, she had a doctoring ceremony performed by a traditional healer. A sweat lodge ceremony where they sprinkled herbs into the fire. By morning the poor kid was dead."

"You can't blame yourself, Isabel. Their suspicions are, in many ways, well founded. And they run deep. You can't come in there and in a matter of months undo attitudes that took decades, over a century, to form."

"Maybe if I'd been able to save Joe . . ."

"Some of them, most likely Will Echohawk, would have stayed away anyway. They'll come back. It'll just take a little time."

"I hope you're right. In the meantime, I hear the native healers are keeping busy." She tried to sound lighthearted, but failed.

"Lehman," Isabel said, "I *have* to save Suzanne. I just have to."

ALISTAIR STEERED THE sleek sportscar around the curve of the Montlake exit. His mood matched the day. Gloomy, oppressive. Already regretting having agreed to meet Mary—his patience with the hand-holding she'd been demanding was growing paper thin—the sight of the long line of cars, at a dead stop in university traffic, made him consider turning around and heading back home. But he'd already merged onto Montlake and now found himself trapped in a sea of cars. He inched forward in the logjam that *Money* magazine had recently declared the nation's third worst. It was always bad this time of day, but today's nasty downpour only compounded it.

Fucking Seattle.

It took almost twenty minutes to travel the two miles from the Evergreen Floating Bridge to the clinic. The rain came in sheets, making it hard to see any distance at all, which is why he didn't notice all the official looking vehicles until after he'd already pulled into the left-turn-only lane that deposited cars directly into the parking lot for the clinic.

Stunned by the sight before him, he counted four, no five, generic white vans with official-looking seals on their doors.

He had just slowed at the parking lot's mouth when a wave of wind and water washed over him, sending new shock waves through him. He turned to see a wet and frantic Mary Pelandini climbing in through the opened passenger door.

"*Back out,*" Mary wailed. "*Now,* no one's coming. Get out of here before they see you."

Alistair glanced briefly over his right shoulder to look for oncoming traffic. He could not see any cars, but then he couldn't really see at all. He slid the gear shift into reverse and punched the gas pedal.

The moment he did so, a horn, followed instantaneously by the sound of rubber screeching against pavement, announced that he'd pulled into someone's path.

"Mother of God!" Mary screamed, but the oncoming red Durango whizzed by, missing them by inches, as its driver vented her fury with a fist held to the horn.

Alistair shifted into drive and accelerated, heading west.

"What the fuck's goin' on?" he asked, eyeing Mary, who'd begun shaking and crying.

"They're raiding us," she sobbed. "They showed up just after we hung up. Like a SWAT team or something."

"Who're they?"

"They called themselves federal agents. There must be a dozen of them. They were watching me. I couldn't call you to tell you not to come. I asked to go to the bathroom, then snuck out the back door so I could warn you."

"This is unreal. What're they looking for?"

"Everything!" Mary cried. "They have a search warrant. It gives them the right to take everything. They're going through every drawer, every file, and packing it all in boxes."

"But they've already been through it once. That's what you told me."

"Now they're back. And this time they're taking everything with them. They even . . ." the sobs returned, ". . . they even videotaped me. Why would they do that? Why would they make me stand there while they videotaped me?"

Alistair could see it coming. Mary was about to crack. She could end up spilling her guts. If he didn't watch it.

"They're just trying to intimidate you," he said, struggling to sound self-assured. "That's all. It's all for show, darlin'. All of it. There's not a goddamn thing there. Not a thing that can hurt us." He reached out and placed his hand on her thigh. Immediately, his touch seemed to calm her. "Now, darlin', I better get you back there. I'm gonna swing around Thirty-second and drop you in the lot of the office park next to ours. You sneak back in there. Tell them you were so shaken you stepped outside for some air. You can't let them rattle you, darlin'. Remember what my friend said? We're practically home free."

"But what about Ariana's fax?"

"You still haven't found that?"

"No."

"Then it doesn't exist."

Alistair had made three consecutive right turns and now approached the office complex adjacent to and north of the clinic.

"What if they start questioning me?" Mary whimpered, reaching for the door handle. "Should I call my lawyer?"

"Absolutely not," Alistair declared. "That just makes it look like you've got something to hide. You don't want that."

He didn't add that any lawyer worth his or her salt would work an immunity deal in exchange for Mary's cooperation in hanging Alistair.

"You have nothing to fear, Mary." He reached for her hand as the car came to a stop and squeezed reassuringly. "Nothing at all. What we've done is nothin' out of the ordin'ry, nothin' that others aren't doin' every single day. Remember that."

Mary gave him a weak smile.

The fear clenching at Alistair's throat relaxed its hold a bit. Mary would be all right. All it took was a little TLC, some attention from Alistair. But he would have to keep a close eye on her.

Alistair did not linger. He was back on Montlake within minutes, this time more preoccupied with his own troubles than with traffic.

Federal agents. No doubt called by the FDA's criminal division. Was this just some kind of bluff? A mind game designed to make someone talk? Alistair strongly suspected that to be the case.

But there was another explanation, and this one was far more difficult to dismiss. This one absolutely had to be explored.

Had somebody been feeding them information?

THE MESSAGE WAS so short, so maddeningly lacking in information, but the note of urgency in Mary Talking Horse's voice was unmistakeable.

"It's Suzanne. Please come."

For the past week, with Suzanne gone, Isabel had formulated her own routine before opening the clinic for the day.

Feed the dogs. With spring came bountiful rodent hunting on the reservation. Most of the pack she'd nourished through the winter had disappeared, but two—the mangy mutt and one of his female friends—continued to be waiting for her each morning. She'd taken to putting bowls of food out for them, out of sight, near the back door of the clinic.

Play back messages on the answering machine. If the message light blinked, she would press the playback button, then listen as she walked around the office turning on lights and checking the appointment book for the day's schedule.

Before this past week, Suzanne had complained routinely of having to wade through too many messages each morning. Today the machine had announced there were only two.

The first was from the CDC investigator who was in town and wanted to schedule an appointment to speak with her.

The second had been Mary Talking Horse's.

Isabel had grabbed the bag she'd just deposited on the counter behind Suzanne's cluttered desk, rummaging frantically for the keys to relock the clinic's front door. There was no time to spare. She would call Mary from her cell phone and, if need be, contact Missoula General to have them dispatch a Life Flight team immediately.

As she sped out of town, Isabel punched Suzanne and Mary's telephone number into her cell phone. No response. She punched the redial button, then pressed the phone back to her ear. Nothing. She tried it again, then raised the phone to look at it. The screen flashed NO SVC.

No service.

Damn. Her cell phone worked just fine between her cabin near East Glacier and Browning, but she'd never tried to use it south or east of town.

She had a decision to make. Turn the car around and find a pay phone, or continue to Suzanne's.

Turning around would cost her at least five minutes.

She'd already learned that with hantavirus, five minutes could cost a life.

She had an ironclad grip on the steering wheel as she pulled off Highway 2. Still, her hands shook as she roared up the nameless gravel road leading toward the trailer.

Isabel realized that she'd done the unthinkable. She'd let herself become too involved. Suzanne's recovery, her survival, had become the only thing that mattered to Isabel. It had caused her to lose good judgment. She should never have agreed to treat Suzanne at home. Perhaps if she had refused, Suzanne would have been forced to do the prudent thing and go either to Cutbank or Missoula, where an entire hospital staff would be available to minister to her. But Isabel had been too afraid to call Suzanne's bluff and so she had acquiesced.

And now this.

Oblivious to the purple lupines dotting the meadows and the hawk circling lazily overhead, catching a light breeze in the cloudless morning sky, Isabel tore down the unmaintained road, the car shaking so violently as the ruts grew deeper and more frequent that her medical bag vibrated back and forth on the seat beside her, giving the appearance of riding on a cushion of air.

A long cloud of dust announcing its approach before the Jeep actually came into sight, Isabel finally rounded the last curve. She saw cars—at least three of them—outside the trailer. One was Suzanne's. As she drew near, she recognized another immediately. It belonged to Father McGrath, the parish priest.

Her anguish literally choking her, Isabel roared up to the white picket fence and approached the trailer door at a run.

It opened before she reached the steps.

Father McGrath, a compact, white-haired Irishman with a smile so benevolent Isabel suspected that it had dictated its owner's destiny, stood in its frame.

Only Father McGrath would smile at a time like this.

"Come in, my dear," he said.

"Am I too . . ." Isabel began, stepping inside, but the air she met stopped her mid-sentence. The unmistakable aroma of just-brewed coffee and baked goods fresh from the oven enveloped her. Not the air of illness or death.

Father McGrath's grin widened as he nodded toward the living room, where a small group had gathered.

Mary Talking Horse. Another elderly Blackfeet woman whom Isabel did not know.

And Suzanne.

Suzanne. Sitting up, fully dressed, a cup of tea in her hand, a big, jubilant grin—the most beautiful grin Isabel had ever seen—taking over her entire face. And, for the first time in days, cherry-red lipstick.

With legs of rubber, Isabel went to her and dropped to her knees, her medical bag falling thickly to the floor beside her.

"What . . . ?" Isabel stammered. "When?"

Suzanne's laughter reached out and enveloped her.

"You did it," she beamed. "You healed me."

"I don't understand. Just yesterday, you'd begun vomiting . . ."

Suzanne placed a hand on Isabel's shoulder.

"I don't understand any more than you. But last night, I could feel it. That the sickness was leaving my body. It was like my body was purging itself of it yesterday, when I couldn't keep anything down. I didn't want to call you and get your hopes up, but I knew. I knew I'd be well again this morning. And when I woke up, I was."

"It's a miracle," Isabel said softly.

The smile left Suzanne's face.

"*No*. It's no miracle. *You* did it. You saved me." She looked at the others in the room. "I owe my life to her. She came to me every day, twice, three times sometimes. She got me through this. She saved me."

Heads nodded all around.

Isabel grabbed Suzanne's wrist and felt for her pulse. Strong, steady. No sign of the tachycardia she'd noticed every other day.

She checked Suzanne's lungs. Clear.

Oxygenation, ninety-eight.

Suzanne had shown improvement in days three and four, fueling Isabel's optimism. But yesterday's nausea and vomiting had sent Isabel's spirits spiraling into the gutter. Now, overnight, her patient had recovered.

Lehman Morris had told her that those hantavirus patients who survived recovered almost as fast as the others died. But never, in her wildest dreams, had she dared hope for this.

"Now I can come back to work." Suzanne grinned as Isabel retracted the stethoscope.

"Not so fast," Isabel said, finally allowing the relief, the laughter that had been bubbling up inside her, to surface. "You're staying right here. At home and in bed. Another couple days at the very least."

"Aw, come on. I'm bored to death out here." Suzanne turned to her aunt. "No offense, Mary. But next time I get so sick I almost die, I'm gonna demand a satellite dish. We're the only ones on the rez without one."

Isabel accepted the tea and fresh fry bread brought in celebration of Suzanne's recovery by Mary's elderly friend Rose, then she stood.

"I should get back to the clinic," she said.

"I'm sorry if we made you miss appointments," Mary Talking Horse said softly. "We just wanted you to see Suzanne for yourself. We thought you deserved that."

"Thank you. And no apology necessary. I haven't exactly been busy recently."

"That's what we heard." Suzanne's expression reflected both concern and embarrassment. "But that's gonna change now. You wait and see."

Isabel's smile was wide. And genuine.

"I hope so. But for now, I'm just happy to see you looking so well. Don't you push yourself too hard, you hear?"

After getting Suzanne and Mary's promise that Suzanne would take it easy for several more days, Isabel took her leave.

The lupines and hawk—now perched on top of a telephone post—that she'd missed on the way out gave Isabel great pleasure on her return trip. As did the blue columbine and the fiery Indian paintbrush dotting the meadows on either side of the road. The sense of relief that she felt surged through her like adrenaline, sharpening the blue of the morning sky. The morning air, still chilled from thirty-degree nights, never felt so pure and crisp as it did now, rushing through her open window. She could not get enough of it. Or of the heady sensation.

Suzanne did not die.

Just once they had beat this dreaded, loathsome disease.

Pulling up to the clinic, Isabel's mood lifted higher still to see two figures waiting outside. *Patients.* Had word of Suzanne's recovery already spread, or were there still some who did not blame her for Joe and Dolores's deaths?

Right now it didn't really matter.

Isabel flashed both patients, Eli Walker and a middle-aged woman whose face was unfamiliar, a smile of greeting. Eli looked clean and sober.

"I'm so sorry to keep you waiting outside like this," she said. She'd never felt so eager to treat a patient, so full of hope.

As she fingered her keys, searching for the one that opened the clinic's front door, she noticed it.

The package, small, thin, rectangular, leaning up against the locked door.

"You just missed UPS," Eli Walker said.

Without looking at its address label, Isabel picked up the package, which was the size and shape of a videocassette, unlocked the door, and ushered her two patients inside.

Then she dropped the package on top of Suzanne's desk and went to work.

CHAPTER

EIGHT

WHEN AN ENTIRE month passed with no new cases of hantavirus, then six weeks, Isabel finally began to breathe more easily.

The CDC investigator had confirmed Isabel's conclusion: that Dolores Birdsong contracted the virus while cleaning out the broken-down truck in her yard. Deer mice caught in Will Echohawk's house were sent for tests and came back confirmed carriers of the hantavirus. Since Suzanne had disposed of the mice caught in the clinic, there was no way to prove that her exposure originated there, but the final report labeled the clinic mice as "the probable source of exposure."

It was never determined how Joe contracted the virus. Anna Winged Foot's house was spotless and free of any signs of rodent infestation. There was no reason to think Joe had been exposed at school, especially in light of the fact that none of the other students at Browning High became ill.

Though Isabel could not control the thoughts that tormented her in the quiet of each night, during the day, she wasn't given that chance. Suzanne's recovery—accompanied by tales of Isabel's dedication—had spread like wildfire across the reservation. Isabel strongly suspected that her assistant had mounted a one-woman campaign from her trailer in the week between her recovery and the day Isabel allowed her to come back to work on a part-time basis. Whatever the explanation, Isabel suddenly found her patient load dramatically increased. Blackfeet residents who had suffered from a condition or ailment silently for years were filtering in to see what the new doctor could do to help. And the fear of hantavirus brought many in for sniffles or aches and pains that once would have been ignored.

The relief and gratification Isabel felt was immense. She relished the hard work, relished the exhaustion at the end of a twelve- or fourteen-hour day, for it represented her only hope for a few hours of mindless, merciful sleep.

This day, like the three before it, had started before dawn and was now ending well after the sun had dropped into the mountains. As Isabel approached the side door to her cabin, she could hear the telephone ringing inside. Flinging the door to the kitchen wide, she groped the wall blindly for the light switch. She told herself she'd start leaving a light on each morning when she left for work.

Dropping her medical bag on the dusty wood floor, she used both hands. After the fourth ring, the answering machine came on. As she heard her voice asking the caller to leave a message, Isabel continued groping the wall impatiently. There, at last, she found it. The kitchen sprang to light just as the caller began to speak.

Isabel's hand froze on the light switch.

"Nice to hear your voice, darlin'," her caller said. "But not nearly so nice as it was seein' your picture in this month's *Journal*." The words came out in the slow, silky drawl that he usually managed to keep more in check but that alcohol inevitably exposed, with long pauses between. "Ah see you're still crusadin' for the underdog. A regular Florence Nightingale."

The bitterness, even filtered through an answering machine, cut through the cabin's cold air like a knife. An irrational fear caused Isabel to stop breathing, for fear that he would hear her and realize that she stood just feet away from the telephone.

"Such a shame that you weren't able to save those young boys. Ah'm sure that's weighing heavy on your mind. Ah 'magine that it's pretty hard to sleep . . . out there in the wilderness."

His snicker ran through her like a current of electricity.

"You know . . ." He was breathing heavily into the phone, and in that moment, Isabel knew what he was doing on the other end. "Ah haven't forgotten what turns you on. How to make you moan. Ah could help you to sleep . . ."

More heavy breathing, and all Isabel could do was stand, a prisoner, and listen.

"Do you remember, Is? What it was like? It's been a long time . . . such a long time . . ."

Isabel pressed her hands to her ears and began breathing again, long deep inhales and exhales, focusing only on her breathing, shutting everything else out, until finally, what seemed an eternity later, she thought she heard the beep that signaled the end of the message.

But she was wrong. He was still talking.

"Did you get the video, darlin'?" In the background she heard the familiar note of Alistair's grandfather clock marking the half hour. "Ah hope you enjoyed it. It's just a little reminder for you. You know, in case you were thinkin' of causing me any more trouble. You looked so beautiful. Ah've been thinkin it's a shame not to share that much beauty . . ."

Dropping her hands, Isabel continued to stand, staring at the phone as if it were alive.

Finally, at last, he hung up.

Isabel crossed the room, grabbed the answering machine, and, holding it first at arm's length—as if it contained something deadly, something even worse than the killer hantavirus—flung it with a savage grunt against the wall. It bounced off a log, clattering noisily to the floor, where she kicked it irrationally, again and again, until it lay shattered in several pieces.

What did he mean about a video?

Isabel's mind spun wildly, dizzily. She reached for the back of a chair and once more forced deep breaths in and out of her lungs.

She'd known Alistair would eventually call. Still, the horror of hearing his voice, the images she was now battling to cleanse from her mind. And what video was he talking about?

His first comment she understood. The article she'd written for the *Journal of the American Medical Association* must have come out. Even now, five months after she'd left him, Alistair was still managing to spoil things for Isabel. No wonder he'd chosen tonight to call. He knew a simple call from him could ruin what little pleasure, or satisfaction, or hope, she might take from the fact that the article had been published.

If Alistair had seen *JAMA*, her copy may have arrived too. Isabel walked into the room off the kitchen. Years ago it had served as a pantry, but she had no need for extra storage—the few cupboards the kitchen provided were practically always bare anyway. She yanked on the metal chain hanging from a lightbulb over the desk she and Gus had found at a garage sale in Ennis.

Envelopes and files littered the desk's surface, but there was no sign of the monthly *JAMA*. How long had it been since she picked up the mail?

Pulling tight her wool sweater, Isabel stepped back into the night and headed down the long gravel road toward her mailbox. The moon, poised above Little Chief Mountain, was almost full. The jagged peaks, maybe even more magnificent in this light than at dawn, were silhouetted against an indigo blue sky. The sight usually sent shivers down Isabel's spine, but tonight she barely noticed, keeping a keen eye instead on the road.

As she approached the end of the driveway, the stand of cottonwoods across from the mailbox caught a headlight. She started, but then remembered the grandfather clock she'd just heard in the background. Alistair had called her from home. Within seconds she recognized another distinctive sound—the muffler on Gus Dearing's pickup. Only Gus was familiar enough with the winding roads to drive at night with such speed.

Gus was Isabel's landlord. His family had homesteaded in East Glacier, just across the reservation boundary, at the turn of the century. Real estate prices on that side of the line and that close to Glacier National Park had made him a wealthy man. Before Isabel came along, he'd had numerous offers to buy or rent the little log cabin where Gus's great-grand-daddy was born. He'd turned them all down. But something about Isabel caused him to reconsider, and they'd since become close friends. Gus lived up the road half a mile in a sprawling log home overlooking the Two Medicine River. He could afford to drive any car he wanted, but he loved tooling around in his old green pickup.

He roared past, coming within a couple feet of Isabel, then, suddenly, gravel flew as the pickup screeched to a halt.

Gus was rolling down his window when Isabel approached his side of the truck.

"Damn, Isabel," he cursed, his bushy white eyebrows coming together in consternation. "I hardly saw you. You oughta carry a flashlight with you so you don't get run down."

"Sorry about that, Gus. I didn't mean to scare you."

Gus's moonlit, weathered face suddenly disappeared behind a mass of moving, golden fur.

"Hey there, Grunt," Isabel said, reaching to stroke the head of the big yellow Lab whose enthusiastic greeting for his friend shook the truck's cab and fogged its windows.

"Get the hell off my lap, will you?" Gus growled. But he simply craned his neck to see over the dog, which stayed put at the window, straddling Gus's legs. "You finally pickin' up your mail?"

Isabel tried for a laugh, but it came out a weak imitation. In Montana, nothing was private.

"Yes. I suppose Benny's been complaining again?"

"He's always got somethin' to whine about. Says if he keeps having so much trouble stuffing mail into your box, the post office'll stop making deliveries. You'll have to start picking it up in Browning."

"Well, tell Benny I'll try harder. Okay?"

Grunt's wet nose pushed at the hand she'd placed on Gus's half-opened window. For a brief moment, Isabel debated asking whether she could borrow Grunt for the night. Alistair's call had shaken her to the core. Even with the knowledge that he was four hundred miles away, she did not relish the thought of spending the night alone.

"You okay, Izzie?" Gus said.

"Of course."

If she told Gus something was bothering her, he would insist that she come stay with him. As appealing a prospect as that now seemed, it was not a solution. She'd never before spoken to Gus about Alistair and right now the last thing she wanted to do was get into it.

"Seems like somethin''s bothering you."

"No, Gus, really. I'm fine. Just tired, that's all. I've been awfully busy. Flu season, you know."

"No more cases of hantavirus?"

"No, thank God. It seemed to disappear as quickly as it showed up."

"Well, I'm glad for that. Drop by to see us one of these days."

"I will, Gus," Isabel said. "I promise."

She waved as Gus and Grunt resumed their way to Gus's ranch, then crossed to the mailbox. True to Benny-the-mailman's complaints, the box was crammed so full that Isabel had to use both arms, cradlelike, to carry its contents back to the cabin. Once inside, she dumped all the mail on top of the layer of papers already obscuring her desk and grabbed the newly delivered *JAMA*.

Before settling down to read, Isabel walked around the cabin, checking to be certain all the windows and doors were locked and curtains drawn. Finally, she went to the closet and from the back of the top shelf, pulled out a thirty-eight-caliber revolver given to her by Gus when she first moved in. He'd insisted that she keep it. In order to avoid an argument, she'd finally acquiesced, but had immediately tucked it away at the back of the closet.

The cardboard box containing the bullets he'd given her had never been opened. She opened it now and withdrew several cartridges, which she slid, one by one, into place in the gun's chamber.

Then, laying it on the bedside table so that it pointed toward the wall, she changed into the sweats and long-sleeved T-shirt she routinely slept in and climbed into bed. She reached to turn on the small lamp next to the bed and, falling back onto her pillows, turned to the *Journal*'s table of contents.

Two-thirds of the way down the page, under "Commentary," she saw it:

Hantavirus vaccine: not possible, or not profitable? by Isabel McLain, M.D., page 1848.

She turned to page 1848.

Then, with the loaded gun beside her, Isabel began to read.

IT DID NOT come to her until the middle of the night.

She awoke, AMA journal still resting on her chest. The lamp was still on.

The video. There had been a package that appeared to be a video delivered to the clinic that day that she locked up to go out to Suzanne's. It had been resting against the door. Eli Walker said he'd seen UPS deliver it.

What ever happened to it?

Isabel vaguely recalled dropping the package on Suzanne's desk, but things had been so hectic that day, and in the ensuing days and weeks. While she was away, a mound of mail and forms had grown on every available surface in Suzanne's office. Isabel had never seen or thought of the package that had been delivered that morning again.

Until now. Until Alistair's call.

She tried to go back to sleep. She would ask Suzanne about it in the morning. Suzanne had probably put it away somewhere.

It was nothing, nothing, she told herself.

Still, she could not sleep.

SOME DAYS IT felt as though she'd fully recovered from her terrifying bout with the hantavirus. Others, like today, Suzanne could still feel the aftereffects. Shortness of breath, tendency to tire easily. And then of course there were the nightmares. She'd watched Joe Winged Foot die of the hantavirus. For all practical purposes, Dolores Birdsong too—though Dolores hadn't actually died, gone flatline, until she was in the helicopter.

Suzanne felt kind of ashamed for the relief she felt about that. That they'd gotten Dolores on the helicopter before she actually died. It seemed a lot worse somehow, to die up there in the air, with her connection to their sacred Earth Mother severed. But Suzanne just didn't think she could've gone through another ordeal like the one with Joe.

'Course she didn't know Dolores all that well. Like she knew Joe.

All she knew, after seein' what she'd seen, watchin' Joe's dying heart go into ventricular fibrillation, then seein' his beautiful body just about jump off the table from them damn paddles—sizzle, sizzle, crankin' the dial up, then sizzle again—was that if she was gonna die of the hantavirus, she'd do it on her own. At home. No paddles for her. No medic squeezing air into the bladder connected to the endotracheal tube that they'd inserted into her lungs. No siree. That wasn't the way Suzanne was gonna go.

But in her dreams, in her nightmares, that's the way it went. Just like Joe and Dolores.

She didn't know why she'd been spared. Who to give the credit.

Isabel?

Maybe. The ribavirin Dr. McLain gave Suzanne might just have saved her life. And no question she received good care from her. Hell, seemed like those dark, pain-filled eyes were peering down at Suzanne every time she came to from one of those awful dreams.

She'd had a few doubts about Isabel before. They'd never quite hit it off. But she was learning—fast—that there was a whole lot more to Dr. McLain than Suzanne ever knew before. And a person'd have to be pretty damn ornery and heartless not to be touched by how hard that woman tried to get Suzanne better.

But Suzanne wasn't ruling out the Black-Tailed Deer Dance either. Mary had wanted to take Suzanne up to Badger Creek, to one of the sweat lodges that Mary's husband, Charlie, used to go to when he was real sick. Suzanne didn't want to hurt Mary's feelings by pointing out the fact that Charlie had died anyway—he was buried up there on the sacred grounds somewhere—so she just told Mary the truth. That she was too sick for the long drive. So instead Mary and her old friend Rose and a couple of the elders conducted kind of a scaled down Black-Tailed Deer Dance where they consecrated the sweetgrass and prayed for Suzanne's recovery. The ceremonies and dancing and midnight feast kept Suzanne up most of that night, but when she did sleep, a deer came to her, just like was supposed to happen. It didn't actually give her instructions about how to get well, like was supposed to happen, but she definitely saw a deer in her dream that night.

Suzanne made Mary and Rose and the two others promise to keep the ceremony a secret. It wasn't that she was ashamed to be callin' on the old ways, not at all. She actually liked the idea, felt like she was covering both bases this way. But if word got out that they'd had the ceremony, everybody on the rez was gonna think *that's* what healed Suzanne, and not Dr. McLain. And both because Suzanne felt a new tenderness toward her boss and because she knew her people—knew that they'd all but give up on Dr. McLain and the clinic if they found out, and that wasn't good—she made everyone promise to keep the ceremony a secret and she made sure to get the word out that Dr. McLain had saved her.

Besides, what was she gonna do if everybody stopped comin' to the clinic? It was her job, after all.

This morning she was surprised to see Dr. McLain's dirty Jeep when she pulled up to the clinic. Suzanne always beat Dr. McLain in, even now.

She was even more surprised at what she saw when she stepped into her office. Dr. McLain, on hands and knees, rummaging through the cupboard that ran below the counter that separated the waiting room and Suzanne's desk. Several of the file drawers had been opened, but not shut fully.

"Whatcha lookin for?"

Isabel McLain's head snapped up.

"Suzanne," she said. She'd been looking a lot more rested recently, but today dark circles framed Dr. McLain's eyes. "I didn't hear you come in."

"Can I help you find something?"

Isabel rocked back to sit on her heels and rested a hand on top of each thigh.

"You haven't by any chance seen a video that was sent here for me?"

Suzanne maintained a blank expression.

"A video?" she echoed.

"Yes. On the day you called me out to your house to celebrate your recovery, UPS delivered something that looked like it could have been a video. It was resting outside, against the locked door. I thought I put it on your desk. Then I just forgot about it."

"Gee, there was a ton of stuff on my desk when I got back to work. But I don't remember any video."

When a flicker of relief seemed to cross Isabel's features, Suzanne couldn't resist pressing for more information.

"Was it somethin' you were looking for? Something you might've ordered?"

Isabel shook her thick head of ebony hair—hair Suzanne had always thought looked every bit as Indian as that on any head on the rez—and snorted a caustic laugh.

"No. Definitely not."

" 'Cause I'll keep an eye out for it, if you're expecting somethin'."

This seemed to startle Isabel.

"Why don't you just put any mail you get for me on my desk?" she said, averting her eyes from Suzanne's stare.

"You still want me to open it for you?"

Isabel tried a light smile.

"You've got so much to do. Why don't you just leave that to me from now on?"

"Whatever you say."

If Suzanne had had any doubts about her actions before, she did not now. It was clear that the video for which Dr. McLain searched so frantically was about as welcome as a case of head lice.

Suzanne had had to trust her instincts when she'd opened that package. She knew right away somethin' wasn't right. After all, there was no return address on it and nobody sends somethin' of any value without putting a return address on it. Unless they don't want the person receiving it to know who it's from.

She'd actually thought it might be some kind of threat to her boss. After Joe and Dolores died, she'd heard talk that a few of the more radical Blackfeet were thinkin' about how they could run Isabel out of town. That's why Suzanne had taken it home, 'cause after all she'd been through recently, Suzanne didn't think Dr. McLain needed anything else to worry about. The lack of return address had made Suzanne suspicious right from the start.

But all Suzanne had to do was watch a couple minutes of the video to figure out who'd sent it. That it had to have come from the guy in it. The same guy who dropped by the clinic tryin' to find out where Isabel lived. No wonder Isabel had flipped out when Suzanne told her he'd been there askin' about her. I mean, this guy . . . There was no question in Suzanne's mind that he'd filmed the two of them in bed without Isabel's knowledge. It was the look in his eye—his awareness of the camera. He played to it like you do when you see your reflection in a store window and you suddenly lift your shoulders, suck your gut in, or when you look in the mirror.

Isabel didn't have that look. Good thing, 'cause what Suzanne saw was enough of a surprise about her boss without thinkin' that she was deliberately putting on a show for the camera.

Suzanne didn't think white women had it in them to make love like that.

Then there was the final clue. If she had any doubts that Isabel didn't know she was being filmed, the one line scrawled along the label of the video itself, where you usually write the date and whatever it is you've taped, was enough to dispel them.

Let this be a warning.

That's all it said. But the meaning had been pretty clear.

This guy was somehow tryin' to blackmail or threaten Isabel. And Suzanne had made the decision, all on her own, that Isabel had had enough to deal with without some slimeball with a southern accent adding to her troubles. She hadn't realized that she had it—that sense of loyalty to her employer. But hell if she was gonna stand by and let that sleazebag make her miserable.

And so Suzanne had destroyed the tape. Not just thrown it out, into the Dumpster. Guys were goin' through those Dumpsters all the time lookin' for drugs and such.

No, she'd pulled the guts out of the thing, the cassette, and ruined it good. Then she'd thrown it all in the trash.

CHAPTER

NINE

PULLING INTO THE Outlaw Inn, Isabel scanned the parking lot for out-of-state plates. When she'd heard Dr. MacStirling planned to drive all the way from Portland, she'd offered to meet him in Kalispell. The only information he'd been willing to offer her over the phone was that he had a "proposal" he'd like her to hear. She'd received several similar calls since her article appeared in *JAMA*. One from a graduate student at Duke who informed her that thanks to her article, he planned to apply for an NIH grant to study the hantavirus; another from a Native American candidate for the state legislature in Arizona who, if elected, planned to propose a bill sponsoring funding for hantavirus research; and one from an investigative reporter who claimed Joe's, Dolores's, and Will's deaths were actually the result of a biological weapons accident in Utah. Her initial elation at the fact that the article had drawn attention to the disease and stirred interest had now ebbed to a cynicism occasioned by the reality that no one with a serious chance of changing things had yet stepped up to the plate.

Isabel had no idea what to expect at today's meeting, but at the very least, she saw it as an opportunity to get out of town for a few hours. Some new scenery would do her good.

MacStirling had been happy to accept her offer to meet him in Kalispell.

"Lovely," he'd proclaimed in a brogue that had a musical ring to it. "That will give me a chance to wander about Glacier National Park while I'm up that way."

A tan Land Cruiser with flashy gold trim and a pricey-looking bicycle mounted on its back stood out among the rows of older-model cars and pickups. Oregon plates. That had to be it. Isabel pulled in next to the

Land Cruiser, then got out, taking care not to brush up against her own vehicle, which had its usual coating of dried mud.

The motel's coffee shop had already emptied of the breakfast crowd. A lone man sat in a booth near the back of the restaurant. He stood and strode her way.

"Dr. McLain." He smiled, extending a hand. He was tall with longish, sandy hair that curled over the collar of his Patagonia jacket. Isabel recognized the accent right away as belonging to Ken MacStirling. "I'm Dr. MacStirling. It's a pleasure to meet you."

He escorted her back to his table, where a waitress with big hair was delivering steaming mugs.

"I hope you don't mind," MacStirling said now. "I took the liberty of ordering you a latte."

"Thanks," Isabel said, settling in to the booth.

There was a moment's awkward silence while both sipped at their drinks.

"That was some article you wrote for *JAMA*," MacStirling said. Just as she'd thought, MacStirling's call had to do with her article. "Some of my coworkers were a mite offended by it."

"Coworkers?"

"Yes. I work for a biotech company called ImmuVac. Our headquarters are in Portland."

"Are you an M.D. or a research scientist?"

"Ph.D. Immunology."

Isabel studied Ken MacStirling to see if he agreed with his coworkers' characterization of her article. She could not get a take on his expression.

"Hantavirus first appeared almost seven years ago," she answered, "and after all that time, we still don't have a vaccine. Or even an effective treatment."

"But to call the medical and pharmaceutical industries racist because they haven't poured millions of dollars into hantavirus research . . . don't you think you're being a wee bit hysterical?"

"Hysterical? If this disease had broken out in Manhattan, or Beverly Hills, or even Portland for that matter, we'd have a vaccine by now. My article merely told it like it is. I hardly think that equates with hysteria."

"You actually believe that no one cares about this disease because Native Americans have borne the brunt of it?"

"You're British, right?" Isabel asked.

"Scottish."

"Sorry. How long have you been in this country?"

"So you're implying I'm a bit naive about this country's treatment of its aboriginal peoples?"

"How else can you explain the fact that victims of this disease today have no better chance of surviving than they did seven years ago, when we first learned it existed? If the right people had died, you better believe that money would have been allocated for research."

MacStirling's rueful smile caught Isabel off guard.

"You find the subject amusing?"

"Well, I rather hate to disillusion you," MacStirling said. "But I've been working on a hantavirus vaccine for three years now."

"You . . . what?" Isabel fell back against the padded booth. "I did extensive research before I wrote that article. BioScreen was the only company at all interested in hantavirus. They'd developed a test to detect it in its earliest stages. But when someone put the numbers to it, they decided it wouldn't be profitable, so, of course, they dropped it." She directed a penetrating gaze at MacStirling. "Why doesn't anyone know about your work?"

"Probably because I haven't exactly had a lot of corporate backing. When I signed on with ImmuVac, it was to help develop an AIDS vaccine. But I managed to talk them into piggybacking my work on the hantavirus. The company's never really gotten behind it, but because they seem to think I've got something to contribute to the AIDS work, they've put up with the hantavirus research I've done on the side."

Isabel shifted forward, her palms flat on the table.

"How far along is your research on a vaccine?"

"It's been ready for clinical trials for over a year now."

"Let me guess. ImmuVac refuses to fund the trials."

"Correction. ImmuVac *refused* to fund a clinical trial. Thanks to your article, they've reconsidered."

"You mean ImmuVac is willing to invest in a clinical trial?" The disbelief in her voice was audible. "Because of my article?"

"Yes."

"That's incredible. Fantastic." Isabel paused. "I owe you an apology, don't I? And ImmuVac."

"Absolutely not. You had no way of knowing about my hantavirus work. If the truth be told, I'd about given up on it myself. ImmuVac has had plenty of opportunity to move forward with the clinical trials, but they chose not to. I couldn't be more pleased that that's changed now. And I have you to thank for that fact."

"But if my article swayed them, caused them to reconsider, ImmuVac is that rare company with a social conscience."

Ken MacStirling leaned across the table, bringing his narrow face within inches of Isabel's to speak in a conspiratorial tone.

"I'm going to level with you, lass. As moving as your article was, ImmuVac is not doing this to right a wrong. Or for the greater good of mankind. Your article seems to have stirred a great deal of interest in hantavirus. ImmuVac now sees the vaccine as a way to attract funding—you know, either larger pharmaceutical sponsors or maybe, if there's a good deal of positive publicity, a public offering."

"I don't really give a damn what their motivation is, so long as someone comes out with a vaccine. That's all that matters to me. That's why I wrote that article."

MacStirling eased back, studying her.

"I imagine writing it was a wee bit therapeutic too. I mean, your grief at the loss of your patients came through loud and clear."

MacStirling's observation was astute—a little too astute for Isabel's comfort.

"Tell me," she said, changing the subject. "When do you plan to begin the clinical trial? And where?"

"That depends."

"On?"

"On you."

Isabel drew back.

"On me? What do you mean?"

"We would like to conduct the clinical trial on the Blackfeet reservation. And we would like for you to head it up."

"You're kidding," Isabel said. "Aren't you?"

"No. I'm not. In fact, I couldn't be more serious."

"Well, then you're wasting your time and mine."

"Good God, girl, don't you want your patients protected?"

"Of course I do. But I'm not about to make guinea pigs of them. Now, if you'll excuse me."

Ken MacStirling reached out and grabbed her by the forearm.

"Please, hear me out. You owe me that much."

"I don't owe you anything!"

MacStirling reached into his briefcase, extracted something, and threw it down on the table.

"Then what was *this*?" Isabel's picture, alongside the *JAMA* article, stared up at her. "Some kind of a charade? How the devil can you write such an article then refuse the chance to participate in the process that will bring about the change you bloody claim to want? The change you say your patients need. Can you explain that?"

Isabel shook her arm free.

"I have nothing to explain. Find another study director," she said, standing so abruptly that coffee went flying.

She'd taken no more than two steps away from the table when she heard him say it.

"I should think I'd have trouble sleepin' if I were you."

She twirled, furious, and returned to the table. She stood above him, grasping the Formica edge as her anger erupted.

"Who do you think you are coming here like this and passing judgment on me?"

MacStirling studied her.

"Then please, explain it to me," he said. "As a professional courtesy if nothing else. How can you deny your patients—bloody hell, the whole world—the chance to be protected from this disease?"

"Now if I've ever heard gross exaggeration, that's it. You're trying to tell me that my refusal to conduct the clinical trial for your vaccine is the equivalent of denying it to the world?"

"Unfortunately, that's just what I'm telling you. Because the simple truth is, if you don't agree to conduct this trial, ImmuVac will not proceed with the vaccine."

"*What?* That makes no sense, no sense at all . . . unless . . . *It's some kind of publicity ploy*," Isabel cried. "Doing the trial on a reservation. The media will eat it up. That's why you need me to be the study director."

MacStirling's gaze would not meet hers.

"You know what you and your company can do with your proposal?"

These words brought MacStirling's eyes back up to hers. They were angry, and anguished.

"Don't lump me in with the rest of your villains."

Isabel turned and stormed out of the restaurant.

IN ANOTHER RESTAURANT sixty miles away, inside East Glacier Lodge, a busload of Japanese tourists had disembarked their Greyhound and now made claim to all but two tables.

Tony Wilderman stood at the dining room's entrance and scanned the room. He hated crowds. But he was hungry, and it was a fifteen-minute drive into Browning.

The mere thought of eating in a Browning restaurant propelled him forward, into the dining room.

At one of the tables not occupied by the noisy tour group, a woman was spoon-feeding a toddler boy who sat on her lap. At the other, a lone man, nicely dressed, read a newspaper. Tony headed in his direction.

"Mind if I sit down?" Wilderman asked.

The man looked up from his paper, then surveyed the room, as if he were about to suggest that Tony go elsewhere.

"Be my guest," he drawled without expression, immediately looking back down at the paper.

Friendly sort, Tony thought to himself. When he spotted several sections of the *Seattle Times* strewn on the other side of the table—his tablemate was engrossed in the business section—he dared to speak up again.

"Sorry to bother you again, but mind if I borrow the sports section?"

"Help yourself."

"Where'd you find the Seattle paper? These Montana papers have the worst sports sections I've ever seen."

"Gift shop in the lodge here carries it."

"You a guest here?" Tony said. "So am I."

Without answering, the man went back to his article, just as a waitress showed up with a glass of iceless water and a menu which she placed in front of Tony.

"You're becoming a permanent fixture around here," she teased Tony good-naturedly as she eyed the other man. "I'll get you a cup of coffee while you decide what you want."

"Already know," Tony grinned back. "Western omelette, wheat toast. And a small juice. And coffee, as soon as it's convenient."

"That's easy enough," she said.

When she returned minutes later, she reached for the white ceramic mug in the upper right corner of the paper placement that contained a map of Glacier National Park, then began to pour.

"So how's the prospecting going?" she asked.

"Now, that's highly confidential," Tony teased. "Suppose you were a spy for a rival mining company?"

"Do I look like a spy for a mining company?" Her laugh was easy and hearty.

"You never know." Tony held up a hand to stop her from filling the cup to its brim. He needed plenty of room for cream. "Thanks. Actually, I'm encouraged by what I've found so far, out past Browning."

"On the reservation?"

"Yep."

"Good luck with that," she said. "Them Blackfeet don't like mines."

"I suspected as much," Tony answered as she turned to the next table.

It was then that Tony realized his tablemate had finally taken his nose out of the newspaper and now regarded him with considerably more interest than before.

"So," the man said, his tone much friendlier now, "you're a miner?"

"A geologist for World Resources, a Canadian mining company. I'm in charge of exploration."

"And you're planning to mine on the reservation?"

"Just doing some preliminary exploration."

Wilderman had just teased the waitress about being a spy. Had he accused the wrong person?

"My name is Alistair Bott," the man said, as he reached into his blazer pocket for his business card. It was gold embossed and stylish.

ALISTAIR BOTT, M.D. CARDIOVASCULAR SURGERY, it said. The address below was in Seattle.

"Tony Wilderman, Vancouver, B.C. Nice to meet you," Wilderman said, shaking the man's proffered hand.

A doctor. That explained the attitude. And expensive clothes.

"What's a heart surgeon from Seattle doing in these parts?"

"Just takin' a short vacation. I come up here from time to time."

"The park's really something, isn't it?" Tony said.

When Bott looked confused, he said, "Glacier National Park. It's something else. Don't you agree?"

How could this guy not know what he was talking about?

Bott hesitated.

"Yes, yes it is. Actually, I've spent most of my time here."

"East Glacier? Not much in East Glacier besides fish. You a fly fisherman?"

"Yes," Bott said. "So you're doing a little exploration on the Indian reservation? That must be interesting."

"The reservation or the exploration? The reservation's downright depressing. You been over there at all?"

"Just a little. You're right. It's pretty bad. And none too friendly, I hear. How do they feel about someone like you snooping around?"

Wilderman snorted.

"Let's just say I watch my back. I've worked on other reservations, but something tells me this one's going to be a real challenge. Usually there's at least some faction of the community that welcomes me, that wants to cooperate because they know what mining can do for their economy. But if there's anybody like that up there in Browning, I haven't run into them yet."

"I suppose that means there's not much chance that you'll actually end up minin' there."

"Not necessarily. There are ways to get the approval we'd need. It just means it'll take more work on our part. A little more diplomacy. There's always a way, a button to push. You know much about mining?"

"Not really." Bott's smile was oddly amused. "But my ex-wife was one of those tree-hugger types. She hates minin' companies."

"She live in Seattle?"

"No. She moved away a few months ago," Bott said. Then, with a joviality that seemed misplaced, he lifted his glass of orange juice into the air.

"A toast to you, Mr. Wilderman. And World Resources. I wish you both the best of luck in your endeavor in Indian country."

KEN MACSTIRLING COULDN'T imagine who would be knocking at the door of his motel room. He'd just returned from dinner after an exhausting day in Glacier National Park, where he'd biked to the top of Going to the Sun Road.

The bathwater he'd been drawing to soak his aching limbs had drowned out his visitor's persistent rapping until he turned the faucet off and returned to the bedroom for a newspaper to read in the tub. Then its urgency could not be mistaken.

Grabbing the robe he'd thrown on the bed, he went to the door and, tying his sash, opened it.

Isabel McLain stood outside.

"May I come in?"

She seemed not to notice MacStirling's garb.

"Aye," he said.

Isabel entered the room, quickly assessed it, and settled into one of two overstuffed chairs under the window that looked out on to Kalispell's busy Highway 93.

MacStirling, his discomfort at hosting a visitor while wearing nothing but a robe overshadowed by immense curiosity, followed suit, settling in the other chair.

"How safe is your vaccine?" Isabel asked.

"Extremely safe. I have two years of animal studies to back it up." MacStirling stood and walked over to the bulging briefcase propped against the wall next to the bed. Extracting a three-inch-thick black binder, he returned and offered it to her. "Here, here's everything on the vaccine. Its mechanism of action. Tests to date. Everything. You can take it home with you. Keep it for as long as you like. Or I can go over it with you, page by page. You make the call."

Isabel took the binder and placed it on her lap. Despite her air of determination, she looked utterly miserable. And exhausted. The white lab coat with her name on it that she now wore over the same jeans and shirt she'd worn earlier that day indicated she must have driven back to Browning that morning after their meeting, put in a day's work, then returned to Kalispell to find him.

"Do you know how difficult this study will be to sell to the Black-feet?" Isabel said.

"No. Tell me."

"They don't trust outsiders. They especially don't trust our medical establishment. They still remember the blankets given them by our government—blankets deliberately infected with smallpox. Like it was yesterday."

"But they trust you," MacStirling said, not unkindly.

Isabel raised her tortured eyes to his.

"Some do. And you're asking me to use that trust in a . . . a . . ." Her voice drifted off, as though she could not bring herself to say the words.

"A clinical trial. One that is without question the safest trial I've ever been involved with. A trial that will save lives. You wouldn't be back here tonight if you didn't believe this vaccine will help your patients. And many, many others."

Isabel remained silent.

"I admitted to you today what my company's motives are," Mac-Stirling continued. "Maybe I shouldn't have done that. But surely you can't attribute the same motivation to me. I mean, I've worked on this vaccine for years now, without a reasonable expectation that it would ever be profitable."

"Why? Why did you choose hantavirus?"

"I don't know," he said, shaking his head. Then, finally, he smiled. "That's not true. I do know. It may sound silly. Westerns are very popular in Europe. I grew up watching *The Lone Ranger* and *Gunsmoke*. I always had empathy for the Indians, for the way they were portrayed, as either savage scalp-takers or straight men for the dashing cowboy hero. Those things you said today—when I called you hysterical—I had the exact same feelings that you described in your article after those people died in Four Corners back in ninety-three. Why isn't someone doing something to prevent this from happening again?" He'd been averting his eyes, embarrassed by sitting there practically naked, but now he raised them to find Isabel staring intently at him. "I decided to do something." He leaned forward, holding the lower half of his robe closed with one hand. "I give you my word that this vaccine is safe. I have already immunized myself. Three times. Over a period of two years. And I've never been healthier."

The silence that followed seemed to MacStirling to last forever.

"I don't know if I can convince them to take part in the study," Isabel McLain finally said softly.

MacStirling's hopes soared.

"If anyone can, it's you."

CHAPTER

TEN

*H*AVE YOU EVER *stopped to think about how a society goes about stealing human rights?"*

As usual, Monty Four Bear's lecture on Indian law was standing room only. Today's lecture was one of Monty's favorites. He sat with legs slung over the edge of the auditorium stage, facing his students. Bracing himself with his hands, he leaned toward them, his dark, piercing eyes roaming over his audience and drawing them in. His legs swung back and forth restlessly as the heels of his cowboy boots thudded rhythmically against the stage.

Ninety percent of the faces staring back at him were brown, like Monty's. Oftentimes when he looked out, Monty recognized faces from classes he'd taught in previous semesters—students who were back for more, auditing a course they'd already taken and, inevitably, passed. Sometimes it took a moment for Monty to recognize them, especially the young men who had worn their hair short when they started his class, but now—inspired by Monty's message of reclaiming their heritage—had returned with braids of their own.

"It's an interesting phenomenon, based on a simple principle." Monty shifted further forward. *"Wouldn't it be easier to steal someone's rights if you could do it with their cooperation?"*

He allowed the heavy silence that sometimes followed his remarks to settle over the hall.

"And how does one do that, get that cooperation? More specifically, how did the United States government gain the Indian's cooperation? Depending, of course, on your perspective, it's a thing of beauty. An art, really. *The art of stealing human rights.* And surprisingly, the United States can't even claim inventorship."

Monty reached into a back pocket of his jeans and withdrew a worn, folded sheet of paper.

"I'd like to read you something. These are extracts from a speech given by Gerry Gambill at a conference on human rights in New Brunswick in 1958. Just a couple years before I was born." This brought a titter from the class, especially the females. "Listen closely, and see if they sound familiar. I present to you the ABCs of the art of stealing human rights."

He began to read.

"Number one. Make him a non-person. Human rights are for people. Convince Indians their ancestors were savages, that they were pagan, that Indians were drunkards. Make them wards of the government. Make a legal distinction, as in the Indian Act, between Indians and persons. Write history books that tell half the story.

"Number two." He held two fingers up in a V. "Convince the Indian that he should be patient, that these things take time. Tell him that we are making progress, and that progress takes time.

"Number three. Make him believe that things are being done for his own good." He looked up from the paper, a smile twisting his mouth. "I love that one. Anyone want to cite an example?"

A hand shot up in the front row.

"Crystal?"

The girl stood. She was dressed in a plain white long-sleeved shirt that hung out over her khakis. Her black hair was tied in a tight ponytail. She was tall, with unusually regal bearing for someone so young. Her baggy trousers accentuated her thinness.

"The Dawes Act," she answered. "The federal government acted like they were doing us some kind of a favor by making Indians property owners."

"When they really wanted . . . ?"

"To divide us, break up our tribal unity."

"That's hogwash," another student called out from the back of the hall. "The Dawes Act gave your people a chance to be landowners. It gave you a chance to control your own destiny."

A husky, wheat-haired farmboy, one of only half a dozen whites in the class, rose in the last row.

Undeterred, Crystal shot back, "Your family's a perfect example of what was wrong with the Dawes Act. Thanks to the Dawes Act, our land ended up in white hands."

"We bought our acreage fair and square. My great grandfather didn't have to twist any arms to buy our ranch. He paid good money for it."

"How much?" Crystal demanded to know.

The boy's fair skin flushed.

"What we paid is beside the point anyway. One of your people wanted to sell and my great grandfather bought. That's how our economy works. No law against that."

"But it's the reason most reservations today are more white than native," Crystal said. "Look at the Flathead."

"The Salish and Kootenai had the same deal you Blackfeet had. They made good money selling to whites."

"That's bullshit," the girl cried. Then glancing back at Monty, she said, "Sorry, Professor Four Bear. You know what the Dawes Act did for my family? I'll tell you. My grandfather worked his eighty acres for thirty years, then when he couldn't pay an eighty-seven dollar grocery bill, they took his land from him. Eighty acres for an eighty-seven dollar bill. He died penniless. We've been renting ever since."

She plunked back down into her seat, still visibly angry.

"Truth is, John," Monty said, "most Indians sold or lost the land they acquired through the Dawes Act. That's the reason the Flathead reservation has far more whites living on it today than natives. The only reason it didn't happen to as great a degree up here is that even the white men didn't want *this* land." The room filled with soft laughter, laughter that had a bitter edge to it. "I agree with Crystal. Though it was couched in the normal rhetoric about being for our good, the Dawes Act was intended to deal another blow to our culture and unity. And it worked."

"No disrespect intended, professor," John said, hands shoved angrily into the pockets of his carpenter pants, "but I'm not so sure you're objective about this kind of thing. I mean, you belong to AIM. That's a pretty radical organization . . ."

The room erupted in groans and angry name-calling.

Monty raised a hand, calling out calmly. "Let him speak." He held the hand high until the room fell silent again. "Go ahead, John."

It was obvious that the commotion he'd caused had started to unnerve John. But his feelings on the subject ran deep, just as deep as those of the Native American students surrounding him.

"I'm sick and tired of being made out to be the bad guy. We've been good neighbors here. Don't cause anyone problems. Go about our own business . . ."

"What's that got to do with AIM?" another male voice shouted.

John's face flushed a deeper shade.

"Nothin'. But anyone who thinks AIM is anything but a group of radicals trying to stir up trouble between your people and mine has a screw loose. They're just a bunch of troublemakers. They don't want us all to get along. What they want is to eliminate people like me."

"Sounds like a pretty good idea to me," one voice called out.

"What they want is fair treatment for Native Americans," Crystal said, rising again. "Right, Professor Four Bear?"

Monty waited for the uproar to die down.

"AIM is a lot of different things to different people. It certainly doesn't surprise me to hear John's perception of it. After the Pine Ridge shootout in 1973, the FBI, with considerable assistance from the media, I might add, succeeded in painting AIM members as radicals who preferred using violence over other means of achieving their objectives."

Monty jumped down from his perch on the stage and crossed the expanse before the first row of seats to stand within arm's distance of his students.

"But AIM is something entirely different to me. I spent three years as an attorney on the Wind River reservation in Wyoming, fighting for tribal water rights and environmental protections whose unpopularity with the ranchers and mining industry consistently resulted in defeat. Then I went over to the BIA. After two years there, I became convinced that I had about as much chance of changing things by working within the established bureaucratic framework as the buffalo did of ever roaming the plains free again.

"I see AIM as a positive force, a way of combating poverty and despair on the reservations. I like what Birgil Kills Straight calls AIM: 'the warrior class of this century.' He says AIM's business is *hope*. That's how I like to think of it."

It had taken a while for anyone to notice, for the students were rapt in their attention to Monty's words, but heads had begun to turn toward the back of the room, where a young woman stood, holding a piece of paper in the air to get Monty's attention.

"Excuse me for a moment," Monty said, waving her in and starting up the aisle to meet her.

"You had an emergency call," the young woman whispered, handing Monty the paper. "From someone named Leroy. Here's his number."

Monty looked down at the paper. He did not recognize the number. His father, Leroy, did not have a telephone, so he must have gone to a neighbor's to make the call.

Monty strode back to the front of the room and looked at his watch. He had another half hour to teach, but he knew Leroy wouldn't call if it wasn't important.

"I have to make a telephone call," Monty announced. "I'd like to ask you to sit quietly for ten minutes. If I'm not back by then, class is dismissed."

He jumped nimbly onto the stage, heading for the exit at its rear, then suddenly he turned, retraced his steps to the edge of the stage, and beckoned at a linebacker-sized youth in the front row.

Wearing a BCC Athletic Department sweatshirt, the crewcut-shorn Blackfeet approached without hesitation.

Bending at the waist, Monty spoke softly into his ear.

"Listen, Russell, I'd like you to keep the peace while I'm gone. Make sure no one hassles John Morris. Got it?"

"Got it," the youth said, clearly comfortable with the role of enforcer.

Monty turned and exited the auditorium through the back door.

Hurrying to his office—a windowless cube cluttered with books, stacks of newspapers and journals, with every square inch of wall space occupied by activist posters—Monty grabbed the phone and dialed. His father's voice, characteristically slurred, even at this hour of the day, greeted him.

" 'Lo?"

"It's me. Where are you? And what's going on?"

"I'm at Edna's." Edna was Edna Northrup, who lived about a quarter mile from his father's small frame house. "Luke's had an accident."

Luke was Monty's nephew.

"An accident? What happened?"

"On his bike. He's bleeding pretty bad. From the mouth. Think he lost a couple teeth. And he said he couldn't see right."

"Does Edna have a car?"

"It ain't running."

"I'll be right there."

•   •   •

"WE HAVE AN emergency," Suzanne Featherheart announced.

Isabel's head jerked up from the questionnaire she'd been drafting for participants in the ImmuVac study.

"What kind?"

"Eight-year-old boy. Rode his bike into a truck."

Isabel threw the yellow legal pad down and stepped into the hallway, almost colliding with a braided man who'd followed Suzanne down the hall. He was carrying a boy, cradlelike, in his arms.

"Where should I take him?" he asked.

Isabel stepped closer and checked to be sure the boy was breathing. Crushed or obstructed airways were always the first concern in a trauma situation. Once she ascertained that he was breathing on his own, she turned back in the direction she'd just come.

"Follow me."

She led the way to a room she'd termed the "shock room" and helped the man ease the boy onto the examination table in the center of the room.

Blood around the boy's mouth and nose had already dried. Isabel went to work, issuing the barrage of questions that had become second nature to her all those years working at Harborview's trauma center in Seattle.

"What's your name?" she asked, checking the boy's pulse.

"Luke."

"Luke, can you tell me what happened to you?"

"I rode my bike into a truck on my way home from school."

"What time was that, Luke?"

"I dunno. 'Bout three."

Isabel looked at the clock on the wall. It was almost four-thirty. How long had it taken them to bring this boy in?

"Was the truck moving?"

"No. It was parked. I just wasn't paying attention."

"That must have hurt. Listen to me, Luke, okay? I'm going to put this collar around your neck, to keep you from moving around until we've had a chance to take some X rays. Okay?"

"Okay."

Once the cervical collar was in place, Isabel began loosening Luke's shirt to inspect his torso.

"What hurts on you, Luke?"

"My head. And my shoulder."

"Tell me about your head. Did you black out when you hit the truck?"

"I don't think so."

"Are you dizzy now, lightheaded?"

"Maybe a little."

Isabel reached into the pocket of her lab coat and shone a light in the boy's eyes. Just as she suspected, his pupillary response indicated he'd suffered a concussion.

"Were you wearing a helmet?"

Luke shook his head no.

"And what about your shoulder? Is it this one, your left side?

"Ouch, that hurts," Luke cried as she ran her hand along it.

"I'm sorry about that, Luke. I'll try not to hurt you, but I need to examine you to see where all you might have been injured. Did you hit the truck with this shoulder?"

"No, I think I landed on it, after I hit the truck."

"Does your neck hurt at all?"

"No."

"What about your belly? Does it hurt when I press on it like this?"

"No."

"That's good. Now I want you to take a deep breath for me."

Luke's chest rose.

"Good. Take another one. Look at me. Relax, you're fine. Relax for me. Deep breaths, okay Luke?"

Isabel was relieved with what she'd seen so far, but she suspected that Luke had fractured his left clavicle. If so, there was always the possibility of pneumothoraxis—the broken bone piercing the lung and causing it to collapse. Luke's respiration was a good sign that that hadn't happened, but an X ray would be necessary to rule it out altogether. And her greatest concern was that the boy might have fractured a cervical vertebrae when he hit the truck.

"Now Luke, I want you to lay perfectly still while we leave the room for just a few seconds to take a couple pictures of your neck and chest."

For the first time since their initial encounter, the man who had brought Luke in spoke up.

"I'll stay with him."

Isabel turned to face him.

"Are you Luke's father?"

"No. His uncle. My name's Monty Four Bear."

"Are Luke's parents nearby, where we can contact them?"

"My sister lives in Denver. Luke lives with my father, his grandfather. He called me to bring Luke in."

"Well, Mr. Four Bear, I'm afraid you'll have to step outside while we take the X rays. But you can rejoin Luke in just a few minutes."

By now Suzanne had arrived. She loaded the film and followed, her eyes on Monty, as Isabel and Four Bear stepped into the hallway.

Once in the hallway, Isabel turned to Monty again.

"We'll know the results of these X rays within a few minutes. But even if they're negative, one thing is certain. Your nephew has a concussion. I'd like to have you take him to the hospital in Cut Bank for a CAT scan."

"If all he has is a concussion, he doesn't need a hospital. Or more tests. I'll take him home and keep an eye on him. I know what to look for."

Startled, as much by the tone in which the words were spoken as by the words themselves, Isabel drew back and studied Monty.

What had she done to elicit such contempt? For wasn't that what she saw in his eyes?

"Are you Luke's guardian? Or should I be talking to his grandfather?"

"I'll have him give you a call. When he sobers up."

So that's what she was dealing with.

"I would assume Luke's school ends around three o'clock. Can you explain to me why it took almost two hours to get him medical attention?"

If there had been any doubt before about the hostility in Monty Four Bear's eyes, the way he looked at her now left room for none.

"My father doesn't have a telephone. He had to walk to a neighbor's to call me at work." That answer, it seemed to Isabel, would have sufficed. But Monty Four Bear had more to say. "Maybe you weren't aware of the fact that most the houses on the rez don't have phones."

Ignoring Four Bear's response, Isabel turned to Suzanne.

"Suzanne, please try to contact Luke's mother in Denver. I'd like to speak to her. Maybe Mr. Four Bear can help you."

After hearing the beep indicating the X ray had been taken, Isabel reopened the door to the shock room. She tried to pull it closed behind her, but Monty had grabbed the handle and stood in the doorway.

"I'll be right back, Luke," he said into the room. "I'm just down the hall. We're going to try to get ahold of your mom. Okay?"

Luke's big brown eyes stared past Isabel at his uncle. The only thing more clear than the close bond between the two of them was the little boy's absolute terror at being there.

"Promise?" he asked.

"Promise."

As the door closed behind him and Isabel turned back to her patient, she wondered just how it had come to pass that she felt like the villain in this whole scene.

"SORRY ABOUT LUKE," Suzanne said. "Try not to worry. He looks like he'll be fine."

"Sherry'll have Dad's hide if he's not," Monty answered. "And mine for good measure."

"You know her phone number, Monty?"

"I have it in my address book, but I rushed out so fast when Dad called that I left it in my office."

"I'll call information," Suzanne said. "Maybe you can start filling out these forms."

"Luke's been here before. That time he cut himself, remember?"

"New doctor, new forms. Dr. McLain's trying to get things organized here."

"Why doesn't that surprise me?" Monty said, half under his breath. Suzanne smiled.

"She's a good doctor. Give her a chance."

Monty did not respond. His eyes had been drawn to a notice posted above the row of blue plastic chairs lining the opposite wall.

As Suzanne dialed directory assistance for Denver, he crossed the room to get a better look.

WOULD YOU LIKE TO SERVE
ON AN INSTITUTIONAL REVIEW BOARD?

ImmuVac Pharmaceutical Company has proposed a clinical trial on the Blackfeet Reservation. Participants will be vaccinated against the deadly hantavirus, a disease which recently struck three cherished members of the Blackfeet family. Would you like the honor of serving on the Institutional Review Board that has the grave responsibility of recommending FDA approval of this vaccination program? This is an opportunity to serve your community. Interested applicants should contact 1-800-334-4000.

When Monty returned to Suzanne, she appeared to be listening to an answering machine message. He held up the notice, which he'd ripped off the wall.

"What's this?"

Suzanne pointed a finger skyward, indicating she'd be right with him, then she began speaking into the phone.

"This is the Blackfeet reservation medical clinic. We're trying to reach Sherry Luster regarding her boy, Luke. If we've reached the right number, please contact us immediately at 406-444-1212. Thank you."

She hung up the phone and turned to Monty.

"They're gonna do a study here on a vaccine for the hantavirus. Isn't that great?"

"I heard about you being so sick," Monty said. "I was praying for you."

"Thanks, Monty."

"I was happy to hear you were okay," he continued, "but even after what happened, they can't just come in here and begin vaccinating people."

"You're right. First the review board's gotta say it's okay. That's what that piece of paper is all about."

"Mind if I keep this?"

"No, but if you're interested in being on the board, it's too late.

They've already picked it. In fact, they're meeting here tomorrow night to learn all about the vaccine."

For the first time since he'd arrived, a half grin played at the corners of Monty's mouth.

"You know me better than that," he said. "What time's the meeting?"

Suzanne looked down and flipped a page on the appointment book on her desk.

"Looks like seven o'clock."

CHAPTER

ELEVEN

MONTY HATED CALLING class off, but after he'd stood by his refusal to take Luke to the hospital yesterday, the lady doctor had given him explicit instructions that his nephew was to be monitored closely for the next twenty-four hours. That meant missing today's lecture, for Monty wasn't about to leave Luke in Leroy's charge. Leroy had promised he'd stay sober, but when it came to Luke's well being, Monty wasn't taking chances.

Like many of his people, Monty had developed an attitude that fell somewhere between a reluctant acceptance of modern medicine and clinging to traditional native beliefs about healing. The difference between Monty and the others, however, was that while most of his people had spent their entire lives on the reservation and based their distrust more on a superstitious fear of the unknown, Monty had lived in the outside world. He'd gone to college in Missoula, law school in Seattle, and, during his stint with the BIA, lived in Washington, D.C. Monty was educated and knowledgeable—and *still* distrustful. In fact, the more he learned—medicine was one of many topics on which he strove to keep his knowledge current—the more his distrust grew, in direct proportion to his respect for spiritual healing.

Monty turned to modern medicine, especially modern medicine practiced by non-Indians, only out of absolute necessity. Many an Indian had recovered from a blow to the head without the aid of white doctors and their machines. The way he saw it, sending Luke to the hospital for a CAT scan represented more risk than keeping a close eye on him at home. It was time to give nature a chance to heal Luke.

Edna, his father's neighbor, had agreed to stay with Luke when she got home from work so that Monty could attend the meeting at the clinic. Driving into Browning after dropping Leroy off at a friend's—Edna made it clear she didn't want to have to baby-sit *both* Luke and Leroy—Monty found himself thinking that if it hadn't been for Luke needing him to stay home that morning, he would have been able to let his students know what was going on. No doubt some of them would have shown up tonight too. Of course, if it weren't for Luke getting injured, he wouldn't even know about this insane plan in the first place.

How had something like this slipped by him? Slipped by everyone?

The meeting had already begun when Monty stepped into the waiting room. Six chairs had been arranged in a semicircle, in the middle of which stood a tall, skinny white guy wearing a blue denim shirt and khakis. Acknowledging Monty's arrival, he nodded in a friendly manner, causing those seated in the semicircle to turn.

Monty recognized Father McGrath, a Jesuit priest from the mission; Ann Garity, a Blackfeet and science professor from the University of Montana; John Turnbull, a tribal elder; and the lady doctor from the day before. One man, African American, was a complete stranger, and the last person, a middle-aged woman, looked vaguely familiar to him. Seated behind the semicircle and now turned his way, Suzanne Featherheart grinned at him.

"Please, come in," the man said. "I'm Dr. Ken MacStirling. I'm with ImmuVac and I was just explaining the responsibilities these ladies and gentlemen have assumed in volunteering to serve on this board."

Monty nodded in response and slipped quietly into the only empty seat in the room, right next to Suzanne.

"As I was saying," Ken MacStirling continued, "the FDA requires the consent of an institutional review board any time human subjects are involved in research, which, of course, is what we have here.

"It's the job of the IRB to evaluate the research based on several criteria. The first is the risk involved to the subjects. Having developed the hantavirus vaccine myself, I can assure you that there is minimal risk involved. This vaccine has already been tested on animals. The results of that research were presented in the package given you upon your selection to the IRB. The compilation of data on pages seven through twelve shows that adverse reactions were practically nonexistent.

"A clinical trial like this is conducted in three phases. Phase I is generally pretty small. Thirty to forty subjects, max. The primary objective of Phase I is to test safety. Once the FDA reviews the data, we move into Phase II. Because it is so safe, I'm confident we'll be able to move quickly to Phase II, which is just like Phase I, only on a bigger scale. In Phase III, large numbers of subjects, in this case thousands, will be injected. All three phases will take place here, on the reservation. Our goal is to vaccinate every resident. Now, all of you must have questions."

John Turnbull cleared his throat.

"What if this vaccine gives us the disease? What if it gives it to every-one on the reservation? The papers you gave us say it was tested on mice and rats. Well, we already know that the hantavirus doesn't kill them. Doesn't even make them sick. So how do we know it won't kill us?"

"That's a good question, but it's impossible for this vaccine to actually transmit the disease. You see, in the past, most vaccines actually consisted of whole microorganisms, alive or killed, of the disease they were intended to prevent. A flu shot, for example, actually works by introducing minute amounts of the virus into your system. This enables your body to produce natural antibodies, which build up and then protect you against the virus later when you're exposed to it. But that's not how this vaccine was made. This vaccine does not actually contain hantavirus. Instead, it contains a canary-pox virus that has been genetically engineered to be so similar to the hantavirus—without causing any of the same effects of the disease itself—that it will produce antibodies that will actually work against han-tavirus. So you see, there's no chance that subjects who get the vaccine will be infected with the hantavirus."

Turnbull made a *hmmpf*like sound.

Ken MacStirling continued gamely.

"At most, subjects might have a little irritation at the injection site. The truth is, the worst part for most subjects will be having to give blood. As the protocol you have states, blood will be drawn at three points. Once before the vaccine, once one week after vaccination, and again at three weeks."

"Lotta blood," John Turnbull grumbled.

This caused Monty to smile. He noticed Suzanne Featherheart grin-ning too.

"The next criteria that you as a board should take into consideration in reviewing the proposed clinical trial is the anticipated benefits to the subjects and others." Ken MacStirling's eyes swept the panel. "I know I don't have to tell you about hantavirus. It is a very deadly disease—one of the deadliest in the world. As you've found out, its victims are often young and healthy and they literally drown in serum from their own blood. It is an experience that no human being should ever have to go through. Especially if there's a way to prevent it. Before now, there has been no way to prevent this terrible disease and once it strikes, very little that medical professionals could do to stop its course. But this vaccine will change all that."

The room had fallen still. Joe Winged Foot, Will EchoHawk, and Dolores Birdsong had been known by most of those present. Their mem-ories hung heavily in the air.

"At what cost?"

Monty's words—spoken with that voice that had proven capable of mesmerizing students and causing young women to fall in love on the spot—broke through the silence with such force that several of the panel members actually started in their seats.

All heads turned to Monty.

"At what cost?" he repeated, rising from his seat.

"I know what you're all thinking. I didn't know Will or Dolores very well, but I knew Joe from the time he was a little kid. He used to follow me on that bike of his, make a pest of himself. Always hanging around me and my friends, begging us to let him in our pickup games. Then I left the rez and when I came back, Joe was all grown up. The last couple years, the highlight of my winters has been watching Joe's games, seeing him kick ass out there on the court. I was already planning my trips to Missoula to watch him play at the U next year."

Monty was in his element now. He had the full attention of everyone in the room. He zeroed in on each person in the room as he spoke, finally allowing his eyes to fall upon the one face he'd not been able to place before. It belonged to a middle-aged Blackfeet woman. Her eyes were those of someone in great pain. It wasn't until that very moment that he realized who she was. Anna Winged Foot. Joe's mother.

"But this vaccine won't bring Joe back," he said, quietly now, out of respect for Anna. "If it could, I'd be the first in line. We *all* grieved when we lost Joe. He belonged to all of us. He represented the best of us. We're all still grieving. But don't let those emotions color your rational thoughts. Don't make an impulsive decision out of grief. Or guilt."

"Excuse me." It was Ken MacStirling again. "Would you like to introduce yourself?"

"My name is Monty Four Bear."

"And you are . . . ?" The scientist was clearly taken off-guard by Monty's speech.

"I am a Blackfeet," was all Monty answered.

"Monty don't need to be introduced," John Turnbull piped up.

"Mr. Four Bear, what exactly are your concerns about this vaccine?"

Several heads nodded. They all wanted to know. Monty noted that the doctor, Isabel McLain, simply stared at him, blank faced. It was too bad she was the enemy because even Monty would admit she was pretty.

"Yes," Turnbull said, "tell us your concerns. And wouldja move to where we don't have to break our necks to see you?"

A twitter of laughter broke the tension in the room, as Monty stepped out to the side of the assembled chairs. He could have joined MacStirling at the center, but he wanted to maintain the distance between them.

"A friend of mine from college served in the Gulf War. In 1991, the government gave the troops experimental vaccines. My buddy, who's a Lakota, tried to refuse the vaccine. He didn't like the idea of being a guinea pig. But he was told he'd be court martialed if he refused. So he let them vaccinate him. He had headaches and dizziness for years afterwards. He's just been diagnosed with lupus. Can't work, can hardly play with his kids. All because he tried to serve his country."

"With all due respect, Mr. Four Bear," the man sitting next to Isabel McLain interrupted. "Your friend can't prove there's any connection between his problems and the vaccine he received."

"How do you know he can't? What makes you an authority?"

"My name is Lehman Morris. I'm a pulmonary specialist from Missoula. Dr. McLain asked me to serve on the review board. And I just happen to have an interest in what's known as the Gulf War Syndrome."

"You actually believe that thousands of vets like my friend are making these symptoms up? That there's no connection between the Gulf War and the fact that many of them can no longer live a normal life?"

"I'm just saying that as of yet, no direct connection has been established."

Monty shook his head.

"What's it going to take for someone to admit that it's not just a coincidence that all these people who got vaccinated ended up sick? You know what the government wants them to believe? That it's in their heads. They want the problem to go away so they won't have to take responsibility."

These words—condemnation of the federal government—seemed to strike a chord within some members of the group, who nodded or murmured under their breath. Ken MacStirling seemed well aware of the fact that things could easily get out of hand if Monty weren't neutralized.

"Mr. Four Bear," MacStirling said, "I don't feel knowledgeable enough to deal with your friend's situation. I would encourage him to continue his efforts to determine whether there could be a connection between the vaccine and his current health. But surely you wouldn't advocate abolition of all vaccines?"

"Don't be so sure."

"What about polio? Measles? Rubella? Many of us wouldn't be sitting here today if it weren't for vaccines. They've saved millions and millions of lives. That is an indisputable fact. Even if there is some truth to your friend's allegations, you can't let one—or even several—unfortunate results with vaccines taint all of them, across the board. That's the purpose of the FDA regulations. Of this panel. To provide safeguards. To ensure that every vaccine that's put on the market is safe, that its benefits have been established and that the risks presented are minimal."

"But just who is being used here to determine whether the risks exist?" Monty countered, his voice rising in anger. "*Our* people. When the vaccine is out on the market, maybe then some of us will choose to use it. I, for one, will not. But until then, let someone else be the guinea pig."

"So that more of your people can die in the meantime? Is that what you want?"

A new voice had entered the fray.

Isabel McLain stood, facing Monty. If her expression had seemed blank before, it was anything but now. She looked equal parts hostile and, oddly, shaken.

"I had some of the same thoughts." Before Monty even had time to respond, Isabel McLain continued. "Why not wait, until the vaccine has been tested? But Dr. MacStirling pointed something out to me. We're talking years, *years*, before this product is on the market. In the meantime, how many more lives will this despicable disease claim? Even if the answer is only one, that's one too many. I will do everything in my power," her voice weakened momentarily, "... *everything*, to make sure that what happened to Joe and Will and Dolores doesn't happen again. Not here. Not on this reservation."

"Let me ask you something," Monty jumped in. "Are you being paid by the patient? Because I read this morning that that's how it's done. An investigator gets paid a certain amount for each patient he or she enrolls in the study."

"See here," Ken MacStirling said, starting toward Monty as though he intended to throw him out. "That's totally uncalled for."

"No." Isabel held her hand up. "It's okay. Let him ask his questions." She turned back to Monty.

"The answer is no. ImmuVac offered to pay me, but I refused. I know it would be a lot easier to sway everyone here if you could show this is all about money, but it's not. In fact, if you think ImmuVac stands to make big money from this vaccine, you're wrong. I'm sorry to disappoint you."

Monty realized, too late, that he'd gone too far. Even John Turnbull was shooting concerned glances Dr. McLain's way. Monty had to give her credit. He knew he'd shaken her up, but she'd held her own against him.

"Are there any other questions? Or comments?"

Anna Winged Foot raised a hand.

"I would like to say something." She spoke softly and slowly, choosing her words carefully. "Joey was a good boy. He loved his mother, and he loved all of you. He was a good boy. He always wanted to help people. And maybe this is his way. The way he can help. Maybe because Joey died other people won't have to.

"And there's one more thing. And no disrespect intended, Monty, cause we all know you're a good man. But maybe it's time we stop blaming everything on the government. They done us wrong. Everybody knows that. And they still do us wrong a lot of the time. But we have to look out for other people. Not just Indian people. Everyone. Maybe if we show we want to do this to help everyone, it will start something. You know what I mean? Maybe things can still change. Joey would have liked that."

The vote for approval was 5 to 0 in favor of endorsing the clinical trial. John Turnbull abstained.

As Monty walked out to his pickup, he felt a tug at his sleeve.

"You were pretty tough on her."

It was John Turnbull.

"She's a good doc, you know. She's been good for us here."

Monty offered Turnbull a ride home, but he'd already made arrangements with Anna Winged Foot. Monty sat in the truck, revving its engine a few times to warm it. The battery had been giving him trouble recently. Tomorrow he planned to drop it off at Lester's gas station and have it charged.

After two or three minutes, Monty backed the pickup up, turning the headlights on as he did so. Crossing the parking lot to a lone Jeep that Monty had parked next to, Isabel McLain stepped into their glare.

She lifted her hand in a thanks to the driver for waiting for her, then recognized Monty behind the wheel and dropped it. For a moment she froze, then she approached Monty's side of the truck.

Monty rolled his window down. Now what?

"How's Luke?"

"Fine. Much better in fact."

"Good."

She hesitated, and Monty could almost see the struggle taking place inside her over whether to give him a piece of her mind.

He'd failed in his mission to turn the IRB against the proposed study, but he'd definitely succeeded in getting under Isabel McLain's skin. Especially when he implied that her support for the study might have been related to payments from ImmuVac. He'd probably hit below the belt with that one, but he'd consider it payback for her inference yesterday that he'd been negligent in taking so long to bring Luke into the clinic. Plus, he'd long ago had to buy into the maxim that—at least where his people's welfare was concerned—the end justified the means. He had to keep focused on the mission. He mustn't let the fact that Isabel McLain had taken good care of Luke, the fact that his nephew had later told him he liked the "white lady doctor," interfere with that, with his mission. Nor the fact that, standing in the half-lit parking lot glaring at him, she looked so damn good.

Abruptly, Isabel McLain turned away.

Monty rolled his window up and watched as she walked to the old Jeep.

He waited until she was safely inside. Then he pulled onto Highway 2 and headed toward home.

TWELVE

ARE YOU ABSOLUTELY certain I can only give forty vaccinations?" Isabel's eyes fell to the stack of papers in her hands. "There must be two hundred applications here."

"Forty is *it*," MacStirling replied decisively. "I told you before, Phase I is always small."

"It's going to be so hard to decide who gets the vaccine and who doesn't."

MacStirling reached across the Formica surface for the applications. They'd taken to meeting at the same table at the Outlaw Inn. Mac-Stirling's visits had become a weekly event, as the initiation of Phase I of the HantaVac study drew near. "May I?"

Isabel pushed the stack his way.

"Be my guest."

While MacStirling perused the applications, Isabel dove in to her breakfast. Usually she grabbed a piece of fruit on the way out the cabin's door, then followed it up with Suzanne's leadlike coffee at the clinic. Hash browns and an omelette were a rare treat. At least she got a decent meal out of these meetings with MacStirling.

Halfway through her omelette, Isabel realized that as he reviewed each application, MacStirling placed it in one of two piles he'd formed in front of him on the table.

"What are you doing?"

"You said you wanted help deciding who to include in Phase I."

Isabel grabbed the pile to MacStirling's left.

"No, I didn't. I just said I wasn't sure how I'd make that decision."

"Well, I'm just helping you."

She recognized several names in the pile she'd grabbed. Jean White, a fifty-year-old patient who had undergone a mastectomy five years earlier but had been cancer-free ever since. Robbie Hill, a fortyish father of five and recovering alcoholic, who at first forbade his wife from bringing the children into the clinic, but who now dropped by himself—never with an appointment—when he wasn't feeling well. Also included in this pile was the application of Arlo Iron Heart.

"Is this your yes or no pile?"

"I'd exclude those applicants, at least from the first two phases of the trial and perhaps altogether," MacStirling answered. He pushed the other pile her way. "*These* are good candidates."

Isabel felt the blood rushing to her face. She'd been so pleased when Robbie had come in one day and asked for an application for the HantaVac study. And after her brush with cancer, Jean White enthusiastically embraced the trial as another means of ensuring her continued good health.

"Why? What's wrong with these applicants?"

"Their histories. While I'm confident the vaccine doesn't present any increased risk to them, their complicating factors could skew the results."

"*Skew the results?* What is that—lab-speak?" Isabel cried. "The people who will ultimately get this vaccine will be *real* people with *real* problems. People like Robbie Hill and Jean White. Let me tell you something, Dr. MacStirling, I will not be part of some carefully manipulated scam to produce results simply to make your vaccine look good. This isn't about data and numbers for me. It's about my patients."

MacStirling looked surprised by the venomous response.

"Now let me tell you something, Dr. McLain," he said, anger twitching his jaw. "I'm a scientist. That's what we do—conduct systematic studies in which we collect and analyze data. I suppose you think I should apologize for that, but if it weren't for people like me, people like you would be a whole lot less effective in saving the world."

Isabel grabbed both piles, placing one on top of the other in clear disregard of MacStirling's attempt to order them.

"I'll take another look at these later," she said.

"We need a definitive list by tomorrow."

"That won't be a problem."

"Good," MacStirling said, using a mellower tone, as if he'd decided that nothing would be served by getting into a shouting match with her. "Then we can begin vaccinations. The pilot lot of the vaccine will be shipped directly to you at the clinic. It will arrive by the end of the week. You can either draw blood prior to the vaccine, in which case I'd suggest you get started as soon as you determine the participants, or you can make life simpler by doing both the same day."

"I've already decided to make it a two-step process," Isabel said civilly, following MacStirling's lead. "It would be easier to draw blood and administer the vaccine in one visit, but I think the study participants might find a single visit too intimidating. I'll use the first visit to draw the control sample of blood and to give them another opportunity to ask questions."

"Suit yourself. You'll be receiving all your supplies, including sterile kits and mailing cartons for the blood samples, within the next few days. Of course, I'll be in regular contact with you."

"Of course."

"There's one other thing." MacStirling shifted uncomfortably in the booth. "ImmuVac's CEO, Dr. Lyons, plans to arrange for a reporter from the Portland papers to be on hand at the inception of Phase I."

Isabel could do nothing but stare, disbelieving, at MacStirling.

"I realize," he said tentatively, "that the participants may not like it, but now that we have their consent, I can't really imagine anyone backing out simply because the trial is being observed by an outsider. They don't even have to know he's a reporter."

Isabel drew a deep breath.

"If a reporter shows his or her face, I will walk away from this study. Is that clear?"

"I think we've already had this conversation. You can't claim to have no knowledge of ImmuVac's desire for some good press for this study. I made that known to you from the start."

"I'm warning you. Publicity can only harm this study."

MacStirling's eyes narrowed on her.

"How so?"

"I've been hearing that there might be organized resistance. Remember Monty Four Bear, from the first IRB meeting? I've heard rumblings that he made the clinical trial a topic of one of his college classes. He apparently compared it to the Tuskegee experiments. I don't really think ImmuVac would benefit much from having *that* reported. Could have the opposite effect you're hoping for. Might actually scare investors off."

"Why haven't you said something?" MacStirling said, clearly agitated. "It sounds like I'd better plan to be there."

"That's why I haven't. Because I can handle this alone. In fact, I'm confident that if there *is* any resistance, your presence would only exacerbate the situation." She leaned MacStirling's way and leveled her brown eyes on his. "This entire experience is something very new to these people. New and frightening. It's taken me a while, but finally, many of them—almost all who've submitted applications—trust me. They are just beginning to see me as one of them. If you're there, I suddenly lose that. I become associated in their minds with you. With a world they've learned not to trust. Faced with Monty Four Bear and any support he's drummed up, it becomes us against them."

MacStirling studied Isabel silently.

"Maybe the reporter's not such a good idea," he said. "But do you promise to let me know if things with this Four Bear fellow get out of hand?"

Monty Four Bear could stage an armed takeover of the clinic and Isabel would still not call MacStirling for help. The mere notion struck her as ludicrous.

"I promise."

· · ·

THAT NIGHT, ON her way home, Isabel made a turn at the fork leading
to Gus's ranch. A full moon dominated the sky, mesmerizing Isabel as she
crept down Gus's long drive. Many a night she'd lain awake observing
the moon through the bedroom skylight in the house she and Alistair
shared in Seattle, but never had she seen anything like the humbling
sight of a full moon in Big Sky country.

Lights were on in the house, but Grunt's barks turned Isabel's attention to the barn where she saw Gus's silhouette. He was shoveling out a
stall. Grunt ran halfway across the corral toward the driveway, barking a
greeting at Isabel, then stopped and looked back at Gus, torn between
the two.

Isabel entered the barn. Years ago all the stalls lining either side had
been occupied, but now Gus was down to a single horse. Isabel walked
the barn's length, then stepped out into the corral. Gus was pushing the
wheelbarrow he'd just emptied back across the corral, toward where Isabel
stood. Bessie, Gus's sorrel mare, followed close behind, her muzzle at
Gus's shoulder.

"Hey, there," Isabel called. "What are you doing out here in the
dark?"

"Full moon," Gus answered. "Plenty of light. Just thought I'd come
keep Bessie here company."

"But it's freezing. I think you're losing it, Gus."

"Not cold if you keep moving."

"Well, I don't have enough energy to start shoveling manure with you,
so how about taking a break and offering your neighbor some hot chocolate?"

The moonlight enabled her to see the twinkle of delight in Gus's eye.

"I was about to do that, if you'd just give an old man some time."

"Old man, huh! I only hope I'm as spry as you when *I'm* eighty."

Isabel had helped Gus celebrate his seventy-fifth birthday in April.

Gus glared at her.

"You better watch it. I never signed any papers when you moved into
that cabin. Keep on insulting me and you might just end up out in the
cold."

Isabel stood on tiptoe and pecked Gus on the cheek.

"How's that?"

"Much better."

When he smiled, Gus's eyes disappeared into folds of leathery skin.

After they'd locked Bessie in her stall for the night, they crossed the
driveway. Grunt, tail wagging and nose to the ground, led the way.

"How's he doing?" Isabel asked.

"He's a tough old bugger," Gus said, laughing. "Limps a little bit in
the morning but it doesn't slow him down none."

"Good. Maybe we can start running again one of these days." For months, Isabel had been in the habit of borrowing Grunt to keep her company on the runs she took several mornings each week. She didn't tell Gus that the reason she'd stopped was fear that Alistair could be nosing around the area and see her. "I've missed it."

"Haven't seen much of you recently. Clinic must be keeping you busy. I heard you got some kind of an experimental vaccine you're gonna be givin' out there."

Isabel shook her head and laughed. "Moccasin telegraph?"

It was what they called the lightning-quick wire through which gossip spread on the reservation. Even though Gus's property bordered the tribal lands, she hadn't expected the moccasin telegraph to extend that far.

"Yep."

Heated by a fire in the massive stone fireplace that dominated an entire wall, Gus's house felt warm and cozy. Isabel followed Gus to the kitchen, pulling a big can of powdered cocoa from the cupboard as he put milk on the stove to warm.

"Marshmallows?" Isabel asked. Gus loved to smother his hot chocolate in them.

"In the fridge."

Standing beside Gus at the stove, watching him stir the milk that didn't require stirring, Isabel felt a sudden sense of peace. Her first two months in the cabin, she'd spent several evenings like this. Those first months had been difficult in so many ways, struggling for acceptance—struggling to get patients to come to the clinic—but it had given her a great gift in Gus. It had been too long since she'd dropped by to see her dear friend.

When they'd settled in front of the fire, Isabel listened as Gus rambled on about the neighboring rancher's poor fence-mending practices. Seems Gus and Bessie had to round up stray cattle on his property every other day or so. Isabel suspected that it didn't bother Gus half as much as he let on, that it gave him something to do with his time. A decade earlier, Gus had run two hundred head of cattle on his property. It always seemed to her that idle time was Gus's worst enemy.

An hour later, the fire and cocoa had taken effect, and Isabel found herself fighting back sleep.

"I'd better head on home," she said, rubbing her sore back as she rose from the sofa. Then she remembered one of the reasons she'd come. "Oh, yeah. I have something for you."

She reached into the back pocket of her army-green cargo pants and withdrew a sheet of paper.

"What's that?"

"It's an application for the vaccine program," she said, handing it to Gus. "I think it's important that you be vaccinated."

"I thought it was just for the Blackfeet."

"Technically, it is. But you just happen to have some pull with the lead investigator."

Gus's withered hand pushed the paper gently away.

"Thanks, but no thanks," he said.

"Why, Gus? I think this is important. You know I wouldn't suggest this if I didn't."

"I know," Gus said. "And I appreciate what you're trying to do. You're a good girl, Izzie. But I don't want any part in some experimental program."

"Gus, what are you talking about?"

"Just what I said. You weren't around back then, but back in the fifties, all of us were given the polio vaccine."

"Yes, and thank God for it."

"Did you know it was contaminated? That they made it from some kind of monkey blood or something . . ."

"The rhesus monkey."

"That's it. Anyway, turns out the monkey had this virus."

"SV 40."

Isabel found herself tensing as Gus continued his explanation.

"That sounds about right. Anyway, they changed the kind of monkeys they used, but not before plenty of people had been given the bad vaccine. They say folks are getting cancer now from that vaccine. No, I'm steering clear of them. Don't even get a flu shot."

Isabel tried to hide the knee-jerk reaction Gus's words gave rise to.

"Gus, you're the last person on earth I expected to hear such paranoia from." The rise in her voice gave away her indignation. "Do you actually think I'd be involved with a vaccine that could be dangerous?"

"Hold on, there, Izzie. I'm not accusing you of anything."

"I certainly hope not."

Gus stared in confusion at Isabel, then at the application grasped so tightly in her clenched fist that it looked like it had gone through the washing machine.

"What's got into you, girl?"

Isabel dropped her hand to her side.

"Nothing, Gus. I apologize. It's just a touchy subject for me, that's all."

"I thought this study you're doin' was somethin' you're happy about."

For an old man with whom she had little in common, Gus possessed an uncanny ability to read her.

"Of course I'm happy about it, Gus," she insisted. "Why wouldn't I be?"

THIRTEEN

ONE BY ONE, at the appointed time, the cars and pickups filed into the parking lot.

Monty Four Bear was there to greet them. He approached the latest arrival, a bumperless red VW with numerous activist stickers on it. I SUPPORT THE BUFFALO NATION. NO NUKES. BLM = ENEMY.

"We're expecting one more," Monty said, his breath visible in the early October air. "You might as well wait in your car, then we'll all spend a few minutes together before we caravan over to the clinic."

"Want to climb in and warm up?" Waylon Eagleplume asked, a thick black braid falling out the window as he rolled it halfway down to stick his head out.

Waylon was one of Monty's repeat students. His mother didn't have money to send him to a four-year school so he'd been attending classes at the community college for four years, working part-time at the Browning Bowl to pay for tuition. As usual, his girlfriend, LuAnn, was with him. Monty would have preferred that Waylon come alone. LuAnn was painfully shy and ill suited to today's task. But for as long as he'd known them, the two were inseparable, and Monty respected their commitment to each other.

"Thanks, but I'm fine. Good to see you again, LuAnn. Here's the literature we'll be handing out at the clinic. It's pretty much the same stuff we went over in class."

"Gotcha," Waylon said, his angular face bisected by a crooked smile.

"Here's Clyde now," Monty said as a newer-model Ford Bronco pulled up. "Give me a little blast on your horn, will you?"

Eagleplume obliged cheerfully as Monty waved all the vehicles' occupants over for a meeting.

They were a scraggly lot, mostly college students, with the exception of Clyde Birdseye, who posed as a cousin of Monty's from Denver but was, in reality, a fellow AIM member. They'd learned early on that if both men were known to be members of AIM, any activity they took part in together would inevitably be classified as AIM sponsored, which tended to close doors and minds.

Monty and Clyde had met at an AIM protest years earlier and formed a close friendship, fueled by the intensity of their shared ideology. Clyde had grown up on the Big Piney reservation. Like Monty, he was in his early forties and had abandoned a professional career, as a reporter for a Denver paper, to devote himself to AIM.

"Okay, listen up everyone," Monty said. "I'm glad to see you. We'll be heading over to the clinic in a few minutes, but I wanted to go over some ground rules first."

"To start with, no physical force is to be used today. These are our people, we're not there to intimidate or scare them. We're there because we care about their welfare, remember that. Keep that first and foremost in your mind. We're there to educate them. If you see someone you know, approach them first. As a friend. There's a good chance that at least one of us will know every participant in this study.

"If the police show up, I don't want to see any resistance. Everyone understand? There are situations where that's called for—any of you who accompanied me to Ward Valley know that—but this isn't one of them.

"I'm handing out literature for you to share with the study partici-pants."

He passed the stapled sheets around, nodding and occasionally smil-ing through the cloud of crystallized breath billowing forth from each of the nine faces surrounding him.

"Any questions?"

"None here."

"No, sir."

Several nods.

It seemed they were all anxious to do what they'd come there to do.

"Okay," said Monty then. *"Let's go!"*

ISABEL'S STOMACH PICKED the worst time to complain about not having been fed. She'd been too nervous this morning for food, and in too big a hurry for lunch. Now, as she arranged chairs in the waiting room, she regretted not taking time to eat. Once the study group arrived, though, she was certain eating would be the last thing on her mind.

They were due within the next half hour.

After spending three days drawing blood for the control sample, she'd decided to split the study group in two and administer all the vaccinations during two consecutive afternoon sessions. She'd been generous in the time she'd given each participant when he or she came in for the blood sample, had patiently answered their questions and gone back over the protocol and scientific data supplied by ImmuVac. Now she felt that the most efficient way to conduct the vaccinations would be in two groups.

That way, each group would have one last opportunity to ask questions before receiving the vaccine. Another big factor in her decision to handle it this way was that she hoped that seeing the other study participants would have a calming effect on each person. Though for the most part each applicant she'd chosen seemed pleased to be included, under the surface, she sensed more than a little bit of nervousness, too.

She was just trying to decide how to arrange the chairs, when she heard Suzanne mutter an uh-oh.

Isabel looked up to see the receptionist staring out the clinic's front door.

"You better come take a look," she said.

"What is it?" Isabel approached Suzanne, her gaze following that of the younger woman's.

A caravan of cars and trucks was pulling in to the clinic's parking lot. The lead pickup looked vaguely familiar. Then it hit her. The night of the IRB meeting. *Monty Four Bear.*

"*Sweet Jesus,*" Isabel muttered, pushing through the front door.

Just as the last of the caravan pulled in from the east, she recognized the car of Arlo Iron Heart, whom she'd included in the Phase I group despite MacStirling's recommendation.

Isabel approached Monty Four Bear's truck. A tall, bony Indian with a hawkish nose, piercing eyes, and long straggly hair tied loosely at his neck stepped out of the passenger side and stared across the truck at her as she waited, with a twisted gut, for Monty to open his door.

"What are you doing here?" she asked when he did.

"Nice to see you again." Monty smiled.

"Answer me. What do you want?"

Monty turned to his companion and introduced him to Isabel over the truck's bed.

"This is my cousin, Clyde Birdseye. Clyde, this is Dr. Isabel McLain. She's the doctor I told you about, the one who's in charge of this study."

Clyde nodded and gave Isabel a half salute that was distinctly mocking.

By now, Arlo had pulled up to the spot nearest the clinic door and another member of Monty's caravan had approached him. Isabel glared at Monty, then rushed to Arlo's side in the hope of escorting him inside before something awful happened. But it was too late.

"Please, just read this literature," a round-faced young man with a shaved head was saying to Arlo. "This study could do you more harm than good."

Isabel grabbed the stapled pages the young man held in front of Arlo's face.

"What's *is* this?" she said.

The top sheet was entitled, in large bold print, HUMAN GUINEA PIGS.

Isabel groaned. By now, the kid had handed Arlo a second copy. Monty Four Bear and two other study participants had joined them.

Isabel turned on Monty.

"How dare you do this?"

Monty's eyes held hers momentarily, then he turned away and surveyed the group, which had grown with more arriving participants.

"We are not here to frighten you," he said. "Please, just give us a few minutes of your time. Let us share some important information with you before you decide to go inside."

Arlo Iron Heart had a look of sheer panic on his leathery face. The other participants appeared nervous and hesitant, but when Isabel opened the clinic door and pleaded with them to come in, no one budged.

"Please, just walk past them," she kept repeating.

"All we're asking," Monty Four Bear was saying to the group in a voice that Isabel found maddeningly reasoned, "is that you listen to us. Or read this." He raised the handout in the air. "These are facts. Actual statistics from sources like *The New York Times*. Or the Food and Drug Administration. Listen to this: The FDA issued a report that says that in the past year, one-point-five million Americans were hospitalized as a consequence of pharmaceutical drugs they were given to *cure* them. You can't assume this vaccine is safe, not when drugs already approved for commercial sale can harm you."

Isabel let go of the door and stepped forward angrily.

"Don't let him do this to you. He's just trying to confuse and frighten you. This vaccine is not a drug intended to cure you—it is meant to protect you from contracting a very dangerous virus. That FDA statistic means nothing in this context. *Nothing*. We're talking about a vaccine here."

"Okay, if you want to talk about vaccines," Monty broke in, "read this." He shook a copy of the pamphlet above his head. "How many of you knew that it is a proven fact—one admitted by the government— that the polio vaccine had been contaminated with a serious virus?"

Isabel groaned inwardly.

Had Gus and Monty Four Bear just read the same article?

"That was almost fifty years ago!" she cried. "It was a terrible accident that the government has admitted." She swept her eyes over their audience, which was growing by the minute. "Many of you might not be here today if it weren't for that vaccine. Please, all of you study participants, come inside. Ignore them."

Her voice fell on deaf ears. It was as if the only words actually ingested by the group were those coming from the mouth of Monty Four Bear. Until Clyde Birdseye opened his.

"Why do you suppose we've been selected to be the subjects of this noble gesture?" Birdseye asked. His voice did not have the lyrical quality to it that Monty's had, but it was strong and angry and could not be ignored. "You've all heard of the Tuskegee Institute experiments, haven't you? Where black men were deprived of treatment for syphilis for thirty-eight years?"

Even Arlo Iron Heart's head nodded in response.

Isabel could take no more.

"That's not why this reservation was chosen for this study and you know it. We were chosen because hantavirus struck here. Because I wrote an article . . ."

"*An article that condemned the medical establishment,*" Clyde shot back. "Called it racist. And now you're trying to deny that this type of thing happens. This one talks out of both sides of her mouth. Don't trust her."

"Don't you twist my words." Isabel gave Birdseye a withering glare. "There's one big difference between all those situations you described and this. A *huge* difference. The tragedy, the *crime*, in all those situations was that the patients were not informed. If what this man says is true," she turned back to the rest of the group, "and I don't for one moment buy into it, that alone should alleviate your concerns. You are protected here. There has been full disclosure. No one is forcing you to participate in this study. In fact, there were far more applicants than we could accommodate during this phase. This vaccine will save lives. It may well save each of *your* lives."

"I've heard it was some kind of vaccine that caused AIDS."

It was a statement that sounded more like a question, coming from one of the study participants, a young woman whom Isabel had first met just two days earlier. She'd directed it to Monty.

Monty nodded. "Some people believe the AIDS virus was caused by a contaminated hepatitis B vaccine given to gay men."

"Could that happen here?" The woman's eyes grew wider. "Could this vaccine be contaminated with something like AIDS?"

"Of course not," Isabel answered, but her words were drowned out by Monty's.

"Anything's possible when there's no independent testing to make sure the vaccine's pure."

"Nobody's tested this vaccine?" Arlo Iron Heart asked. "How can they tell us it's safe then?"

Isabel's flush gave away her flustered state.

"Mr. Four Bear is correct in stating that the FDA does not test each vaccine for purity. Quality assurance is the responsibility of the vaccine manufacturer. All of you received detailed information, results of tests and page after page of data, which demonstrates this vaccine's safety."

"I dunno," Arlo said softly. "Sounds a little risky to me."

"I've got two babies to feed. I ain't takin' chances with somethin' that's not even been tested," the same woman said, turning back toward the parking lot.

Isabel reflexively clenched her fists and set her jaw as she noticed two of Monty Four Bear's companions exchanging a high five at the back of the crowd.

"YOU WHAT?"

"I agreed to send the vaccine out to an independent lab for testing."

Ken MacStirling's breathing, which Isabel could usually hear over the telephone, ceased.

"Are you out of your mind?"

"No, I most certainly am not. It was the only way I could salvage this study. I told you, I was faced with an army of opposition. An *armed* army. They came well supplied with data and information. If I hadn't agreed to the independent testing, we'd have lost every volunteer there. And the more I thought about it, I decided it was a reasonable request."

"I knew I should have been there," MacStirling huffed. "I would never have allowed this to happen. This is insane. Lyons will have my head for this."

"I don't understand what the problem is. Unless you think the testing might turn something up."

"I've never seen anything like it."

"Like what?"

"A study investigator so paranoid about a study. I don't understand you. You write this article demanding that the pharmaceutical industry come up with a vaccine for hantavirus, then put up roadblocks every step of the way."

"All this independent testing costs us is a little time," Isabel answered defensively, "and I'd rather lose time than lives. In the long run, this will give the study that much more credibility. I could tell it made an impression on them, our being willing to send the vaccine for testing."

"*Our* being willing? This was a decision you made unilaterally. I don't want any part of it. In fact, you can't just send the vaccine out. You signed a confidentiality agreement. That vaccine is proprietary to ImmuVac."

"I have to have my patients' trust. I will not participate in this study without it."

"Is that another threat?"

"It's not intended to be. It's merely a statement of fact."

"Well, I'll keep that in mind."

There was a long silence.

"Will you grant me permission to send it out?" Isabel pressed. "In writing?"

"I want your word that you will not disclose the lab results before

I've had a chance to adequately address any adverse findings—which, of course, I don't anticipate."

Isabel hesitated for a moment.

"The full report has to be released to the study participants, regardless of the findings. As long as you agree to that, I'm agreeable to giving you whatever time you need to address it first. After all, I want this to put to rest, once and for all, any concerns that anyone—my patients *or* that damn Monty Four Bear—have."

"*Amen.*" Ken MacStirling sighed.

FOURTEEN

SOPHIA WHITE THUNDER winced as the needle penetrated the skin of her fleshy upper arm.

"I told you not to contract your muscles," Isabel scolded.

"Couldn't help it." Sophia smiled.

Isabel massaged the injection site for a moment before placing a piece of gauze and tape over it.

"Now don't forget to keep a journal of any reactions you have to the vaccine," Isabel said as she walked Sophia to the door. "Even if it doesn't seem related—if you're just tired, or achy—I want you to make note of it. Okay?"

"Sure, Dr. McLain. I'll do it. And thanks for letting me in the study. I know you had more people wanting in than you could vaccinate."

"We'll get them in Phase II and III." Isabel smiled.

When Suzanne came into the exam room a couple minutes later, she found Isabel lying on the exam table. She lifted her head and grinned at her assistant.

"What a day it's been."

"Ever give that many shots in one day before?"

Isabel laughed. The independent laboratory had confirmed the purity of the HantaVac, and she had just completed Phase I.

"No. Can't say that I have. Thirty-nine's a record for me. I just wish Arlo had shown up, but Monty Four Bear must have scared him off. It's a wonder more of the study participants didn't back out after seeing all that propaganda Four Bear and his group handed out."

"Dolores and those boys dying, that really scared everyone. Besides, they trust you. You wouldn't be doing this study if it wasn't a good thing for us."

Isabel had heard that same sentiment repeated throughout the day. Her patients trusted her, trusted that this study would safeguard them from what had happened to the others, that Isabel and ImmuVac had their best interests at heart.

The only flack she'd taken all day long had come from Lester Clay, a wiry, crewcut Blackfeet in his early thirties, whose ambivalence at participating in the clinical trial came through loud and clear.

"Probably shoulda listened to Monty and the others," he'd told Isabel.

"You're still welcome to change your mind, Mr. Clay," Isabel had responded, feeling somewhat guilty, for she knew that if it had been another of her patients, she would have done more to assuage any lingering concerns.

"Didn't say I wanted to change my mind. Did I?" Clay snapped. "What I want to know is if you're giving *yourself* the shot."

"I'm not allowed to participate."

"Why the hell not? Too dangerous?" he'd snickered.

But after he left, Isabel found herself regretting that she hadn't insisted on receiving the vaccination herself. She'd raised the issue once with MacStirling, and he'd told her it was forbidden, that for the study investigator to also participate in the trial would constitute a conflict of interest. He'd even pointed out that there was a limited amount of vaccine and that her participation would only deprive one of the Blackfeet of the protection it offered.

Isabel had to concede that there were probably situations in which the conflict of interest rule made sense, but surely this was not one of them. How could she ask these people to put their trust in her without subjecting herself to the same risks—if any existed—that she was exposing them to? Isabel had never believed in following rules that made no sense. And there was another consideration. Despite the explicit instructions she'd given each study participant, she knew that her patients had spent a lifetime ignoring symptoms—waiting, hoping to ride out an illness without having to resort to doctors and clinics. It was their nature to make light of aches and pains. Could they be counted on to report every symptom, even those they might be inclined to deem insignificant, that might or might not be related to the vaccine?

Suzanne had joined her, hoisting herself up on to the edge of the exam table.

"Guess we can call it a day," she said. "Want me to help you clean up in here?"

"No, you go ahead. I can take care of the exam rooms. You go on home. I shouldn't have let you work such a long day. You're still recovering."

"I'm fine now. It was important to me to be here."

"I can see why it would be. Thank you. I couldn't have done it without your help, but go now. Before that sky opens up."

It had been threatening rain all day, but with the evening temperatures dropping in to the mid-twenties, snow was a distinct possibility now.

"Winter's almost here, enit?"

Isabel nodded.

"Drive carefully."

"You too."

Isabel waited for the sound of the deadbolt turning in the clinic's front door. Then she stood and walked to the small refrigerator which sat atop the exam room's counter.

She opened the door. The refrigerator was empty save for the bottom half of a cardboard carton labeled IMMUVAC HANTAVIRUS VACCINE: FOR CLINICAL TRIAL USE ONLY.

A single vial sat in the grid that earlier in the day held forty. A vial intended for Arlo Iron Heart. Isabel reached for the small glass container, which held three millimeters of clear fluid.

She shook it, then reflexively rolled it back and forth briskly between her palms as she had the other thirty-nine vials, letting friction warm its contents to minimize discomfort when it was injected.

She'd been deeply disappointed when Arlo Iron Heart failed to show up for his four-fifteen appointment, but maybe it was a good thing after all that he had changed his mind.

She'd seen the fear in each of the study participants' eyes as they watched her pierce the rubber dam at the end of the tiny vial and draw its contents into a syringe. What must each have been thinking? An experimental drug, never before tested on a human being. Created by outsiders who belonged to a people who had systemically gone about killing and torturing their ancestors, who to this day showed neither remorse nor concern for the likes of Suzanne Featherheart, or Joe Winged Foot, or the countless other gentle and destitute souls living on godforsaken reservations across the country.

She hadn't realized until just that moment the extent of the courage and trust each of the participants had demonstrated in casting aside those fears, overcoming the terror that surely had resulted from Monty Four Bear's campaign of warnings—for Isabel belonged to the "chosen" class, was herself a medical doctor, and even *she* entertained a fleeting fear as she rolled up her left sleeve.

What if, just what if, this vaccine had unanticipated side effects? What if, in protecting its recipients from the deadly hantavirus, it exposed them to other, potentially dangerous consequences?

Nonsense. What was she thinking? Surely she hadn't let Gus's or Monty Four Bear's paranoia get to her.

Dabbing her upper arm with an alcohol-soaked cotton ball, Isabel reached for the syringe and, feeling like a contortionist, twisted her left bicep as far forward as possible to enable her to see the meatiest portion of her arm.

She was just lifting the syringe when a sound stopped her right hand in midair.

What was *that*?

She listened, thinking it had probably been her imagination, but when it occurred again, there was no mistaking the fact. Someone was banging on the clinic door.

Setting the syringe down, Isabel walked to the door and stepped into the corridor. Suzanne had flipped the clinic's outside lights on before leaving, which enabled Isabel to make out the identity of this late visitor, who stood pounding the glass with the heel of one hand.

With mixed emotions, Isabel walked down the long hallway and let Arlo Iron Heart in for his vaccination.

"THE MUNICIPALITY OF Barskoon has filed suit," Pierre Sabin said. "They're asking for twenty-five million dollars and an injunction. They want all activity at the mine shut down until after trial. And from what I'm hearing, this is just the first of several suits. The family of the dead woman has retained an attorney. And GreenEarth is in the area, so we can expect them to jump on the bandwagon."

Jon LeCoque swiveled in his chair, turning away from the company attorney and toward the blue expanse below his window. This was just what he feared, the last thing WRI needed right now, with all the bad press they'd received over Essiquibo.

Twelve stories below, LeCoque could see activity on *Chesire*. He anchored the yacht in Vancouver harbor and often chose to spend the night there instead of returning home to his wife of thirty years. He would have to remember to call the steward and ensure that the liquor cabinet had been restocked, as he had the feeling that tonight would find him sleeping in *Chesire*'s state room. He turned back to Sabin.

"What's happened to the fucking moron who drove the truck into the river?"

"We let him go."

"Let him go? We should have him thrown in jail. He's the one responsible, not WRI."

"Jon, you know the law. He was working for us at the time. According to the suit they filed, the truckers routinely drove that route at excessive speeds. The police have records of complaints from citizens, and meetings with mining supervisors."

"I want names."

"Pardon me?"

"I want the names of any supervisors who were aware of the fact that the imbecilic drivers were speeding. That just proves my point, it was the driver's fault."

"There's no doubt that the driver was at fault. But ultimately the liability will be WRI's, especially if they can show that mining supervisors had been warned about the speeding."

"Have you talked to any of the supervisors involved?"

"Yes. One. He verified having received a warning."

"Then why the fuck didn't he do something about it?"

"He claims to have given the drivers a stern warning. He also faxed a request to fund a security officer to accompany the drivers up and down the mountain."

"Who'd he fax it to? I want answers and I want them now."

"He faxed it directly to your office. On June sixteenth." Sabin slid a sheet of paper across the desk. "Here it is."

LeCoque snatched it up and stared at it. It looked vaguely familiar.

"Never saw it before."

Sabin, looking as though he'd rather be anywhere on earth but sitting across from WRI's CEO, slid another paper LeCoque's way.

"Here's your response."

Omar operation is already over budget. I suggest you worry more about output than finding more ways to spend money. Request denied.

At the bottom, in his oversized scrawl, was LeCoque's signature.

"How the hell can I keep track of every request that comes through this office? If the supervisor knew about the problem he's responsible, along with the driver."

"This shows we were put on notice. It's very damning. Even without it, agency law would make WRI responsible."

"Have you researched this? Whose to say Kyrgyzstan has the same laws as we do?"

"They've petitioned the Canadian courts to hear this case. If their petition is granted, Canadian law will apply. WRI will be responsible."

"What are the chances the court will grant the petition?"

"It would be a first. But that's not necessarily good. Because it would have such far-reaching consequences—every company that does business on an international basis, from mining companies to Nike, will be nervous as all hell about the prospect of being held accountable at home—the whole world will be watching to see what the court holds. So in that sense, even if the court denies the petition, we lose because of the bad press we're sure to receive. And, of course, then we face litigation in Kyrgyzstan."

LeCoque turned back to the window. He hated attorneys and their fucking negativity. Just once he'd like someone to come to him and say,

"Jon, you've got a problem, but I can solve it." Just once. Instead all he ever got were dire predictions. He was sick to death of Sabin and his doomsaying.

Without taking his eyes off the uniformed man scrubbing the decks of the *Chesire*, LeCoque delivered his dictum.

"You're in charge of legal affairs. Take care of this damned thing. Make it disappear. And don't come back to me until you do."

CHAPTER

FIFTEEN

SERGEI KIROV COULD inevitably be found hunched over his lab table, bifocals in danger of sliding off a nose that looked like it had been lopped off two-thirds of the way down, wild, prematurely gray hair stabbing the air. Despite the comfortable temperature, his lab coat invariably bulged and gathered over the sweater he'd worn back home, working in a now-defunct Soviet lab.

Kirov had once served as director at the State Research Center of Virology and Biotechnology in Vector. But with the collapse of the Soviet Union, Kirov's position, along with most of the 70,000 scientists and technicians employed in the secret Soviet germ weapons program, had been eliminated. When James Lyons contacted him, he'd been working in a lab with neither heat nor electricity, oftentimes going without pay for months at a time. The sweater, it seemed, was a remnant of those days and just one of several things that set him apart from his coworkers.

Sergei and his coworkers were an odd lot. In the laboratories at ImmuVac, white-coated scientists routinely went about their business in a focused manner. The social atmosphere contrasted sharply with the friendly atmosphere common to most small companies, where camaraderie and team spirit usually flourished and most employees started with one basic common bond—the fact that they were local people working for a local company. The culture in the labs of small biotech firms reflected a transient, disparate grouping of employees. Talent was recruited from other countries and other labs. Scientists came and left with such frequency that bonding with other employees was a concept given little to no consideration. Fully half of the employees at ImmuVac were in the country on temporary working visas. The rest had been imported from the National Institutes of Health or any number of other ground-breaking research institutions, most of them concentrated in the East. Scientists followed funding. Period. It made for little stability. Those friendships that did form were based on nationality or previous institutional affiliations.

As the only Russian at ImmuVac, Sergei had no friends. That was okay with Kirov. He was just trying to survive, hoping the checks he sent home to his wife and children, who had been denied passports in an effort to lure Sergei back to the country, would ensure their survival as well.

Tonight, as the lab emptied of ImmuVac employees, not one of the departing scientists or technicians looked Kirov's way when calling out their farewells. Everyone had grown used to Kirov being the last to leave for the day. After all, he did not have a family waiting for him at home. If Kirov noticed the fact that he was regarded as little more than a piece of furniture, he did not let on or seem to care.

This was actually his favorite time of day, when he had the labs to himself. Which is why, thirty minutes after the last employee had departed, the sound of footsteps brought a scowl to his round features.

"Thought I'd find you still here."

Kirov looked up to see James Lyons, CEO of ImmuVac, towering over him. Sergei's contact with Lyons was minimal, which—to Sergei's way of thinking—was just as well. Lyons had lured him to ImmuVac with promises of big money in support of Sergei's immunization research. The promises had proved hollow from the start, and recent developments at ImmuVac had so angered Sergei that he'd begun thinking of returning to his homeland.

Sergei pushed back his lab stool and stood, but even then the short, stocky Russian found himself eyeballing Lyons's prominent chin.

"Yes, well," he stammered, taken aback from this unexpected visit, "I like the—what is it you call it?—solitary of working alone at night?"

"Solitude."

"Yes, solitude."

"May I pull up a chair?" Lyons said, already reaching for the lab stool at the next table.

"Of course."

Kirov settled back onto his own stool as Lyons noisily dragged the metal perch across the linoleum floor and plunked down on it.

"I understand your 2453 work is going well."

"Yes." It was about time Lyons paid some attention to his work. "By incorporating extracts from the mice's own tumors, the vaccine stimulates their immune system, teaching it to attack cancer cells. Sixty percent of subjects demonstrate reductions in tumor size."

"Impressive results," said Lyons. "But what concerns me is Angio-Genics. They're about to complete Phase III, and I hear the study's going well."

"The mechanism of AngioGenics's vaccine is much different than mine. Theirs reacts against sugar molecules on the outside of the cancerous cells. Mine stimulates heat shock proteins, which serve as natural stimulants of the immune system."

"Isn't GeneFactor working on the same principle?"

"Yes. But their Phase I results were disappointing. I assure you, our clinical trials will not prove disappointing."

Lyons stroked his mustache.

"I'm afraid we're not in a position financially to be rushing into clinical trials of 2453. That's what I came here to discuss."

Sergei drew a deep, shaky breath. Americans were all the same. Liars who could not be trusted.

"I came to the United States to escape this . . . this . . . handcuff of finances. If money is in such short supply, why is ImmuVac conducting clinical trials on Dr. MacStirling's hantavirus vaccine? It is a comedy, putting resources into a vaccine like that. How many deaths have there been in this country from hantavirus? Not even a hundred." He stood, slamming his hand down angrily on the desk. He was shouting now. "*Cancer.* I am working on a way to prevent cancer! And you tell me my research must take a backseat to this ridiculous study being conducted on savages somewhere in . . . in . . ."

He stood there, face flushed with anger, his heart battering his rib cage ferociously. Lyons seemed undisturbed by this display.

"Montana," Lyons finished for him. "Browning, Montana. On the Blackfeet reservation." He studied Sergei, who now felt foolish standing but could not bring himself to be seated again either. "I didn't realize you felt so strongly about MacStirling's vaccine."

"I'll tell you how strongly I feel about it. I will not stay where my work is not appreciated. I would return first to my homeland, return to the labs without electricity or heat. At least there I am close to my family."

"But how will you feed your family if you return?"

Sergei had no answer.

"Listen, Sergei," Lyons said, "you may not approve of ImmuVac funding Ken MacStirling's hantavirus vaccine, but we believe it makes good business sense. And that's what I came here tonight to discuss with you. Another idea I've had. One that involves your work, and that I believe could make even more sense than the hantavirus vaccine. Will you please sit down and listen to me?"

Lyons had piqued Kirov's curiosity. For a man who had once enjoyed status and special privileges in Russia as a member of the scientific elite—as director of Vector, Sergei had lived in a spacious, well-appointed apartment and been invited to the most important state functions—ImmuVac's failure to showcase his considerable talents had been hugely disappointing. Maybe that was about to change. He lowered himself back onto his stool.

"Go on."

"I'm curious about something," Lyons began. "In your work at Vector, you were involved in developing and testing biological agents, weren't you? Anthrax, plague, smallpox. That's true, isn't it? How about the Marburg virus?"

Sergei had never seen his boss like this before, so attentive, so eager.

"Russian scientists studied many biological agents that had the ability to be used as weapons," Kirov spoke slowly and precisely, the subject matter exaggerating his usual need to think through his choice of English words.

"And this work went on even after the 1972 treaty banning the development of germ weapons. Didn't it?"

Since coming to America, Sergei had never discussed this secret past life of his, despite the fact that he took great pride in his accomplishments. This pride now overcame his natural reticence about the subject.

"It actually escalated after the treaty. In secret, of course. Different centers specialized in different diseases. At Obolensk, lethal bacteria. At Kazakhstan, anthrax. We made and studied several different viruses at Vector. But our specialty was smallpox."

Lyons's usually dull eyes were bright now with excitement.

"Smallpox," he echoed. "How many strains?"

There was a long pause.

"Maybe fifteen thousand."

"Fifteen *thousand* different strains?"

Kirov nodded.

"And how many of those were deadly? How many could have been considered for the warfare program?"

"Maybe one hundred had potential as weapons. Ten, maybe twelve had already been targeted."

"What happened to them? Were they all destroyed?"

"Officially, yes."

Lyons leaned closer, his arm pressing into Kirov's. It was one of those moments where you had to trust your instincts. Kirov could have lied to his boss. He had been conditioned to lie, for the good of his homeland. But something told him that this was a moment for honesty.

"What about *unofficially*?"

"Unofficially?" Kirov replied, the wariness cultivated by years of secrecy giving way to a sense of inexplicable anticipation. "That's another story."

•   •   •

WINTER IN THE Pacific Northwest was a miserable affair. Today's torren-
tial rains were accompanied by winds gusting to sixty mph. Though shel-
tered in the harbor, *Chesire* rocked furiously, causing the steward to steady
himself with a hand on the cherry dining table before depositing an ap-
petizer of oysters on the half shell in front of his boss, Jon LeCoque, and
WRI's attorney, Pierre Sabin. The plate delivered, the stately server
topped off LeCoque's and Sabin's wine, then disappeared back into the
ship's kitchen.

"Not ideal conditions for dining onboard *Chessie*," LeCoque apolo-
gized, "but I wanted to have our conversation in private."

"No problem," Sabin said, reaching for a shell.

They ate a dozen oysters in silence. LeCoque was a man of few
passions, but food happened to be one. Discussion of WRI's legal problems would come later. He would not allow it to sully the meal he'd
ordered prepared.

As Sabin downed the last oyster, the steward appeared again to clear
their plates.

"May I open a new wine to accompany your main course?"

LeCoque nodded.

"Let's try that Beringer cabernet."

Impressed with its bouquet, LeCoque had purchased half a dozen
bottles of the 1994 Private Reserve from Napa Valley at a recent wine
tasting arranged by his wife. It was one of the few things the two did as
a couple anymore. Two years earlier, they'd toured Northern California's
wine country. When they returned home, they'd hired a contractor to
convert their basement into a wine cellar. Stocking it had become an
activity that gave both LeCoque and his wife pleasure.

The men ate the meal served them—lamb tagine with lemon and
olives, couscous, and green beans—with gusto; however, midway through,
Sabin began to look somewhat green, the yacht's rocking having grown
more violent. The wind's roar and rain pelting against the windows added
to the sensation of being caught in a squall at sea, but LeCoque rather
enjoyed it. The previous year on a voyage to Kauai, he had piloted *Chesire*
through forty-foot waves. On a subconscious level, LeCoque's lack of fear
at crossing oceans compensated for his paranoia about flying.

With dinner over, LeCoque pushed back from the table.

"Well, I think we've delayed the inevitable long enough," he said.
"Why don't you tell me about the proposed settlement?"

Sabin pulled the green linen napkin from his lap, wiped his mouth,
and stood, heading for the briefcase he'd left on a chair.

"*Sit,*" LeCoque barked. "Just give me the basics. I don't need all the
legalese."

Sabin cleared his throat.

"Basics. Okay. I received a written offer of settlement today from the

City of Barskoon and the dead woman's family. The city will settle now for twenty million, Canadian. The woman's family wants two."

"What about the fucking environmentalists?"

"They haven't filed suit yet."

"But they will."

"I believe they will; however, the terms of settlement with the city may be enough to placate them."

"How so?"

"One of the conditions of settlement is that the lease will not be renewed in 2002."

"Those bastards. If we don't find another deposit, that could kill us."

"I thought Wilderman is on to something in the States. Montana."

"He is. But turns out it's on an Indian reservation. We have to go through the tribe for approval to do more exploration."

"When's that happening? Maybe I should be there."

"Next week. Tony can handle it. I want you to stay focused on this Kyrgyzstan thing. Now, what about resumption of operations? I suppose they're gonna fight to keep that injunction in place."

"Actually, no. They're amenable to resumption of operations, provided some safeguards are put in place."

"You know why that is, don't you? Because the fucking economy over there depends on that mine. Shut it down and their people start going hungry. What kind of morons would cut off their nose to spite their face like this?"

"Morons worried about their environment and their health, I guess."

"Twenty-two million is an outrage."

"It's a lot of money. But Zellman-Tusky settled out of court for thirty-eight million for their cyanide leaks in Montana. And North Country fought all the way, only to end up paying a seventy million dollar judgment." North Country Mining Corporation was a Saskatchewan mining company sued when a sealed drainage tunnel at a tailings pit at their Pomater Mine in the Philippines collapsed, sending cyanide-laced tailings into the Boac River. "And I have to tell you, the damage alleged from the Philippines accident was considerably less than what we saw in Kyrgyzstan. Plus there were no deaths linked directly with it."

"That doesn't mean *we* can't win," LeCoque said. "I'm not sure I wouldn't take the odds. Seventy million or walk away free, versus a guaranteed hit for twenty-two million. A betting man would go for the chance to walk away. Or file for bankruptcy protection like Zellman-Tusky did."

"It's my legal opinion that WRI would not walk away free," Sabin said. "And there's the publicity to consider. As I told you before, if the Canadian courts approve their request to hear this, it will be a first. It's already getting a lot of press. Settling now nips that in the bud."

LeCoque was sick and tired of running scared from environmentalists and lawsuit-happy opportunists.

"You fucking lawyers are all alike. No balls."

"*Balls?*" Sabin repeated. "Okay. You want to talk balls? Well, how about this? The Philippines government filed criminal charges against four of North Country's top executives."

This news hit LeCoque precisely in the body part they'd been discussing.

"Reckless imprudence, violation of the Mining Act, Water Code, and Pollution Control Law," Sabin continued. "They could each get up to eighteen years in a Philippines prison. And to my knowledge, they hadn't received any warnings prior to the accident. We did. We received several warnings.

"Do you have the guts . . . er, excuse me . . . to use *your* term, the *balls*, to risk the same thing happening to you in Kyrgyzstan? Or would prudence dictate that we settle and move on. Turn our focus elsewhere?"

"WHAT'S THIS ABOUT Sergei going overseas?"

Bob Blount, head of medical research and a lifelong friend of Lyons's, had dropped by James Lyons's office unannounced.

Lyons looked up from the patent application that legal had sent over for him to review.

"What part don't you understand?" he said.

"Well, he made this sound like a company trip."

Lyons hesitated. Kirov's work would be highly secretive. Still, if his mission proved successful, it would probably be impossible to set up a new lab without some assistance. And of all the people in research, not only did Bob Blount stand to be the most helpful, he was also the one person Lyons felt he could trust.

"Sit down," he said.

When Blount had settled into a chair, Lyons continued.

"I've sent Sergei over to the Middle East, where he plans to meet with some of his former Soviet associates."

"You have Sergei recruiting for us now?" Blount's voice had risen an octave, signaling his indignation at the thought that Lyons had turned to one of his underlings for help in finding new research talent. "I thought we were looking at downsizing, not hiring."

"He won't be bringing back other scientists."

"James, do me a favor, will you? Stop playing games with me. As head of research, I feel entitled to know what this is about."

"You're right. But this is a very sensitive issue, one in which you would eventually have become involved. I was just waiting to see how things pan out."

Lyons stood and walked to the door. He looked into the outer office, but his secretary was nowhere to be seen, which explained why Blount's arrival had gone unannounced. He closed the door and returned to his desk.

"Ever since the disappointing Phase III results on our cancer vaccine, I've been racking my brain, trying to come up with some new path for ImmuVac. A golden egg. I knew it had to fit two requirements: It couldn't cost too much and it couldn't take too long."

"I thought that's why we decided to proceed with the clinical trial for the HantaVac. To attract a new partnership, bolster the stock by getting some good press."

"It is. But there are no guarantees that strategy will pay. We all know there's no money to be made in the HantaVac vaccine, but it does stand to draw attention. And since MacStirling had already done the work, it satisfied both of my requirements, the cost and time factor."

"You're not thinking of abandoning it, are you?"

"Absolutely not. But I've never believed it was *the* answer. It would be foolhardy for us to put all our eggs in that basket. I've spent days going over our finances. We can continue operating, on a shoestring, less than two years."

"Define shoestring."

"Everybody but research and absolutely essential support staff gets laid off. Hopefully, within that time frame, the hantavirus vaccine will have attracted another partner, someone with deep enough pockets to fund our other therapeutics in development."

"But if it doesn't?"

"If it doesn't, then we'll have to close down shop. That is, unless we come up with a new product, one that fits those two criteria *and*, unlike the hantavirus vaccine, has strong commercial potential." Lyons leaned forward, lowering his voice and locking eyes with Blount. "That's what I believe I've finally come up with. *Listen to this. A smallpox vaccine.*"

Blount's head snapped to attention at these last two words.

"This is some kind of joke, right?"

"I couldn't be more serious."

"Smallpox was eradicated in the 1980s. The World Health Organization's planning to destroy the last stock. The disease has vanished from the wild."

"It may have vanished from the wild, but there's still plenty of it out there. And the World Health Organization's never going to destroy the last official stock held by the United States and Russia."

"But that's the plan."

"That may be the official line they've handed out these past two years, but even the United States has backed down from it. We know, it's an established fact, that Russia continued to work with the smallpox virus

after the Biological Weapons Convention treaty in 1972. Hell, Sergei himself admits it, as have a number of Russian scientists who've defected to
the United States. Smallpox was their number one biological weapon.
They grew it by the ton. There've been rumors for years of it being passed
from country to country. After the Russians closed the Biopreparat institutes, a lot of scientists had to choose between going hungry and selling
the only thing of value they had. Their knowledge. That's why the United
States has been pouring money into Soviet labs and cooperative ventures.
To stop what they call the brain drain. To give unemployed scientists an
alternative to leaving their country, to going to work for Iran, Iraq, North
Korea. That's how we got Sergei. Because the situation in Russia became
desperate. And you can be sure there were some scientists smart enough
and desperate enough to smuggle the biowarfare agents they'd been working on out of the labs. And out of the country."

"You're saying smallpox is already in the hands of bioterrorists."

"Exactly. And someone, somewhere is eventually going to use it. We
read about it every day—the threat of bioterrorism. So far it's just been
that. Pretty much a threat. Mostly hoaxes. But if smallpox is out there
and in the hands of terrorists, it's not a matter of 'if.' It's a matter of
'when.' And since we long ago stopped vaccinating for smallpox, there's
a damn good chance that no one will have any protection. Those of us
who were vaccinated twenty-five years ago probably don't have any immunity left. Which means that a ready-made vaccine will be a thing of
considerable value. Priceless, really."

"What if the government is already working on a vaccine, as we
speak?"

"You know how the government operates. With the efficiency of a
slug. And we have something the government doesn't. Sergei. No one
knows this virus better than he does. Who are you going to bet on in a
race to develop a vaccine for the inevitable day that bioterrorists unleash
this on us: a government scientist, or the man who led the Russian smallpox program?"

"Do you mean to tell me you sent Sergei to get the virus?" Blount
asked, incredulous. "He'll be bringing smallpox back with him?"

Lyons nodded. "If he succeeds."

"It's no wonder you've been secretive. This is insane. Not to mention
highly illegal."

"We'll be setting up a separate lab. Level Four. No one but Sergei
will have access. As far as the rest of the company is concerned, we'll tell
everyone Sergei decided to stay in his homeland."

The room fell silent. Lyons studied Blount for his reaction.

"Well, what do you think?"

When Blount reached to straighten his glasses, his hands were shaking.

"I told you. I think it's insane," he said. "But it might work."

Both men grew silent again.

"What if Sergei gets caught with it? At the airport?"

"That won't happen. Once we began discussing this, I learned a great deal about Sergei. He's thrilled by the prospect of resuming the work he'd been doing in Russia. And, of course, I promised he'd be rewarded handsomely if this all works out."

In reality, Kirov's enthusiasm had erased any doubts Lyons had about the proposed project. The Russian had assured him that his earlier work would speed the creation of a vaccine. In addition, during their conversation it had become clear that Kirov had no doubt that smallpox had, indeed, fallen into the hands of terrorists and that he fully expected it to be used.

All the elements that Lyons needed to put WRI in a position to come to the world's rescue—and reap the resultant acclaim and profit—existed. He only needed to make them fall together.

"Everything hinges on whether he can get his hands on the virus," he said, his thoughts returning, as they had so many times these past days, to Sergei's words. "If he does, we're in business."

CHAPTER

SIXTEEN

REALLY *HAVE* to get going," Suzanne declared, energetically scrubbing the counter of the exam room. The scent of isopropyl alcohol lingered as she paused in the doorway.

It was almost six-thirty. Isabel had miscalculated how long it would take to do the follow-up and blood work on the twenty study participants she'd scheduled to come in today.

"How many more are waiting out there?" Isabel asked.

"Just Sophia."

Isabel wiped a stray wisp of hair from her forehead. Tucking it behind her ear, she noticed for the first time how nice Suzanne looked. She wore a long denim dress and an exquisite turqouise pendant.

"That necklace is gorgeous."

"Thanks. It was passed down from my grandmother."

"Got a date?"

"No. Tribal council meeting at seven, and I want to grab a bite to eat first."

"Since when do you attend council meetings?"

"The council's thinking about leasing reservation land to some mining outfit. I'm sick of them leasing out our land cause nobody on the rez ever makes any money from it."

"Mining *here*? On the Blackfeet reservation?"

"Yep."

"That's appalling. What kind of mine?"

"Gold. My cousin lives on the Alamosa River in Colorado. Few years back a cyanide spill there poisoned seventy miles of the river. Same thing could happen here. They'll come in, ruin the land and water, take all the money, then leave us to deal with the whole mess."

"Why haven't I heard anything about this mine?"

"I dunno. I heard about it from Monty. He wants all of us to be there." Suzanne headed out the door, then turned back and said, "You ought to come."

"*Me?*" Isabel asked.

It was the first time she'd been invited to a meeting of the Blackfeet, and it took her by surprise.

Isabel put the council meeting out of mind while she finished up with her last appointment. But after she'd closed the clinic down and climbed into the Jeep for the half-hour ride home, Suzanne's words just kept pricking at her.

Suzanne had heard about the meeting from Monty.

Who the hell was this Monty Four Bear? Did he just go around looking for causes, people to blame and hate and strike out at? I mean, the guy seemed to be everywhere. He shows up at the clinic on the night of the IRB meeting. He's there the first day vaccinations were scheduled. And now he's rallying the troops for tonight's tribal council meeting. He obviously had a chip on his shoulder the size of a small planet.

Still, news that the Blackfeet reservation could end up mined disturbed Isabel tremendously. Her father had always been an ardent environmentalist. He used to rail against mining companies. Even as a small child, Isabel could remember him ranting about their environmental impact. It had always made her proud of him, for none of the other adults that inhabited the world in which she'd grown up seemed to care much about anything that didn't directly effect their everyday creature comforts.

"Once we destroy this earth," he used to tell her, "we won't be able to bring it back."

It used to scare Isabel—the mere proposition that the earth was capable of destruction. But if her mother overheard such remarks, she'd be sure to bring some levity to the situation, saying something like, "Oh,

Tom, don't be so dramatic. Honey, your father's just a bleeding heart who wants to save the whole world."

She always said it like it was some kind of disease, but Isabel had been proud of her dad's passion.

She never could understand how two people as different as Nada and Tom McLain ended up together. Or stayed together for all these years.

Taillights on the highway ahead cut Isabel's reflection short. She braked. The right turn signal of the vehicle in front of her indicated it planned to turn into the drive of the Blackfeet tribal headquarters, but even from where her Jeep now sat, waiting for the car to turn off the highway, Isabel could see the lot was full.

When the car in front of her spurted forward, then took a quick left into the parking lot of the Dairy Queen, which also appeared near capacity, Isabel surprised herself by following suit.

TONY WILDERMAN HAD been there, done that. Nothing surprised him anymore, not even the packed meeting hall where the Blackfeet tribal council held its meetings.

It had been a real challenge to find out when the monthly meeting was held so that he could get WRI on the agenda. Hell, he'd even had trouble finding the tribal headquarters. No one in town wanted to give him any information. Word had apparently gotten out about who he was and why he was there, and everyone appeared to have made a pact to provide as little cooperation as possible. But finally he'd stumbled on to the building on the outskirts of Browning. A GONE FOR LUNCH sign had resulted in his sitting outside in his vehicle—appropriately, a Ford Explorer—almost ninety minutes, but finally, when she returned, the receptionist had given him Thomas Rose's phone number. Rose, tribal president, had been reserved but polite.

"If you want to talk to the council, I can't stop you," he'd said. His final words—"Guess I'd better not plan on getting much else done that night"—were his way of acknowledging the uproar the inclusion of WRI on the agenda would give rise to.

Now as the six council members, five men and one woman, settled behind the long table at the head of the room, Wilderman walked purposefully through the maze of gathering Blackfeet and seated himself in the front row of seats intended for the audience. He debated briefly about introducing himself to the council, but several of its members had looked his way, then averted their eyes when he tried to make eye contact.

The meeting was scheduled for seven P.M. At thirteen minutes past, one of the council members—a rangy, sharp-nosed man wearing a flannel shirt and jeans with a turquoise-studded belt buckle—pushed back his chair, stood, and banged a wooden gavel on the table three times.

"This meeting will come to order."

Wilderman recognized Thomas Rose's voice from their phone conversation. The leathery skin and salt-and-pepper hair put Rose's age in the late fifties or maybe even early sixties, but in other respects he appeared decades younger—broad shoulders and a flat stomach, and the posture and movement of a man whose daily activities kept him in excellent condition.

Those who had been standing seated themselves immediately, and the room fell silent.

"Been a while since we've seen this much interest in anything the council was doing," Rose said. "I guess most of you are here to hear what the mining company has to say, but before we get into that, Penny's going to read the minutes from the last meeting."

The lone female member of the board stood. Her charcoal hair was pulled back in a tight bun, showcasing high cheekbones and large, almond-shaped eyes. The size of the group seemed to make her nervous, but she read slowly in a strong, low voice that had a musical, rhythmical quality.

"The first item on the agenda last month was funding for a new elementary school," she started. "The council invited Susan Giles, the principal of Browning Elementary to speak about the condition of the school. Mrs. Giles reported that several windows are broken, the lunchroom has a leak in it, and some of the equipment on the playground is dangerous. She also said that a lot of classes don't have enough books for students, the computer's broken, and two of the teachers have given notice that they plan to quit at the end of the year. The council told Mrs. Giles that they'd have the windows and roof fixed but that there isn't enough money in the budget for new equipment or a new school. There was a unanimous vote to begin efforts to fund a new school. Thomas will talk with the tribal bank. The council agreed that this should be its top priority but they informed Mrs. Giles that there's not a very good chance she'll get a new school. They'll try to borrow enough to at least get a new computer and new books for next year. And someone's gonna take a look at the playground equipment and remove anything that's dangerous.

"The next item on the agenda was complaints about road maintenance."

At this, laughter broke out across the room.

"What road maintenance?" someone called out.

Penny cracked a tight smile and continued.

"There've been several complaints about potholes and such. The council decided there wasn't enough money to do anything about most of them, but Arnie Holmsby says on some of the side streets the holes are so bad they're ruining his truck and he won't keep pickin' up garbage if we don't do somethin about it, so the council voted five to one to fill some of the biggest holes with gravel." She looked up. "I'm in charge of arrangin' that.

"Ann Beam asked if we could keep the tribal headquarters open on Saturdays so that members who worked off the rez during the week could use the copier and typewriter. The council decided it's our responsibility to support everyone's efforts to find a job, or maybe a job closer to home, which would be hard to do without a typed résumé, so Ann's request was approved. The Ping-Pong table and rec room will stay open too."

She looked at Thomas Rose.

"That's about it," she said.

Rose, still seated, asked for a motion to approve the minutes. The motion was made and accepted.

Finally, Thomas Rose slowly unfolded his lanky form again and stood to introduce Tony Wilderman.

"Everyone already knows that one of the speakers tonight is someone from a Canadian mining company called World Resources. Now, I know this isn't going to be a popular subject for a lot of you, but let's hear what Mr. Wilderman has to say before we go getting all stirred up. Mr. Wilderman, please come on up and tell us what's on your mind."

With that less than enthusiastic introduction, Wilderman strode to the front of the room. Seeing no podium from which to speak, he positioned himself to one side of the long table, where both the audience and council members could see him. He'd decided against bringing any visual materials along, as experience had told him that in situations where his reception could be counted on to be chilly, the more low-key he played it, the better.

"Good evening," he said in a tone that avoided being overly friendly—over the years, he'd also learned that being too solicitous only caused the level of suspicion to rise. "I appreciate this opportunity to speak to you tonight. As Mr. Rose explained, I'm here as a representative of WRI—World Resources, Inc. We are a Canadian mining company, but as the name implies, we operate worldwide. Our primary emphasis is on the production and exploration of gold, but we also mine uranium, which is used by electric utilities in the generation of electric power.

"Our interest in your reservation is based on our belief that minable gold may exist in the northwest corner of the reservation, between the North Fork and the South Fork of the Milk River. WRI would like to take a closer look at that region, conduct further exploration. We'd get set up over the winter, then, depending on the weather, begin next spring."

At that, a strikingly good-looking, braided man who'd been standing at the back of the room, stepped forward and interrupted him.

"What do you mean *further* exploration? That would indicate you'd already done some preliminary exploration, and if that's the case, what authority did you have?"

Though he fully expected to be under a magnifying glass tonight, the question and the manner in which it was presented took Wilderman aback somewhat. Intuitively, he knew to proceed with caution, that his interrogator was not someone to take lightly. Before he could respond, another member of the audience rose to his feet from the belly of the audience.

"He's been nosing all over the rez," this older and grizzled man, with a head of hair that had never seen a barber, said. "I seen him up there, near Duck Lake, coupla times. He was even nosin' up around Ghost Ridge."

Wilderman recognized the second speaker. The only thing missing was the shotgun that he'd aimed that day at Wilderman's back.

"My understanding is that Ghost Ridge is public property," Wilderman said politely. "If I strayed on to private property last time I was up here, I apologize. It's entirely possible, considering the fact that the only maps of the reservation I could get my hands on were pretty sketchy."

"They got *maps* of the *rez*?" someone called out in an incredulous tone, causing widespread laughter.

Thomas Rose banged the gavel.

"Now I told you, let Mr. Wilderman talk. Then we can ask him questions."

Wilderman nodded Rose's way.

"Thank you. I would be happy to answer your questions. But first I'd like to give you an idea of just what we have in mind when I say WRI wants to do more exploration.

"WRI would conduct an airborne magnetic and electromagnetic survey over the property involved. This, plus detailed mapping, soil geochemistry, and ground geophysics, would enable us to locate drill targets. Somewhere between six and eight diamond drillholes totalling twenty-five hundred to three thousand meters would be drilled. The drillholes enable us to test the down-dip extensions of the zone in which we expect to find gold and to test soil geochemical anomalies to the east and west of the zone."

Looking out, Wilderman couldn't tell whether he'd lost his audience or whether they were just waiting to pounce. The response to his next comment provided his answer.

"WRI would be looking at spending almost half a million dollars for this exploration program. That's a lot of money. Money we'd be investing in your reservation."

"*Investing in our reservation?*" It was "the interrogator" again, angry now. "You make it sound like some kind of investment *on our tribe's behalf*! Companies like yours think they can come onto sacred native lands, lease them for a fraction of what they're worth, make millions, then leave the land scarred and so full of dangerous chemicals and pollutants that our cattle and our kids start getting sick. And you try to make it sound like it's some financial plan you're putting in effect for our benefit."

Several "Right-on"s and "Go get him"s could be heard, as across the room heads nodded defiantly and eyes pierced the distance between Wilderman and his audience, which seemed to grow shorter by the moment. Any trace of humor in the meeting hall's air had evaporated.

Wilderman looked to Thomas Rose for order, but Rose simply stared back at him.

"I'm not saying all of those things haven't occurred. They have. And the mining industry is responsible. But WRI doesn't operate that way. Our policy is to have ongoing field surveillance and auditing throughout the mining process." It was a bold lie, but a necessary one. He would deal with it later. "We would work hand in hand with your Environmental Protection Agency to ensure . . ."

Mention of the EPA brought another strong reaction, this time from the man standing to the interrogator's right. He stood several inches taller than the interrogator and looked much meaner.

"All we natives can count on from the EPA is institutional racism. As some of you know, I am a Cheyenne. Northern Cheyenne. We Cheyenne fought for ten years to get the EPA to acknowledge that the tribe is a government, that the Cheyenne have a right to establish their own Tribal Air Quality Implementation Plan." His sharp eyes scanned the group and Wilderman recognized that in both men, he was up against skilled orators. "If we let him tell us that the EPA is going to look out for us and our reservations, we're going to become the proverbial sheep being led to slaughter. We learned long ago that as a people, we have few allies. The EPA certainly isn't one of them."

Between the two men at the back of the room, it was clear the crowd was becoming agitated.

"What about Duck Lake?" someone called out. "And all the rivers? Mining'll kill all the fish. Poison all the wildlife. We'll all go hungry."

Another voice jumped in.

"My ancestors are buried up in that area. I don't want anybody messin' up there."

Wilderman knew it was a pivotal moment. He was about to lose them altogether.

"Please," he said, lifting his hand in the air like a cop stopping traffic. "Let's reason together. I *hear* what you're saying. I'm not unaware of this industry's track record. And I know the EPA has let many Native Americans down. But does that mean that change is impossible?"

"Unlikely," someone opined loudly.

"Unlikely and impossible are two different things. Change is not only possible, but in this situation, we realize it's *essential*. All I'm asking is for you to hear me out. We have some basic facts here that I think we need to lay out. Give me a few more minutes of your time. They could turn out to be the most wisely spent minutes of your collective lives."

Without giving anyone time to object, he continued.

"Fact number one. The world, this nation in particular, is heavily dependent upon gold. It's used as currency and as a basis for international monetary transactions. It's used in coins and jewelry, photography, dentistry, and now, it's even being used in biological research and the treatment of cancer. I know what you're thinking: Why do we care, because chances are none of these uses are high on any of your priority lists."

For the first time, Wilderman saw that he'd managed to elicit a smile or two.

"Here's why you care: because of fact number two. A fact that the minutes from the last meeting illustrated quite painfully. Your tribe needs money. Your children desperately need a new school. You all need better road maintenance. And at the risk of being impertinent, I'd say you could also use a new facility for your headquarters."

He could see he was beginning to get their attention now.

"The discovery and mining of gold on your reservation can give you all that. Your new school. Better roads, better health care and facilities. The fact is, my company will continue mining gold. If it's not here, it will be somewhere else. Why shouldn't you be the ones to benefit? Along with WRI, of course. There's no doubt we will reap benefits—that's our business. But there's enough to go around. We can address your concerns. Each and every one of them. But why turn your backs on what could be a winning situation for both parties?"

"*Bullshit,*" one of the men from the back of the room—the one without braids—cried out. "He's full of shit. Don't you see?"

Wilderman felt a dash of satisfaction, and hope, at seeing one of his adversaries step off his intellectual soapbox and resort to the use of profanity. Both emotion and reasoning could be powerful tools with a group like this, but the expressions on most the faces in front of him told Wilderman that, with a little luck, calm logic and reasoning might just have a chance of winning the day.

Seeming to sense the peril, the braided man placed a restraining hand on the speaker's arm and stepped forward.

"Clyde's right. This is classic manipulation, textbook. Promises of wealth, enough money to fix all our problems. It's a technique these companies have used for over a century. *We must not let ourselves be fooled by it.* Listen to what he's promising. Then look back at our history. Since when have the promises made to our people been kept? Each and every one of you in this room knows all about promises. We can't even trust our trustee—the federal government—to keep its promises. That's why we're filing a class action suit against the BIA. We're suing them for a billion dollars."

The room erupted in cheers at this announcement.

Monty lifted a fist into the air, then continued, "It's time we get what's coming to us. Whenever we've leased our lands to companies like WRI, we never see the money we're promised anyway. The only ones getting rich from reservation lands are non-Indians. But that's all going to change with this lawsuit. We're going to teach the rest of the world what it costs to cheat us. Millions, maybe billions, of dollars. In the meantime, we can't keep repeating our mistakes."

More cheers resulted in three loud *thwacks* of Thomas Rose's gavel.

As the room quieted, the low rumble of a throat being cleared turned Wilderman's head back to the front of the room.

It had come from a wide-faced, portly man seated at the end of the council member's table opposite where Wilderman stood.

He "hrumphed" again loudly, waiting for the complete attention of everyone in the room.

"Seems to me we're puttin' the cart in front of the horse here," he said.

MONTY FELT THINGS were going well until old Rock Peacock opened his mouth.

"How's that, Rock?" Thomas Rose wanted to know.

"Well, we're all getting into some kind of a frenzy over something we don't rightly know for sure yet." Rock squinted in the direction of the audience. "Whether there's even gold on the reservation."

He turned and measured Wilderman with his large brown eyes.

"Let me ask you something. How much damage does that drilling you were talking about a few minutes ago do? And don't go getting tricky with me cause you can bet that we're gonna to do some looking into all of this. We want honest answers here."

"Where are you coming from, Rock?" Monty could hardly contain himself. *What the hell was Rock trying to do?* "That's what all this is about. We don't *want* them drilling on our land. Period. Aren't you listening to what's been said here tonight?"

"Do me a favor, Monty. Let me ask my question. You're the one who teaches our kids about what our rights are. And I know damn well I have the right to ask this man any question I please. It's time to let someone else do some talking." He paused, as if waiting for more grief from Monty. When none came, he continued. "Here's how I see it. It's the council's job to take care of our tribe. That takes money. More than we have now. That means that we have a responsibility to give serious consideration to any financial opportunities that come our way. I'd say maybe we're shirking our duty if we don't even take this thing to a level where we find out if there *is* any gold to be fighting about."

"It's the council's responsibility to listen to the people," Monty declared from the back of the room.

"What's your problem, Monty? Now shut that big trap of yours up for a couple minutes and let me finish. We're only talking about a couple of holes here. No one's even *thinking* about letting them actually start mining. If and when that happened, it'd be down the road some. I don't see the harm of finding out just what the facts are. *If,* that is, this man can tell us this exploration plan of theirs wouldn't harm our land."

Wilderman jumped quickly on the life raft tossed him.

"The environmental impact of the tests we'd be conducting, including the drilling, would be negligible. I can bring you photos of other sites where we've done the same thing, put you in contact with people who can verify what I'm saying."

"If that's true," Rock said, "what's wrong with finding out just what we're sitting on? Good God, we all know we need some way to produce income on this rez. I'm as concerned as any of you about taking care of our Mother Earth—she is sacred to all of us. But we've been trying to find a way of bringing industry up here. The tribally owned bank is a great idea, something we're all proud of. But the truth is, we don't know if it's gonna even make it, and if it *does* make an impact financially, it's gonna take a while. We got no jobs to speak of, other than the pencil plant and the seasonal stuff during the summer. I mean, how can we afford not to at least take a look at this?"

Monty could literally see the tension in Clyde Birdseye's body as he stepped forward to respond.

"The Cheyenne have sacrificed many things to protect our homelands. We, too, would like new schools and better housing. If you think *this* is the answer, think again. Many years ago, the BIA, the same trustee you Blackfeet would be dealing with, leased over half our land to coal companies for stripmining. They sold the coal for eleven cents a ton. No environmental safeguards were put in the leases. We spent the next fifteen years fighting to get those leases voided. And during that time, conditions on our reservation did not improve, I can assure you. But we have decided that we would rather live without roads or indoor plumbing than allow any more desecration of our lands."

"This is Blackfeet territory," a voice called out, "not Cheyenne."

Monty had cautioned Clyde not to bring too much attention to the fact that he was not a Blackfeet. He should have known Clyde would find it impossible to keep his mouth shut.

"The Cheyenne are our brothers," Monty said calmly. "And Clyde here is my cousin. That gives him an interest in what we do here. If we

Indians don't stand together, if we let the white man divide us on the basis of where we live or what tribe we belong to, we'll never have a chance to change things."

A young woman rose from the front row.

"I know this won't make me a whole lot of friends, but I have three kids at home. The oldest starts school next year. And I want them to have a better life than me. I never finished high school. Got pregnant and started havin' babies. That's not what I want for my kids. I want them to go to a good school, one that will help them make somethin' of themselves. If a gold mine on the reservation can do that for my kids, I'm all for it."

"Maybe you oughta just move off the rez, then," someone called out.

Another bang of the gavel indicated Thomas Rose had decided it was time to take back control of the meeting.

"Now all of you were welcome here tonight. You're always welcome at our council meetings. But the council will make this decision. We've heard your input. Now it's time to put this thing to a vote."

"No way, Thomas." Monty was halfway down the aisle before Rose had finished proclaiming his intention to put the drilling to a council vote. "This is too important to the whole tribe for the council to handle it alone. I demand a tribal referendum."

"Another word from you, Monty, and you're out of here. Understand?"

"The six of you have no right to make this decision alone." It was Clyde, right behind Monty.

Pandemonium was beginning to break out and Thomas Rose knew it.

"Where's the sheriff?" he called, scanning the room.

An imposing figure, clad in brown police uniform, stepped out from the shadow of the back corner of the room.

"Okay, Monty," Bud Wolfkill said, approaching Monty and Clyde. Bud had been a linebacker in high school, and a friend for most of Monty's life. Still, it was apparent he was about to put duty ahead of friendship. "You two are outta here."

Clyde twirled around to face Bud, raising his fists as though ready to put up a fight.

"Cool it," Monty told him. "You don't want to mess with Bud."

The last thing Monty heard, before being ushered out of the hall, was Thomas Rose telling the rest of the group that the next person who opened his mouth would end up out on the sidewalk.

With Monty and Clyde.

THE MEETING HAD already started when Isabel slipped into the back of the packed hall. Jim Robinson, a patient, turned to see Isabel standing just inside the doorway and rose from the last row of chairs, insisting that she take his seat. Isabel noticed Monty Four Bear, standing along the back wall, in conversation with the same loathsome companion he'd had at the clinic the day of their protest, and felt grateful when he didn't notice her.

The number of Blackfeet in attendance surprised Isabel. Years ago, at her father's urging, she'd attended a similar public hearing in Wenatchee. Of course the proposed mining site that time had not been located on a reservation. Only a handful of locals had shown up to hear the proposal. With the exception of the objections raised by her father and two of his friends from the Sierra Club who had accompanied them, it went through without a hitch. Yuppies, she'd decided, had better things to worry about than driving a hundred miles across the Cascades to express concern over the environment.

Within minutes of watching Tony Wilderman at work, Isabel came to the conclusion that WRI had sent their best man for the job of negotiating with the Blackfeet. Wilderman was slick, playing on the economic poverty on the reservation, making clear what WRI's mine could do to turn life around for the reservation's inhabitants. Isabel took an instant dislike to the man and what he stood for.

Monty Four Bear was equally reprehensible. But at least this time she shared his passion for protecting the reservation from the decimation of WRI's mining.

Had the same kind of passion driven Monty to try to stop the clinical trial? For the first time, the possibility that Monty was someone truly driven by the desire to protect his people and culture entered Isabel's consciousness.

Monty and Clyde's ouster from the meeting had broken the backbone of the opposition. In near silence, the audience watched as the council approved WRI's proposed exploration by a four-to-two vote. Attached to the approval were two criteria required by the tribal council: that an agent designated by the council have access at all times to the drill sites, and that the approval could be withdrawn at any time and for any reason.

Wilderman had in turn insisted upon only one condition. In consideration for its investment, WRI wanted a right of first refusal in the event the tribe did, indeed, decide to proceed with mining. WRI did not want another mining company coming in and out-negotiating them for a lease after they'd spent half a million dollars finding the gold.

"Seems fair enough to me," Thomas Rose said. "What do the rest of you think?"

Anxious to dispose of the mining issue altogether and adjourn for the night, the rest of the members had agreed and the meeting was about to come to an end when Isabel's eyes settled upon the back of a head in the second row.

How could she have missed it—the sandy hiccup in row after row of black locks? But the man to whom the precisely styled waves belonged sat at the end, near the wall, and Isabel's attention had been focused ahead, on the speakers.

Thomas Rose had barely begun to announce the results of the vote when Isabel jumped up and began excusing herself, stepping on several toes in the process, but not stopping to apologize. Panicked, she pushed open the door at the back of the room, rushed down the hallway to the exit, and, stepping outside, came face to face with Monty Four Bear and Clyde Birdseye.

"*You*," Birdseye said. It was an accusation.

Monty stepped forward. "What happened in there?"

Isabel glanced over her back nervously.

"The council approved the exploration proposal," she said breathlessly, without stopping, but as she passed, Birdseye grabbed her by the arm.

"That probably pleases you, doesn't it?"

"Let me go," Isabel said.

Monty grabbed Birdseye's forearm and jerked it off Isabel's.

People had begun filing out the door. Without another word, Isabel turned and ran across the parking lot. She was so shaken that when she started to cross the two-lane highway to the Dairy Queen, she nearly stepped into the path of an oncoming car.

"Watch where you're going," its occupant screamed at her, swerving into the next lane, which, fortunately, was empty. As the older model Dodge retreated, through its back window Isabel saw a hand raised in an obscene gesture.

TOO RATTLED TO go home, Isabel stopped by Gus's.

It was obvious from his disheveled hair and shirt and the way he blinked at the light above the front door that she'd awakened him from a nap in front of the fireplace.

"I didn't mean to disturb you."

"Aw, nonsense," Gus said. "I can sleep anytime. Me and Grunt would love some company, wouldn't we Grunt?"

Grunt pushed a wet nose into Isabel's hand, his body nearly convulsing with excitement at her arrival. She crouched down and threw her arms around the dog's thick neck. Deep folds of extra skin around his forehead and neck gave Grunt a Sharpei-ish look. Isabel buried her face in his warm fur.

She stayed that way—unable to face Gus, for she could no longer hide her emotions—until she felt the old man's hand on her shoulder.

"Okay, girl. You been lookin' like a scared rabbit lately. It's time you told me what's goin' on."

Isabel looked up into Gus's kind eyes and fought back tears.

"It's a long story, Gus."

"Well how 'bout I get each of us a glass of wine and you can tell it to me?"

They settled on either end of the long leather couch with Grunt in between them, his head taking up all of Isabel's lap. She stroked it as she told Gus the entire story, starting with when she first met Alistair, in med school.

For the most part, Gus maintained an expression that was difficult to read. But half an hour later, when Isabel reached the final days of her marriage—the events that led to her packing her bags and leaving town—he did not attempt to hide his shock.

"Someone shoulda beat the livin' daylights out of the son of a bitch," he huffed. "And you mean to tell me he's tracked you down now?"

"Yes. With the help of my mother."

"Some mother."

Isabel managed a half smile.

"She doesn't know much about what happened, Gus. I never told her."

She wondered what she saw in Gus's eyes now, which studied her. Pity? Disapproval? She could not bear to let him down.

"So go on. What happened tonight to bring you to my door?"

"Let me backtrack a little first. Remember that night I saw you out by the mailbox? When you told me the mailman's mad at me?"

Gus nodded.

"Well, he'd called me that night. He was just leaving a message when I came in from work. He made it sound like he knew where I lived, but I was pretty sure he was just playing one of his sick games."

"I remember that night. I *knew* somethin' was wrong. But you wouldn't come clean."

"I guess I thought that if I ignored it, it might just go away."

"But it didn't."

"No. It didn't." Isabel thought back to the shock that had run through her entire body just thirty minutes earlier. "He was there tonight, Gus. At the tribal council meeting." The wine in Isabel's glass jumped with her shaky hands. "I saw him."

"Did he see you?"

"No. I'm sure he didn't. I got out of there the minute I recognized him."

"You're sure it was him?"

"I only saw the back of his head, but, yes, I'm sure."

Gus watched her closely, his brow furrowed into three deep folds, as she stroked Grunt.

"Why would he go to a tribal meeting? You think it has something to do with what happened between you?"

Isabel shook her head.

"I have no idea. That's what I keep asking myself. What's he up to now?"

"Well, one thing's for damn sure. You're staying here tonight. With me and Grunt."

"I really don't think that's necessary, Gus. Alistair can't know where I live. If he did, he'd have shown up at the cabin by now. And I've got that gun you gave me. I've had it loaded ever since that night."

"You listen to me, Isabel McLain. You ain't goin' nowhere tonight. You hear? And in the morning, I'm gonna find that SOB and send him packing."

"Good God, Gus, I don't want to drag you into this. Promise you won't do anything foolish."

He smiled at her then, easing her worries, and placed his misshapen hand on top of where hers rested, on Grunt's back.

"Don't you worry. How much trouble can an arthritic old man get into anyhow?"

"Knowing you, plenty."

This comment clearly pleased Gus. The gleam in his eyes erased a decade, and Isabel had a momentary glimpse of a younger man full of righteousness, piss, and vinegar.

"You're really something, Gus Dearing," she said. "You know that?"

"In my day maybe," he chuckled. "Now, how about a little more wine?"

Thanksgiving was three days away and they made plans to spend it together. Isabel had invited Gus and Grunt to dinner at her cabin. They were in the middle of planning the menu when Isabel closed her eyes to rest them for just a few seconds.

Sometime after midnight, she awoke to find herself still on Gus's couch. The fire had burned down to a crimson glow of smoldering embers. Grunt, stretched out the length of the couch, which had been vacated by Gus, snored loudly. Before going to bed, Gus had covered Isabel with a lambswool Pendleton blanket.

Shaking her head to clear it, Isabel stretched and stood, then folded the blanket. Then, tiptoeing to keep from waking Gus, she went to the kitchen where she scribbled a note:

Gus, Went home. Promise I'll be fine. Please don't worry. Love, Is

She left it on the kitchen table, then stepped into the cold night air and turned the key in her Jeep's ignition.

Maybe it was because she was there, at Gus's house, that his earlier warning came to her just then.

"Those tires of yours are gettin' bald," he'd told her the other day when she'd run into him in town. "You better get your studs on. Winter's gonna hit any day now and you'll be in a heap of trouble trying to get up to your cabin with those."

"I know. My snow tires are stored in the shed. I've been meaning to bring them into town with me and have them put on," Isabel had answered.

As she eased the car out of the driveway, she hoped that Gus was sleeping soundly. If he heard her leaving, he'd jump up and try to make her wait 'til morning.

That thought undoubtedly explained why Gus's words of warning had sprung to mind.

Or maybe Isabel simply had a premonition.

CHAPTER

SEVENTEEN

THE ROAD BETWEEN Gus and Isabel's houses hugged the shores of the Two Medicine River, and while it provided spectacular views during the day, Isabel knew to exercise caution at night. Montana's lack of guardrails along roadways that dropped off steeply had shocked her when she'd first moved to the reservation, but like everything else, she'd long since grown accustomed to the status quo.

Since she still felt sleepy and there was no moon to supplement her headlights tonight, Isabel proceeded even more tentatively than usual, her Jeep kicking up gravel as it began the long climb up the last ridge before the turnoff to her cabin. She hadn't warmed the car up, so its interior was frigid, and for a moment she regretted leaving the warmth of Grunt's company and Gus's couch. The fear prompted by seeing Alistair had shrunk to a manageable size. For the first time, she admitted to herself that it was just possible she'd been mistaken. After all, she'd only seen the back of a head. Maybe if she hadn't rushed out of their half crazy, she'd have discovered it was someone else. Alistair wasn't the only man with curly blond hair. She was even beginning to feel a bit silly for reacting so irrationally. She could hardly wait to get home and climb under her down comforter.

She became aware of the presence of a car behind her when, rounding the first of a series of S curves, she glanced in the rearview mirror. Had she imagined it, or was that a flash of light? She looked again. Her rearview mirror reflected a near total blackness outside. But then it happened again, and with a start, Isabel made out the outline of another vehicle, following dangerously close behind her. Something, perhaps her taillights as she rounded the curve, or a break in the cloud cover, had reflected off its front window.

At the realization that the vehicle was traveling without lights—an act of pure insanity on this road at night—her heart began to pound so ferociously that she fleetingly wondered which presented more danger: cardiac arrest, or this inexplicable company?

The answer to the question became clear momentarily, when Isabel slowed to round the next curve. A jolt, shockingly rough and unexpected, threw her entire body violently forward, into the razorlike restraints of the Jeep's frayed seatbelt.

Now that the vehicle had announced its presence by ramming her, its lights—blinding in their proximity and the mirror's reflection—ignited, making it impossible for Isabel to see her pursuer and even difficult for her to see the road in front of her.

Keep your head. Keep your head.

The isolation and solitude of her chosen home, which had previously held such allure to Isabel, now meant that there was nowhere to turn for help.

Pushing down on the accelerator, Isabel managed to put several car lengths between them. But just as she crested the hill, the increasing intensity of the glare in the rearview mirror warned her that her pursuer was about to ram her again.

Isabel tensed.

The hit sent the Jeep skyward. Isabel's grasp on the steering wheel became viselike. She could not allow herself to lose control. This time, prepared, she managed to ride with it. As the Jeep thudded back to earth, Isabel gunned it again. Her only hope was to outrun her anonymous predator.

In the next few seconds, it seemed she was gaining ground. The pursuing vehicle's lights receded, first just a couple car lengths, then more, as much as the length of a basketball court. Were they playing with her? Giving her a false sense of hope? Or did her old Jeep actually have enough life left to outrun the other vehicle? Choosing to believe the latter, Isabel began to formulate a plan. Ahead, several miles past the turnoff to her cabin, there was a ranchhouse. If she could beat them there, she would arrive with horn blasting, drive through the fencing surrounding the corral if she had to to get their attention.

But suddenly, Isabel recognized her precise location on the dangerous switchback road. As that realization hit, instantaneously, she lifted the foot she'd pressed to the accelerator and slammed it down, hard, on the brake pedal.

They were racing toward a hairpin turn.

The realization had come too late. Her bald tires spun wildly, failing to gain purchase on the pebble-strewn road, and Isabel's Jeep began sliding sideways into the turn. Isabel knew this section of the road well, had even pulled over one gorgeous August morning and gotten out of the Jeep to pick flowers and walk the dozen steps to the precipice, so spectacular was the view.

It was just ahead that she'd stood, the pinnacle of the road that separated her house from Gus's, to gaze down at the frothing waters of the Two Medicine, two hundred feet below. She'd marveled that day at the fact that such a perilous section of the roadway, which ran so dangerously close to the steep dropoff, was not protected by guardrails.

Behind her, the oncoming vehicle had also slowed.

Heart pounding, her breath held, Isabel brought her full weight and strength to bear on the brake pedal. As if in slow motion, the Jeep, moving sideways now, continued its slide. When it reached the hairpin, the smooth ride across the roadway gave way to a shock of bumps. The Jeep was on the shoulder now, crossing the stretch where, throughout the summer, wildflowers had enchanted Isabel on her way to work.

And then a miracle occurred. Just as Isabel reached for the door handle to try to jump free, the Jeep came to a standstill. Snapping her head forward, Isabel saw that the headlights pierced nothing but the blackness of night. They illuminated not a single object.

The Jeep had stopped its uncontrolled slide at the very edge of the dropoff.

So terrified was she of the impending freefall, that Isabel had momentarily forgotten about her pursuer.

But a nudge, softer this time than the previous two, changed that.

And with the door partially open and Isabel grasping frantically for the release on her seat belt, the Jeep toppled over the rocky edge to the rushing waters below.

WHEN ISABEL CLOSED the front door behind her, a disappointed Grunt padded down the hallway to Gus's bedroom. Nudging the partially closed door with his nose, Grunt entered the room and took a flying leap onto Gus's big bed, where the big dog routinely slept alongside his beloved master.

"Settle down now," Gus groused sleepily.

Then he heard the car door slam. Jumping up, Gus hobbled to the window in time to see Isabel's Jeep backing out of his driveway. His creeky, arthritic knees would not allow him time to stop her, so Gus stood watching his friend back from the driveway onto the road.

Isabel had just disappeared down the road, heading north toward her cabin, and Gus was about to turn away when the floodlight on the arch over the mouth of the driveway picked up a surprising sight: a car—some kind of sport utility vehicle—following a short distance behind Isabel's Jeep. What startled Gus was the fact that it did not have its lights on, though once it passed, he could see brakelights, indicating the driver was deliberately hanging back.

It usually took a good thirty minutes for Gus to shake the early morning kinks and aches out of his bones, but now he moved quickly.

"Come on, Grunt," he called, grabbing a rifle from the antique oak gun cabinet that filled one wall along the foyer.

Holding the door open for Grunt, Gus climbed into his pickup and punched the gas pedal, shooting backward down his long drive. In his entire life, Gus had never had a car accident. He prided himself in his driving skills. Last time he went in to renew his license, old Esther Robank, who'd had a crush on him for as long as Gus could remember, winked as she told him his record was so spotless that she'd reissue the new license without requiring Gus to take the test all seniors over the age of seventy were required to take.

But adrenalin and age now combined to distort his reflexes, and by the time Gus realized he'd turned the wheel just a smattering too far to the right, it was too late to stop the truck from going off the drive and into soft, damp earth, where it lodged.

"Damn it to hell," he cried, rocking the truck between first and reverse, time and again. This only served to deepen the rut Gus had created. As soon as he realized the pickup was there to stay, he jumped out and half hobbled, half ran into the house for the keys to what he affectionately called his "beater"—a 1963 International Harvester Traveler.

The Harvester fired up on Gus's first try.

Frustrated by the delay, Gus tried to make up time as he followed in the direction of Isabel's cabin, taking curves faster than he'd ever dared before.

It was when he was approaching the last switchback to Isabel's turnoff that Gus came upon the bizarre sight of a beam of light shooting skyward. It originated beyond the cliff and lit up several tree tops along the cottonwoods lining a portion of the ridge.

As Gus pulled the Harvester over to the side of the road and jumped out, his sense of apprehension soared.

Grunt disappeared over the edge before Gus could stop him.

When Gus reached the spot of Grunt's descent, a slippery, steeply sloped and rocky section that, under other circumstances, Gus would never get near, it was with a sense of absolute terror that he recognized Isabel's Jeep, twenty to thirty feet below.

It had rolled onto its roof, and now lay wedged between the rocky surface of the hill—a thirty degree slope—and a stand of three medium-size cottonwoods, its front end pointing toward where Gus stood, the lights piercing the sky.

"Oh my God, Izzie."

Gus could hear Grunt's whines as he nosed around the car, which looked to be perched none too securely against the trees—which themselves looked none too sturdy.

Gus started down, but loose rocks immediately took his feet out from under him. He grabbed the bare branch of a thistleweed to stop his descent. He would never be able to negotiate the steep terrain without help.

"Isabel," he yelled, cupping his mouth with the free hand. *"Isabel!"*

Grunt had by now reappeared at his side, and as the devoted dog hovered nearby, Gus managed to climb back to safety by pushing himself along the rocky ground on his rear end. Once back on solid ground, Gus rushed to the Harvester and opened the back door. The backseat and floor were strewn with trademarks of the ranching life—empty cans of chewing tobacco, worn out leather gloves, boots, used tubes of worming meds, a horse pick, several used shoes, newspapers. Gus rummaged frantically through it all until finally, hidden deep, on the floor, he found what he was looking for. A coil of rope.

Now the question was: Would it be long enough?

Gus started up the Harvester, backed onto the road, eased it forward, then backed it on to the shoulder again, leaning out the open door to watch his progress. He would need every inch of that rope to reach Isabel. That meant he had to back the Harvester as close as he dared to the edge of the precipice. When the ground illuminated by his taillights broke away into blank space, he stopped and pulled hard on the old vehicle's emergency brake. He tried not to think about the fact that for years, he'd been meaning to replace the brakes—one of those things that he'd just never gotten around to.

One thing a rancher learns just about as well as the rest of the world learns such basic tasks as buttoning a shirt is the art of tying knots. Luckily, like everything else littering the backseat of the Harvester, this rope had seen plenty of use, which made working with it easier. Deftly, Gus formed a slip-knot and looped it over the trailer hitch, then he snaked his hands to the other end of the coil and knotted it around his waist. He realized then that he'd forgotten something. Straddling the rope as he walked, he returned to the backseat and grabbed two mismatched gloves.

He gathered the loose length of the rope and coiled it as best he could, then, shooing Grunt out of the way, Gus began his descent. His weight supported by the rope, he leaned into the void behind him and slowly walked his way backward, down toward where Isabel lay in her Jeep.

If you're listening to me up there, please give me enough rope to reach Izzie.

The prayer almost worked. The rope ran out less than two yards from the overturned Jeep.

"*Izzie!*" Gus yelled.

Grunt whined and pawed at the vehicle.

"*Izzie.*" Gus dropped onto his rear end, bracing himself against gravity with his feet, and cursed as his damn fingers made untying the knot around his midsection difficult. But soon he was free, and as he inched his way to the Jeep, scooting on his rear end, he finally heard it. A soft cry.

"Gus?"

He covered the last yard of ground in a heartbeat.

"Izzie. I'm here. Don't move. Do you hear?"

The cottonwoods against which the Jeep was braced were leaning at close to ninety degree angles from the hillside, so strained were they by the weight. Gus surveyed the situation. The driver's side was wedged against the trees. He would have to get to Isabel through the passenger door.

The roots of the trees had formed something of a woven platform filled with loose soil as they'd grown. Gus kneeled on it as he struggled to get the Jeep's door open. But it was lodged tight against rocks and exposed roots.

"Turn your head, Izzie," he said. "I've got to kick this window out. Try to cover your face, do you hear me?"

"Yes. Go ahead, Gus. Just get me out of here."

Relief flooded Gus at hearing her speak. She was conscious, and understandably terrified.

Standing, he kicked out the window with his boot, then stamped along its lower edge—the upper edge, were it upright—trying to eliminate any shards. He would have to pull Isabel out through it.

When he dropped back to his knees, he stuck his head in the window and finally saw her.

"Good God, Isabel," he cried at the sight of her hanging upside down. He was inside now, crawling to her across the inside surface of the roof. "Can you find your seat belt? I'm here, I'll catch you."

He reached up to help her, but then heard her say, "I've got it. *Here I go.*"

She tumbled into his outstretched arms and as she did so, they both heard it. The unmistakable crack as one of the trees snapped—their movement, and Gus's added weight, had strained the slender trees to their limit.

EIGHTEEN

GRUNT BEGAN BARKING, and as Gus inched back out the broken window he could feel canine teeth on his pant leg, pulling.

"Hold still," he whispered to Isabel, as though raising their voices might be enough to send the Jeep toppling down the hillside.

Isabel slung an arm around Gus's neck and began using her feet to propel herself in the direction of the open window.

Gus had one knee out of the Jeep and on the rocky ground, when the roof began to lift under them.

Pulling her free of the car, Gus fell back with Isabel in his arms. They both lay still, in horror, watching as the Jeep swayed once, twice—its weight supported now by just two trees and the remainder of the one that had broken. Then it grew still.

"Let's get you out of here," Gus said, turning to look for the rope.

QUESTIONS OF JURISDICTION were nothing new to Bud Wolfkill. When the call came in, he'd known the incident occurred just beyond the boundaries of the reservation. Other members of the tribal police force might have used that as an excuse to kick back and let the county sheriff's deputies respond, but not Bud. East Glacier County was understaffed, over one hundred miles long and eighty miles wide. Chances of a sheriff's deputy being in the vicinity were remote.

"You're sure you don't need to go to the hospital in Cutbank?" he asked the lady doctor. He'd heard plenty about Isabel McLain, and had seen her earlier that evening at the tribal council meeting, but this was the first time he'd actually met her.

"I'm sure. After all, I am a doctor. I'll be sore for a couple days, but I don't have any broken bones or internal injuries."

"Well, from what Gus here's told me, it's a miracle you don't. Soon as we're done, I'll head on up the road to see for myself."

"By now, that old Jeep might be floatin' down the river," Gus said.

Wolfkill grunted, *"Hrrmphf."*

"You're sure it was deliberate? That someone forced you off the road?"

"Absolutely. As I told you, he came up behind me with the lights out. Then he rammed me hard. Twice."

"I can vouch for the lights being out," Gus interjected again. "That's what really spooked me about it. Drivin' around in town, you might not know you forgot to put your lights on, but out here at night? Nobody *forgets* to turn 'em on."

"Wouldn't think so," Wolfkill said. He turned his dark, sleepy eyes back to Isabel. "So go on. You were trying to outrun them when you reached that hairpin." He looked back at Gus. "We used to call it Suicide Elbow."

"Yes. I'd slammed on the brakes when I realized I was approaching the turn, but it was too late—my car kept sliding toward the edge. But then, finally, it stopped and I thought I was safe. Next thing I knew, he'd driven up over the shoulder behind me and he was nudging me over the edge. I tried to jump out of the Jeep, but I couldn't get my seat belt undone. That's the last thing I remember."

Wolfkill scribbled a word here and there on a notepad, more to give himself time to think than anything else. He didn't know that many white women. Most those he did weren't to be trusted, 'cept of course Allison Becker, his son's fifth-grade teacher. But Ms. Becker was the exception to the rule. He'd seen too many white women who came on to the reservation to drink and look for good-looking Indian men to get laid by. Maybe it wasn't fair to judge them all by the ones he'd come in contact with. This Dr. McLain didn't seem like the hysterical type. And just about everyone who went to the clinic had good things to say about her.

Still her story was pretty hard to believe. Bud had never seen anything like that in all his years on the reservation. Over the years, he'd responded to more than his share of incidents of violence. Hell, violent crime rates, even murder, were almost twice the national average on the rez, but they were always the result of personal relationships, too much booze, emotions getting out of hand, that kind of stuff. This kind of faceless violence, well, it was something entirely different.

"You keep saying 'he.' Did you get a look at who was driving this car?"

"No."

"Have any idea who might do something like this to you? Enemies, patients who might be mad at you, something like that? Pretty hard to believe this was something random."

"It's not random . . ." Gus said, eyeing Isabel. "Tell him."

"Tell me *what*?" Wolfkill wanted to know.

Gus had fixed his gaze on Isabel.

"Tell him what you told me earlier tonight. About your ex-husband."

Wolfkill put the paper down on his knee and turned his complete attention on Isabel.

"Tell me about this ex-husband of yours."

The subject appeared to cause the lady doctor distress.

"We're not divorced yet. He's been showing up here, on the reservation. A couple times recently. I saw him tonight, at the council meeting."

"Has he contacted you? Threatened you in some way?"

"No."

"Do you have a restraining order against him?"

"No."

"Recognize the car?"

"No," Isabel cried. "I did *not* recognize the car. But don't you think it's a bit of a coincidence that the same night he shows up at the meeting, I end up pushed over the fucking cliff?"

Wolfkill saw that he'd pushed some sensitive buttons with this line of questioning.

"Ma'am, I can understand how frightening that must have been for you. And it's apparent you're not very happy about this ex-husband of yours showing up here on the rez, which I can also understand, but I can't arrest a man based on coincidence."

"You can look for him," Gus interjected, "can't you? Find out what the hell he's doing here in Browning."

"I certainly can do that. And I will. But it's a free country. If she doesn't have a restraining order against him and he's not breaking the law, he's entitled to be here. All I'm saying is we'd need a lot more evidence than that to bring him in."

"Well then why don't you deputize me," Gus huffed, shifting impatiently in his chair, "and I'll get you that evidence?"

Wolfkill stifled the urge to smile.

"Now, Gus, I doubt this lady wants you goin' gettin' yourself in trouble on her account. You leave this matter to the sheriff's office."

Isabel McLain, who'd paced back and forth during the interview, stopped and placed her hand on Gus's shoulder.

"He's right, Gus. I need you right here."

Gus's arthritic fingers, balled into fists, looked ready to strike out. He glanced from Isabel to Wolfkill.

"You find the SOB who did this to her, you hear?"

"I'll do my best," Wolfkill answered.

NINETEEN

BUD WOLFKILL WAS clearly ill at ease. It wasn't just that his large frame dwarfed the metal folding chair in which he now sat, the lack of leg space between the chair and Isabel's desk forcing his knees up at unnatural angles. He also just happened to be someone who was not comfortable sitting still. Especially when he had nothing worthwhile to report and his constituent was clearly not happy with him.

"But it's been almost a month," Isabel said, frustration echoing in her voice.

"I know that, Dr. McLain, but we still haven't come up with any evidence that it was your ex-husband who tried to run you off Suicide Elbow that night. Two officers from the police department over there in Seattle questioned him. He admitted being on the reservation that day. Going to the tribal council meeting. But he says he drove straight back to the lodge in East Glacier after the meeting."

"What about his car? Did they check his car?"

"It was a rental. He couldn't produce the rental records. All he could tell them was that he picked it up at one of the rental counters at the Kalispell airport. I've sent a guy over there to try to track the car down and see if there's any evidence indicating it could have been the car that rammed your Jeep, but you said it was a sport utility vehicle. Most of them have bumpers like steel tanks. Wouldn't do much damage to give your Jeep a little bump."

"It was more than a *little bump.*"

"Sorry. Poor choice of words." Wolfkill pushed a hand through his head of thick black hair, as if stalling for time. "Unfortunately, your ex also has an alibi for later that night, the time you and Gus said the accident took place."

It didn't escape Isabel's attention that Bud was now calling it an "accident."

"An alibi? Like what?"

Wolfkill cleared his throat.

"Umm, a lady friend. Someone who works there at the lodge. She's apparently willing to vouch for him. Says she spent the whole night with him. I talked to her myself."

Wolfkill looked startled when Isabel let loose with a laugh.

"Classic," was all she said.

Wolfkill lumbered to his feet, nervously fingering his brown felt uniform hat.

"I want you to know that we'll keep looking for whoever did this to you. We're not giving up. We'll track down the car he was driving that night, and if there's anything suspicious, we'll bring him in. And his lady friend."

Suddenly his eyes jumped up and to the left, to the half-opened door behind Isabel.

Isabel swiveled in her chair to see Ken MacStirling standing in the hallway.

"Dr. MacStirling," she said, taking a quick glance at her watch. "You're early."

"Sorry about that," MacStirling said. "When I flew in and saw the snow, I decided to give myself plenty of time to drive up from Kalispell—I guess maybe I gave myself a wee bit too much." He eyed Wolfkill. "I can come back in a while, if you'd like."

Wolfkill moved quickly toward the door.

"I'm on my way out," he said. Nodding at Isabel, he added, "We'll get back to you if we find anything else about Dr. Bott."

"Thank you, Officer Wolfkill," Isabel said. "Not just for your work, but for coming here to talk to me in person."

Her words of appreciation seemed to surprise Wolfkill.

"You're welcome, ma'am. And you can call me Bud. Everybody else does."

Ken MacStirling had stepped aside for Wolfkill's passage, but even now, after the brown uniform had disappeared down the hall, MacStirling did not move.

"Please, come in," Isabel said.

MacStirling entered Isabel's office looking confused and took up the seat just vacated by Wolfkill.

"Bott?" he finally blurted out when he could contain himself no more. "*Alistair* Bott?"

"Were you standing out there listening?" Isabel's eyes narrowed in accusation.

"Of course not. All I heard was what that officer just said. That he'd let you know if they found out anything about Dr. Bott. Did he mean Alistair Bott, the cardiologist from Seattle?"

"Dr. MacStirling, the meeting between Officer Wolfkill and myself dealt with private personal business."

"Listen here now, this is my clinical trial," said MacStirling, furious. "Anything that might affect it *is* bloody well my business."

Suddenly the realization of what MacStirling had to be thinking came to Isabel and she let out a soft groan. He was right. She had no choice but to tell him.

"What?" MacStirling said, his gaze boring through her. "What is it?"

Every ounce of air went out of her as Isabel raised her eyes to meet MacStirling's scrutiny.

"Alistair Bott was my husband," she said softly. "Correction, he still is—until our divorce becomes final."

"Your husband? How can this be? How could I not know this?" MacStirling said, wild eyed.

"Why *would* you?"

"Well, for starters, you should have told me," MacStirling said indignantly.

"I DON'T SEE what my soon-to-be-ex-husband's identity has to do with my heading up the HantaVac study."

"Under ordinary circumstances," MacStirling said, "that might be true. But not when your husband was accused of being paid millions of dollars for studies for which he faked results . . . I heard he even listed patients that had died as study participants! You don't think that's relevant here? That it merits mention?" He shook his head incredulously. "Please tell me he's had nothing to do with the HantaVac study. Is that why the police were here? Something to do with my study?"

"Calm down, Dr. MacStirling. This has nothing to do with *your* study."

"Then what? Why was that officer just here?"

Isabel had always refused to worry about what anyone thought of her. And she guarded her privacy fiercely. But in this instance, she felt a duty to breach both longstanding rules. In all fairness, she couldn't blame MacStirling for his reaction. A scandal like Alistair's could ruin a career. She'd known that all along. But she hadn't let it stop her.

With years of research and the HantaVac study at stake, MacStirling deserved to know the truth.

"Just before Thanksgiving," Isabel began, "a car ran me off the road. Actually, over the cliff. I reported it to the police. I also told them that I believed it was Alistair behind the wheel of that car. Officer Wolfkill was here today to report to me on his investigation."

MacStirling looked even more confused than he had when he first entered the office.

"Why? Even if you're divorcing him, why would your husband want to harm you?"

"Because he blames me for everything that happened."

MacStirling's spine went stiff.

"You mean the clinical trials? *You* were involved? Bott holds you responsible?"

"In a sense, yes."

"Oh my God."

MacStirling dropped his head into his hands, and began rocking back and forth slowly.

Isabel reached over and gently squeezed his shoulder.

"Ken. Listen to me, will you?"

MacStirling raised weary eyes to hers.

"There's a reason my husband blames me for what happened."

The memory was still so fresh, so disturbing. Still something she didn't want to talk about. But now she must.

"He blames me," Isabel continued, with a sigh of resignation, "because I'm the one who turned him in."

CHAPTER

TWENTY

ISABEL HAD KNOWN for some time that something was not right. Alistair was devoting more and more time to conducting clinical drug trials and less to his lucrative surgical practice, yet the new cars, expensive clothes, and high-tech gadgetry—one state-of-the-art laptop was not enough; Alistair had recently come home with two—indicated that money had never flowed more freely. When Alistair called from his car, ten minutes away from their house, and announced he'd just purchased ocean-front property in the Cayman Islands, Isabel's suspicions had driven her upstairs, to the third floor office loft where Alistair was spending more and more time.

"When was the last time you operated on a patient?"

The pleased-with-himself grin he'd worn into the house disappeared as Alistair threw the FedEx package containing the signed real-estate documents for the Cayman property onto the hall table.

"What the hell is that supposed to mean?"

"Just answer my question. When was the last time you did a bypass? Or even *saw* a cardiology patient? I mean, that's what you are, isn't it? A cardiovascular surgeon? Or have you given that up altogether now, to conduct drug studies?"

"Do you ever get tired of riding that moral high horse you're always on?" Alistair said. They were standing in the foyer of their million-dollar home. Isabel had been waiting for him to come in from the garage. "You don't know how easy you have it, working in the ER. Insurance companies aren't tyin' your hands every fuckin' step you try to take. Hell, it was getting to where I couldn't even perform the tests I needed to make a diagnosis."

"That's such a bullshit cop-out," Isabel cried. "I know how maddening managed care has become. I sympathized with you, but that doesn't mean you just quit. That you give up saving lives with those incredible hands of yours—hands that performed miracles—and just sell out to any greedy drug company that comes along and asks you to run a trial for them. Look at this. It just came through on your fax machine. *Read it*," Isabel found herself practically screaming as she shoved a sheet of paper under his nose.

Improve Your Cash Flow
Discover the secret for obtaining more funded studies. List with our service and your name will go out to hundreds of pharmaceutical companies looking for doctors to test their products. Investigator grants average $48,000 per study. Top recruiters can earn as much as $1 million a year.
SO GET BUSY!!

Alistair glanced at the fax, then threw it down with the FedEx.

"Calm down, Isabel. How do you manage to turn every fucking move I make into some loaded issue? How do you think your ER patients would do without drugs? I mean, some guy comes in with a smashed face and you don't have anything to kill the pain. How would that go over? Or a diabetic in shock? And just how do you think those drugs are made possible? Because of studies, that's how. Because of people like me, who conduct them."

"For money." Isabel's chest heaved with each angry breath. "*Bonuses*. There's another fax in there. It says Warner-Bick will increase the four thousand dollars they're already paying you for some diabetes study you're doing to five thousand for every new participant you enroll in the next thirty days. Have you seen that one? It's hard to keep track of them. There's a stack of faxes an inch high. How many of these studies are you doing?"

She'd heard that some doctors were turning away from their private practices to conduct lucrative clinical trials, but she'd had no idea how much money an investigator stood to make. Nor that Alistair had become so heavily involved.

"Pharmaceutical companies are a business. And time is money. They provide incentives to enroll patients as quickly as possible."

"Just what are you doing conducting a study on a diabetes drug anyway? You're a cardiologist. What do you know about diabetes?"

"I could do a diabetes study blindfolded," Alistair answered with undisguised disdain. Then he turned on her. "What are you doing in my office anyway, snooping around my fax machine?"

"Your office? Since when is it your office? We always said that it would be both of ours. But it just so happens my *medical practice*," she couldn't help but goad him, "doesn't give me time to spend in it."

"That's it. That's why this all gets to you. You resent my success. It drives you crazy to see how well I'm doing." His expression mellowed just enough to test the waters. "I've told you, Is, you can get in on it. All you have to do is start referring your patients to me. Most of these pharmaceutical companies will pay you five hundred dollars just for the referral."

Isabel simply stared at him.

"You've turned patients into a commodity. Money machines."

Disgusted, Alistair stormed up the stairs, into his office, and slammed the door.

They didn't talk for two days after that, which actually wasn't all that big a jump from their usual state of affairs. Over the past few months, they'd almost made a concerted effort to steer clear of one another.

After that day, when Alistair was out of the house, Isabel began exploring his office, reading the faxes that came through, sometimes dozens in a single day. Her busy work schedule usually meant taking only a twenty-minute lunch at a deli near the hospital, but now she found herself running home for lunch to see what had come in over the fax machine.

Many of the faxes were generic solicitations from drug companies wanting doctors to head new studies or recruit patients for existing studies. Without question, the majority, however, came from the same fax number, and a person named Mary, who Isabel soon surmised to be Alistair's study coordinator for the clinical trials he was already conducting. From what Isabel could see, it appeared that Alistair was involved in no fewer than a dozen trials. He was testing products ranging from angina medications to acne treatments to prostate cancer therapies.

During one such lunch hour, when she was up in Alistair's office, the telephone rang. Isabel picked it up before the third ring, but heard only a dial tone. Thinking the caller must have changed his mind at the last minute or realized he had the wrong number, Isabel hung the phone back up, but then, on an impulse, she picked it up again and this time, heard the interrupted signal that indicated a message had been received. She dialed the access number she always used and punched in her four digit password, but was informed by a mechanical sounding voice that she had no messages.

That couldn't be true—the dial tone clearly indicated they had messages.

Isabel took a closer look at the phone. It wasn't until then that she

realized that the phone number written on the plastic-covered plate dif-
fered from the number for the rest of the phones in the house. Alistair
had apparently installed a separate line into his office without telling her.

She dialed the number written on the plate and immediately, after
just one ring, Alistair's voice came on the line.

"This is Dr. Alistair Bott. If you are calling regarding a clinical trial,
please feel free to leave a message. If this is a medical emergency, please
contact my study coordinator, Mary Pelandini, at 206-282-1789."

Before the beep sounded, Isabel pressed "zero" and was instructed
to punch in her password. She tried Alistair's birthdate, 12/14, and was
told by the same mechanized voice to try again. Their anniversary, 09/21,
received a similar response.

Then she tried 1962, the year Alistair was born, and was immediately
informed there was one new message:

"Alistair, this is Mary. Mrs. Hougham's blood pressure keeps rising,
ever since she started the study drug. She was already on an antihyper-
tensive when she entered the study, and I added that other one you told
me to try, but they're not working either. She's complaining about dizziness. I know she's the last patient we needed to complete this study and
get final payment, but I'm wondering whether you want me to drop her.
Will you call me back immediately?" There was a pause. "Oh yeah, I also
wanted to let you know that I've signed James Burgdorff up for the asthma
inhaler study." She chuckled, then added, "Good old James."

Isabel hung up the phone, stunned.

Could they be talking about Bernice Hougham? Bernice was an especially sweet elderly patient Isabel had treated just two months earlier
at the hospital emergency room. She'd come in complaining of chest
pains. Isabel had run an EKG on her and determined that she was not in
danger of imminent cardiac arrest, but her blood pressure had been on
the high end, and she'd urged Bernice to see a specialist.

She had not referred Bernice specifically to Alistair. Despite the fact
that Isabel considered Alistair one of the city's best cardiovascular specialists, she never referred patients to him, deeming it a conflict of interest. If, however, a patient or coworker enquired about Alistair, Isabel felt
confident and comfortable recommending him.

Could the Mrs. Hougham this Mary was talking about be the Bernice
Hougham Isabel had treated? She thought back to the evening Bernice
had been brought by ambulance to the hospital.

With a sick dread in the pit of her stomach, Isabel grabbed the stack
of faxes that Alistair had allowed to pile up on the machine and began
perusing them.

It had become clear that Mary routinely faxed new information, pri-
marily study data, to Alistair. Isabel began running her finger down lists
of names of study participants. On a sheet labeled Warmer-Bick Phar-

maceuticals, a study for a drug to treat hypertension, she ran across the name of James Burgdorff, but no Hougham.

Another study, this one for a drug called TriGlys, listed almost a hundred participants. Near the top, she again came across the name Burgdorff.

Many of the names sounded vaguely familiar to her. Perhaps because Alistair had mentioned them as patients.

By the time she was done going through every sheet in the stack, she'd found James Burgdorff listed on four study lists. But she never found a reference to Mrs. Hougham.

Ariana Pitts, the regular admissions clerk, was not on duty the next day. Isabel asked one of the other clerks on duty to pull the records on a Mrs. Hougham. Later, the clerk handed her a sheet of paper. *Bernice Hougham*, it said.

Isabel subscribed to the belief that there are few coincidences in life. This was not one of them.

She'd planned to call Bernice Hougham that day, under the guise of following up on her visit to Harborview's ER. But she'd never had a moment's rest at work, and that night, Alistair seemed so determined to make amends for the strain between them that she'd not been able to sneak away from him to make the call.

It had almost seemed as though he were courting her again. But later, in bed, despite the wine, which he'd poured liberally, Isabel had turned away from him. They had once shared a passionate love life, but increasingly Alistair had displayed an appetite for sexual practices that Isabel found disturbing, and when he touched her now, she could barely refrain from pulling back in revulsion.

The next morning, when Isabel awoke—later than usual from the wine—Alistair was nowhere to be seen. She tiptoed up the stairs to the third floor office, reached for its door, and found it locked.

Furious—her instincts telling her she'd been had—she began pounding.

"Alistair? Are you in there?"

When he failed to answer, Isabel ran down both flights of stairs, flung open the garage door, and saw that his Jaguar was gone.

Stopping in the kitchen for a steak knife, she raced back to the office and jabbed at the keyhole, jiggling the knob repeatedly. She hadn't even realized the door had a lock on it. In fact, when she thought about it, she knew that it had not. Not until now.

She was about ready to give up trying to jimmy the door open when it occurred to her.

There was a small ledge that ran outside the third floor bathroom and the office.

In the bathroom, she climbed on top of the toilet, opened the window, and, her bare foot groping for purchase on the rain-slicked composition roof, stepped out, keeping a tight grip on the windowsill. Her nightgown lifted with the breeze off Elliott Bay.

The ledge was only three feet wide, and sloped gradually.

Don't look down, she told herself.

The distance between the bathroom window and the first of three office windows was no more than two yards. Midway between, there was a decorative column of tan shingles. Isabel tugged on one of the shingles. When it held, she let go of the windowsill. Changing hands and shingles, she inched her way through the galeish wind to the first of the paned office windows. She breathed a sigh of relief to see it was unlocked. Still grasping hold of a shingle, she used her free hand to force the window up and, moments later, lowered herself inside the office.

She turned and immediately saw something missing—the stack of papers on the fax machine. The phone light blinked. She picked it up and dialed the number on its plate, then again punched the four digits of Alistair's birth year, but this time was told that she'd selected an incorrect password.

Every file drawer she tried to open proved locked, and a search through the desk yielded no keys.

Now she understood the previous evening—why Alistair had been so attentive, why he'd insisted they open the bottle of Duckhorn merlot they'd been saving. He must have come up to the office during the night, cleaned it of any information regarding the clinical trials, and changed his password to his voice mail.

But why? And why last night?

SHE'D DRESSED IN record time, rushing so much that as she climbed into her car she realized she'd left the information the clerk had given her yesterday in the lab coat that she'd thrown into the dirty clothes. She ran back into the house and retrieved the sheet of paper from a pocket.

She had only asked for Ms. Hougham's first name and telephone number. Fortunately, the clerk had also jotted down her address.

601 Summit, Apt 2.

Isabel steered her Jeep across the Magnolia Bridge, then followed Denny Avenue along the waters of Elliott Bay before it curved east, toward Capitol Hill.

She climbed over Interstate 5, then, at Summit, turned left and slowed, watching for the 600 block. Six-oh-one was a three-story frame house, with a recent coat of yellow paint and turquoise trim. Ignoring the warning signs, Isabel parked in front of a fire hydrant and climbed the four steps to the porch, where three metal mailboxes were aligned. Each one had its own buzzer.

Above each box was a unit number and name, two handwritten—Gilbert and Ochoa—and a third, this one typed. MacNaughton.

Isabel took three steps back to recheck the numerals on the column at the top step.

601.

She pressed the buzzer to apartment two. No one answered.

She pressed again.

Still no answer.

Then, through the glass panes of the front door, she saw a head pop out of a door just inside the hall. A slender woman, her red hair in tight pigtails, stepped into the foyer and opened the heavy walnut door.

"Are you trying to get into Bernie's apartment?" she asked. "I heard you buzz."

"Yes. Do you know if she's home?"

"Are you family?"

"No. A friend. Actually, I'm a doctor. I treated her a couple months ago at Harborview's emergency room."

"She told me about you," the girl said, finally smiling. But Isabel thought it an oddly melancholy smile. "She said you were so nice."

"That's always good to hear. Listen, I'd like to talk to her, if you think she's home."

The girl's eyes suddenly filled with tears.

"You didn't know?" she said, swiping at them with the sleeves of her gray sweatshirt, which was inscribed with the letters PAWS over a gigantic pawprint.

"Bernie died," she sniffed. "Yesterday."

ISABEL WAS PACKING the last of three suitcases when the front door of the house slammed shut so violently that the framed Bev Doolittle over the bed she and Alistair had shared the night before threatened to fall off its mounting.

Alistair appeared in the doorway moments later.

"Are you out of your mind?" he screamed at her.

Isabel did not turn to face him. Instead, she continued transferring clothes and personal items—a photo album, birthday cards she'd saved over the years, hair clips and pins—from the dresser to the suitcase.

Seconds later, he was on her, grabbing her by the shoulders and jerking her around to face him.

"Look at me," he bellowed. "Are you out of your fucking mind? You called Warmer-Bick? Told them I'd killed a patient in my study?"

The veins in his neck looked like slender blue snakes leading to his face, which was the color of a fiery sky just before sunset. Isabel refused to flinch under his glare, or from the force with which his hands squeezed both shoulders.

"How did you get to her?" she hissed at him. "How did you get Bernice Hougham to join your study?"

"I don't know what you're talking about. I've never even heard of her."

"You're a liar! She was my ER patient that night you picked me up at the ER for the Fred Hutch dinner. Someone named Mary left you a message about her just the other day, told you she was having problems with Warmer-Bick's hypertensive."

One of Alistair's hands let go of her shoulder and slapped her across the face so forcefully that she felt, and heard, a distinctive *pop* in the back of her neck.

"You bitch! You listened to my messages. *What have you done?*"

She had seen many ugly emotions in her husband's eyes. Greed, anger. But now she saw something she had never before seen. Terror. And hatred.

"If what you're saying is true, if your patient was enrolled in my study, they'll think it was *you* who enrolled her. I'll make sure they do. I'll bring you down with me. You'll never be able to practice medicine again."

"I didn't just call Warmer-Bick. I called LaRouche too," Isabel said. "And Angiogenics. I told all of them that you had the same person enrolled in four different studies."

Alistair released his grip on her other shoulder as he fell back.

"You'll never be able to prove any of it."

"The attending physician at Swedish said Bernice Hougham's heart attack was caused by the antihypertensives. She was on three of them. You killed her."

"I told you, I don't know what you're talking about. I meet the patients who enroll in my studies once. Do you actually think I remember all of their names? If this woman was one of your patients, you must have referred her to me."

"That's a lie."

"Who's to say?" Alistair smiled.

Then, suddenly, his face transformed.

"Don't you see what you've done, Isabel? Don't you?" They stood facing each other.

"You've just made the biggest mistake of your life."

TWENTY-ONE

ISABEL KNEW THE moment she awoke that something was different. She lay cocooned in her down comforter, trying to figure out what it was. And then it came to her.

Silence. The absolute lack of sound, inside or outside her cabin.

Turtlelike, she inched her head out from under her comforter. The cabin's frigid morning air condensed each breath into a short billowing cloud. She inhaled, pursed her lips, and exhaled in a silent whistle, sending a stream toward the ceiling, where it quickly drifted into oblivion.

Dreading getting up to build a fire, Isabel briefly entertained the idea of staying in bed all morning, but then she remembered what day it was. Almost simultaneously, she heard the first sounds of the morning.

A man's muffled voice, then a *woof*.

Isabel jumped up and hurried to the window. Pulling open the curtain, she drew in her breath at the sight that met her eyes.

Outside, the world had been transformed overnight. Huge, soft flakes drifted lazily from a ceiling of low clouds. A solid, undisturbed white velvet blanket spread as far as Isabel could see, silencing the world, covering even the trees, whose branches hung low with their weight. The only thing breaking the moonlike expanse were two narrow ribbons created by the horse-drawn wagon approaching the cabin.

Urged on by Gus, who wore a fringed jacket and Daniel Boone–style cap, Bessie plodded forward, unfazed by the weight of the sleigh, tossing her head occasionally, while Grunt balanced uncertainly on the seat beside his master.

Scurrying back to the bed for her comforter, Isabel wrapped it around her shoulders and ran through the kitchen, where she threw open the door and stood watching her friends in childlike glee from the doorway.

"Merry Christmas!" she called as Gus stepped down into thigh-high snow.

Grunt jumped off the sled and, running toward her, porpoised his nose in and out of the snow. Once under the shelter of the porch, the exuberant dog executed a shake that started at his head and traveled, wavelike, down his back, sending snow flying into Isabel's eyelashes and bangs.

As Gus literally climbed his way to Isabel through two and a half feet of fresh fluff, the mini-icicles that had formed on the longer strands of hair protruding from his cap and at either end of his mustache became visible to Isabel. Gus clapped his gloved hands together and began scolding her even before he reached the first step.

"I don't see any smoke coming out that chimney. How do you propose to entertain Christmas guests?"

Isabel's laughter drifted like a bell across the morning stillness.

"Mercy, Gus. I slept so soundly I let the fire go out. And I don't even have coffee to offer you. Grab a handful of kindling and let's get the woodstove going again."

"I'll start it up, but just so's the pipes don't freeze while you're gone. You get yourself dressed and we'll head on over to my place. I already got a big old fire going. I'll cook us a rancher's breakfast that'll knock your socks off."

"I was planning to put the turkey on here this morning, then bring it over in time for dinner."

"Even with that fancy new truck of yours, you're not going to make it anywhere until the plows come by. Bessie was itchin' to get out in this stuff. Let's just pack up the whole kit and kaboodle and put it on at my place."

Nothing sounded better to Isabel right now than a day spent in front of Gus's fireplace, and cooking in his spacious kitchen.

"You got yourself a deal," she said, giving Gus a big hug as he stepped inside the kitchen. "But I *have* to have a cup of coffee before I venture out."

"I'll make the coffee," he said firmly. "You get dressed."

When Isabel returned minutes later, dressed in blue jeans and thermal T-shirt, over which she'd slipped a red wool sweater, the woodstove was spitting and crackling and Gus was spooning instant coffee into two mugs.

He gave her a mischievous smile, then reached inside his jacket and extracted a pint-sized pewter flask.

"This'll warm you up for the ride," he said, unscrewing its cap.

"Why not?" Isabel laughed, watching as he poured watery brown liquid into both mugs. "Whoa, Gus, go light on mine!"

She'd begun bagging the groceries she'd bought the day before for their Christmas dinner when the phone rang. Isabel froze and turned anxious eyes toward Gus. The caller would not be her mother. She'd already had a long talk with her the night before.

"Want me to get it?" Gus asked.

"Would you mind?"

Gus's "hello" was decidedly more gruff than Isabel had ever heard before. He listened briefly then placed his calloused palm over the mouthpiece.

"Some guy named Ken MacStirling," he said. "Want me to tell him to get lost?"

"I'll take it."

Isabel grabbed the phone from Gus.

"Hello?"

"Merry Christmas," MacStirling said. Isabel could hear children's voices in the background.

"Same to you. I certainly didn't expect a Christmas call from you."

"Well, I've been wanting to apologize for the other day. What better day to do it?"

"I don't blame you for anything you said or felt, Ken. I should probably have told you about Alistair, but it's not . . ."

"Please, no," MacStirling interrupted her. "I didn't call for explanations. The more I've thought about what you did, turning your own husband in, the more impressed I am. Now I understand your reluctance to get involved with the HantaVac study."

"Well, don't be too impressed. My attorney tells me there's a good chance that Alistair will get away with little more than a slap on the wrist. The pharmaceutical companies don't want any of this making the news. She's heard they're prepared to make the whole thing go away. They've pulled Alistair off most of their studies, but they're saying they don't have proof of intentional wrongdoing, that it can all be attributed to sloppy paperwork."

Bud Wolfkill's words came back to her then. *We haven't come up with any evidence that it was your ex-husband who tried to run you off Suicide Elbow that night.*

Alistair was an expert at eliminating proof of his misdeeds.

"I should think the FDA would get involved. It would be terrible if Bott isn't made to pay," MacStirling said. "Still, if you think your actions were wasted, you're wrong. I can tell you, that whole incident opened plenty o' eyes. It spread through the industry like wildfire. Truth is, there'd been a lot more of that goin' on than anyone wanted to say. Let's hope what happened to that coof you had the misfortune of being married to changes all that. If it doesn't, people like him are going to end up ruining things for important trials, like the HantaVac study.

"But listen, no need to get so serious on such a joyous day. I also received some good news and wanted to share it with you. Thought it might add to your holiday cheer."

"What's that?"

"We'll be getting on with Phase II. Following the holidays. Lyons gave me the go ahead yesterday. I tried callin' you last night, but your line was busy."

"That *is* great news. I already have the Phase II participants signed up. I was just waiting for the go-ahead."

"Well, now you have it. You can start drawing blood immediately. The new vaccine lot will be shipped to you the first of the new year. Things are going so well, we should be into Phase III by late spring, early summer. Aye, I almost forgot. ImmuVac got more good news yesterday. One of the biggest pharmaceutical companies in the nation, Pfister, is interested in a partnership. Thanks to our study."

Isabel couldn't help but smile—it was back to being "our" study again.

"Congratulations. Sounds like you have a lot to celebrate."

Gus had handed her a mug and now Isabel took a long sip from it. The old man's throaty laughter rattled through the kitchen as he watched Isabel's expression when the whiskey burned its way down her throat.

"We both do," MacStirling said. "I have the feeling it's going to be a very good year for both of us."

WHEN SHE WAS a child, Christmas day often left Isabel with an emptiness that stacks of presents and plates piled high did not touch. There were always invitations from other physicians and family friends, but early on, Nada made it a rule that the three of them—Nada, Tom, and Isabel—spend the day alone together, as a family. Isabel had always secretly hoped that they'd accept one of those invitations.

While she couldn't put a name to it when she was young, later she decided that the joy at her household on Christmas Day always seemed particularly forced. Nada McLain seemed determined to create an atmosphere of gaiety and celebration with lavish gifts. Isabel's father, who did not have a materialistic bone in his body, never complained—throughout their marriage, Isabel had never heard him criticize Nada—but Isabel sometimes sensed he escaped times like that by going somewhere far away in his mind, which only made Isabel more lonely.

Christmas Day with Gus turned out to be the simplest Christmas Isabel ever spent. Just Isabel and Gus in front of the fire, exchanging modest but thoughtfully selected gifts—a leather-bound world atlas for Gus, handmade moccasins for Isabel. They'd feasted on turkey and stuffing, potatoes and green beans, then worked some of it off outside, shoveling Gus's driveway, then grooming Bessie and mucking out her stall. Afterward, Gus produced a mammoth pumpkin pie that he'd bought at Sandy's Diner, for which Isabel whipped real cream.

Gus also broke out his homemade Irish cream, which they drank straight at first. Then, after downing a third of the bottle, they added it to the coffee Isabel brewed.

"What a magical day it's been, Gus," Isabel said, smiling at him across the dinner table, her face flushed with alcohol, heat from the fire, and happiness.

"Hell, Is, I would've thought today was a disappointment for you."

"How can you say that?"

"Well, Grunt and me here have been celebratin' Christmas alone for a long time. Having a little company's a real treat for us. But I would've thought you'd be used to a lot more excitement than this."

"No, Gus, I'm not. This has been perfect."

They both grew thoughtful, sipping their creamy coffees.

"Gus?"

"Yep?"

"Would I be a busybody if I asked you about your wife?"

The smile that graced Gus's eyes was slow and sweet.

"Hell, no. What'd you want to know?"

"Anything. Everything."

"Well, let's see. Her name was Marian." A tenderness and warmth laced Gus's words. "She died two weeks short of our forty-third anniversary. And there wasn't a single day in all those forty-three years that I didn't thank my lucky stars for her."

Isabel felt a catch in her throat. What would it feel like to be loved like that?

"What was she like?"

Gus grew thoughtful.

"Patient. Marian was a patient woman. She just kinda rolled with the flow, which is a good way for a rancher's wife to be. And she didn't mind bein' alone. Course she had so damn many critters that I had to fight for my spot on the bed every night. That woman just loved animals. Which is a good thing, 'cause many a night they were about all the company she had."

"You were gone a lot?"

"I traveled some, but it wasn't that so much. The weather and cattle, they don't pay much attention to a clock. Runnin' a ranch is a twenty-four-hour proposition. Marian accepted that. Hell, she'd always have a warm meal waitin' for me, no matter what time of day or night I was called out to tend to things."

"How did you meet her?"

"Marian grew up on the Flathead reservation."

"She was Indian?"

"No. But her grandfather bought eighty acres 'bout the time of the Dawes Act and then he just kept buyin' up the stuff around him as it became available. I used to drive down there for my alfalfa. That's how I met Marian. I bought hay from her old man . . . What is it, Isabel? You look like you've just seen a ghost. Did I say somethin'?"

Isabel's voice grew soft and tentative.

"Did I ever tell you my father was a doctor on the Flathead reservation? That he spent a year there just before I was born?"

Gus's eyes widened to the size of silver dollars.

"What was his name?"

"Tom. Tom McLain."

"Holy Toledo. *Dr. Tom*. I can't believe I didn't make the connection. But then it's been so long, and the only name I ever really heard him go by was Dr. Tom."

Isabel's entire body went taut.

"You knew him?"

It was an odd thing, Isabel would recall later. Watching Gus at that moment. His initial surprise seemed to transform itself into something else. Something Isabel couldn't quite put a finger on.

"Well, no. I never actually met him."

"How'd you remember him then?"

"Well, Marian had this friend." Gus's words seemed measured somehow. "Her name was Hattie Bay. The two of them grew up together. They went to school together, on the reservation. It was Hattie who knew your father."

It struck Isabel as strange that Gus would remember a man who had only lived on the Flathead reservation for one year, and whom he'd only heard about because his wife's friend had known him. Still, Isabel couldn't hold back the excitement that she felt building inside.

"Did she work with my father at the clinic? Was she a nurse?"

"No. I think Hattie was just a patient of his."

"Hattie's Indian?"

Gus nodded. "Yup. Salish."

"Do you suppose I could find her, Gus? It'd be so incredible to meet her and talk to her about my dad. That time meant so much to him, but it wasn't exactly a popular subject around our house. I'd just love to meet her."

"Hattie died, Isabel. A long time ago."

Isabel's heart dropped back into her chest, where it belonged.

"Were they friends? Hattie and my father?"

Gus pushed back from the table so suddenly, and with such force, that it actually startled Isabel.

"You know, that's about all I remember on the subject. It was a long time ago." He stood. "Now, I better hitch Bessie back up and see you home, girl, before I pass out from all that good food and drink."

SOMETHING WAS AMISS. She first noticed it when she went into the bathroom. The wall just to the right of the toilet had a small, old-fashioned window that opened outward, to the back of the cabin. When Isabel moved in, she'd replaced the cheap steel rings intended to hold towels with a long brass rod that she'd positioned directly beneath the window.

On warm summer days, she liked opening the window so that her towels could absorb the scents of the mountain air and flowers.

It was that—a towel—that tipped Isabel off. She'd done laundry yesterday, and last night, before going to bed, she'd folded a fresh towel over the rod. Just as Isabel had a thing about installing toilet paper so the paper always rolled off the top of the roll, not the bottom, she was fastidious in the way she folded towels. Lengthwise in thirds, not halves. It was one of those little, admittedly anal idiosyncrasies.

But as Isabel reached for the forest green towel to dry her face, her hands froze in midair.

The towel was folded in half. Not thirds.

And there was no way, no way at all, that she had folded it like that.

Immediately, her eyes went to the window, which was secured with a latch that rotated its way clear of the locking position.

She'd kept it locked all winter. But it was not locked now.

Lowering the lid to the toilet, Isabel stepped onto it and pushed the window out, a blast of cold air immediately turning her breaths into clouds.

Snow, falling thickly, made it difficult to see far. The square of light from the small window illuminated a patch of snow below.

It afforded Isabel just enough light to make out the imprint of a boot in the snow beneath the window. She watched, momentarily transfixed, as it filled with snow.

"YOU HAVE TO report it."

Isabel had waited until morning to call her attorney in Seattle with her discovery.

"I'm telling you, K. T., it won't do any good. Look what happened when he tried to push me into the Two Medicine." Anger seized Isabel's chest and tightened around her throat, giving her voice an ugly edge. "I've turned him in to the authorities twice now. It just makes it worse when they come back and tell me they can't find any evidence against him. I can practically feel him mocking me, taunting me. And that just makes me crazy."

K. T. Seinberg sounded just as disturbed as her client.

"I don't agree with you, but it's your decision. Okay, then. What's missing? What did he take?"

"Nothing. At least nothing that I can tell. But it's clear he was looking for something. He turned my entire office upside down."

K. T.'s silence indicated she was deep in thought.

"He obviously knows where I live now," Isabel continued. "If he wanted to hurt me, he could have."

"Don't count on that. My guess is Alistair would have no problem with hurting you. But he's too smart to break in to your cabin and harm you. He knows he'd be the prime suspect. But there has to be a reason he won't leave you alone." She mulled this over for several seconds. "He's either trying to frighten you, or he's actually looking for something."

"I agree. But what?"

"I don't know. Remember all those documents you found in his office, on his fax machine?"

"Yes."

"You never kept any of them, right?"

"No. I've told you that. I could kick myself, but he locked me out of there before I became suspicious enough to actually do something."

"Which is why, from what I've heard, they haven't been able to prove any serious wrongdoing. The agent I talked to said it appeared that Alistair and his assistant had done a very thorough job of purging their files."

"If I'd only had the presence of mind to take them when I saw them," Isabel sighed. "I know those faxes would have led somewhere."

"That's it," Seinberg cried suddenly.

"What?"

"Alistair must think you *did* have the presence of mind. He must think you took something. Something that could hurt him."

Isabel mulled this over a moment before responding.

"That would make sense of his comment that night he left the message here for me . . ."

"That's right. What was it he said? That the video was a *reminder?*"

"Yes. He said something like 'in case you were thinking of doing me any more harm.' Something like that."

"You never did figure out what video he meant," Seinberg said. "Did you?"

"No. Never." Suzanne continued to claim that she never saw a video, despite Isabel's clear recollection of UPS delivering one that day. "Listen, K. T., isn't this enough to go after him in court again? Get a court order, a restraining order?"

"You still don't have any proof, Isabel. None. It's all too circumstantial. Any judge is going to see it that way. Unless you call the police and they can come up with something. Like fingerprints. Or even footprints."

"I really don't want to call the police. Besides, we're in the middle of a blizzard. The footprints are long gone. And Alistair's too smart to have left fingerprints. We both know that. I just have to figure out what it is he's after."

"He's like a wounded animal," Seinberg mused. "And that's when they're most dangerous. When you shoot, you have to shoot to kill. You didn't do that. Turning Alistair in for the fraud you suspected him of just nicked him. Just made him that much more dangerous."

K. T. was right. Isabel had blown it. She'd naively assumed the drug companies would be eager to hear her suspicions about Alistair. Instead, all she'd succeeded in doing was giving him a warning, a chance to clean up his files, destroy any evidence of wrongdoing. But if K. T. was right, Alistair was still nervous about her. About Isabel's power to hurt him. And Isabel knew only too well what Alistair was capable of when his back was to the wall.

"Maybe if I find out what it is he's after," she said with more optimism than she felt, "I can finish him off. Bury him, once and for all."

"Let's hope you can," K. T. Seinberg, who never minced words, answered. "Because I have no doubt that he'd bury you in a heartbeat if he felt it could save his own sorry ass."

CHAPTER

TWENTY-TWO

YOU KNOW, MARY, darlin'," Alistair stared over Mary Pelandini's shoulder at a striking blonde who'd just entered Starbucks, "this hysteria of yours is becoming tiresome."

Mary's shock at Alistair's words, let alone his tone of voice, caused her fleshy jaw to drop.

"Hysteria? Do you understand what I'm telling you? They found at least six invoices from Laticia that were labeled *urine samples*."

"Who made those invoices? Whose handwriting were they in?"

"Mine," Mary practically screamed.

"How could you have the stupidity to label the invoices like that?"

Alistair thought Mary might pass out from shock at his behavior. But he'd had about enough of all this. And the fact that the invoices for the urine they'd routinely purchased from a former nurse at the clinic—urine with high levels of protein, which was a prerequisite to enrollment in the GenSci trial—were written by hand, *by Mary*, was really some of the best news he'd had in a long time. He could just hear himself now, telling the FDA investigators of his devastation upon realizing that his study coordinator had been commiting fraud of such unimaginable proportions.

But that would be a last resort. Mary knew so much. So very much. Who knew if, when told to destroy all the evidence against him, she'd held back something incriminatory? As annoyingly emotional as she was, she could also be cunning. He had one final card to play before he would resort to that plan.

"Listen, darlin'," he said, eyes now making contact with the blonde, who had moved to the line waiting for drinks, "I think it's time we change tactics with my former wife." Isabel and Alistair's divorce had become final just that week. "I think it's time to throw the blame on her."

"What do you mean?"

"I mean, the investigators are so fucking hung up on the fact that some of our study participants were former patients of Isabel's. Aside from the invoices, which are an unfortunate new development, you did such a good job of cleaning up the files, that's about all they can hang their hat on. I think it's time we tell them that it was all Isabel's idea."

Mary drew back in shock.

"But the fax from Ariana. If she has that . . ."

"Will you please forget about that fucking fax? She doesn't have it. I've searched her cabin high and low for it. I've told you all along, it doesn't exist."

"You're absolutely certain?"

"Yes, I'm certain. Believe me, if Isabel had that fax, she'd have used it by now. Especially now."

"What do you mean, especially now?"

"Now that the divorce is final. Now that she undoubtedly realizes that I'm the one who broke into her cabin."

He didn't add the thought that was foremost in his mind.

Now that she's seen that video.

He'd felt certain that the video was the one weapon that would guarantee Isabel's cooperation. But, to his amazement, he'd been wrong. He'd expected Isabel to come crawling to him after he sent it to her. Begging him to let her off the hook. He'd expected that video to really scare the bejesus out of her. After all, the one thing Isabel held dearest was her pride. And her goddamn arrogance. The threat of having their kinky love-fest broadcast to the wonderful world of online perverts . . . well, he was pretty sure she'd do just about anything to prevent that from happening. Instead, she'd ignored the damn video altogether and even had the nerve to send some fucking redskin cop to question him about breaking into her cabin. Which was, of course, a joke, since Alistair had been a little too smart to actually leave fingerprints that night. What did she think he was, a fucking idiot?

He glanced in the direction of the good-looking blonde, just in time to see her flash a giant smile at a broad-shouldered jock who had joined the line next to hers. The slob was dressed in sweats and a pitted-out jersey, wearing his hat backward like some punk kid, but the blonde didn't seem to mind. When her eyes swept across the tables moments later, they skipped right over Alistair, returning quickly to the jock.

Alistair felt as if he would explode. Sorry bitches were all alike.

"It's definitely time," he said, his anger growing as the blonde's transgressions brought back thoughts of Isabel's refusal to fuck him that last night. She'd pretended to be asleep, but Alistair knew it was an act. He knew she could hear him, that she realized what he was doing next to her in bed. He knew how disgusted it would make her.

Which was half the fun.

He realized then that Mary was staring at him.

"Time for what?" she said.

"I just told you, darlin'. Time to make Isabel pay."

TWENTY-THREE

SHE WAS SO shaken and frazzled—the call had awakened her only two hours earlier—and she'd used every spare minute in the early hours, before dawn, on the telephone, arranging for a Cutbank doctor to cover for her in her absence. She hadn't had time to put on any makeup whatsoever, or do anything with her hair. She told herself she regretted that fact only because she knew it would disturb her mother to see Isabel dressed in jeans and looking like she'd just rolled out of bed. It certainly wasn't because she happened to run into Monty Four Bear.

What were the chances they'd both be on the first flight that morning from Kalispell to Spokane?

What were the chances that when she rushed out onto the tarmac to climb into the small Dash 8—the single flight attendant having held the door open for her, their last-minute passenger—the only remaining seat on the plane would be next to him?

Upon looking up to see his new seatmate—for whom the plane had been held a good ten minutes—Monty's expression signaled that he was no less chagrined at this development than Isabel.

"Figures," he muttered.

"Pardon me?"

"Figures you'd be the one who kept us waiting."

Furious, Isabel pursed her lip, ready to launch her defense. But then she realized just how near to tears she was over the news that her mother had had a heart attack. Too close to trust herself by trading barbs with Monty Four Bear right now. She would not allow him to see her cry. And so, buckling her seat belt, she refrained from answering.

Isabel had always been a nervous flyer. In fact, she'd steadfastly refused to fly in anything less than a full-sized jet. But the only way to get to Seattle before noon was the little Horizon puddle-jumper that was now taxiing out to the runway.

As the propellers kicked in gear and the plane began its takeoff, Isabel gripped the armrests on either side of her.

Monty Four Bear looked up momentarily from his newspaper. When his eyes stopped to rest on Isabel's white knuckles, she instructed her fingers to release her grip, but they refused to cooperate.

The ascent out of Kalispell went smoothly, and by the time the flight attendant came along, Isabel had finally let go of the armrests. Isabel had been surprised to see a flight attendant on such a small plane. This one, older than most and decidedly more cheerful, stopped at their row and bent over Isabel's shoulder.

"Are you doing okay?" she asked with concern that was unquestionably genuine.

Isabel startled.

"Why, yes," she answered. "I'm fine."

"Good. I'm so sorry about your mother." She gave Isabel's shoulder a light squeeze. "You just let me know if there's anything we can do for you."

When Isabel called the ticket counter from her car, pleading with them to hold the seven A.M. flight so that she could get to the hospital in Seattle, where her mother lay in critical condition, she hadn't expected that that information would be passed along to the crew.

"Thank you. And thank you for holding the plane."

Red-faced, Isabel reached for the *Horizon* magazine in the seat pocket in front of her and began flipping through it. She could feel Monty Four Bear's eyes drifting her way.

"Your mother's ill?" he finally asked.

Isabel did not meet his eyes.

"Yes. I just got word she had a heart attack."

"I'm sorry."

"Thank you."

There was a pause.

"I'm also sorry for my remark about making the plane wait."

Isabel's eyes drew upward, toward Monty's.

"That's all right," she said, smiling involuntarily.

The smile seemed to disarm Monty, whose own eyes dropped quickly back to his newspaper.

The flight attendant had just served beverages—water for Isabel, V8 for Monty—when the plane suddenly began to shudder. As the pilot came on the loudspeaker and warned them they might experience "a little turbulence," the plane suddenly dropped out from under them.

Seconds later, Isabel had a lap full of water and an ironclad hold on both armrests.

"He'll get us out of this in no time," she heard Monty say.

She could only nod.

True to the pilot's promise, the plane soon leveled out. As if possessed of eyes in the back of her head, the flight attendant showed up almost immediately with a stack of paper napkins.

"Here you go, dear," she said, offering them to Isabel.

Isabel, by this point emotionally numb, simply nodded and took them. She set about pressing them against the large wet spots on her blue jeans, and it was while she was doing that that the tears began. Not many, not the all-out good cry she needed, but several big drops from each eye. She was grateful she'd not tied her hair back, for it shielded her face from Monty and made it impossible for him to see her.

Suddenly his hand came into her field of vision. It held a red bandanna. The kind movie cowboys tied over their mouths on a cattle drive.

"Thank you," Isabel mumbled, taking it and wiping dry each eye. For the rest of the flight, she did not look at him. She could not.

When the plane rolled to a stop in Spokane, where Isabel was scheduled to switch to an Alaska Airlines flight, she gathered up her bag and finally, with no small amount of effort, glanced Monty's way.

Most of the passengers stood, but Monty remained seated, seat belt still buckled.

"Aren't you getting off?"

He shook his head.

"I'm going on. To Moscow."

Moscow. The University of Idaho. A touch of curiosity arose in Isabel.

"Oh," she said. "Listen, I'll get this back to you." She raised the fist still clutching the bandanna.

"No need," Monty Four Bear replied.

Isabel stepped in line and, keenly aware of Monty's eyes on her, inched her way toward the plane's exit.

STEPPING BACK INSIDE the corridors of Harborview Medical Center, corridors she'd walked for more than six years, Isabel's body and mind switched involuntarily, unreasonably, into fight-or-flight mode.

Silently, eyes cast downward—she was in no mood for reunions—she headed for the elevators. Cardiac ICU was on four.

If anyone should have been prepared for what she would see when she entered the large room housing four beds, four critically ill patients, it should have been Isabel. Patients fresh from surgery, with tubes running from nose and mouth, neck, arms, and any other exposed surface. Overworked nurses, one for every two patients, huddling over a semiconscious form, checking monitors, listening. Always listening, needing to distinguish that one cough or groan that signaled one of his or her charges were in trouble. Monitors everywhere, mounted in each corner of the room for easy visibility.

And the smell. Isabel remembered that smell.

Isabel knew to expect it all.

But knowing and being prepared turned out to be two entirely different matters. As she entered 4A and stepped around the first partially drawn curtain, it was a wonder she even recognized Nada McLain.

Nada lay unconscious, tubes extending from her nostrils, both arms, and protruding from under the groin area of her hospital gown. A ventilator stood nearby. Nada's white hair, usually perfectly coiffed, lay flattened against her head. In repose, her features seem sunken and frail, much more frail than Isabel remembered.

Isabel eyed the monitor above the bed. Nada's blood pressure was low: 94 over 55.

"What are you doing here?"

Isabel turned. A young nurse with perfectly drawn brown lips stood eyeing her warily.

"I'm her daughter," Isabel said. "Isabel McLain." She did not preface her name with "Dr." "How is she?"

"She's had a rough night. She was only sent up here from her angioplasty five or six hours ago. We're planning to keep her sedated most of the day. It's unlikely she'll even know you're here."

Isabel had long ago learned to quickly peg a nurse. She had the utmost respect for nurses, and sympathy. They did the real grunt work, especially in surgical wards. But all the credit went to the doctors. She'd found that those nurses who stayed in the profession for any length of time were in it because they truly cared about the patients, not about glory or gratitude. But there were some with an attitude.

"I see."

"Maybe no one told you, but visiting hours are quite restricted in ICU. You're only allowed to be here from . . ."

"Dr. McLain? Is that you?"

Both women turned to see an anesthesiology resident standing in the doorway.

"Dr. Arati." Isabel smiled. "How are you?"

The young man, a handsome East Indian, stepped forward, extending his hand, his face all toothy grin.

"It's so good to see you," Dr. Arati said. "Last I heard you were running a clinic in Montana. This doesn't mean you've decided to return to us here at Harborview, does it?"

Isabel felt a flush of satisfaction at his obvious pleasure at seeing her.

"No. I'm actually here on a personal matter. My mother had a heart attack last night."

Dr. Arati's eyes roamed to the bed where Nada McLain lay.

"Oh, I'm so very sorry. How is she doing?"

Isabel looked at the nurse, straining to read her name tag.

"I was just asking . . . Kathy that very question."

Kathy's jaw jutted out defiantly as if to say *How the hell was I supposed to know she's a doctor?*

"She's stable for now. I'll be keeping a close eye on her."

"As will I," said Isabel.

"I'll check in on her also," Dr. Arati said in his formal, clipped English. "I'll leave you alone with your mother now, but I would love to buy you a cup of coffee when you're ready for a break."

"Thank you."

When Dr. Arati had departed, Kathy attempted to get back on track with Isabel.

"There are a couple chairs at bed three. Let me grab one for you." When she returned, she deposited the chair near the foot of Nada's bed.

"Feel free to stay as long as you'd like."

NADA MCLAIN CAME to only briefly, late in the evening. Isabel jumped up from her chair, bending low over her mother's shrunken form as she stroked her hair back off the shriveled forehead.

"Isabel?" Nada said weakly.

"Mother. I'm here. You just take it easy now. Okay?"

The corners of Nada McLain's thin lips lifted ever so slightly into a smile.

"You're a good girl, Isabel."

She mouthed it more than voiced it, but Isabel caught every word.

The new nurse on duty, Annette, whom Isabel took an immediate liking to, appeared instantly.

"I'm going to give her more sedative," she said. "Dr. Holmes wants her to stay as quiet as possible."

Isabel watched as she injected the clear liquid into the IV line running to Nada's elbow.

"You really should get some rest," Annette said to Isabel. "She's not going to open those eyes again until morning."

"I suppose you're right," Isabel said, stifling a yawn. She hadn't eaten all day and felt ready to drop. "Maybe I'll head to my mother's house to catch a few hours. I won't be much good to her tomorrow if I don't."

•   •   •

BUT BACK AT the house in which she'd grown up, a house in which she had not slept for over half a decade, Isabel found herself too overcome by nostalgia to sleep. She ate a bowl of cereal, then padded from one room to another, taking everything in. Over the years, she'd visited Nada and Tom at this house, and then Nada alone, but now, with both absent, she took everything in as if it were the first time she'd returned since childhood. The fireplace mantel lined with photos of Isabel as a child, Isabel in her teens, Isabel's graduation from college. Isabel and Alistair's wedding. Photos, mainly of Isabel, lining the stairwell to the second floor. In Nada and Tom's bedroom, more photos still. They were everywhere. And with each new photo she discovered, as if for the first time, the pain in Isabel's chest grew sharper.

It was like a shrine to Isabel. A heartbreaking shrine.

And what had she done to deserve such adoration? True, she'd been, in some ways, the "perfect" daughter. Good student, popular. Active in school. The pictures were testaments to the pride Nada took in those accomplishments and Isabel took some satisfaction, some consolation in being reminded of that.

Isabel may even have married Alistair in large part to please her parents, for both Nada and Tom McLain had shown more enthusiasm for Alistair than just about any other man she'd ever dated.

Wasn't that enough? Hadn't Isabel done enough to please her parents? Why did she feel so unbelievably guilty right now?

It was because, when it came down to it, even while she was achieving, and marrying, and becoming a doctor, just like her father, Isabel was rejecting her parents, her life with them. She resented it. Resented how wrong it all felt.

And finally, her actions had caught up with her innermost feelings and—despite the fact that she knew the effect it would have on Nada McLain—she had fled. Moved away. And not just away, but to a Montana reservation. Just as her father had done decades earlier.

How was that for gratitude? For making a statement?

Her bedroom looked exactly as it had the day she left for USC. Isabel took off her shoes and lay back on the pillows, studying the figurines Nada had collected for her—Lladro, which Isabel detested. There was a crack in the corner of the ceiling above her bed, where the plaster bubbled. The roof must be leaking.

Everything looked the same. Everything except the trunk sitting against the wall, underneath the window that looked out on Nada Mc-Lain's gardens, which were now overgrown.

Isabel rose and went to the trunk. She lifted its lid.

Inside were scrapbooks. She picked up the first one. The photos inside were all old and yellowed, but the scrapbook, like the trunk, was clearly new.

Nada McLain had been making scrapbooks of Isabel's life.

There were almost a dozen of them, along with yearbooks, programs from dance recitals, award certificates for good attendance. Letters Isabel had written home from camp.

What did Nada plan to do with all of it?

With a twinge of melancholy, the answer came to Isabel. Everything in the trunk related to Isabel. It was as if Nada knew that Isabel would never make the effort, never care enough to organize the mementos that symbolized her life.

The contents of the truck represented hours of labor on Nada's part. It was as if Nada feared that once she was gone, Isabel's history, their life together, would just cease to exist.

Nada McLain was preparing to die.

Isabel spent hours going through the photo albums and scrapbooks, one by one. Each one had been put together which such care, so much thought. Sitting on her bed, legs crossed, Isabel stepped back in time, and she realized something. That there had been good times. Many of them. For some reason, she'd thrown them away, like worthless trash, but now, before her eyes, she saw them. Relived them.

Finally drowsy, Isabel put the last of the scrapbooks back into the trunk. That's when she noticed it. Beneath all the scrapbooks and albums, a clear plastic file.

It contained documents of some sort.

Isabel could tell that much even before she lifted the flap and reached inside.

"I HEARD YOU were back in town," the voice cried from the hallway.

Isabel pulled her eyes off of Nada McLain's pained features—even in her sleep, Isabel could tell her mother was in agonizing pain—and looked toward the door.

"Candace," she said, rising to give the director of human resources a hug.

"I'm sorry about your mother, Isabel," Candace said, throwing both arms around her. Isabel took a deep, shaky breath, inhaling Candace's perfume, which had always reminded Isabel of Nada's cherished rose gardens. "The whole staff is praying for her."

"Thank you," Isabel said, pulling back to face the disarmingly vivacious Candace.

"Is there anything we can do for you? Have you seen the chaplain?"

"Yes, he's been here. I think she's getting excellent care and I appreciate that." Isabel lowered her voice. "According to Dr. Holmes, her heart suffered massive damage. It may just be beyond repair."

Candace Abrahams reached out and squeezed Isabel's hand.

"Page me if you need anything. Anything at all."

"Okay," Isabel said, turning back to Nada, who had begun stirring.

"Isabel?"

The voice was cracked and dry, like Nada's poor lips, to which Isabel had gently been applying Vaseline.

Isabel lowered herself on to the bed next to Nada's tiny form and took her hand.

"Right here, Mom."

"I'm so happy you're here, honey." The words came slowly. "Thank you for coming."

Isabel swallowed against the lump in her throat.

"Of course I came, Mom. I love you."

Nada's fingers curled around Isabel's palm and squeezed.

"I want to tell you something, Isabel," she whispered.

"You just rest now, Mom. We can talk later."

"No," Nada's head rolled from side to side in protest. "This . . . has . . . to be . . . said."

A nameless terror gripped Isabel.

"You shouldn't strain yourself, Mother. I want you to relax now. Please."

"I loved you so much, but in some ways, I wasn't a very good mother."

The fear escalated when Isabel realized that Nada's voice came out in the thinnest of whispers as much by choice as necessity. She did not want the nurse to hear her.

"Stop that," she scolded. "You were. You were a wonderful mother."

"But I did you such a grave disservice, Isabel. I should have told you . . ."

Isabel could not bear to hear the words.

"Mother, you must stop this right now. You listen to me. I love you dearly. I could not have loved you more." Isabel's tears began falling freely, on to Isabel and Nada's clasped hands. "You gave me a wonderful life. You did what you thought was best for me. I'll be grateful to you forever for that."

As she studied her sobbing daughter, Nada McLain's eyes suddenly took on a clarity. And in that moment, Isabel knew her mother understood what Isabel was trying to tell her.

"I was afraid I'd lose you, like I lost your father," Nada's whisper was fading fast.

"You didn't lose Dad, Mother."

"Yes . . . I . . . did . . . long . . . ago."

Isabel could not stop the tears.

"Sleep now, Mother. Sleep."

As Nada McLain closed her eyes, Isabel leaned over to kiss her forehead. Then she whispered into Nada's ear.

"I love you, Mother. I love you so much."

A very small smile tilted Nada's once lovely mouth. She squeezed her little girl's hand.

And then she drifted peacefully away.

MORNING, BROTHER." CROUCHED in front of the fire, one hand raised over its flames for warmth while the other grasped a mug of steaming coffee, Monty Four Bear nodded at Clyde Birdseye as he emerged from the teepee.

His Cheyenne friend had slept in the blue jeans and flannel shirt in which he'd arrived the night before. A boldly striped blanket, wrapped around his shoulders, had since been added to the ensemble. Wild hair that had escaped its ponytail during the night, as well as only four hours of sleep, made Clyde look more ill-tempered than usual.

Monty studied him, imagining him as a warrior of years ago, awakening on the day of battle. The imagery worked.

"Pour yourself some coffee."

"Thanks," said Clyde, reaching for the blackened aluminum kettle perched on a rock at the edge of the fire. "*Shit*. Colder than a polar bear's toenails out here."

Monty grinned.

"Springtime in Montana."

Just the day before, the mountain passes had been closed and showers in the valley had come in the form of coin-sized snowflakes. Still, there had been several mild stretches of weather over the winter, enough for WRI to move in equipment and erect chain-link fencing around the first drill site.

Actually drilling two thousand feet into frozen earth would be another matter though. WRI's exploration in earnest had had to wait for spring. But despite outward appearances, spring had now come and today's date had been circled for a good long while on many a reservation calendar.

For this was the day that WRI's drilling was to begin.

Monty had also put the time since the tribal council meeting to good use. Lulled into a false sense of security by the lack of further visible opposition to the mine, WRI had never even given consideration to posting a guard at the site, which enabled last night's execution of Monty's months of planning to go off without a hitch. During the night, three teepees—two canvas and one buffalo hide—had been assembled in front of the fenced entrance to the drill site. Now, as Bobby Lighthouse's drum punctuated the predawn sky, the hardy souls who had slept in the teepees were beginning to stir.

"What time are the rest due?" Clyde asked, using his coffee mug to cover a toothy yawn.

"Soon," Monty answered, reaching for a stick. He poked at the coals on the perimeter of the firepit, rolling them back into the flames, while Clyde, fueled by caffeine, slowly came to life.

"So what's going on with that class action?"

Monty shook his head.

"Did I ever tell you about what Sky Thomas said at that meeting we had?"

"Who's Sky Thomas?"

"The oldest living Blackfeet. A visionary. Sky was at the trust affairs meeting. She told us trouble was coming. That we should hold off on the suit until the trouble passed."

"And you let her change your plans?" Birdseye snorted in amusement.

"When Sky talks, I listen. Wasn't long after that meeting that the hantavirus killed three of our people. Anyway, I've started some preliminary discovery. Maybe this summer, after we shut this baby down, I'll actually have time to get the suit filed."

"Hell, even if we get this thing shut down by then, there'll be another mine, or someone murdered, or *something* to keep you too busy to get to your lawsuit."

"You know the problem with you?" Monty said, tossing his stick at Clyde good-naturedly. "You're always so full of good cheer."

Birdseye chuckled.

"It's early. Wait 'til I warm up."

Suddenly a pair of lights drew both men's eyes to the horizon. A vehicle was approaching from the south. Soon several other vehicles followed. The two stood, watching the vehicles' progress in a silence punctuated by the drumbeat and increasing activity around the tents. As the first vehicle neared, they could see it was the bus Monty had arranged. It would be filled with students from Monty's classes.

"Just in time for the sunrise ceremony."

Several protesters had begun dancing around the fire to the beat of Bobby Lighthouse's drum. Monty and Clyde stepped in line, their feet stomping the ground slowly at first, gracefully, their heads bobbing with the rhythm. As bodies filed down from the bus and other arriving vehicles, the loosely formed circle grew.

In a low, strong voice, Clyde began to chant the words to the Cheyenne Sun Dance Song.

E ya ha we . . . ye he ye ye
He ye . . . ho we . . . ye whi ye ye
E ya ha we . . . ye he ye ye
He ye . . . ho he we . . . ye hai i yi hi ha

Monty could not help but thrill at the experience of gathering with his brothers and sisters, dancing rhythmically at the first light of day, as they prayed for the protection of their sacred lands. The rocks, water, and all living things. Sunrise was the most powerful time of day, a time when prayers would be most far-reaching. Monty prayed for wisdom and strength, for the ability to influence the day's outcome.

He . . . yi ha i . . . ya ha ya ya
Ha ai ya ha ai yo yu ai ye ye
Ha ai ya ho ho o ya
Ho ai ho ho ho . . . o ya
He ye he a ya

The dancers continued for almost ninety minutes. As the sun began its climb up the distant slopes of the mountains, the ceremonial firekeeper, Victor Green, walked around the human circle, cleansing each participant with smoke from a sage bundle. Then he offered each a pinch of sacred tobacco.

A large crowd had by now assembled in the camp, with as many watching the dance as participating. There was a festive atmosphere, with food and drink passed around freely. Monty knew most of those present. Some had come from as far away as Nevada, where Monty had placed a call to the Shundahai network for support. Many of those faces were new to him.

As Monty took the tobacco given him by Victor and threw it into the fire, something drew his eye to where two non-Indians stood, several yards away from the circle, observing. There were other non-Indians—strangers—in the crowd that had come up from Nevada. But these two Monty recognized. He had seen the man before. An old rancher who'd lived in the valley forever. Monty couldn't remember the rancher's name right now, but he knew his ranch, just off the reservation, along the Two Medicine.

And his companion. He had not seen her since his trip to give a guest lecture on Indian activism at the University of Idaho.

Before he had a chance to look away, she'd caught sight of Monty, and for the briefest of moments, he found himself staring into the eyes of Isabel McLain.

•   •   •

ALL WINTER LONG, Tony Wilderman thought the silence too good to be true. Monty Four Bear and Clyde Birdseye—he'd made sure to familiarize himself with the names after the tribal council meeting—had impressed him as serious, perhaps even violent, activists. Too serious to let the proposed drilling go forward without further resistance.

Still, the sight that met Tony and his crew's eyes upon rounding the last bend in the gravel road leading to the drill site left Tony's fleshy jowls resting on his even fleshier neck.

"What the fuck?"

Tony, driving the lead truck, slowed to a crawl.

Ahead, the only part of the equipment he'd installed over the winter that was visible were the tops of the rigging poles. The fence, tractors, and red canvas lean-to had been swallowed by the crowd. There had to have been a hundred gathered there, directly in front of the only entrance to the drill site. Maybe more.

If Tony hadn't known better, he'd think he'd stumbled, uninvited, upon a party, so festive the scene appeared. But Tony knew better. And three teepees, plus the reaction of the crowd upon its recognition of WRI's vehicles, left little room for doubt as to the purpose of the gathering.

Two hundred yards from the group, Tony stopped his truck. The three vehicles behind him followed suit. Stepping out, his eyes trained on the scene in front of him, Tony could hear the approaching footsteps of his workers.

"We're not goin' in there, are we?" one asked.

"You told us those Indians approved the drilling," another added.

Tony peeled his eyes off the scene awaiting them and bore them instead into the men assembled behind him.

"Calm down," he ordered. "Do you hear? You sound like a bunch of old women."

The last of the crew, Rod Sokaski, a six-foot-three, broad-shouldered ex-hockey player from Calgary, had just approached the rest of them from the last truck. Rod had played for five years for the Vancouver Canucks. Now he was the star of Calgary's recreational league.

"It don't bother *me* to go in there," Rod said, spewing chewing tobacco through the gap in his front teeth that used to house his upper right canine. "I'll beat the shit out of anyone who tries to stop me."

The others, stung by Wilderman's rebuke, made halfhearted noises of agreement, although it was clear no one but Rod felt exhilarated by the sight of the protestors.

Reaching into the truck, Wilderman grabbed his cell phone and dialed 911.

"We've got trouble at the WRI drill site. You better get some of your people out here."

"What kind of trouble?" the operator wanted to know.

"Demonstrators blocking the site."

"Has there been any violence?"

"No."

"Has anyone threatened violence?"

"No."

"Are you certain this is an emergency?"

"It will be just as soon as we get back in our trucks and drive onto the site."

"Just where is the drill site located?"

Wilderman let out a sigh of exasperation.

"On the Blackfeet reservation. The tribal police know where. Get someone out here. *Now.*"

He threw the phone back into the truck and turned to assess the situation.

The road leading to the gate of the enclosed area was blocked, not only by protestors bearing banners, but a large teepee painted with murals had also been erected dead-center in the road. Several protesters were dressed in traditional Indian war bonnets. Upon seeing the WRI vehicles, the festivities had stopped and the group had begun forming a human chain around the fenced area. The fact that they'd succeeded in circling the entire site told Wilderman that, if anything, he'd underestimated their numbers.

From this distance it was impossible to identify any of them, but Wilderman knew he would find Monty Four Bear and Clyde Birdseye among them.

"Climb back in your trucks," Wilderman ordered.

"We're going in there?" one of the men said tentatively.

"You bet your sweet ass we are."

"*All right,*" Rod Sokaski exclaimed.

With Wilderman's WRI-logoed truck in the lead, the convoy started back up.

The protesters, hand in hand, had begun chanting.

We . . . will . . . protect . . . our . . . land.

As Wilderman's truck inched forward, displaying no sign that its occupant would allow the human wall to deter him, reinforcements positioned themselves in front of the section of the human chain that blocked the road. In just seconds, Wilderman was making eye contact with them.

With only yards separating the protesters and the truck, Monty Four Bear stepped into the gap between them. Crossing his arms over his chest, Four Bear braced himself and glared at Wilderman, daring him to proceed.

Motherfuckin' Indian. I oughta just run you down and get rid of you once and for all.

Wilderman was considering doing just that when sirens filled the air.

With the approaching tribal police car in his rearview mirror, Wilderman braked.

Wouldn't do to run someone over in front of the police.

Instead of toning things down, the arrival of the police and the proximity to Wilderman and his crew, who were all alighting from their vehicles, agitated the crowd.

Wilderman had just turned to yell instructions to his men when something large and wet hit him in the back of the head. His hand shot up to his scalp and came back full of smashed tomato.

Laughter and shouts rose from the crowd.

This was the final straw for Rod Sokaski, who charged into the crowd. *"I'll kill you sons of bitches."*

Several of the WRI men had been holding back. One had even jumped back in his truck. But Rod's daring inspired two others, who followed, fists swinging, in Rod's path.

A free-for-all broke out, and the lone officer who'd responded to the 911 call seemed helpless to stop it. Wilderman saw him run back to his car to radio for reinforcements.

Wilderman kept his head down and plodded forward slowly through the crowd, keys to the gate in hand. Most of the attention seemed to be directed now toward Rod and his coworkers. Many of the activists were trying to stop those that had stepped into the fray, but passions ran high, and even if one protester was persuaded or physically restrained from striking out, another stepped in.

Rod Sokaski had taken on two and three Blackfeet at a time. Blood dripped from his nose and a gash above his left eye, but he showed no sign of surrender. Fueled by memories of many a ruckus on the hockey ice, Rod continued charging the crowd like a bull.

Wilderman could no longer see any of his other men, though waves of activity and shouts hinted that at least one had ended up on the ground.

Wilderman had one goal in mind.

Opening the gate to the drill site. No motherfucking Indian was gonna stop him from doing what he'd come here this morning to do.

Pushing his way through the outer perimeter of the crowd, he finally saw it. The chain lock on the gate. He'd just extended his hand to reach for it when someone jumped him from behind. His assailant on his back, Wilderman fell to the ground, where the two men twisted and grunted, his attacker clinging like a monkey to him, preventing Wilderman from being able to land a single blow. Maintaining a tight grasp on the ring that held the key to the lock, Wilderman had just managed to break his parasitic attacker's ironclad hold on him when a heavy boot came down on his wrist.

Wilderman's eyes followed the worn cowboy boot skyward to see Monty Four Bear's cold black eyes staring down at him.

"I'll take these," Four Bear said, bending to take the key ring.

At the tightening of Wilderman's grasp, Four Bear stomped down harder on the wrist, which felt to Wilderman like it might shatter. Reflexively, his fingers opened and Four Bear grabbed the keys.

At that moment, the first shot rang out.

BUD WOLFKILL AIMED his .45 skyward, away from the crowd and into the distance, and pulled the trigger. He'd just been clocking out at the station after another night shift when the call from Jason Prather came in. Prather needed reinforcements out at the WRI drill site.

By the time Bud arrived, a wild brawl—worthy of the reputations of both Montana and the Blackfeet reservation—was underway. Prather, fresh from the criminology program at the University of Montana, was so green he hadn't even broken up a good bar fight yet. He scuttled from one fisticuffs to the next, breaking protester from miner, but without assistance, he felt helpless to make any arrests.

The crowd barely noticed Bud's sirens as his squad car squealed to a halt, raising a cloud of dust.

But all heads turned at the blast of the .45.

"Next jackass that throws a punch gets a free ride to jail."

For a moment, the crowd seemed inclined to comply with Bud's command, but then a rock sailed overhead, shattering the windshield of a white truck bearing the WRI logo, and once again all hell broke loose.

Grabbing Officer Prather by the arm, Bud had to yell in his ear to be heard.

"Who the fuck started this?"

"Don't know," Prather, wild-eyed, answered.

"Indians or miners?"

"Far as I could see, they've both done their fair share."

Frustrated, Bud snapped, "Well, don't just stand there. Arrest someone."

He watched as Prather approached a miner who was on the ground, surrounded by protesters. Prather looked back, uncertain as to who Bud wanted him to arrest. Bud pointed at an Indian about to boot the downed miner in the rear end. Prather grabbed the offender by the elbow, jerking him around. The Blackfeet protester's fists came up, and in the instant before they connected with the fresh-faced officer's jaw, Bud fired another shot into the air.

"You don't wanna do that, Riley. Assaulting an officer, resisting arrest. Assault and battery on that fella you been kickin'. Be a long while 'fore you'd be back home with Tana and the kids."

Riley glared at Prather, then dropped his fists. Prather promptly snapped a pair of handcuffs on them.

The gunshots and arrest had finally succeeded in capturing the attention of the crowd.

"The rest of you," Bud roared, "I can fit three of you in my car, and three in Junior here's car. Who's next?"

More fists fell, as did one or two rocks. The WRI employee on the ground rose slowly, brushing dirt off his shirt sleeves and jeans.

Bud surveyed the crowd.

"Where you at, Monty?" he called.

"Here."

The voice came from the back of the gathering.

The protesters split as Wolfkill strode toward the fenced enclosure.

Bud found Wilderman and Monty Four Bear in front of the gate, standing side by side—though from the looks of Wilderman's clothes, he had recently spent a little time on the ground.

"What the hell's going on here?" Wolfkill demanded to know.

"We're just demonstrating our opposition to the mine, that's all," Monty said. "Nobody's breaking any laws."

"Since when's it legal to destroy property and break noses?"

"You're right. Destruction of property isn't legal. Trouble is, I don't know who threw that rock, and I doubt very much if you know either, Bud. And as for breaking noses, even demonstrators have the right to protect themselves."

Wilderman's face turned a bright red.

"That's the biggest crock of shit I ever heard."

Monty Four Bear smiled.

"Your gorilla threw the first punch. Everyone here saw it. What happened after that was self-defense."

Wilderman turned to Wolfkill.

"Are you gonna let this . . ." both Monty and Bud waited for the racial slur, but Wilderman came to his senses before continuing. "Are you gonna let *him* get by with this? This bullshit about self-defense? Me and my men were just trying to go to work. To do the job your tribal council gave us permission to do. And this is what we have to put up with."

Bud looked both men over, then answered in his usual unhurried manner.

"Monty's right about one thing. No law against demonstratin'. And this is reservation land, so there's been no trespass. If Monty's tellin' the truth and your man threw the first punch, I'm not sure any of his people broke the law."

"What about my truck's windshield?"

"You might have something there, if you could identify who threw that rock."

"You know damn well I can't identify who threw it. It came from the crowd."

"Pretty hard to arrest a whole crowd. Don't got enough cells to hold 'em."

Wolfkill turned to Monty.

"Monty, like it or not, you're gonna have to let these men get in there and do their job."

"We *can't* get in," Wilderman said. "Not without keys to my truck and the gate."

"Where's the keys?"

Wilderman glared at Monty Four Bear.

"*He* took them. Then he threw them back into the crowd."

Bud had to stifle a grin at this revelation.

He turned back to the crowd, a large section of which had gathered around the three men.

"Okay, who's got the keys?"

This inquiry was met with looks of surprise and shoulder shrugs that proclaimed innocent ignorance.

As Wolfkill stood waiting for someone to cough up the keys—or at least giving the appearance he was waiting for someone to cough up the keys, for in reality, he knew that the chances of that happening were somewhere between slim and none—his attention was drawn to a commotion near the center teepee.

Breaking back through the crowd, Bud approached the teepee, where a heated argument was taking place.

Isabel McLain was ministering to a big bloke of a man, who had blood spouting from a three-inch gash on his forehead. The man sat propped up against one of the teepee's support poles. Isabel's medical bag was open on the ground, next to her patient, while she rummaged through it.

Standing over them was a very angry Clyde Birdseye.

"What do you think you're doing?" he railed at Isabel. "What the hell are you doing helping him?"

At first, Isabel refused to acknowledge Clyde, but when he tried to grab the bandages she'd finally located, she flew into him.

"*Get your hands off me.*" One errant strand of black hair hung over Isabel's dark eyes—which surprised Bud with the intensity of the hatred they bore for Birdseye. "Don't you dare interfere with my treating this man."

Clyde turned to face the protesters gathering around them.

"See. She's one of them. I knew it. Are you really going to trust this woman with your lives? Take your kids to her when they're sick? Allow her to vaccinate you as part of some perverted experiment on Indians?"

Bud could see Isabel's hands shaking as she stood to face her accuser.

"I came today to protest the mine," she said. "I don't want this mine on the reservation any more than you do. But that doesn't mean I will sit by and allow an injured man to go untreated. Now get out of my way before I ask Sheriff Wolfkill to arrest you."

Bud hadn't seen her until now. If he had, he'd have escorted her right to his car, out of harm's way. But as bodies parted at the frontline of the onlookers, a frail Sky Thomas, bent nearly double over her cane, stepped forward.

"What makes you think she's not one of us?" Sky barked angrily at Clyde Birdseye.

"One of us?" Clyde hooted. "You crazy old . . ."

Wolfkill grabbed his arm and stopped him.

"That's enough, Clyde," he said. "You show Sky some respect. And let this lady do her job. Now get out of here."

NOTHING COULD HAVE surprised Isabel more than the sight of a yellow taxicab sitting in the driveway of her cabin when she returned home from the protest. She hadn't even known there were cabs in Browning. One look at the door of this one and she saw it had come all the way from Kalispell.

As Isabel pulled into her driveway behind the cab, blocking it, a back door opened. A tall, dark woman with strong features and stylishly short hair emerged.

"K. T.," Isabel called, jumping out of her truck.

K. T. Seinberg didn't walk, she flowed. The effect was enhanced by her tendency to wear long, loose skirts that hid the fact that, with a sixty-hour work week, she spent more time lunching with clients than working out. The two women embraced.

"My God, Isabel, you told me you'd moved to the country, but this is ridiculous."

"How did you find me?"

K. T. lowered dark sunglasses to the tip of her nose and eyed Isabel over their frame.

"I practically had to bribe that damn assistant of yours. She wouldn't give me the time of day until I convinced her I was actually your attorney and that I was here to help you."

Isabel let out a brief laugh.

"Suzanne can be a force to reckon with. It's wonderful to see you, but I have to say, I'm more than a little surprised."

"Listen, dearie, this isn't a social call. Let's go inside. I have news for you."

"News that you didn't want to deliver over the telephone."

"That's right."

With a sense of dread, Isabel steered K. T. up the path to the cabin's front door. Isabel ignored the shock that registered on her attorney's face upon seeing the modest accommodations.

"Should I make us some tea?" she offered.

"Right about now I could use something a little stiffer than that."

"I think I have a cheap pinot."

"Let's open it."

Isabel had finally mastered the woodstove so that she could leave for the better part of the day without it burning completely out. Keenly aware of K. T.'s penetrating gaze, she opened its door, threw two pieces of wood on the bed of coals, unwound the damper to let it stoke up. Then she went to the cupboard above the sink and located the bottle of pinot noir.

"That's how you heat this place?" K. T. asked.

"That plus the fireplace."

"Who cuts the wood?"

"My landlord usually does, but if I'm home, I help him."

Isabel's curiosity was killing her, but still, she did not ask the question hanging in the air.

They each took a sip of the wine she'd poured.

"You ever miss Seattle? Or your old house?"

Isabel smiled.

"You're not doing a very good job of hiding your shock."

"I'm not trying to."

"No. I don't miss my old house at all. And for the most part, I don't miss Seattle either. In fact, the longer I'm here, the more I begin to suspect that I was never actually happy there. Even before Alistair."

"That's sad."

"Yes. It is." It was Isabel's turn to stare now. "But I am happy now, K. T. Truly happy. Not in some fairy tale kind of way, but in a very basic way. It's not something I can explain."

K. T. did not respond, instead she stared at the jelly jar holding her wine.

"As I said, I have news. News that I wanted to deliver in person." She raised her eyes to Isabel's. "You have become the subject of a criminal investigation by the FDA."

CHAPTER

TWENTY-FIVE

SABEL'S HEAD SNAPPED back.

"For what?"

"Conspiracy to commit fraud in a number of clinical trials."

"This must be some kind of joke."

K. T. Seinberg reached across the table and grabbed Isabel's hand.

"I'm sorry, Isabel. But it's no joke. The drug companies were willing to turn their heads to what was going on with Alistair's trials, but the FDA came in. They've had half a dozen agents scrutinizing all of his records. It didn't take them long to see a pattern with the patients Alistair was enrolling in the different trials. Many of them had been patients of yours in the ER shortly before enrolling in his studies."

"You mean it wasn't just Bernice Hougham? There were more?"

K. T. nodded her head.

"Quite a few more."

"But how could he have known who my patients were? How is that even possible?"

"According to Alistair, you gave him that information. Routinely."

Isabel yanked her hand loose from K. T.'s, spilling her wine across the table as she did so.

"That's ridiculous. I was the one who turned him in. As soon as I learned about Bernice."

"That's what I've told them."

"You've been talking to them?"

"They came to me looking for you. Listen, Isabel, if you didn't give Alistair that information, he had to have gotten it some other way. How? How else could he have known your patients? I mean, he contacted most of them at home. He had their addresses. He wrote them a letter introducing himself as your husband. Saying you'd provided their names to him because you believed they stood to benefit from whatever clinical trial it was he was trying to get them to sign up for. How could he have gotten that information?"

Isabel had the childish urge to press her hands to her ears and scream gibberish, anything to block out what she was hearing.

"I don't know," she finally said. "I simply don't know."

• • •

"Fancy meeting you here."

Tony Wilderman looked up from the fax he'd picked up at the front desk on his way down to breakfast. After yesterday's riot at the drill site, half the crew had requested reassignment. He'd called WRI's headquarters first thing this morning and asked to be faxed a complete list of all WRI field workers. He'd been going down the list of names and addresses, checking off those who'd requested transfers, and drawing stick-figure stars next to those who were already on the Blackfeet crew and willing to stay, and those men he knew personally from other crews around the world.

"Dr. Bott," he said. "I didn't expect to see you back here again so soon."

"I'm developing a bit of a fondness for this place, even if they don't serve grits," Alistair Bott grinned. "Mind if I join you?"

"Of course not. I could use some company."

As Bott settled in, he signaled the waitress.

"I heard about what happened yesterday," he said, "out at your drill site. Ugly business."

"You got that right. Fucking Indians. And the damnedest thing is that the tribal police say they've got a right to be there. They've been no help at all."

"What do you expect from their own people? Sounds like you're in a bit of a bind."

"Bit of a bind?" Wilderman scoffed. "It's a hell of a lot worse than a bind. WRI's had big expectations for that mine." He refrained from telling Bott that LeCoque, furious at yesterday's turn of events, had told Wilderman the company's future may well rest on the Montana deposit. "It just burns me up to think a bunch of Indian radicals might put an end to those plans."

"Surely you don't intend to capitulate?" Bott said, an expression of shocked disapproval on his face. "I mean, if it were me, I'd fight fire with fire."

The waitress had arrived with coffee and orange juice.

"Mornin', Alistair," she cooed, sliding a menu to him. "Be right back for your order."

"Fight fire with fire?" Wilderman repeated. "We tried that yesterday. I've got one real goon on the crew who went ape-shit on those Indians. Used to be a hockey player on the Vancouver team. The rest of my men were scared shitless by the time all was said and done, but I swear to God, Rod got off on it. But all *that* did was turn the tribal police against us. They told us we were there as the Indians' guests. That the protesters had every right to be there too. And that if we used violence again, we'd be arrested and charged."

"Now, you obviously can't count on the local police." Bott's "police" came out POE-leece. "Maybe you just need to be a little more covert in dissuading these troublemakers."

"I'm not following you."

"Let me tell you something. As you may have guessed, I'm from the South. Now, my daddy, he wasn't exactly a role model, but I do have to give him credit for teaching me some things. Especially about getting by in the real world. You see, Daddy was a Klansman . . ."

"The Ku Klux Klan?" Wilderman made no attempt to disguise his shock.

"That's right. Nasty business, that Klan stuff. As I said, my daddy wasn't exactly my hero. But you have to give the Klan one thing. They knew how to silence their opponents. Some fire-breathin' liberals'd come to town, tryin to stir up trouble," as he talked, Bott seemed to slip back into time, into a lazier drawl, "and the Klan, they knew how to shut them right up. Those folks are all hot air. Daddy always said it just took findin' their weakness—he never said it, but I always knew what he meant, their wives, or kids—and they'd back down real quick-like."

Bott slipped back into the present and smiled. He could have been talking about the weather, so matter of fact was he over this disclosure about his past.

"You find the ring leaders, and give them a little of what they gave you and your men yesterday," he finished. "I promise you, you'll be back in business in no time."

Wilderman thought about what the doctor from Seattle seemed to be suggesting. When the waitress returned to take Bott's order, he studied him. He was an odd bird. Dressed to the nines all the time. Refined acting. Yet what he was suggesting was not only illegal, someone could easily end up getting hurt.

The waitress took Wilderman's empty plate and headed toward the kitchen with Bott's order.

"What did you say that ex–hockey player's name was?" Bott asked casually.

"I didn't say."

Bott laughed then.

"That's right. You didn't."

WHILE ISABEL, THROUGH K. T. Seinberg, had been the one to request the meeting, it soon became clear that it would only have been a matter of time before the FDA investigators came looking for Isabel.

K. T. had requested that the meeting be held away from Browning. They settled on Kalispell, where they rented a conference room at the Outlaw Inn.

Isabel and K. T. agreed to get together that morning, in K. T.'s room, to discuss what to expect. K. T. had ordered room service. With their breakfasts eaten, they finally got down to business.

"Here's how I see it," K. T. began, pacing back and forth as she spoke, while Isabel, seated near the open window, focused on staying calm. Isabel always sensed that her attorney hated seeing her clients in trouble but relished the actual battle. K. T.'s energy this morning declared her primed for their meeting.

"Ever since those congressional hearings last February got so much media attention—you know, the hearings called to look into deaths of patients in clinical trials—the FDA's been looking for a scapegoat. The pressure's on. Someone has to be held accountable. The NIH is blaming the FDA, and the FDA's blaming the NIH. The drug companies just want the whole thing to go away before it becomes impossible to recruit patients for their studies. Your ex-husband could hand them what they all want on a silver platter. A scapegoat. The villain who will take all the attention and pressure off the rest of this sorry lot."

"But what does that have to do with me?" Isabel replied. "I'm as outraged by what I've been reading about those poor patients as anyone else. If Alistair did what they think he did—what I suspected him of doing—he *should* pay. I want that as much as they do." She laughed then, a short joyless laughter. "Probably more."

"That's the problem. We may learn otherwise today, but from what I see, almost everything they have on Alistair is circumstantial. They're desperate to change that."

They spent half an hour discussing K. T.'s expectations and strategy, then left the room, heading for the meeting.

"They need someone who can drive the stake through Alistair's heart," K. T. predicted as they approached the conference room. "And they think you're that someone."

"WE ARE LOOKING at research fraud of audacious proportions," the lead FDA investigator, a small, pinched man by the name of Earl Wittren, started out. His cohort, a humorless, oversized Dane named Hans Thomasen, sat by his side, making notes. "Cutting corners, inventing data, fictitious patients. Failure to report study deaths. You name it."

"But I had nothing to do with that," Isabel protested. "Nothing."

"Dr. McLain, we are conducting an extensive investigation into the clinical trials conducted under the supervision of your husband."

"*Former* husband," K. T. Seinberg inserted.

"Former husband," Wittren conceded. "A cross-check of your ER patients and Alistair Bott's study participants seems to contradict your statement that you had no involvement."

"I never gave my former husband a single patient's name for his trials. I didn't even know he was so heavily involved in them until a couple weeks before I called the drug companies and told them of my own concerns."

Wittren's sparse eyebrows shot up.

"You never mentioned your patients to Dr. Bott? Not even in conversation? After all," he said in a conspiratorial, almost lascivious tone, "you were husband and wife."

Isabel thought back to the night Bernice Hougham came into the ER. Alistair had waited patiently for her to finish with Bernice. And then, in the car on the way to the fund-raising dinner, he'd questioned Isabel about her patient's condition. And Isabel had provided answers.

"You're right. On occasion I probably did mention my patients. But only in casual conversation. And it happened so rarely."

"One doctor sharing information with her spouse, who also happens to be a doctor, does not constitute a crime," K. T. Seinberg said. "If you've got something of substance, fellas, let's hear it. Otherwise, both my client and I have better things to do."

Isabel actually found herself trying to stifle a smile. Leave it to her feisty attorney to threaten to walk out on a meeting they had called.

"Were you aware that your husband enrolled patients for studies who were taking medications prohibited by the study protocols?" Wittren pressed on.

"No."

"Were you aware that records were falsified according to the requirements of a particular drug study? For example, if a certain blood pressure was required for a patient to participate in a hypertension study and your husband had a willing patient, but that patient's blood pressure was too low or too high, the records would be falsified?"

"No."

"What do you know about urine your husband routinely paid for because it contained high levels of proteins—just the level needed for patients to qualify for one of his studies? Urine that was then falsely attributed to study participants? We actually have invoices issued from your husband's office for these purchases."

Isabel jumped to her feet, clenching an angry fist.

"I have *never, ever* in my entire career deliberately misrepresented or fabricated patient data. Nor have I ever knowingly put a patient in a position of danger."

K. T. had risen too and now placed a steadying hand on Isabel's forearm.

"Take it easy," she said under her breath. "Don't let them bait you."
She turned to the investigators.

"Are you implying that my client was the source of this urine?"

"No."

"Because if you are, maybe we can just settle this matter once and for all. With a urine sample. Because I don't understand what the hell this has to do with my client if you're not planning to accuse her of either providing this extraordinarily valuable urine or buying it. And you've already told us the invoices were from Bott's office. They had nothing to do with my client. What will it be, gentlemen? Would you like my client to provide you with a sample? Here and now?"

Both men turned red-faced and appeared too startled to respond.

"Let's stick to matters that directly involve my client, gentlemen. Or else cut this meeting short."

Wittren cleared his throat and stared at Isabel, waiting for her to take her seat again.

Slowly, Isabel lowered herself into it.

"Do you recall an ER patient of yours by the name of Alice Richards?" he asked.

"The name isn't familiar, but you have to understand, I had dozens of patients each shift."

Wittren took the paper handed him by Thomasen and began to read.

"Mrs. Richards came to the clinic after injuring herself—her knee—in an adult soccer game."

"May I see that?" Isabel asked, reaching for the paper.

Wittren hesitated, then pushed the document across the desk to her.

It took only seconds for Isabel to remember.

"Yes. I remember this patient."

"What was the diagnosis?"

"A partial tear of the anterior cruciate ligament."

"What treatment did you render?"

"It's here, in the file. I took an X ray. Prescribed anti-inflammatories. I sent her home with instructions to alternate hot and cold compresses."

"Did you recommend surgery?"

"No. I told her she should consult with an orthopod. Sometimes a slight tear will heal on its own, without surgery. I wasn't qualified to make that recommendation."

"Did you relay—during casual conversation—any of this information to your husband?"

"*No.*"

"You're certain of that?"

"Absolutely."

He glanced knowingly at Thomasen, who handed him another paper from the same file.

"Here is a sworn affidavit from Mrs. Richards," Wittren said, making no attempt to hide his glee. "It states that your husband contacted her at home just two days after her visit to Harborview's ER. Dr. Bott told her that you had suggested that he contact Mrs. Richards, that if she were lucky, she might just be a candidate for a study he was conducting on a new product that could stave off arthritis. He asked her to come to his office for a meeting.

"When Mrs. Richards arrived at his office, she attests to feeling pressured by your husband. He told her that an injury like hers almost always resulted in arthritis, oftentimes so severe it ultimately impaired one's mobility. As a very athletic young woman, Mrs. Richards was very concerned. Still, she had some reservations about the study, but your husband rushed her, forced a decision that very day by telling her they had only one spot left in the study. That he couldn't hold it for her and that she'd regret her decision for the rest of her life if she didn't act right then. Needless to say, she signed up."

Again, he slid his "evidence" against Isabel across the table toward her and K. T.

"As you can see in the affidavit, in addition to being frightened by the prospect of developing arthritis in that knee, Mrs. Richards stated that she didn't want to make either you or your husband mad."

"That's outrageous," Isabel cried.

"We agree."

"Does Mrs. Richards's affidavit claim that she had any direct contact with my client? Other than her visit to the ER?" K. T. Seinberg cut in.

"No."

"That's because she did not. My client knew nothing of any of this. She had no way of knowing her husband was contacting her ER patients and using her name—and the relationship she'd already established with the patients—as an introduction. And you can't prove otherwise."

"No, Ms. Seinberg," he finally said, "we do not have unequivocal proof of your client's knowledge or involvement. But just how do you think Alistair Bott obtained such sensitive information as this? Mrs. Richards's case is just one of dozens. If Dr. McLain didn't supply this information to her husband, then who did?"

He was speaking to K. T. Seinberg, but his eyes were trained on Isabel.

"Dr. McLain. We are willing to work with you. We may even be able to strike a deal with you, let you off the hook, if you agree to provide us with the proof we need to convict your husband."

"*Let me off the hook?*" Isabel practically hissed. "Aren't you listening? I haven't done anything wrong. Nothing. I'm the one who turned my husband in."

"We've talked to Dr. Bott. According to him, that was simply a clever but desperate attempt on your part to distance yourself from these studies. Your husband claims that you're the mastermind behind the whole thing. That he wanted to report the death of Bernice Hougham, but you refused. That when Bernice died, you became frightened and turned on him. He says you initiated contact with the pharmaceutical companies to throw us off, to make it look as though you were innocent. He also suggests that we keep a close eye on the study you're currently involved with."

Isabel was so stunned and enraged by the lies Alistair had fed them that she found herself speechless. Wittren continued.

"Dr. McLain, I ask you: Without hard evidence, just who are we supposed to believe?"

CHAPTER

TWENTY-SIX

ON THE ELEVENTH day of what had become widely known across the reservation as the Encampment, Monty and the half dozen remaining protesters awoke to the deafening roar of a helicopter, flying low across the draw between the two ridges.

On several occasions over the past week, WRI employees had ventured near the protesters' occupation zone, each time coming a little closer to the protesters themselves. They would sit in their trucks in silence, observing, then retreat. There had been no further confrontations or violence of any sort, which was beginning to get on Monty's nerves, because he didn't believe for one moment that WRI had reversed its decision to proceed with the drilling. They were playing some kind of a waiting game.

And Monty was not a patient man.

With the exception of two trips to Browning for supplies, Monty had not left the site. The initial adrenalin rush of battle had long faded and even the solace he derived from the traditional customs the protesters had agreed to observe—daily sunrise ceremonies, storytelling, and songs of war and victory—had been wearing thin. Until last night.

The mescal religion was an ancient Indian faith that had in the past few decades been revived and adopted by younger Indians. Mescal, or peyote, came from the tip of a cactus. The disk-shaped button induced a druglike effect that produced feelings of lightness and visions of beauty. It had been used for centuries for pain relief.

Two of the protesters still remaining at the drill site belonged to the Shundahai network. They'd come to Montana from Nevada, bearing a precious gift from the Southwest for their fellow activists.

Mescal buttons.

On the previous night, as darkness fell, the six brothers and one sister—all Native American—had entered the center teepee, where a fire was kept burning all night. Sitting cross-legged and blanketed in a circle around the fire, Monty, Clyde, and the other protesters each solemnly ingested one of the buttons. Heads bowed, some with blankets drawn over their heads to enhance the imagery, throughout the night each person took turns singing. Most of the songs contained no words, simply sounds that invoked that the truths of the universe be revealed to the singer. A small buckskin drum was passed around from one person to the next.

Monty had experienced a sensation of release, as though he were floating above the earthly troubles that had been sitting, like a wounded buffalo, on his shoulders. The fatigue brought on by a week of sleeping on the ground dissipated, and the anger and sadness that had filled his soul gave way to joy at visions of spectacular sunsets, glorious mountains, brooks singing to him of the power to heal.

As it was intended to do, the mescal ceremony helped Monty to see the road before him, to see the truths of life and the spirit. It renewed his hope.

And then, just before dawn, it lulled Monty and his brothers and sister to sleep.

Now the roar of a helicopter bearing a WRI logo had shattered that peace, and Monty's anger exploded skyward.

Grabbing a rock from the fire pit, Monty heaved it skyward at the passing helicopter.

"*Sons of bitches.*"

In a rare turn of events, the restraining hand on his shoulder turned out to belong to Clyde.

"No offense, bro, but you're no Joe Montana." He shouted over the helicopter's din, giving Monty's shoulder a short squeeze. "Don't let them rob you of the spirit, man."

Monty turned to face Clyde. The mescal ceremony still lingered on his prematurely lined face.

Monty ran both hands through hair that hung loose to his shoulders. The two stood watching the helicopter retreat.

"You're right," Monty said. "It's not like I thought they'd given up."

"No, we knew that wasn't gonna happen anytime soon. Looks like they've just decided to begin the aerial survey." Clyde paused. "Only way we'll stop that is firepower."

"No violence. We agreed."

"Not yet anyway."

They'd just finished breakfast—scrambled eggs, coffee, and toast, all cooked over the fire—when the patrol car pulled up.

Bud Wolfkill emerged slowly, an unusually serious expression on his round face. He approached the group, who were seated around the fire. It wasn't until he stopped in front of where Monty sat on a large rock, plate balanced on his knees, that Bud made eye contact.

"I've got some bad news, Monty," he said. "You better come with me."

THE HOSPITAL IN Cutbank was a nondescript brown brick affair that, at four stories, claimed honors as the highest building in town.

Monty followed Bud Wolfkill through the lobby and to the elevator. When it failed to come immediately, he scanned the corridor for an exit sign and, finding one, made a beeline for the stairwell.

"Meet you up there," he told Bud over his shoulder.

He took two and three stairs at a time.

A nurse had just left room 414 when he stepped into the hallway from the stairwell.

"How is he?" Monty called.

She turned his way. The nameplate identified her as Julie Watson, R.N. Up close, she looked too fresh-faced and young to be a full-fledged nurse. Maybe without the short bangs and pageboy cut of her chestnut hair.

"He's sleeping right now. We've got him on morphine. Are you a relative?"

"His son."

"You can go in, but please don't disturb him. Sleep is probably the most powerful medicine for him right now."

"When can I see the doctor?"

"I'll let him know you're here."

Slowly Monty pushed the door open. The first bed was unoccupied. A white cotton curtain had been pulled around the bed by the window.

Monty stepped around it.

Asleep, drugged, illuminated by the sunlight pouring through the window, Leroy Four Bear appeared to have shrunk to a fraction of his normal five-foot-eight self. His formerly straight and aristocratic nose—the feature of which he'd always been most proud—was, however, twice its former size and no longer traveled a steady course. His upper lip, in particular the left side, had also at least doubled in size. Over his right eyebrow, a three-inch gash had already been stitched.

Monty felt Bud Wolfkill's presence, but did not turn. It wasn't because he did not want Wolfkill to see his tears, but because he could not take his eyes from his father's beaten form.

He heard Wolfkill steal back out of the room, closing the door behind him.

Monty settled on to the window ledge, shading his father, and sat watching the clear liquid drip, one precise drop at a time, into the clear tubing that ran from the bag hanging over Leroy Four Bear's head to somewhere under the white sheet covering him. His father's breaths were short and shallow, like those of a small animal. He did not stir.

"Mr. Four Bear?"

Monty turned toward the door. A wiry, bald man with glasses, wearing a telltale white smock and stethoscope, gestured for him to follow.

Out in the hallway, Bud Wolfkill joined them.

"I'm Dr. Sharp. Your father is lucky to be alive. Aside from a broken nose and two fractured ribs, there are no broken bones. He was in a great deal of pain when he came in, which is why I've got him on morphine. Those injuries will just take time. I'm more concerned about internal injuries. And his concussion. The CAT scan shows a good-sized bruise on the brain. He sustained one hell of a blow. Or maybe a series of blows. But he was alert throughout his admission and the subsequent testing, so there's every reason to be hopeful that there's no permanent damage."

"You mentioned internal injury."

"Yes. Nothing showed up on the X rays or CAT scan, but there are a couple reasons I want to monitor him closely. First, his abdominal region is extremely tender. Considering the beating he took, this fact alone might not have that much significance."

The beating.

Monty had assumed Wolfkill had come to the drill site to arrest him, that WRI had finally managed to force the tribal police into action.

But when they'd climbed into the squad car, Wolfkill had turned to him with the news.

"It's about Leroy, Monty."

Luke had awakened in the middle of the night to the sounds of Leroy's screams. He'd rushed to his grandfather's bedroom, where a "giant" of a man with the crushed and distorted features of a monster stood over Leroy's limp form on the ground.

Luke had rushed the giant, pummeling him with his fists.

"Leave my grandpa alone."

With one swat, the giant had sent Luke flying.

"Out of my way, kid."

He'd reached down, grabbed Leroy by the shirt collar—Leroy always fell into bed in his clothes from the previous day—and pulled the old Indian's face up to within inches of his.

"You tell your son to back off," he'd said.

"Or I'll be back."

He'd kicked Leroy in the ribs, which sent Luke flying onto his back. "Fuckin' kid."

Luke rode him halfway down the hallway before being tossed into the wall. Shaken, but amazingly reasoned for what he'd just witnessed, Luke had returned to the bedroom to make certain Leroy was alive. When he determined he was, he'd run the quarter-mile to Edna's house to call 911.

"Where's Luke now?" Monty had demanded of Wolfkill. "How is he?"

"He wanted to go to school," Wolfkill had answered. "Tough little guy. Edna offered to have him stay with her tonight."

"No, he'll stay with me."

"You sure that's a good idea?" Wolfkill had responded.

It took Monty a second to get Wolfkill's point. If Luke wasn't safe at Leroy's, he certainly wouldn't be safe at Monty's house.

Monty could not afford to lose control. Not when Luke and Leroy needed him. But now, standing in the glare of the harsh hospital lights, hearing a doctor describe the injuries sustained by his sixty-nine-year-old father—as a result of Monty's actions—the anger and guilt threatened to explode into a hurricane that would rattle even Monty Four Bear.

"But in addition to the tenderness," Dr. Sharp continued, "your father's blood work, the hemoglobin in particular, is borderline. We'll monitor it, and his urine and stool for signs of internal bleeding. We'll be keeping him on IVs for several days."

"And if there is bleeding?"

"Then we'll operate."

"Is he in any kind of condition for that? For surgery?"

"If there's bleeding, we'll have no choice."

A NEW NURSE, Julie Watson's replacement for the night shift, kicked Monty out at precisely eight P.M. She and Monty had already butted heads over the fact that earlier that day they'd brought another patient into the room.

"There are plenty of empty rooms," Monty had complained at the nurse's station after his father's roommate had been there two hours. "I've seen them. There's one right next door. This guy's gonna keep my father up all night with his coughing. And he's got that goddamn TV up so loud it's hard to think. I want him moved."

Nurse Ratchet, as Monty had quickly nicknamed Julie's fiftyish, brusque replacement, gave him a look designed to intimidate. With the shoulders of a linebacker and wiry gray hair pulled back so tightly into a bun that her temples were stretched like a rubber band, the look really wasn't that difficult for her to achieve.

"Take it up with the administration office tomorrow."

Case closed.

Now, at Monty's resistance to leaving his father's bedside, she employed similar subtlety.

"Out."

Monty, still perched on the windowsill, looked at his father. Leroy had awakened several times during the day, usually when the nurses came in to take his blood pressure and make sure he hadn't lost consciousness from the head blows. Each time, he'd acknowledged Monty's presence with a look, or a word or two, but for the most part, he'd slept. A deep sleep—despite the short, shallow breaths, which Julie Watson explained were the result of the broken ribs. Even the simple act of breathing, she told Monty, would be painful for Leroy for a while.

Now Leroy's eyes, the left lid still puffy, opened again.

"Go home," he said softly. It obviously hurt to talk too. "I'm okay. Luke needs you."

"I just talked to him. He's at Edna's. He sounds okay."

"Go home. I'm juz gonna sleep. Come back tomorrow."

"You sure, Pop?"

" 'Course I'm sure."

Monty bent to kiss a leathery cheek. When was the last time he'd kissed—or even hugged—his father? He'd spent so much time these past few years—hell, most of his life—being angry with Leroy for letting the family down. Giving him a hard time about the booze. Wondering why he'd never even tried to get a job.

Monty flushed with sudden shame.

All that mattered was that Leroy was still alive. Monty would not take him for granted again.

"I love you," he said, standing there.

Leroy's eyes popped open again.

"Not gonna die on you, if that's what you're thinking."

The annoyance was feigned. Monty could tell the display of affection pleased his father.

Monty stopped in the lobby to telephone Edna and Luke again.

"I'm just leaving the hospital. Thought I'd stop by and check on Luke," he told Edna.

"Boy's already sleepin', Monty. I'd let him be."

"You'll call me if he needs me?"

"You bet."

"You got your doors locked, Edna?"

"We're locked in tight. And nobody gonna get within hundred feet of here with Grizz outside."

Grizz was Edna's rottweiler.

"Plus I've got that .45. Only good thing that no-good husband of mine left me. And I know how to use it."

"Okay, then. I'll stop by in the morning, take Luke to school."

"He'll like that."

The thirty miles to Browning passed in a blur. Monty's anger was beginning to take hold, get the best of him.

He mustn't let it. Intimidation of activists was not new to him. He even taught a short section on it in his lecture on activism. Telephone threats and harassment, arson, even violent assaults like the one on Leroy. He'd taught his students that they were a price an activist could end up paying. That they were intended to make advocates think twice before taking a public stand, or, as in this case, to force them to back down from a stance already taken.

It's not personal, he'd said. It's simply a political act committed by your opponents in an effort to silence you.

But Monty's father lying in a hospital bed was personal. Very personal.

When Monty pulled up to his small white frame house, two miles outside Browning, he sensed immediately that something was not right. It was dark by now, and hard to see the unlit house, but as he walked up the dirt path to its front door he put his finger on it.

The curtains in the living room had been drawn. Monty couldn't remember the last time he'd closed them.

Monty stood, silent, frozen on the cement stoop, listening.

Nothing.

Slowly, he reached for the doorknob. It took only a light touch for the door to creak open. He'd left it locked.

He stepped inside the darkened living room.

When Monty was a boy, Leroy used to tell him he would have made a good Indian scout, so fine-tuned were his senses. Now these senses told Monty the house was empty.

He reached for the light switch on the wall.

And saw that a storm had swept through the living room, upending furniture, smashing framed photographs of Monty's deceased mother and grandmother. The little black-and-white TV that formerly occupied a table in the corner lay in pieces against the far wall.

Monty strode past all of it, through the tiny kitchen that he could see had not escaped the assault, into his bedroom. He stepped over a lamp on his way to his desk. The digital clock, untouched, shed enough light for him to see that the space usually taken by his laptop now sat empty. His feet slid on loose papers scattered over the floor.

He reached for the desk lamp, then, unable to find it, returned to the lamp he'd stepped over. Fumbling to locate the electrical outlet in the dark, he managed to plug it in, but the bulb had been broken.

He retreated to the kitchen, where he found a new bulb.

He was angry about the stolen computer, but he knew that it would be next to impossible for anyone to penetrate the AIM files it contained. His biggest fear, he realized as he retraced his steps to the bedroom, concerned his paper files. They contained everything from research he'd conducted on WRI and other mining companies with bad environmental records, to pamphlets he'd prepared, to names and addresses of other activists. It was these, the identities of other activists, plus plans for further disruption of WRI's activities, that he most feared falling into enemy hands.

The light revealed that his filing cabinet had been literally torn apart in a search. One drawer hung open, the other lay next to the bed on its side. Every file had been perused. Papers—those apparently holding little interest—had been flung across the floor.

It took just minutes to determine that while many files had been perused, then left behind, several were missing.

His WRI and ImmuVac files. And the entire file on the BIA lawsuit.

"HOW YOU DOING today, Pop?"

"Better," Leroy grunted, barely audible over the *oohs* and *aahs* emanating from the wall-mounted television. On its screen, above the subtitle "I used to be a geek but look at me now," a curvy brunette strutted to the applause of an appreciative audience. She embraced Sally Jesse Raphael before settling seductively into her seat of honor.

Monty drew the curtain between Leroy and his roommate's bed, eliminating Leroy's view of the TV but giving the two of them more privacy. He cracked the window open half an inch, then settled in his seat on the sill.

Leroy's color did look better today. And while he'd remained flat on his back all the day before, he could sit up now, at least at the thirty-degree angle his nurse had raised his bed. But his face still looked as though he'd walked in front of a train. And he was still hooked up to an IV. Monty would have to ask the doctor about that.

"How's Luke?"

"Luke's fine. He's just worried about you, that's all. Edna is taking good care of him."

"Tell him not to worry 'bout me. I'll be home 'fore he knows it. He oughta just enjoy Edna's fry bread while he can."

Monty chuckled.

"I had a piece this morning when I picked Luke up for school. Hot off the grill. Edna's fry bread's somethin'."

"Enit? Maybe you can bring me some."

"You bet, Pop. I'll bring you some tomorrow."

They settled into silence, listening to Sally Jesse Raphael, but not really paying much attention.

"So what you gonna do about this?" Leroy finally said, turning to study his son.

Monty's gaze met that of his father.

Monty shrugged.

"I'm not sure."

He did not mention the fact that his house had been ransacked, most likely by the same person who'd broken into Leroy's house and attacked him.

"Putting myself in danger's one thing. This happening to you . . . well, that's different."

"Don't let them bastards get away with this," Leroy said, his anger causing him to lean forward suddenly. "That's just how they want you to start thinkin'. *Don't do it.*" Involuntarily, Leroy took a deep breath, which caused him to grimace. He beckoned Monty closer with his index finger.

"Get your ass back out there at that drill site," he whispered, "and raise hell. You hear me?"

Monty put his hand on his father's shoulder and managed a sad half smile.

"I don't know if it's worth it. Endangering you. What if they go after Luke next?"

Leroy raised a withered hand and reached for the collar of Monty's blue flannel shirt. Latching on to it, he pulled his son closer.

"You listen to me, boy." His words came in short, breathy stretches. "That's our land you're trying to protect. Blackfeet land. Nothing's more important. *Nothing.* You send Luke to Denver, to his mama. Then you get back out there. You hear me?"

The old fingers shook with emotion.

Monty curled his own hand around that of his father's.

"You sure about this?" he asked.

"Damn right, I'm sure."

TWENTY-SEVEN

ALL OF THE material had been packaged neatly in a cardboard filing box. Now he lifted the lid and withdrew the first of half a dozen files, the one labeled WRI.

Inside were personnel records, including employee names, phone numbers, addresses. A profile on Jon LeCoque gave the names of his wife, grown children, and two grandchildren. A picture of LeCoque's residence along with his yacht, *Chesire*, were even included, along with their addresses.

Tony Wilderman's impressive résumé included several awards garnered from the world and Canadian mining communities. Wilderman was credited with finding the company's two biggest money producers to date: the Krygyzstan mine and the Essiquibo mine. Wilderman's family history even included a special note about his Irish roots and his fondness for St. Patrick's Day.

He sat back momentarily, impressed. This clearly was not the product of one man working alone. Only a skilled and well-funded network could put this much information together.

He moved on to another file.

CLASS ACTION: BLACKFEET VS. BIA

Inside, lawyer names. Plaintiff's names. An unauthorized copy of something called the Morris Audit.

He thumbed through the twelve-page document, stopping to read the last page, which contained a summary of the independent audit's findings. It concluded that the BIA's recordkeeping was a joke. That the Indians had been cheated out of substantial amounts—perhaps even as much as $2.4 billion.

He let out a low whistle, then pushed the lawsuit file aside as another file caught his eye.

IMMUVAC STUDY

He reached for it.

The first page he opened to was a stapled document entitled HUMAN GUINEA PIGS. He began to read.

Vaccines couldn't be trusted, it proclaimed. Too many were contaminated: the polio vaccine, contaminated with a simian virus, had caused hundreds of thousands of deaths from cancer. Vaccines given to soldiers during the Gulf War resulted in Gulf War Syndrome. According to the literature in his hand, even AIDS was a result of a contaminated vaccine.

He flipped to the last paragraph of the second page.

This is a call to all Blackfeet, and to all our brothers and sisters. To participate in this study is suicide. To allow it to go forward could result in genocide, since ImmuVac plans to vaccinate every resident of the reservation against hantavirus. Did you know that? Every resident.

We must all stand together in opposing this insane, genocidal plan.

His heart beating harder and faster, he rifled quickly through the rest of the file. There was a notice for the formation of an Institutional Review Board. A list of Phase I and Phase II study participants. A profile on ImmuVac, the company sponsoring the study, and Dr. Ken MacStirling, the research scientist responsible for the HantaVac's development.

The identity of the study's lead investigator.

It was perfect. Almost too perfect.

AT THE APPOINTED time—midnight—Clyde Birdseye showed up at Monty's door. He was dressed in black, head to toe, as was Monty.

"All our people out of there?" Monty asked. Monty had had a brief meeting with Clyde after returning from the hospital in Cutbank, then he'd gone by Luke's school to pick him up. Clyde had agreed to oversee the speedy dismantling of the teepees and encampment while Monty drove Luke to the airport in Kalispell, where he put his nephew on an Alaska Airlines flight to Denver. Luke's mother would be waiting on the other end. Monty had only been home from Kalispell twenty minutes when headlights from Clyde's four-wheel-drive swept across the living room wall as it pulled into Monty's driveway.

"Yep. Everyone went home," Clyde answered, watching as Monty grabbed a dark ballcap from a coat tree standing near the door and pulled it down low over his thick hair. "Nobody put up much of a fight. They were all burned out. Tired of waiting for something to happen."

Monty snickered softly as he pulled the door shut behind them and stepped into the night.

TWENTY-EIGHT

IT WAS WITHOUT doubt the most difficult telephone call she'd ever made. She had put it off until after her meeting with the FDA investigators. She had wanted to verify for herself what K. T. had told her before going to Ken MacStirling with the news.

But Isabel left her meeting with the investigators from the FDA with little doubt. She was, indeed, a subject of investigation. And the stakes were high—much higher than she'd ever dreamed possible. It was time to talk to MacStirling.

Twice during the day she tried reaching him at his ImmuVac office. Finally, on her third try, she'd left a message saying it was urgent that she speak with him.

Still, she hadn't expected MacStirling to return her call at night, and somehow the simple act of discussing the sordid, awful business there, in the cabin she considered her refuge, only managed to magnify the situation.

"I'm sorry to be calling you so late," MacStirling began. "I had to make a quick day trip down to the San Diego area today. You'll like hearing this. I went down to take a look at a manufacturing facility down there. We've begun discussions on the commercial manufacture of HantaVac."

At any other time, this news would have produced the desired response in Isabel. But tonight it simply made things worse, if that was possible.

"Did you hear me?" MacStirling pressed. "ImmuVac is already planning for the manufacture of the vaccine? Isn't that brilliant?"

Isabel's sigh rose from the depths of her soul.

"Yes, Ken. It is. But I'm afraid I have some bad news for you. And it regards the HantaVac trial."

A stunned silence followed.

"What?" MacStirling finally said, his voice high and tight. "What news?"

"It's about me. I received word recently that I'm under investigation by the FDA. A criminal investigation for fraud in Alistair's clinical trials."

Isabel expected Ken MacStirling to fall apart at this news. What she hadn't expected was no reaction. No reaction at all.

"Ken? Are you there? Listen to me, I'm resigning from my position as lead investigator. I'll do everything in my power to ensure that the HantaVac trial isn't prejudiced by this."

"You will not." MacStirling's voice was forbidding, and stiffly Scottish.

"I promise. I give you my word. I'll talk to the investigators, make sure they know that I've removed myself from ImmuVac's trial. I give you my word."

"No," MacStirling said. "I didn't mean it that way. What I meant is that you *will not* resign from this trial. I will not allow it."

"I don't understand. Didn't you hear me? I'm under investigation. For fraud involving numerous clinical trials. Don't you realize what this could do to the HantaVac study?"

"Not if you're cleared."

"But I may not be cleared. I had a meeting with the FDA just yesterday. It seems hopeless. Just hopeless."

MacStirling took a long breath before answering.

"I have a confession to make," he said. "I also had a meeting with the charming agents from the FDA."

"You met with them, with Wittren, and . . . and . . ."

"Thomasen. Charming laddies, aren't they? Yes. They came snooping around. Said your ex told them you were heading the HantaVac study. That he warned them to keep an eye on you."

Isabel could feel the crimson rush of blood to her cheeks. She felt grateful that this conversation was taking place over the telephone and not in person. All that she'd worked for, gone. Destroyed by Alistair's vengeful, twisted mind.

"Isabel? Isabel?" MacStirling chanted. "Isabel?"

"Yes."

"Aren't you interested in what I had to say? In what I told the self-righteous sons of bitches?"

"What?"

"I told them that they were pathetic. That it was obvious they'd failed miserably in building a case against your husband and so, to save their own fat fannies, they'd targeted you. I told them that they could search high and low for the rest of their lives and they would never, ever come up with solid evidence against you because you, Isabel McLain, just happen to be a person of the highest integrity. I told them that I feel exceptionally honored and secure having you head the HantaVac trial, and that they are welcome to sit on my or your doorstep and hover over our every move, but that it will be time wasted, time when they could be pursing legitimate villains. Like your ex-husband. That, my dear, is what I told them."

Isabel took in a deep breath, filling her lungs.

"What makes some people so incredibly decent," she sighed, "and others so terribly depraved?"

MacStirling was quiet for a moment.

"I don't know the answer to that question," he said. "I don't know how a man fortunate enough to have you for a wife could want anything more from the universe."

Any other time, these words would have made Isabel uncomfortable. But tonight they repaired her damaged soul. Tonight they helped her sleep.

SHE'D ONLY BEEN asleep a short while when the cabin's walls shook with the pounding.

Groping blindly, Isabel smacked her hand down on her reading glasses, knocking them off the bedside table. Then her fingers found the gun.

She rose slowly, eyes glued to the front door, where the relentless pounding continued.

Isabel crept up to it.

"Is anybody home in there?"

The voice sounded vaguely familiar, but it did not belong to Alistair. She relaxed her grip on the gun.

She stepped to the window and pushed back the curtain. At first, in the darkness, she saw nothing. But when her eyes adjusted, she made out two figures, both male, standing on the wooden porch. The smaller of the two had an arm slung over the shoulder of the other, who stooped forward to accommodate the difference in height and provide support.

"Open up. He's hurt."

That voice. The peachfuzz hair at the nape of Isabel's scalp bristled. She froze, her professional instincts slowed by sudden recognition.

But any hesitation was fleeting. She was a doctor and someone needed help.

Placing the gun on the floor, she grabbed hold of the thick iron bolt that locked the door by sliding in place. She had to wrestle with it, for, over the years, the door had shifted in its frame and the bolt had rusted. That, plus the fact that it could only be locked from the inside, had prompted Isabel to mainly use the kitchen door, upon which Gus had installed a deadbolt.

Finally, with Isabel's grunt, the bolt gave way. She bent to retrieve the gun, flipped on the bare lightbulb above the door, then pulled the door open.

The taller of the two had raised his hand reflexively to shield his eyes from the light's glare. But Isabel had no trouble recognizing Clyde Birdseye.

Monty Four Bear, slouched against Clyde, did not bother covering his eyes, for they were closed. The front of Monty's blue flannel shirt, mostly its right side, was drenched in blood.

Momentarily stunned, Isabel squinted in disbelief at the sight before her.

"He's been shot," Birdseye said.

"Bring him in here."

"I will when you put that gun down."

Isabel placed the gun on the table under the front window, then opened the door fully. She hurried ahead of Clyde, turning on lights as she directed him inside.

"On the bed."

Together they lowered Monty to the bed. He fell back, semiconscious.

Isabel had already begun unbuttoning Monty's shirt.

"Is this the only wound?"

"I think so, but I'm not sure."

"Go into the kitchen. Put some water on to boil," Isabel ordered.

Monty's semiconscious state troubled Isabel, but he was breathing spontaneously. Blood, however, continued to seep from the upper right quadrant of his chest, and the extent of the staining on his clothing indicated he'd lost a great deal—which most likely explained his lack of consciousness. Decreased circulating blood volume caused blood vessels to narrow, limiting the perfusion of blood to vital organs, such as the brain. If circulation wasn't restored, the brain could become starved for oxygen and hypoxia could develop.

Ultimately, uncorrected, all his organs would fail and Monty would die.

She unbuttoned his shirt, pushing it back off his chest on the left side. She would like to have removed the shirt covering the wound, which appeared to be just below his clavicle on the right side, for a better assessment, but the rule of thumb was never to remove dressings covering areas of active, heavy bleeding.

Eyeballing the bullet's entry point, she realized Monty was a lucky man—same position on the left and it would have punctured the heart. She was concerned, however, that, depending on its trajectory, the bullet might have penetrated the right lung.

Isabel rushed to grab her medical bag. Withdrawing the stethoscope, she moved quickly to place it over Monty's heart and lungs. Both normal. The bullet had missed the lung.

Hemorrhaging appeared to be the most immediate problem. A small stream of fresh blood continued to seep from the wound. Upon entry, the bullet had taken some of the shirt's material with it, imbedding it in Monty's tissue. When Isabel tried to peel the shirt back for a closer look, a surge of blood indicated she'd dislodged a partial clot.

Clyde had returned.

"Grab one of those white packets from my bag and put gloves on," Isabel said, reaching for one of her bed pillows. She ripped its case off and folded it into a neat square, which she placed over Monty's chest.

"I don't need gloves."

"Suit yourself. But throw me a pair. Then come over here and put pressure on this while I find some makeshift dressings."

"Don't we have to clean it first?"

"No. We have to stop the hemorrhaging before we do anything else."

She didn't add what she was thinking. *If we don't, he'll bleed to death.*

She ran to the built-in wooden cabinet along the wall beside the fireplace, pushed aside the floral curtains she'd hung there when she first moved in, and grabbed several hand towels.

The pillowcase was already soaked clear through by the time she returned to her bed. She replaced it with two towels, one stacked on top of the other.

"Harder, press harder. There, that's better. And keep your hand steady. We want a clot to form. Any movement at all could dislodge it."

It was a horrible place for a deep wound. An extremity could be tourniqueted. With a chest wound, short of surgery, pressure was the only means of stopping the bleeding. The question was: Would it be enough?

Monty moaned softly.

A blur of motion now, Isabel grabbed two pillows from the couch and placed them under Monty's legs. Then she extracted her blood pressure cuff from her bag and took a reading.

108 over 55. For most patients, low. But Monty was young and fit. Another reading in a few minutes would be key.

Heart rate still at 73 beats per minute.

She ran her hand over Monty's shoulder, feeling for a fracture of the clavicle. She slid her hand under his right shoulder, looking for an exit wound, but found the shirt there intact and dry. The bullet had lodged somewhere in the upper right quadrant of Monty's chest.

"Okay, I'll take over now, but don't release the pressure until my hand's in place."

As Isabel placed her hand on top of Clyde's, she felt his entire body tense at her touch.

"Slowly," she cautioned.

As instructed, Clyde pulled his hand out from under Isabel's slowly and steadily. As he stepped back, Isabel said, "Now, go call 911. Tell them we'll be transporting him to the hospital in Cutbank. We'll need a surgeon on hand. And blood."

She looked down at Monty. The poor lighting in the cabin made it difficult to assess his color. How much blood had he already lost?

She called out after Clyde.

"How long ago did this happen?"

Suddenly she realized that Clyde still stood beside her.

"I told you to call 911," she snapped.

The look in Clyde's eyes spelled trouble.

"We can't do that."

"What do you mean? We have to. He's going to bleed to death if we don't."

"I'm not gonna bleed to death."

All eyes fell on Monty. His own had opened, only to narrow slits, but Isabel could see their pupils.

"Just clean . . . me up, then . . . we'll leave."

"You're out of your minds. Both of you. I'm calling for help."

In fewer than half a dozen long strides, Clyde reached the kitchen. Isabel watched as he jerked the phone away from the wall, severing the line.

"Nobody's calling for help," he said, returning to the bedside. He stared down at Monty. "You sure you're up to traveling?"

Monty nodded, closing his eyes again.

"He's not going anywhere," Isabel said. "This man needs medical treatment. Are you his friend, or are you *trying* to kill him?"

"Why do you think I brought him here?"

Monty appeared to slip into unconsciousness. Still leaning over him, applying pressure to his chest wound, Isabel glared at Birdseye.

"What's going on here? And don't bullshit me."

Birdseye studied her before answering.

"We had some trouble tonight. Out at the mine site."

Isabel's unflinching eyes bore down upon Birdseye, demanding further explanation.

"There was an explosion . . ."

"I thought you said this was a bullet, not shrapnel," Isabel cut him off.

"It *is* a bullet. There was a guard at the site," he continued. "We didn't realize it until it was too late. We exchanged gunfire. Monty was hit."

"And the guard?"

Clyde did not respond.

"The guard?"

Birdseye's black eyes, the coldest, hardest eyes Isabel had ever looked into, rose to meet hers.

"The guard's dead."

"You killed him? You murdered a man?"

"It was self-defense. He started the shooting. We didn't even know he was there. Son of a bitch was hiding in the brush. Ready to ambush us. He could have stopped us before we doused the site with gasoline, but he actually waited for us, then while we were standing there watching it burn, he opened fire."

"You expect me to believe that?"

Birdseye's contempt filled the air between them.

"Ordinarily, I wouldn't give a damn what you believe. But since you hold my friend's life in your hands, I'll humor you. Have you heard about Monty's father, about Leroy?"

Isabel nodded. Yes, she had heard about Leroy. For the past twenty-four hours, it had been all anyone talked about on the reservation.

"You heard who did that to him?"

"I heard it had to do with the mine."

What Isabel actually heard—though something, most likely their past history, prevented her from phrasing it this way—was that WRI had hired some goon to beat Leroy Four Bear to a pulp. That it had been done to force Monty to back down from the mining protest. Isabel refrained from saying all that. Just as she refrained from disclosing how deeply disturbed—in fact, downright crazy with anger and disbelief—the news had made her.

"So you tell me. Do you actually think someone who'll break into a home where a sixty-seven-year-old man and an eight-year-old boy are sleeping and beat the shit out of the old man, in front of the boy . . . you find it impossible to believe this same person would open fire on us after we'd just set fifty thousand bucks worth of equipment on fire?"

"But one of you *killed* him."

"Lady, when you're being shot at, you shoot back."

"Then tell that to the authorities. Tell them it was self-defense."

"Ever hear of Leonard Peltier?" Birdseye asked, his voice full of cynicism.

"Of course. He was convicted of murdering two FBI agents at Pine Ridge."

"Exactly. He's been in Leavenworth for more than twenty years. Problem is, he didn't do it."

"You don't have to lecture me about Leonard Peltier. I've written letters protesting the medical care he's received, demanding his clemency."

Birdseye snickered.

"You find that funny?" Isabel sneered right back at him. "Letters a bit too civilized for people like you? You'd rather use violence, wouldn't you? So that people like your friend here end up dying."

Clyde's hand came up, encircling Isabel's upper arm like a vise.

"You're not going to let him die."

"Take your hands off me."

Their eyes met over Monty's half-conscious form.

"I want you to go," she said. "Leave. Now."

"Get him ready to travel first."

Isabel placed a hand on Monty's forehead. His skin was diaphoretic, pale and cool to the touch.

The bleeding, however, appeared to have stopped. Maybe she could stabilize him here, without help. It wasn't ideal, but Monty had a whole lot better chance there at the cabin with her than traveling in his condition, on the run from authorities.

"I didn't mean the two of you," Isabel said. "I mean you. He stays. You go. If you take him now, in this condition, he'll die."

The way she saw it, she had no choice really. Monty Four Bear had come to her for help. She could not turn her back on him.

"You mean you'll take care of him?" Birdseye mumbled. "I don't get it."

Isabel raised her eyes to meet Birdseye's puzzled stare.

"I'd treat him either way, but I believe you. I believe that it was self-defense."

"And the explosion?"

"I don't agree with that. But destruction of property is a far cry from gunning a man down."

For the briefest of moments, Isabel thought she saw a flicker of relief in Clyde Birdseyes's expression. A brief respite from the disdain.

"They'll be looking for him. For both of us."

"I'll handle that. Now *go*."

WITH CLYDE GONE, Isabel turned all her attention back to Monty. Checking his blood pressure, she saw that the diastolic pressure had risen slightly.

Heart rate was up to 95, elevated from the last reading, which indicated Monty's heart was working overtime to compensate for the blood he'd lost.

The external bleeding had stopped. That didn't mean Isabel's work was done. Restoring circulating volume would be critical to averting hypovolemic shock.

Isabel prepared an intravenous catheter, choosing a large diameter tubing—the mini-drip or small-bore catheters didn't deliver fluid quickly enough for this situation. If she were at the hospital, she would have chosen a 0.9 percent sodium chloride solution—the only solution that was safe to run in the same IV line with blood products, which Monty would undoubtedly need. But her home supplies only contained lactated Ringer's solution. It would have to do.

Monty stirred as she inserted the needle into his right forearm.

"Where's Clyde?" he said, his voice weak, dry mouthed.

"Clyde's gone. I insisted that he leave you here with me."

"You *what?*" Despite the excruciating pain it had to have caused, he struggled to a sitting position. The movement jerked the needle, which Isabel had just begun taping to his forearm, out of his vein. It dangled, loose, from the tape stuck to his skin.

With a hand on his uninjured shoulder, Isabel tried to push him back down on to the bed.

"Lie still. Look what you've done to the IV."

Using his good left hand, Monty ripped the tape, with attached needle, off his right arm, which hung limp from the shoulder wound.

"To hell with an IV. I'm not staying here."

The way Isabel saw it, there was just so much she could do to force Monty's cooperation. Wrestling him back to bed was not an option. She watched as he pulled himself up off the bed. He stood, wobbling, the effort bringing beads of sweat to his brow.

"I suppose you're going to walk back to town," Isabel said. "Or hitchhike. Now *that's* a good idea. I don't suppose a wounded Indian hitchhiking would draw any attention."

Monty shot her a quizzical look.

"How much did Clyde tell you?"

"Everything. Or at least, enough. Enough for me to know he had to get out of here."

"Son of a bitch left me here," he said in disbelief, almost to himself. He reached out then for the headboard, steadying himself.

Isabel didn't know why she felt the sudden tug of sympathy for Monty. After all, he was a felon. Perhaps even a murderer.

"He'll be back. He made me promise to tell you that. He tried to tell you himself, but you were out cold."

"When? When will he be back?"

"When you're well enough to travel. He told me to tell you he'll be taking care of things. Whatever that means."

"I can catch up with him," Monty said, turning toward the cabin's front door. He stepped out away from the bed, but as he did so, a wave of intense dizziness crumpled him, taking him to his knees.

Isabel caught him before he doubled over.

"You're not going anywhere."

Ducking under his good arm—the left one—Isabel wrapped her right arm around Monty's waist. She tried to rise, lifting him, but his 180 pounds felt like twice that.

"Maybe you can help me a little here?"

"Loan . . . me . . ." his words came with short, shallow breaths, "your car."

"You're out of your mind. You're in no condition to drive, you . . ."

Suddenly she felt a slow, thick warmth wash over the index finger of her right hand.

Monty's shoulder wound had started hemorrhaging again.

At the same instant, Monty's entire form went limp as he once again slipped into unconsciousness.

Awkwardly, trying to support his head to prevent it from hitting the stone hearth in front of the fireplace, Isabel sank with Monty to the floor. Rolling him from his side onto his back, she spotted a gray sweatshirt on the floor and grabbed it. She pressed its soft fleece against Monty's grossly bloodied shirt, directly over the wound.

"Clot, damn you," she ordered.

The steady flow and dark red color she watched saturate the sweatshirt indicated venous bleeding. Had the bullet ruptured Monty's subclavian vein? Isabel chastised herself. Why hadn't she taped a compress over Monty's chest before starting the IV? Monty had been only half conscious, at best, while laying on the bed. She'd assumed he'd stay that way (which did not take into account his macho reaction to the news Clyde had left without him), and decided that building his circulatory fluids took precedence over dressing a wound that had already stopped bleeding.

Not a decision without a rational basis, but as every doctor did when a decision turned out to be the wrong one, Isabel's choice now anguished her. Monty had already lost so much blood. Time was running out. And there was just so much she could do with the supplies she routinely kept at home.

Luckily, the hemorrhaging this time proved easier to stay. She kept steady pressure on it and once again elevated Monty's legs.

This time when she inserted the IV catheter into his forearm, Monty offered no resistance. In fact, he did not stir. Isabel would have been relieved if he had. But the night had taken its toll on him, and, for the first time, Isabel wondered whether the decisions she'd made since answering the door—especially the decision to go along with Clyde and Monty's insistence that no other medical personnel be called in for help—would wind up costing Monty his life.

She pulled the bloodied comforter off her bed and placed it across Monty's midsection, tucking it gently around his legs, then she secured the compress by wrapping elastic bandages around Monty's chest. Again, he did not stir.

Isabel had always managed to maintain her professional detachment with patients, but the intimacy of the moment unnerved her. Ministering to this proud man, whose passions and political beliefs forced him to don a demeanor of such anger and invincibility, especially in his current helpless state, gave rise to a sense that she was an intruder, trespassing on that part of Monty that was most sacred to him.

Each life she touched as a doctor had always weighed heavily on Isabel's mind and heart. Too heavily, Alistair had often declared. But never before had she experienced this, this tremendous sense of responsibility. A feeling that more, much more, than a single life was at stake here.

Did that explain why Monty's simple nearness unnerved her?

She pressed a hand to his forehead. His body temperature was subnormal. Once she was certain the IV flow was steady and adequate, Isabel wadded up a section of the previous Sunday's paper, stuffed it under a web of kindling she constructed hastily in the fireplace, and set it ablaze.

She returned to Monty's side, keeping a close eye on the IV, monitoring his pulse and, in between, staring into the flames.

What a bizarre evening it had been.

Monty and Clyde showing up at her door.

A WRI guard dead.

Too much to digest in one dose. Too much to sort out. Better to put her overactive mind on hold, focus on her patient.

When fire had swallowed most of the kindling, Isabel placed two pieces of tamarack into the heart of the flames, then settled back against the frame of the bed, wondering how the long night would end.

THE SIMPLE ACT of turning his head away from the blinding morning sunlight that had been creeping steadily across the cedar-planked floor toward where he lay gave rise to a razor-sharp arrow of pain that started at Monty's shoulder and radiated down the right side of his torso.

An involuntary shudder followed. This set Monty's entire body in motion, tensing in spasms of shivers, despite the fact that during the night he'd been wrapped, papooselike, in a down comforter. An unfamiliar tightness about his scalp caused him to pull his left arm free of his cocoon and touch his head. Instead of hair, his fingers met the coarse wool of a ski cap.

Inhaling, the faint smell of alcohol assaulted his nostrils and lungs, causing a wave of nausea to wash over him.

Monty opened his eyes.

With his awakening, the events of the past six or seven hours came back to him, all too real.

Less than a yard away, seated on the floor, her head tilted back at an awkward angle against the top of the mattress, Isabel McLain slept. Her hands lay clasped, prayerlike, on her lap. Her gray sweatshirt rose which each deep, slow breath. Monty spied the offending bottle of rubbing alcohol, minus its top, on the floor next to her. Several discarded white wrappers with writing his eyes could not yet focus to read and a roll of white medical tape also lay scattered within Isabel's reach.

Still groggily piecing together fragments of memories from last night's semiconscious state, Monty's eyes followed the clear plastic tube from his right forearm to a nearly empty bag of clear fluid hanging from a twisted wire coat hanger that had been looped over the post of the bed's headboard.

The sight immediately brought Leroy to mind.

How quickly would news of what had happened at the drill site reach Leroy? And what would his father make of the fact that neither Monty nor Clyde were anywhere to be found?

A loud sigh diverted Monty's attention away from that troubling thought.

Isabel, still deep in sleep, sat so close to him that if his right arm were any good, he could reach out and touch her.

His eyes came to rest on her hands. Long, slender fingers with nails unpolished and short. No jewelry.

Nothing of the city about her, especially now, dressed in a sweatshirt and loose-fitting, weathered Levis. Her feet were bare, their bottoms dirty from the dusty hardwood floor.

It took a moment for one oddity—a single concession to vanity or feminity or, perhaps, unpredictability—to register. Her toenails were painted a soft pink.

A single tendril of hair had escaped the knot at the nape of her neck. It dangled over one eye, floating in and out of her parted lips with each breath.

Despite the fact that she'd taken him in last night, as he studied her, Monty tried to work up his usual disdain.

Like Clyde, Monty had from the start categorized Isabel as one of those misguided do-gooders for whom he had no use. He'd worked with them before. Sympathy for the plight of Native Americans had become chic, the politically correct thing. He'd lumped Isabel into a category of people who moved through phases of do-gooding. This year it might be "righting" the wrongs done Native Americans, the next saving the tropical forests. All in an effort to make sense of their own sadly lacking, screwed-up lives.

Despite the courage demonstrated by her response last night, Isabel was no different from the others. And now he also blamed her for something else: Clyde's leaving him behind.

When Isabel began to stir, Monty chose to risk the pain caused by turning away rather than let her catch him studying her.

He closed his eyes, in order to delay interaction with her, but when Isabel's breathing resumed its steady rhythm, opened them again. The sun had climbed, creating a new pattern on the cabin's floor that allowed him to look around now free of its glare.

The cabin's furnishings were remarkably sparse. Just a rocking chair and a bed, a table under the front window, through which Little Chief Mountain declared its rule. On top of the table an assortment of framed photos provided the only personal touch of the cabin's inhabitant. Two were black and white—one of a white couple on their wedding day, both wearing forced smiles, and another of a toddler with hands clasped on her lap, much like Isabel's now. A built-in floor-to-ceiling bookshelf overflowed with volumes. Those books that couldn't fit upright had been laid sideways on top of the neatly ordered rows.

"Have you been awake long?"

Monty turned his head. Just a quarter turn, so he faced the ceiling, not Isabel.

"Couple minutes."

Out of the corner of his eye, he saw her stretch her arms out into the air, shake her head, as if trying to clear it of sleep, then push the errant lock behind an ear.

Then she bolted upright.

"I let the fire burn out."

She reached his way and placed her hand lightly across his forehead. The effect—most likely the warmth—was remarkably soothing.

"Your temperature's fallen." She leaned forward, studying him. "You're shivering."

Isabel scrambled to her feet and flattened a hand on either side of a bag of fluid hanging from the bedpost.

"Damn. It's too cold. How long has that fire been out?" she said to herself. "I can't believe I let myself fall asleep."

Pushing aside the flowered curtain to shelving built into the wall, she grabbed a new bag from a cardboard box labeled LACTATED RINGERS, then headed into the kitchen. Monty watched her standing at the sink, running hot water over the bag, which she kept turning over and over.

"Here," she said as she went about replacing the old bag. "This solution will help warm you. I can't believe I fell asleep."

"Take it easy. I'm fine," Monty lied. In reality, he'd never felt so awful.

"You're *not* fine." Her hands worked quickly, first clamping shut the IV line, then substituting the warmed bag for the old one. "You need to go to the hospital. Immediately. I should have insisted last night. You could be bleeding internally. That could be another reason your temperature's dropped. Now I *do* insist."

Without thinking, Monty's right hand shot out, grabbing hold of Isabel's blue jean–clad ankle. The movement caused a bolt of searing pain, but he did not let go.

"You're not taking me anywhere."

Isabel glanced briefly down at him, her hand still poised on the clamp for the tubing. Then, ignoring his grasp on her leg, she slowly, deliberately released the clamp, until the warmed liquid filled the tube.

"Now," she said, turning her attention back to Monty, *"let go of me."*

Monty met her angry, determined stare with one of his own, but released his grasp.

Isabel sunk to her knees on the floor beside him.

"Don't you see? I'm limited in what I can do for you here. You could die if we don't go for help."

"That's a decision for me to make, not you."

"Hell it is. You've pulled me into this drama of yours. I didn't ask for you and your buddy to show up at my door in the middle of the night. And you're not going to die here in my charge."

"That's really what this is all about, isn't it? Your ego. Your not wanting this kind of responsibility. I mean, a dead Indian, one running from the law, on your hands—pretty messy stuff, huh?" Each word exacted a price, but his face didn't betray that fact. He'd had a whole lifetime in which to learn the art of hiding his pain. "When it comes to actually taking risks—not just quitting a good job and moving to an uncivilized Indian reservation—*real* risks, you fall back on your middle-class-America rules to justify taking the easy way out."

Isabel simply stared at him as he delivered this blistering indictment.

"Don't worry, I'm leaving," Monty finished.

He began to rise, but the force with which Isabel pushed him back down flattened him.

"Don't you *dare* to think you know me, to patronize me with your Indian racism." She huddled over him wild-eyed and visibly exhausted. "Everything is about you, isn't it? The atrocities your people have suffered—they don't give you a blank check to step on the rest of us, mock our purpose or our dignity. Unless, of course, the only thing that matters to you is getting even. And if that's the case, then what makes you any better than the rest of us? In fact, if the truth be known . . ."

"*What?*"

Isabel stood there, staring at him angrily.

"Let's get you on the bed," she said. "This floor isn't helping the situation."

Monty had expended all his energy. He knew he wasn't going anywhere. He didn't have the strength. And Isabel McLain obviously knew it too.

Maybe he would, indeed, die without further treatment.

He did not want to die.

TWENTY-NINE

JAMES LYONS PULLED absentmindedly on one end of his mustache, then the other, as he paced back and forth, waiting for Sergei Kirov. He was oblivious to the sound made by his loafers as they crunched across the crumb-littered linoleum. He had purchased this building—an abandoned schoolhouse in Gaston, a rural community twenty miles southwest of Portland—to ensure that Sergei's work would be conducted in secrecy. No one was supposed to know that Sergei was back in the Northwest. ImmuVac employees had been told that Kirov decided to stay in his homeland. The redbrick structure that formerly housed a school for Gaston's children was close enough for Lyons to visit on a weekly basis, but distant enough that no one from ImmuVac would inadvertently happen by. From outward appearances, the building looked as if it had been converted to a residence.

Lyons had called ahead from his car and asked Sergei to meet him on the first floor. He rarely entered the lab on the third floor when he visited. Didn't like having to struggle into the awkward self-contained, oxygenated suits imperative in Level IV labs. And not even an oxygen mask made him comfortable entering the room in which Sergei conducted his work with the deadly smallpox virus.

Finally, Lyons heard the soft slap-slap of the Russian's Nikes descending the wood stairs. Dressed in a crumpled white lab coat and baggy brown cords, Sergei carried a green plastic tray balancing two Styrofoam cups.

"Coffee?" Sergei extended the tray.

"No." Lyons would starve to death before accepting food or beverage offered by Sergei. "This place is a pigsty. When was the last time you swept the floors?"

"I am a scientist, not a janitor. If you want clean floors, hire someone to sweep them."

"You know we can't do that. We can't let anyone near this place."

"Then you'll have to stand on dirty floors when you visit. They don't bother me."

Motioning for Lyons to do likewise, Sergei settled in one of two ladderback chairs that faced a small table dominated by a TV with a built-in VCR. He placed the tray with the extra cup of coffee on the table, next to the TV. On the floor beneath the table lay two videos: *Armageddon* and *The Godfather*.

"How did you get those?" Lyons scowled, pointing an accusatory finger toward the floor.

"A little store in town rents them."

"We agreed you wouldn't go into town."

"It's just a little market. No one from Portland would have reason to go there."

"But I bought you several videos. I bring you supplies every week. You don't need to go into town. All you have to do is tell me what you want."

"Sometimes what I want is to go to town."

"Listen here, Sergei. You knew damn well what you were getting into when you signed on to this project. All it takes is one ImmuVac employee to spot you and this whole thing could come tumbling down on both of us."

The Russian placed his cup on the tray, rose from his chair, and zeroed in on Lyons.

"You come here, in your fancy car, and drop off supplies like I'm some kind of slave. Or animal. Doing your dirty work. I came to this country to be treated like I deserve to be treated, not to be hiding out, forbidden to leave my lab."

"Well then, maybe it's time we call it quits," Lyons said. "Between what I read in the papers this morning and Pfister Pharmaceuticals, maybe this project should be shut down."

"Pfister Pharmaceuticals?"

"Yes. They're very enthused about our HantaVac study. Thanks to Dr. MacStirling's work, it looks like they may be interested in a partnership."

Lyons could see the effect this information had on the Russian. Sergei's jaw jutted forward while he let loose with an animated stream of Russian. The only word Lyons recognized was "MacStirling."

He finally switched to English and continued his diatribe.

"Comparing MacStirling's vaccine to mine is like comparing a . . . a . . ." his sparse eyebrows furrowed into thin commas above intense, beady eyes, "*insect* to a magnificent Kodiak. My vaccine is *revolutionary*. The day will soon come when it will save millions. The world will call us saviors. Geniuses. Who will be saved by MacStirling's work? *Indians*. The same Indians your country shows such contempt for. Such stupidity would be unforgiveable."

The intensity of the Russian's bitterness forced Lyons back a step.

"Have you read today's papers?"

"How am I to obtain a newspaper when I am forbidden to leave?"

Lyons ignored him and relayed the information he'd just read.

"Intelligence sources are reporting that Iraq and Russia have concealed large stockpiles of smallpox for military use. Apparently this was reported to the president and the Pentagon at the end of last year. The article I read this morning says the U.S. has already begun work on a vaccine." Lyons paused to let this news sink in. "If the government comes up with a vaccine, your work will be obsolete."

"We already knew that military or bioterrorist attacks utilizing smallpox are certain to occur. Long before your government spent millions of dollars to discover what the rest of the world has known."

"But that's the whole point. If the government develops a vaccine in preparation for military or civilian defense, ours loses all its value."

The faintest trace of a smile lifted the corners of the Russian's mouth.

"The government's vaccine will be for the vaccinia strain of vareola. I've told you there are many, many deadly strains."

"You may not have much respect for our government scientists, but you can be sure they're working on several different vaccines. Or a single vaccine that's effective against multistrains."

"That assumes that they've been able to acquire all the different strains. That's a big assumption."

"I agree. But you're not the only former Soviet scientist to emigrate to the United States. You can bet others have been willing to sell samples to the government."

"Even if they have, you have nothing to fear. Any vaccines they develop will be ineffective."

Lyons knew Sergei would be difficult to reason with.

"You're talking nonsense. Smallpox vaccines aren't like trying to develop a vaccine for AIDS. We perfected them years ago."

Sergei locked eyes with Lyons.

"Tell me, years ago, staphylococcus infection was a simple thing to treat. Many different antibiotics were effective. Vancomycin was the—how do you say it?—the drug that always worked when others did not. How do you say that?"

"You mean the last resort?"

"Yes. That's it. The drug of last resort. It always worked. And then what happened? Now some patients with staph infections are not responding, even to vancomycin. Why is that? Tell me."

"Because the staph has mutated. The new superbugs have developed a resistance to all known antibiotics. Even vancomycin."

"Exactly. Now what if scientists created new strains of smallpox—strains that were genetically engineered to resist all known vaccines?"

"You mean . . . ?"

Sergei's chest lifted with pride.

"My Russian comrades have genetically engineered strains of smallpox that U.S. scientists have never seen, never even heard of. Mutant strains that will be resistant to any vaccine the government makes. It's like stapphylococcus. The only difference is that the smallpox mutations did not occur naturally. They've been manipulated, genetically engineered. Specificity will be absolutely essential in creating a vaccine that protects against these new strains. These strains were sold. They are now in the hands of the Iraqis. And North Koreans."

"How do you know this?"

"It was a theory I had proposed during Biopreparat. My pet project actually. I'd been looking at genetically engineering existing strains of smallpox with two goals in mind. The first was trying to target certain gene pools. I believed it possible to manipulate the vareola DNA to create a new strain that could be selective in who it infected."

"Like Hitler. Or Kosovo." Despite his repugnance, there was a note of admiration in Lyons's voice. "A way to wipe out the enemy, purify the population."

"Exactly. Of course, the Union collapsed and my research was never completed. But I told you my work was two-pronged. I'd also been exploring the possibility of creating the smallpox equivalent of the staph superbug. An entirely new strain, one that would be resistant to all known vaccines."

"An artificially contrived human pathogen?"

"After I left, two of my colleagues continued the work I'd begun. They extracted genes from *bacillus cereus* and inserted them into the DNA of existing vareola strains. They created an entirely new pathogen, with new capabilities. And then they took it with them to the Middle East.

"I can assure you, your government's vaccine will not be effective against these new strains. To create a vaccine against the new strain, even to develop a test to detect it, you'd need a supply of the new organism. The U.S. government can't possibly have that. And once there's an attack, millions will die or go blind in the months it will take to get enough vaccine produced."

"Why the hell didn't you tell me this before? If what you're telling me is true, *we* can't even create a vaccine for these new strains."

"That's where you're wrong. Follow me."

Sergei turned and headed for the stairs.

"I don't have time to suit up for the lab."

It was a lie, but Lyons did not want to go to the third floor.

"We're just going up to the kitchen."

The second floor hosted Sergei's bedroom and kitchen, as well as half a dozen former classrooms that had been boarded off.

Entering the kitchen, Sergei strode to the refrigerator and opened the door. When Lyons caught up with him, he could hardly believe his eyes. Milk cartons and juice, a jar of peanut butter, a carton of eggs, stood alongside culture dishes and test tubes. He had to stifle a gag at the thought that Sergei actually ate the food.

Sergei, either oblivious or indifferent to his boss's repulsion, reached inside to the back of the refrigerator. Very carefully, with the steady hands of a surgeon, he withdrew a small glass vial.

A clear liquid filled two thirds of the 10-mm tube.

"Voila," he beamed. "The newest strain of vareola. So new it hasn't even been named."

Lyons drew back in horror.

"Are you out of your fucking mind? Exposing me to some deadly virus?"

He began to turn and flee, but a sudden fear came to him. What if, just what if, the Russian were crazy enough to remove the plug, deliberately expose him to it?

"You didn't seem too concerned about me traveling across two continents with this in my briefcase," Sergei snapped.

"This is crazy. Put it back."

Sergei rotated the vial slowly, allowing the light from the window to filter through it.

"There's enough in there to wipe out half of the city of Portland. That's all it would take," he said gleefully. "Amazing, isn't it?"

"Put it back in there, goddamn it."

Lyons had begun backing out of the kitchen.

Sergei finally dropped his eyes from the vial and laughed.

"Okay," he said, "have it your way."

Turning, he replaced it in the refrigerator, using the same degree of caution with which he'd removed it.

Back downstairs, Lyons declined his offer, but Sergei insisted on walking him outside.

"I need to get some fresh air," he explained.

After what had just happened, Lyons was in no mood to argue. All he wanted wanted was to put as much distance as possible between himself and the crazy Russian. As they crossed the front lawn to Lyons's green Range Rover, his heart thumped against his rib cage crazily.

"So you see," Sergei said as Lyons climbed into his car. "There's no need for you to worry. No need at all. I can do more for you than Pfister Pharmaceuticals. I can make you a champion. A visionary."

"I see that," Lyons mumbled as Sergei watched him go.

IN ORDER TO avoid suspicion, the driver of the dark blue Jaguar had driven right on by the redbrick building when James Lyons's Range Rover pulled into its drive. It proceeded up the road a short distance, until, just out of sight of the building, it reached an opening, apparently a turnaround for the narrow two-lane road. The positioning was perfect. Still well within the range of the equipment he'd secured just the day before from a friend of a friend who now worked for the FBI.

He reached over and, using both thumbs, flipped open the latches on either side of the attache. Raising the lid to the digitized intelligence system, he mentally walked through the checklist given him by his friend: flicking the first switch to Operate, making certain the recorder switch was on Automatic, then pressing the Battery Test Button. As promised, everything checked out.

Switching the receiver switch to the on position, he turned up the volume. Then he turned his attention to the channel selector.

Initially, a blast of static assaulted his ears, but he adjusted to it quickly, and as he rolled the selector knob between thumb and forefinger, it did not take long to find just what he'd been looking for.

Voices. First the strong, fast clipped, typically American voice of a mature male. Anxious. Impatient.

Then another, even more distinctive, voice. This one much slower and deliberate. No note of panic in this one, only confidence.

He found himself straining, leaning closer to the speaker, trying to make out the words of the second voice. It wasn't that the reception was bad. It was, in fact, crystal clear.

No, the reason he was having such a difficult time understanding the second speaker wasn't the equipment, it was the speaker's thick accent. An accent that indicated its owner hadn't been in this country very long.

A heavy, Russian accent.

CHAPTER

THIRTY

YOU SURE YOU'RE feelin' okay? Maybe you should've taken today off, too."

Suzanne Featherheart's big brown eyes peered at Isabel from over the pages of her month-old issue of *People* magazine.

"It's just the same flu that kept me home yesterday," Isabel answered. "I'm still not one hundred percent."

"Lucky thing then that today's so quiet. Just one more appointment. You'll be outta here in no time."

"That'd be nice. Seems kind of strange that we didn't have more walk-ins today. Especially since I missed yesterday, and today's Friday."

Patients often rode out an illness all week, but then, when Friday came along, panicked at the thought of the clinic being closed all weekend. Inevitably, some of them showed up Friday afternoon.

"Everybody's kind of spooked right now, what with the explosion and all. And Monty and Clyde missing. That kind of thing gets a person's mind off his own troubles."

Isabel tried not to register any sign of discomfort at the turn their conversation had taken.

"Any new news on what happened to them? To Monty and Clyde?"

"Nope. Bud Wolfkill came out to the trailer last night, wantin' to talk to Mary. Thought mebbe she'd know something. But Mary told him she didn't know a thing. It's not like Monty would've talked to Mary 'bout somethin like that. Bud's desperate to find Monty."

"Well, a man died. The authorities *have* to take it seriously."

"You ask me, WRI was askin' for trouble. I don't like seein' anyone get killed over all this, but what did they expect after beatin' poor Leroy like that? Only bad thing is that now Monty's in big trouble. And Monty's a good man. No way he shot that guard first. Monty would never do somethin' like that. Never."

"Did Bud say that? That Monty's in trouble?"

"Bud says everyone figures Monty lost his head over Leroy. The FBI says that the explosion was just a cover-up. That Monty murdered the guard, then blew things up to hide the evidence. He didn't say so, but I know that's the reason Bud's so desperate to find him. Cause he wants to find him before the FBI does."

"What if Monty shot the guard in self-defense?"

Suzanne's thick black eyebrows drew together in clear amazement that Isabel could be so naive.

"You really think that anyone but the tribal police would believe that? Would even listen? Now that the FBI's involved, Monty doesn't stand a chance. Which is too bad cuz Monty's the best thing this rez had going for it. I'll miss him—everybody will—but I hope he's long gone. Him and Clyde too."

Throughout Isabel's last appointment of the day—a two-year-old with an ear infection—Suzanne's words continued to echo through her mind.

Monty didn't stand a chance of fair treatment if he turned himself in, or if the authorities found him. And apparently Bud Wolfkill was searching high and low, hoping to find Monty before federal agents did.

Isabel had just finished giving the toddler's mother two sample boxes of antibiotics that had been left recently by the pharmaceutical sales rep on one of her rare visits to the reservation, when Suzanne stuck her head in the exam room doorway.

"Sorry to disturb you, but did you want me to call for a pickup for this blood that was in the 'frigerator?"

Suzanne raised a half-full tube of blood in the air. It was the tube that Isabel had taken from Monty the morning before. She'd brought the sample in first thing in the morning, before Suzanne arrived, to type Monty's blood and pick up more supplies.

In her hurry to get out of the clinic before Suzanne arrived, Isabel accidentally left the tube in the refrigerator.

"Thanks, but no. That's actually an old sample."

"Should I toss it?"

"*No,*" Isabel cried. Then, with forced casualness, she said, "Just stick it back in the fridge. I may decide to take another look."

Suzanne rotated the tube.

"No name on it."

"That's right. Forgot to label it. It's from . . . from . . . from my neighbor, Gus Dearing."

"Really? Never seen Gus in the clinic before."

"He hasn't been feeling well. I dropped by his place to check on him the other day and took a sample home with me."

"Oh." It was a statement but it sounded more like a question. "I'll label it for you."

"That'd be great."

"By the way, you get your phone fixed yet?"

The day before, when Isabel snuck into the clinic before it opened, she did some blood work on the sample she'd drawn from Monty, grabbed medical supplies to replenish what she had at home, and quickly jotted a note to Suzanne.

I drove in to get some meds and let you know I'm staying home today. I have a touch of the flu, nothing to worry about. Unfortunately, my phone's out of order, but I can either be reached on my cell phone, or if that doesn't work, through Gus Dearing in case of an emergency. And I'll be in tomorrow.

She'd jotted down Gus's phone number, reminding herself to recharge her cell phone so that it would not become necessary for Suzanne to try Gus.

"Not yet."

"Want me to call the phone company for you before I leave?"

"No thanks. I've already talked to them. They'll be out soon. In the next day or two."

•   •   •

WHEN SHE PULLED up to her cabin, the first thing Isabel saw—the *only* thing she saw—was a beat-up green pickup sitting outside.

Gus.

She'd stopped by Gus's house on the way home from the clinic yesterday morning. Monty's condition, combined with his status as a fugitive, made it impossible for her to call the phone company out to repair the line Clyde had cut. But as a doctor, she simply could not leave her patients with no means of contacting her. Her decision to leave Gus's phone number for Suzanne had been impulsive, but necessary. After doing so, she had no choice but to drop by Gus's and inform him.

"Line's just dead," she'd told Gus. "And I'm staying home today, don't feel well, so I gave the clinic your number in case there's an emergency. Hope you don't mind."

" 'Course not," Gus had answered. "You call the phone company yet?"

"Yep. They'll get it fixed right away."

She was making decisions—and lying—right and left, and by the seat of her pants. She hoped no emergencies arose that would result in someone calling Gus, which would have sent him to the cabin to find her. If something did come up, she decided, she'd deal with it then.

Luckily, yesterday had passed without word from Gus that she was needed.

As an added precaution against his coming over to check on her while she was gone, she'd also stopped by Gus's house again this morning and told him she felt better and was heading in to work.

But there sat Gus's truck.

Her heart beating wildly, Isabel parked her own truck behind Gus's, then approached the kitchen door tentatively.

Monty was in no condition to put up much of a fight, but he was also a desperate man. Who knows how he had responded when Gus showed up.

Isabel had no idea what to expect when she opened the door. Certainly not the sight of Gus's long legs splayed across the kitchen floor.

"Gus!" she screamed.

Gus's head came up and peered at her from over an arm that held a screwdriver to the phone jack in the wall.

"You scared me to death," Isabel scolded. "What are you doing here?"

"Fixing the goddamn phone. What's it look like?"

"But . . ."

Lifting onto his elbow, he leveled his gaze on her. "You mighta told me you had company."

Isabel's eyes scanned to the living room. Monty looked exactly as he had when she left him that morning, still sleeping in her bed. She crossed to where he lay and placed a hand on his forehead.

He still had a slight temperature. The antibiotics she'd given him intravenously the day before, and again by injection this morning before leaving for work, had helped, but they hadn't succeeded in getting it down all the way.

Monty mumbled incoherently, but did not open his eyes.

"He don't look so good to me," Gus said over her shoulder.

"How long have you been here?"

"An hour or so."

"Was he awake when you got here?"

Gus snickered.

"You might say so. Damn fool started a wrestling match with me before he realized who I was. I'd used my key to let myself in and fix the phone. Once we had a little talk, and I assured him I wasn't gonna turn him in, he settled down. But I think that took it all out of him."

Isabel lifted the comforter and saw immediately that the dressing over Monty's chest was covered with fresh blood.

"I tried to change that," Gus said, following her eyes. "But he told me you wouldn't want me to. I just put pressure on it and it stopped soon enough."

"Thank God for that. He can't afford to lose any more blood. Not until I find a way to replace it."

"That why he's so darn weak?"

"That plus the fact that there's a bullet in his shoulder and his body's trying to reject it."

Isabel could feel Gus's eyes on her. She turned to face him.

"You sure you're doin' the right thing?" he asked.

"Sure? No. But I think I am." The exhaustion of the past two days swept over her suddenly, weakening her to near tears. "I just don't know if I can do enough, though, Gus. What if I can't save him? What if he dies here, when a trip to the hospital would save his life?"

"If that's how it turns out, you can't blame yourself. Monty made this decision. He told me that. He wouldn't want you to feel responsible."

"But it's my job to try to save his life, not to protect him from the law."

"Honey, a white man's dead. Believe me, one way or another, what you're doing could save his life."

"Not if I don't get my hands on some blood for him. I may have to drive to Missoula, Gus. Try to get a couple pints there. I think Lehman Morris might be willing to help. But I hesitate to put him in that position."

"If you have to go, I'll stay here while you're gone."

"Would you? I didn't want to leave him alone today, but he insisted. Said they'd send someone out here for sure if I missed another day of work, and he's probably right. And of course I have other patients who need me. I'd hoped I could make a couple calls from the clinic, get ahold of some AB-positive for him. From a friend in Seattle. The only one I have there who'd be willing to break the rules for me. But she's on vacation. She'll be gone another week." She shook her head, discouraged.

"Wouldn't you know I'm rH negative. I'd been praying he'd turn out to be negative too. But of course, he's not."

"What does that mean?"

"You're either rH positive or negative. And then you're either A, B, AB, or O."

"And you gotta get an exact match for it to work?"

"Not necessarily. O-positive is a universal donor. It works for any rH-positive recipient."

Isabel could tell by the expression of concentration on his face that Gus had been paying close attention to her explanation.

"Maybe *I'm* a match. Or that universal type you just mentioned."

This simple, sweet gesture did it—unleashed the tears that Isabel had been holding back. She stepped toward Gus and threw her arms around him.

"You dear, dear man," she said, laying her head on his bony shoulder, her body trembling with exhaustion.

But it wasn't just exhaustion overcoming her. It was fear—fear for Monty's life, fear for what her actions could do to her career, fear from feeling her life so horribly out of control.

"There, now," Gus said, stroking her hair gruffly, like she'd seen him stroke Grunt dozens of times. "We gotta stay strong. We gotta take care of this young man here."

Isabel pulled back, locking eyes with Gus.

"You mean it, Gus? That you'd be willing to give Monty blood if you're a suitable donor?"

"Way I figure it, I'm an old geezer who isn't much use to anyone anymore. If a coupla pints of my blood can help save this young man, it's my opportunity to make a difference in this world."

"Okay, then," Isabel said, "let's go find out if you're a match."

CHAPTER

THIRTY-ONE

I SHOULD THINK Pfister's a wee bit pleased about this."

Ken MacStirling's eyes remained fixed on the CDC report. Lyons had received a preliminary copy of the report only an hour earlier. After reading it, he'd called MacStirling into his office.

"I haven't shared the information with them yet. I'll bring it to our meeting next week. I want to give it to them in person so I can see their reaction when they see these new statistics."

"By then," MacStirling said, "they'll probably already have seen it. Not that that's a bad thing. Our own marketing department couldn't come up with anything so brilliant."

Lyons laughed. Things were finally looking up and he felt good.

"You can say that again. But I still want to be the one to present this to Pfister. They won't have seen this yet. I have a close friend at the CDC who released the findings to me early. The official report won't be out for another month."

"I knew the hantavirus had spread and that the number of cases had increased, but this is just shocking," MacStirling said, shaking his head.

Lyons always marveled at Ken MacStirling's puritanical approach to what he did—his burning desire to wipe out disease contrasted sharply with the motivation of many of his colleagues, who often lost sight of that end somewhere along the way in their pursuit of acclaim and recognition.

"Thirty states have seen deaths from it now," Lyons said. "As you can see from that graph, the number of cases has climbed exponentially. And the pattern's changing. First couple of years, no one got sick until late spring. Now we're seeing it in February."

"The only thing that seems to be holding constant," MacStirling replied, "is the death rate. Still about forty percent."

"And did you read the CDC's plan?" Lyons sneered. "The report says the first priority should be to study mouse populations so they can learn how the virus is spread among the rodents."

MacStirling snorted his contempt.

"Not one word about funding a vaccine."

"Thank the Lord for that."

Pfister's interest in a long-term partnership with ImmuVac had only grown over the past few weeks. This report had the potential to seal the partnership deal.

"I assume you've been working on your presentation for next week's meeting."

"Yes," MacStirling answered. "As you know, I've already presented the results from Phase I to Pfister. Next week I'll present Phase II's results, which were better than I could have hoped for. And I'll lay out the plans for starting Phase III."

"Are we on target with Phase III?"

"Yes. Isabel McLain is enrolling subjects now. She's hoping to vaccinate ninety percent of the reservation population by the time we're through."

"I haven't heard tales of any opposition recently. What's happening on that front?"

MacStirling took a deep breath.

"Apparently this Canadian mining company came in right about the time Phase I was completed and began doing some exploration on the reservation. Monty Four Bear, the Jimmy who'd caused us so much trouble, turned all his attention to fighting the mine instead. Then things really got weird. There was some kind of explosion at the mine site where a guard was killed and Monty Four Bear disappeared, with another activist friend of his. Horrible mess, I guess. But at least we don't have to worry about him anymore."

"I guess that's what the son of a bitch gets for meddling in affairs that are none of his business."

"Funny thing is," MacStirling added, "Dr. McLain seems sympathetic to him when it comes to this mining situation."

"She's a strange one, if you ask me."

"I don't know. I quite admire her," MacStirling said defensively. "And I'll tell you one thing, without her, this study would never have succeeded."

"I hope you're keeping your relationship with Dr. McLain entirely professional."

MacStirling's fair cheeks flushed. "I don't appreciate that. When have I given you reason to question my professionalism?"

"You're right. I apologize." It wouldn't do to offend MacStirling right now. He needed him for these Pfister negotiations. "That was uncalled for. Now, tell me more about Phase III."

MacStirling hesitated. Then he cleared his throat.

"As I was saying, since the FDA's given us the go-ahead for Phase III, I'll begin production of the next batch of vaccine immediately. By the time Dr. McLain finishes enrollment, we should be ready to go."

"That's great. Let me know if you need any additional resources. I'd like to move this along as quickly as possible. Pfister is very eager to get this vaccine to market." He leaned toward MacStirling. "I want you to know I appreciate the job you've done for us on this one, Ken. If this Pfister partnership goes through, you'll have earned a promotion. How does director sound to you?"

"Thanks, James," MacStirling said, rising. "But you know I don't care about titles. Just keep funding my work."

As MacStirling left Lyons's office, Chris Finch slid by him.

"You have a call on two," she told Lyons.

"Who is it?"

"He wouldn't say."

"Why would you even waste my time then?" he chided, reaching for the Biotech Resource Library DVD on the corner of his desk. "You know I'm not going to talk to someone who won't even identify himself."

"I knew you'd say that, but . . . his voice sounded familiar. Maybe it's my imagination, but I think it could be Dr. Kirov."

Lyons's hands froze in midair.

"I'm sure you're mistaken," he said with a casual air that he hoped didn't sound forced. "But I'll take it. Close my door on your way out, will you?"

"WHAT THE HELL are you doing calling me here?"

"You're not answering your cell phone," Sergei accused. "Don't you pick up your messages?"

Lyons had, indeed, picked up his messages. There had been two from Sergei, saying he needed to talk to Lyons. But Lyons hadn't yet decided the fate of Sergei's work. After the episode with the mutated vareola, he realized he had to think things through carefully before making any announcements to Sergei.

"I told you never to call me here at the office. My secretary recognized your voice."

"Tell her she was wrong."

"What do you want?"

"What have you decided?"

"Nothing. I told you. I won't have any decision made until I find out what happens with Pfister."

"I've been wondering what you plan to do with me if things work out with Pfister."

Lyons paused.

"We'll find something for you, you know that."

"But my work here?"

"Let's take one thing at a time. When we know about Pfister, we'll make that decision."

"When will you know?"

"MacStirling and I have a meeting with them in New York next week. Tuesday through Thursday. I'll have a better idea after that."

"That must mean you're proceeding with Phase III of the hantavirus vaccine."

"Yes. Of course. I told you when I was out there, the hantavirus vaccine is the main reason Pfister is interested in ImmuVac."

"When do you expect to begin Phase III?"

"Soon, goddammit," Lyons said. Then he hesitated. "Why do you care when we begin Phase III? That study has nothing to do with you."

"I'm only curious. That's all. How do you think it feels to be out here, cut off from everyone else? I just like to hear what ImmuVac is planning. After all, the partnership with Pfister will mean more money for research, including mine. Didn't you just say that?"

Lyons felt Kirov was testing him somehow.

"Yes, of course," he said, trying to sound sincere.

"Well, then, tell your secretary that's why I called. Because I may be coming back before too long."

Lyons hadn't decided to pull the plug on the smallpox vaccine quite yet, but only because the Pfister deal hadn't been sewn up. Once it was, he'd be foolish to risk proceeding with Sergei's work.

One thing he *had* decided. Once he closed down the Gaston lab, there was no way in hell he'd hire Sergei Kirov back. He'd always thought Kirov a bit eccentric, but his last visit to Gaston left him convinced the Russian scientist's problems amounted to a lot more than eccentricity. He was dangerous. And—and this was the really scary thing about him—watching the scientist twirl the vial containing the modified smallpox in the air, Lyons had also realized that Sergei, at least when it came to the deadly vareola virus, was fearless.

A deadly combination.

THE FIVE MEMBERS of the Blackfeet tribal council mingled in the hallway outside the meeting room as they waited for Penny Runningwind to arrive. Penny had warned Thomas she might be late. She worked as a sales representative for an office supplier out of Helena, and when Thomas had called her the night before to tell her about this afternoon's impromptu meeting, she told him she'd have to drive up after a sales call in Polson.

"C'mon, Thomas," Rock groused, "let's get the show on the road."

Thomas looked at his watch. Five thirty-nine.

"Penny should be along any minute. I guess we can get started. Provided you're willing to take notes, Rock."

"Why me?" Rock grumbled.

" 'Cause you're the one in such an all-fired hurry, that's why."

"Ahright. Let's go."

The group of five men sauntered into the meeting room, arranging themselves in their usual positions around the long, battered pinewood table that had hosted many a tribal council meeting over the past two decades.

"What's up with the tie, Thomas?" Jimmy Schroeder, sitting to the tribal chief's left, wanted to know.

Thomas had abandoned his customary jeans and denim shirt and today wore nicely pressed black slacks, a white shirt, and a bolo tie. He ignored Jimmy and started the meeting.

"I called this meeting 'cause I've heard now from just about all of you—everyone but you, Rock, I guess—that you think it's time we re-evaluate the permission we gave WRI to drill for gold."

"Re-evaluate?" Jimmy echoed. "Hell, that's not what we said. We've already re-evaluated. What we want is kick them off the rez, once and for all."

Murmurs of agreement rose from around the table.

"Now, I know everyone's pretty upset about what's happened this past week, and I'm not saying I haven't changed my mind on this thing, too, but I want to make sure we don't just react out of anger."

"How else do you expect us to react?" Dave Matthews asked. "I mean, look what they did to Leroy Four Bear. It's no wonder Monty and Clyde blew that equipment up. I'da done the exact same thing if Leroy was my dad."

"We don't know for sure that WRI had anything to do with what happened to Leroy," Rock Peacock said. "Bud Wolfkill says they're still investigating."

"Hell, Rock, you know damn well that's who did it," Matthews said. "The boy heard them threaten to come back if Monty didn't back off his opposition to the mine. What is it with you?"

"What it is with me is that I'm not going to make a rash decision that could end up hurting this reservation. That gold mine could be the answer to our prayers. Could pay for a new school, fix our roads, maybe even allow us to hire a couple emergency medical personnel. When the clinic's closed, someone could die of a heart attack while they waited for that lady doctor to drive into town."

"At least she's living here," Charlie Spencer piped up, "not just coming here twice a week like old Dr. Hammer did from Kalispell. That Dr. McLain's the best thing to happen to this reservation, if you ask me. Her and that vaccine. I got my whole family signed up to get it."

"Really?" Matthews asked. "I been thinkin' about it, but I don't know. Still have a bad feeling about it."

"I'd rather take my chances with the vaccine than risk dying of hantavirus," Penny Runningwind said as she settled in to her customary seat to Thomas Rose's right. "It's been over eight months since Phase I of the trial. Between Phase I and Phase II, almost two hundred Blackfeet have been vaccinated. And not one of them's gotten sick as far as I know."

Rock pushed the pad of paper he'd been scrawling on across the table to Penny.

"I'm signed up," he said.

"This meeting isn't about the clinical trial," Thomas Rose said testily. "Now let's get back to WRI. There's no doubt that the proposed mine's caused plenty of trouble here already. And I think we all have good reason to be concerned. But the question is—and it's a serious question that we have a responsibility to answer wisely—whether or not the mine still stands to be a benefit to our people, as Rock just said. I think we have to separate what happened to Leroy, and what happened out there the other night, from that question. Let law enforcement deal with the rest. We need to decide whether we want to let WRI continue to explore."

"You *can't* separate them, Thomas," Jimmy said. "Don't you see?"

"I don't know," Rose answered. "I just don't know. Maybe you're right."

"And as for letting law enforcement deal with the rest," Matthews chimed in, "do you really think that's how this whole mess should be resolved? With the FBI crawling all over the rez, do you think Monty and his cousin are gonna get a fair shake? We all know what happened out there the other night. Monty was mad, rightfully so if you ask me, about what they did to Leroy. And we all know Clyde was more than happy to help him get even by setting that equipment on fire. But no way Monty killed that guard without him firing first. No way. I'd stake my kids on that. This whole mess is WRI's fault, and letting them stay here will only make things worse."

"Get them off the rez," Jimmy echoed.

"I agree," Penny said, looking up from the notes she scribbled on the pad.

"Me, too," Charlie said. "And I also think we should kick the FBI off."

"That's not easy to do," Rock said.

"Everything that happened happened on reservation land. Far as I can see, that makes it a matter for the tribal police, not the feds."

"The way things stand," Penny said, "we'll never see Monty again."

Thomas Rose banged angrily on the table with his fist. "That's another matter entirely. We can take it up at another meeting. Will you people please stick to the subject here? Rock, you're the only one we haven't heard from. What's your vote on this thing? Do we kick WRI out, or let them stay?"

"You haven't voted yet yourself," Rock responded.

"Okay," Rose said. "I vote to rescind the permission we gave WRI to explore for gold on the reservation. Everyone in agreement, say aye."

A chorus of ayes greeted him.

"Anyone opposed say nay."

A single nay, from Rock, could be heard.

"The ayes have it," said Thomas. "I'll notify WRI to pack up."

THIRTY-TWO

AS HE'D DEVELOPED a habit of doing at the same time each day, Monty found himself glancing frequently at the old bell-shaped oak clock that dominated the mantel.

Four-forty. Isabel would be home soon.

Rolling onto his right side, he pushed himself up onto his elbow. He waited in that position until the dizziness passed. He'd learned from experience that if he stood too quickly, he might end up doing a face-plant on the floor—the position in which Isabel had found him two days earlier when she'd returned from the clinic.

Today he'd decided to demonstrate his improved condition by building a fire and greeting Isabel, not from her bed, but instead from the rocking chair. It wasn't just a matter of pride. *That*—his pride—had taken such a beating already that it was no longer salvageable. Sleeping in Isabel's bed while she slept next to him on the hard floor. Lying, shivering, wrapped in her comforter, wearing her wool ski cap, sipping lukewarm soup from a straw. Relying on Isabel to help him to the bathroom, where she stood just outside, listening in case he should fall—this, of course, only after the first few days where, after his absolute refusal to catheterization, Monty had urinated into a glass mayonnaise jar.

Glass so that Isabel could see it, examine it, to make sure that his urine did not contain blood.

It brought back memories of his mother, in the days before the cancer finally took her, decrying the fact that the blasted disease wasn't content to take just her life, that it first insisted on taking her dignity.

No. The simple act of building a fire could hardly restore his lost pride. But by demonstrating his improved condition, it might help him convince Isabel to drive him to Kalispell, where he could board a bus to Wyoming. He had to get to the Wind River reservation. He'd not heard from Clyde since he left, but Monty knew that's where his friend would have gone. Clyde and Monty both had ties there. Friends who could harbor them while they planned their next move. For they still had work to do. Monty and Clyde might not be able to maintain a visible presence in the fight against WRI's mine, but through their network, they could ensure that the disruptions to WRI's plans continued.

Shuffling slowly across the wood-planked floor, Monty crossed to the kitchen. He opened the door and stood there on its sill, breathing in the spring air dampened by a light mist of rain. That, the simple act of taking a normal breath, in itself showed progress.

He hungrily sucked the air deep into his lungs, savoring it.

Monty had always been able to smell the seasons, to distinguish each from the other by the texture and perfume of the air. Closing his eyes, he inhaled the honeysuckle and wild grasses, the blanket of deep blue wild Camas from the moist meadow in front of Isabel's cabin. There was a freshness to the scent, a newness, that he'd always loved. The season of rebirth. Rivers flush with winter runoff, fawns taking their first wobbly steps. Eagles and hawks and osprey focused only on feeding the gaping mouths awaiting them in their treetop nests.

He loved this land. This reservation.

Soon he would leave. He had no choice. Would he ever be able to return? Had his actions doomed him to become a permanent fugitive?

His wounded shoulder only allowed him to carry two pieces of wood at a time, so Monty shuffled back and forth between the fireplace and Isabel's winter supply of firewood—low now, no more than half a cord—which was stacked neatly at the far end of the porch that ran along the side of the house. After the second trip, on his way back for the last armload of split tamarack, he paused in the kitchen, leaning against the heavy table, exhausted by the effort.

The crunch of tires against gravel announced Isabel's arrival.

Damn, she was early.

He eyed the rocking chair in the living room. Judging he didn't have time to make it there, he decided to stay put.

Two booted footsteps on the porch, and Isabel appeared in the open doorway.

"You're up!"

Her hair, usually tied back, fell over the shoulders of her chamois jacket in a wild pattern. For the past week that he'd been there, Isabel's features had rarely altered from their reflection of her intense anxiety. Even in sleep, when he'd studied her, lying on the floor, her face lit by each night's dying fire, the worry had been there. But her eyes now were clear and bright and she approached him with a smile.

"I have good news." She placed a hand on his shoulder. "Please. Sit down."

Isabel pulled out one of the heavy wooden chairs for him, and Monty lowered himself into it. She positioned herself across from him then and placed both hands flat on the table's surface, as if she were trying to bridge the distance between them.

Monty had developed a level of comfort with the relationship they had forged in the past few days. A relationship where each kept to themselves; where, aside from a few angry exchanges over Isabel's refusal to help Monty leave the reservation, emotions were kept in check. He sometimes wondered if Isabel's concern for him had taken on a new dimension, felt that she had begun looking at him with different eyes; and, if the truth be known, the admiration and gratitude he felt for her had only grown as the days passed. But the expression of any such feelings had, until now, appeared as unthinkable to Isabel as it was to Monty. This—this display of enthusiasm—startled him.

"What is it?"

"The tribal council held a special meeting last night. They voted to rescind WRI's rights to drill on the reservation." Isabel's smile transformed the planes of her face, accentuating her high cheekbones. "You *did* it. There will be no mine on the reservation."

Overcome, Monty dropped his head into his hands and offered a silent prayer of thanks.

When he felt Isabel's grasp on his forearm, he lifted his eyes to hers.

"Congratulations," she half whispered.

"Thank you."

When he was promoting a cause, or teaching a lecture, Monty never lacked for the right words. But now he found himself unable to express the flood of emotions washing over him.

"What?" Isabel said, tightening her fingers around his wrist. "What are you thinking?"

He shook his head.

"I don't know. It's crazy. But I'm thinking maybe I should turn myself in."

Isabel drew back.

"You can't do that."

"We've accomplished what we set out to accomplish. If what you heard is true, our land won't be destroyed. I planned to run, to stay in hiding, so I could continue to fight the mine. Make sure that it never happened. Now that's been done." He paused. "Maybe I'm willing to spend some time in prison for what I did. After all, I broke the law. Destroyed property. If that's the price I had to pay to rid my people of the mine, if that's the price I have to pay to be able to return to my home one day, it would be worth it."

"But you could be convicted of murder."

"It was self-defense. We were fired on."

"I can't believe we're having this conversation," Isabel said angrily. "That now I'm the one sitting here telling you you're out of your mind if you think any court will buy that."

Monty stared at her.

"I would've thought you believed in our system of justice."

Isabel's laughter, bitter and caustic, shocked him.

"What is it?" he asked. He could see he had touched upon something very personal and painful for her. It was in her eyes, which she'd averted.

When she brought them up to meet his, he saw an entirely new side of Isabel. A bitterness he would not have thought her capable of.

"Have I told you I'm also the subject of a federal investigation?"

Monty managed to keep the shock from his face. He remained silent.

"You of all people should appreciate this," she said. "My ex-husband gave up his cardiology practice to conduct clinical trials. The drug companies were paying him lots of money, obscene amounts. I had no idea. And then one day I learned that a former emergency room patient I'd treated had been enrolled in one of his studies. She died. He'd given her three different medications, two of which were prohibited by the study. She should never have been in it in the first place. Her blood pressure was too high."

Isabel eyes focused on the wall, the table. Anything but Monty.

"I turned him in. That's when I left him. And now he's sucked me into it. Turns out it wasn't just Bernice Hougham. He'd enrolled many of my former patients. I don't know how he did it. How he got the information. I would never have given him that, never have allowed it."

"Have you talked to them? Told the investigators?"

Isabel issued another short, harsh laugh.

"Oh yes. I certainly did. But they're convinced I provided him names and medical conditions. In fact, Alistair has them believing it was my idea to start with."

She tried to smile.

"How's that for justice? I may lose my license. In fact, I may end up in prison. Right next to you, if you insist on this foolishness. If you turn yourself in."

Slowly he reached for her, placing his hand, palm up, on the table in front of her. Isabel placed her own hand on his, wrapping her fingers around his.

"I'm sorry," he said softly.

"You can't do it, Monty. You can't turn yourself in."

"But if I run, I may never be able to come back."

They both heard it at the same time. A soft rumble coming up the road. It sent Isabel running to the door as Monty rose to retreat to Isabel's study. Since it was the only room without windows, they'd decided early on that he should hide there if anyone ever came to the door when Isabel was away.

"*It's Gus.*"

Relieved, Monty remained at the table. But moments later, as Gus hobbled into the kitchen, the adrenaline rush returned.

"The FBI," Gus huffed. "They just left my house. They're heading this way."

"How do you know?" Isabel asked.

"They knew you lived up this way. Asked about how to get here. I steered them in the wrong direction. Told them to go up Carnation Creek, then cut over to the river road. I bought us some time. But not much."

"Quick," Isabel said, turning to Monty. "Get in my truck."

"No," Gus said. "I'll take him to my place. I think it's better if you stay here and talk to them."

"Excuse me, you two," Monty interrupted, "but would you mind if I had some say in all of this?"

"Not much time for that," Gus wheezed, "but go ahead."

"Gus, you've done enough for me. Giving me your blood was one thing, taking me in is another."

"So you're just gonna stay here and let yourself get caught? What about Isabel? You know how much trouble she'll be in when they find out she's been hiding you?"

Gus was right. He couldn't do that to Isabel.

He turned to her.

"Let me use your truck."

"No. Go with Gus, Monty. *Please.*"

WHEN GUS'S HARVESTER disappeared, with Monty lying, hidden by a blanket, on the backseat, Isabel tore through the small cabin, tossing any evidence of his having been there into a black plastic garbage bag. Rolls and pads of gauze, a prescription bottle of Keflex, betadine solution, syringes, IV bags, tubing, anything that hinted at her having treated an injury or illness—it all went into the bag, which she stuffed into the back of a shelf in her clothes closet.

Next she rolled up the sleeping bag she'd been using each night and shoved it under the bed. Hurriedly she straightened the bedding, and as she arranged an assortment of decorative pillows that had proved helpful in making Monty comfortable, she heard the car pull up.

A quick glance out the front window showed her a black sedan parked in the spot just vacated by Gus. When the door on the passenger side opened, she did not wait to see who disembarked, but instead ran to the kitchen, where she grabbed the roast she'd fixed two nights earlier, on Sunday, threw it into the oven and turned the heat on. At the same time, she turned the flame on under a pan of water.

It had to appear she was not expecting them.

Simultaneous with the knock on the front door, Isabel ripped open a package of pasta and dumped it into the water.

Her struggle to unlock the front door brought back thoughts of when she'd opened it a week earlier to find Monty and Clyde on the stoop.

This time, however, the two men waiting outside were very clean cut, all business. And white.

"Dr. McLain?" The taller of the two stepped forward.

"Yes."

"We're from the FBI. I'm Agent Tierney and this is Agent Jacobs. May we come in?"

"Of course."

Agent Tierney, tall, slender, with a head of sandy waves and wire-rim glasses that gave him the appearance more of an accountant than an FBI agent, seemed to be the designated communicator. As he explained the purpose of their visit to Isabel, the other agent, Jacobs, stood to the side, out of her line of vision. Isabel suspected immediately that this positioning was designed to enable Jacobs to examine the room while Isabel's attention was focused on Tierney. It made her very nervous. Had she overlooked anything?

"So we've basically been going door to door," Tierney continued his explanation, "trying to find someone who might have seen either of these two men in the past week."

He opened his blue blazer and withdrew two photos from the inside chest pocket.

Isabel waved the photos away.

"There's no need," she said. "I'm familiar with both men. I'd recognize them if I saw them."

"And have you?" Tierney asked. "Seen them, that is?"

Isabel had never been a good liar, but she looked the agent straight in the eye when she answered.

"No. Not since the explosion."

Agent Jacobs had now moved in the direction of the kitchen. Isabel could see him turning to peer inside her darkened study.

"When was the last time that you saw either Four Bear or Birdseye?"

"Let me see. I guess that would be at the rally out at the drill site. That was maybe two, two and a half weeks ago."

Tierney raised an eyebrow.

"You participated in the disturbance that day?"

"Disturbance? No. I participated in a rally. I oppose mining on the reservation and I went that day to lend my support. Along with maybe a hundred others, I might add. Ninety-nine percent of whom were peaceful."

"Just how involved were you in this movement?"

The FBI clearly characterize any protest against the mine as subversive.

"Movement? I'm not sure I'd call it a movement. I just attended the rally that day. Nothing more."

APRIL CHRISTOFFERSON

Jacobs had now taken two or three more steps toward the kitchen.

"Have you attended other meetings with Four Bear and Birdseye?"

"Yes. I have." Now Jacobs froze where he stood. Isabel was getting annoyed. "I attended the tribal council meeting where a vote was taken on whether to allow WRI to explore for gold."

"And?" Jacobs returned to Tierney's side, having now decided that Isabel's testimony was more interesting than the cabin.

"And I was also at a meeting of the Institutional Review Board that Monty Four Bear attended."

She had both agents' full attention.

"Go on," Jacobs said. "Tell us more about this meeting."

"I'd be happy to. It was a meeting to seek approval for a clinical trial being proposed for the reservation. Four Bear was there to oppose it."

The two men shot sideways glances at each other.

"Were there other protesters, besides you and Four Bear?"

Isabel laughed.

"You don't understand. I'm the lead investigator on the study. I was there that night to convince the IRB to go forward with the study. Monty," she'd slipped in using his first name, "he was there to try to stop the trial."

Now both men looked totally confused. So much so that for a moment neither one spoke.

"Gentlemen, with all due respect, anyone on the reservation can tell you that there is no love lost between Monty Four Bear, his cousin, and me. In fact, you'd have no trouble finding witnesses to the fact that the last time I saw the two of them, the day of the rally, Clyde Birdseye confronted me. He basically told me to go home. Get off the reservation. So if you think I may have some involvement in what happened the other night, you couldn't be more mistaken."

Agent Tierney cleared his throat.

"Of course not," he said. "If we'd suspected you might be involved, we'd have been out here long before now. As I already told you, these men are wanted for questioning on two very serious matters. The sabotage of WRI's mine site. And murder. It's our job to find them and bring them to justice. I'm sure you understand that."

Bring them to justice.

"Of course." Isabel should have known better, but the assumption of Monty and Clyde's guilt implicit in these words temporarily disabled any common sense. "By the way, are you also investigating the beating of Leroy Four Bear?"

"That's not a federal matter."

How she wanted to argue this response. Both Leroy's beating and the incident at the mine site took place on tribal land. Both allegedly involved one or more Blackfeet·and WRI. Why the difference in treatment?

But she'd already said too much.

"Is there anything else I can do for you? Any further questions you'd like to ask? I'll be eating cinders if I don't see to my dinner."

"There is one question I'd like to ask," Jacobs said. Now that he'd entered the conversation, Isabel had her first opportunity to take a good look at him. He was an average kind of guy, not someone she'd ordinarily find menacing, but he had eyes that bored right through you. "We believe that one or both of the suspects were wounded in an exchange of gunfire at the mine site. There was a trail of blood that led to their vehicle. But there are no records of any gunshot wounds being treated at any of the hospitals in a four state region. Can a man who's lost that much blood survive without treatment?"

"It's impossible for me to answer that, Mr. Jacobs. Even if you were able to tell me exactly how much blood he'd lost, I'd have to know the nature of the injuries."

"But it would be difficult, would it not, for a man who'd lost enough blood to actually leave a trail behind, to travel, wouldn't it? I mean, the son of a bitch couldn't get far without help of some sort."

"Anything I say would be pure speculation."

"Go ahead," Jacobs challenged, "speculate."

"Okay. Assuming the hemorrhaging is external only, that it can be stopped before he literally bleeds to death and that there are no other life-threatening injuries, there's no reason to think he couldn't travel. Someone with elementary knowledge of first aid could apply a pressure compress, elevate his legs, force liquids. In theory, it would be quite possible to travel, despite the blood loss. Your suspect could easily be in Canada, Arizona, or even Mexico by now. Maybe you ought to consider widening the scope of your search."

"But alone? Could someone who'd lost a fair amount of blood travel alone?"

"I thought you said he had his cousin with him."

Jacobs's eyes never stopped roaming the room.

"Would you like to take a look around?" Isabel invited.

Before Jacobs could answer, Tierney nudged him with an elbow.

"Let's let the lady eat her dinner in peace. I'm hungry myself."

THIRTY-THREE

WHEN THE FBI agents had been gone several minutes, Isabel reached for the phone to call Gus. She dialed the first three digits of his number then, suddenly, hung up.

Agent Jacobs had disappeared into the kitchen. Could he have planted a bug?

Turning off the oven and burner, she grabbed her jacket and hurried outside to her truck.

When she pulled into Gus's driveway, there was no sign of the Harvester. Gus had probably pulled it into the garage to make sure the coast was clear before Monty crossed from the garage to the house.

Was she being paranoid, thinking that the agents might have returned to Gus's, or perhaps even followed her there? Could they be watching? Playing it safe, she stifled her impulse to run to the front door and instead crossed Gus's front yard at a leisurely pace.

Gus had seen her coming, for the door opened before she reached for its knob.

"How is he?" she asked.

"Nervous, like you'd expect. But doesn't seem like he's any worse for the wear."

"He's probably running on adrenaline now. Like we all are."

With Grunt padding behind both of them, pushing a cool, wet nose against Isabel's hand, Gus ushered Isabel into a spare bedroom at the back of the house, where Monty sat braced by both arms on Gus's ornate brass bed. He looked surprisingly strong. And startlingly handsome. Isabel had grown so used to seeing Monty in the prone position, weak from loss of blood or a fever, bundled in ski cap and blankets, that the sight of him now, his long hair pulled back, exposing his strong jaw and classic profile, disarmed her momentarily.

"Are you alright?" Monty asked.

She nodded.

"I'm fine. They didn't stay long. One of them nosed around while the other asked me how I knew you and when I'd last seen you. They know you were wounded and asked me hypothetical questions about whether you could travel."

"What did you tell them?"

"That in theory, with basic first aid administered to you, you might have been up to traveling quite a ways. Then he wanted to know whether I thought you could go very far on your own."

"Sounds like someone caught sight of Clyde," Monty muttered.

"Could be," Gus said.

All three fell silent. Had Clyde been caught? Would Monty be next? And, if so, what price would Isabel and Gus pay for helping him?

"It's time for me to leave," Monty finally said. "Follow Clyde. I think I know where he is. All I need is a ride to Kalispell. I can take a bus from there."

"Don't you realize they'll be checking the bus stations?" Isabel said. "And airports? You can't go. Not now. Besides, you're still not strong enough to travel alone."

"You better listen to Izzie," Gus said. "She knows what she's talking about. They'll have your picture plastered all over every bus depot and train station in the state."

"But I can't ask either of you to continue hiding me. You could be arrested because of me. I can't live with that."

"Son, the truth is, we've already committed some crimes and we know it. Running now just ups the risk that all of us *will* end up in jail. You need to stay put and think through what you want to do nice and slow. I agree with you on one count, though, and that's that Isabel shouldn't be involved anymore. You're welcome to stay here, and let her get her life back to normal."

"No. He's coming back to my place."

Isabel hadn't intended to raise her voice.

She could feel both men's eyes turn on her. Embarrassed, she continued.

"It makes no sense for you to stay here, Monty. You still need medical care. And Gus, you've done enough now."

If it weren't for Isabel, Gus would never have been put in this precarious position. She had to minimize the chance of his involvement being discovered by the authorities. She was doing this for Gus's sake.

"What if the agents come back to your house?" Monty asked.

"There's no more reason to think they'd come to my place than Gus's. Besides, I told them about the clinical trial. That we've been enemies from the start. If they ask around, everyone will tell them I'd be the last person you'd turn to for help."

"You're sure about this?" Gus asked. Isabel could see the concern in his eyes, but for some reason, he wasn't putting up his customary fight.

"Yes."

While they waited for darkness to descend upon the reservation, Isabel prepared a meal of venison burgers and fried potatoes. Gus hovered near her in the kitchen, quieter than usual, while Monty rested in the back room.

When Gus cleared his throat, Isabel knew that he had something important to say.

"I'm worried about you."

Isabel focused on the diced onions she was scraping into the skillet of potatoes.

"There's nothing to worry about, Gus. Things will be fine. I promise."

"You know you can't promise any such thing."

He grew quiet again and Isabel realized just how deep Gus's concern for her ran. She finished stirring the onions into the potatoes, flipping them to brown evenly, then rested the spatula in the skillet and turned to face him.

"Tell me," she said. "What is it you want to say?"

Rivers of bright red capillaries mapped the whites of Gus's tired eyes, but Isabel still thought them beautiful.

"I know what you said a while ago. What we both said. But do you really understand what you're getting yourself into?"

Isabel reached for Gus's hand.

"Yes. I do. And I'd be lying if I told you I wasn't frightened by what's happening. But it's as though I have no choice, Gus. I think you feel it, too, don't you?"

Gus drew a deep breath between front teeth stained by years of chewing tobacco.

"I think what you and I are feeling are two different things. They may have started out the same, but that's changed."

Isabel dropped her eyes momentarily, then raised them again to meet his.

"So what am I supposed to do?" she said softly.

Gus shook his head; whether in sadness or resignation, Isabel could only guess.

"Just be careful. You and he come from two different worlds. He's a good man, I'd be the first to admit it. But sometimes that's not enough."

WHEN ISABEL AND Monty arrived back at her cabin, she had him wait just inside the kitchen while she checked the rest of the cabin for anything that looked out of place.

"Okay," she finally called from the living room, turning on a lamp.

Monty walked slowly to the bed and sank onto it, falling onto his back, his legs hanging over the edge.

"Need some help?"

"No," he said, watching as she stacked kindling on the fireplace grate. "So much for my plans."

"Plans?"

"To have a roaring fire going by the time you came home from work." Isabel smiled.

"Thanks for bringing more wood in. That's a big help."

After washing up and changing into a long flannel gown and robe, Isabel settled into the rocker, rocking softly and watching until the flames had swallowed the kindling. Then she rose and placed two of the lengths of tamarack Monty brought in earlier on the grate, six inches apart and parallel to each other. Moments later, she laid a third on top of and at right angles to the first two.

She watched for a few minutes, then scooted on hands and knees over to the bed where she pulled at the down sleeping bag she'd stuffed under it when the FBI agents arrived.

Monty had by now climbed under the covers. Isabel hadn't realized he lay watching her until he spoke.

"There's room for both of us," he said.

"What?"

"Here, on the bed. There's room for both of us."

"But your shoulder. You need plenty of space."

"I'm sleeping on my back these days. I'll take the right side. You take the left."

She stared at him, still crouched next to the bed, not knowing how to respond.

"Come on, Isabel."

It was the first time he'd used her first name.

"You've slept on the floor long enough. It's not much—just a good night's sleep in your own bed—but it's about all I can offer right now. Allow me that. Please."

After all they'd been through—from the shared danger to the intimacy forced by her tending to his injuries—sharing a bed seemed a harmless practicality. Monty was a proud man for whom she knew such invitations could not come easy.

She lay the sleeping bag down and rose. One by one, she turned out the lights in the cabin. Then, framed by the fire's light, she dropped her flannel robe to the floor and climbed under the covers.

She expected to be immensely uncomfortable, to have trouble falling asleep. But the truth was that it felt good to be in her bed again, under her down comforter.

Neither spoke, and in a matter of minutes, the sound of Monty's now familiar pattern of slow, deep breaths signaled he'd fallen asleep. It didn't take long after that for Isabel to drift off too, but she slept lightly, waking often. With the curtains shutting out any light, it was impossible to see him, but each time she awakened, the steady rhythm of Monty's breathing told her he was sleeping soundly. But just before dawn—in the darkness, the only indication of the hour was the song of a family of swallows nesting under the cabin's gutter—Monty had fallen silent.

That realization, however, did not hit Isabel immediately because of another, more alarming one—the fact that, in her sleep, she'd rolled onto her side and slung her leg across Monty's, as she once used to do with Alistair.

Praying that Monty was still sleeping, Isabel shifted her weight to lift her leg and move away. Immediately, a warm hand came down on her thigh.

"Don't leave," Monty murmured sleepily into her hair.

Isabel took a deep breath, aware for the first time of a scent other than the smells of sickness and medicines that had become familiar. This was musky, distinctively male.

She did not *want* to leave. And so, instead of doing so, she lifted her head and placed it on Monty's good shoulder.

"I didn't mean to wake you."

"Don't talk."

She could hear the smile, and the thrill, in his voice, because she felt both too.

Without thought, she lifted her mouth to him and in the next instant, his lips found hers.

The love they made was silent, and sweet, and gentle. Afterward, laying in his arms, she found herself wondering whether Monty was always so gentle a lover, or whether his injury made it a necessity this one time. She also wondered if she would ever have the opportunity to learn the answer to that question.

When they'd each exhausted the other with pleasure, Isabel at last fell into a deep sleep. The sleep of someone at peace.

HE WAS PROPPED up on his elbow and staring at her when she finally opened her eyes to the daylight that had filtered in around the perimeter of the curtains.

"Still think I'm the enemy?" he whispered.

She expected to see a teasing grin, not the serious eyes and turned-down lips.

"What do you mean?"

"You told those feds that we were enemies. Do you still feel that way?"

"No. Of course not."

He smiled then, and tilted his head to study her. During their lovemaking, he had tried to help her slip out of her nightgown, but with only one good arm, he'd been pretty much useless. In the end, Isabel had helped him out of the blue jeans he'd climbed into bed wearing. She lay next to him now, her eyes drinking him in, storing for future recall the pleasure of the moment.

"Are all Indians such gentle lovers?" she asked playfully.

"Just the wounded ones." His smile deepened the lines at his eyes.

Isabel could feel him studying her, his gaze lingering on her bare shoulders, covered only by strands of her long black hair.

"My turn," he said softly. "Do all white women look this good in the morning?"

She'd been holding back from him. Perhaps because she was still digesting the information herself. Perhaps because she'd feared that voicing it would make it more real, and in doing so, dishonor Nada in some way.

Or perhaps the real explanation was that she had not fully accepted the truth yet. Until now.

Her lips slipped into an uncertain smile.

"I think there's something you should know..."

CHAPTER

THIRTY-FOUR

SERGEI KIROV'S MOOD was downright jubilant as he steered his battered Dodge across the Ross Island Bridge, heading for the business district southwest of downtown Portland. He hadn't realized he actually missed Portland until this moment, nor that it would feel this good to return. And, of course, his mission tonight ... well, how could he *not* feel a strong sense of anticipation?

He knew from his long nights in the ImmuVac labs that at this hour, just past ten P.M., he would find the building empty. Lyons's news last week—that both he and MacStirling would be out of town this night, on the East Coast, selling their souls to Pfister—had disposed of any serious concerns Sergei might otherwise have had about his ability to pull tonight off.

There was no reason to think his security passkeys would not get him inside both the building and the labs. While he was still working at ImmuVac, an employee had been caught downloading patent information from the legal department's computer network. She'd been promptly fired, and all locks and security codes throughout the building changed. For weeks, it had caused problems—employees locked out, a re-examination of who should have access where, which led to numerous disputes and ill feelings. In the end, the action, while necessary, had so irritated the rest of ImmuVac's employees that Sergei felt confident Lyons would not have made another change because of Sergei's departure. Besides, as Lyons told it, Sergei was out of the country. And, of course, Lyons supposedly trusted him. After all, he'd set him up in Gaston, doing work that could land them both in jail if either were to slip up.

Sergei also had an ace in the hole. While the property posted numerous signs boasting of twenty-four-hour security, he knew that the night guard, Vinh Dang, wasn't scheduled to arrive until eleven P.M. And in reality, Sergei also knew from the many nights he'd worked until early morning that Vinh Dang rarely arrived until midnight. The fact that Sergei had kept his mouth shut about these late arrivals had on several occasions prompted Vinh Dang to tell Sergei, "I owe you one." He could always wait until the guard showed up and talk himself inside if need be.

Still, in spite of his confidence, Sergei's pulse quickened as he pulled up to the ImmuVac parking garage. His passkey gained him immediate access.

When working at ImmuVac, his routine had been to travel directly from the parking garage to the labs on the second floor, but tonight when he stepped into the elevator, he pressed the button for the fourth floor, which housed quality control and the manufacturing facilities, which were minimal.

Like most small biotech companies, ImmuVac was in many senses a virtual company. It farmed out a great deal of its work. When the grand day finally arrived that one of ImmuVac's products received FDA approval and went into commercial production, the job of manufacturing and packaging would be delegated to a large plant in the San Diego area. Federal regulation of the manufacture of commercial pharmaceuticals, especially vaccines, was so stringent that it made the cost of manufacturing prohibitive for small companies like ImmuVac.

In an effort to assure consistency, prevent errors, and avoid contamination, federal regulators closely reviewed manufacturing procedures to ensure compliance with what was known in the industry as GMP—good manufacturing processes. Commercial vaccines were manufactured in large lots. Prior to release, each lot was subjected to stringent testing for potency and lack of contamination. This drove the cost of manufacturing sky high, while giving the public good reason to feel confident about the safety of medications sold commercially.

But something the average person didn't realize was that these stringent regulatory safeguards did not apply to medical studies. The only regulations pertaining to medical studies involving humans had been adopted by the Department of Health and Human Services and the FDA in 1981—and these regulations applied only to those studies funded by the government. Private entities, such as drug companies, could, in theory at least, ignore the antiquated rules. These loopholes allowed small companies like ImmuVac to produce their own vaccine lots for clinical trials.

Sergei headed for the labs where the HantaVac lots would be manufactured. Exiting the elevator on four, he hurried past a door marked QUALITY CONTROL, then stopped at the juncture of two corridors. He peered both ways, then turned left, down a poorly lit hallway.

At its end, a door declared MANUFACTURING, AUTHORIZED PERSONNEL ONLY. Sergei stopped in front of the small black box posted next to the entry. Raising his hand, he pressed his right thumb against the small screen, then waited, breath held.

Several seconds passed, then a familiar click and the flash of a small, pen-sized green light indicated he'd been authorized for entry.

Sergei pulled the door open, stepping inside a vast, semidark space filled with the hum of machinery. Walking quickly and surely along an aisle between rows of tables that contained computers, autoclaves, electron microscopes, electrophoresis apparatus, and row upon row of cultures and test tubes, Sergei headed for the annex off the main room.

Entry to the annex was strictly limited, for it was in the annex that ImmuVac manufactured and stored vaccines to be used in clinical trials. The purity of the vaccines, stored in large stainless steel vats, could not be compromised, as the success of the trial and safety of the participants rested on that basic assumption of purity.

In a small locker room outside the annex, Sergei found the oxygen-equipped suit he was looking for. The only two ImmuVac scientists who ever had occasion to use the suits had been Ken MacStirling and Sergei. He remembered the day the suits had arrived—any time new equipment arrived at ImmuVac, the scientists who stood to benefit most stayed close at hand to protect their interest in it. He and MacStirling had argued over the suits. One suit was a large, the other extra large. Both men had eyed the extra large, which allowed greater freedom of movement. But MacStirling, taller than Sergei, had prevailed, laying claim to the extra large. With Sergei out of the picture, it was likely the second suit now served as a backup in the event the bigger suit became punctured or developed problems with its oxygen. Knowing MacStirling would pick up on any change in the oxygen level, Sergei made sure he held the smaller of the two suits, then stepped clumsily into it

Only then did he raise the lid of the insulated cooler he'd carried with him. He'd bought it that morning at a convenience store in Gaston.

BUY TWO SIX PACKS OF BEER AND WE'LL THROW A MINI-COOLER IN FOR ONLY $3, a sign on the counter read.

Extracting the small glass vial from the crude stand he'd fashioned inside the cooler, Sergei retraced his steps to the annex.

THIRTY-FIVE

T HAT'S RIGHT," KEN MacStirling said, "tomorrow. The first shipment of the vaccine for Phase Three should arrive by ten A.M. I'm sending shipments of one thousand vials at a time. You'll receive a new shipment every two weeks."

"Great," Isabel said. She'd been waiting for MacStirling's call to confirm the vaccine's arrival. "I've devoted two days a week for the rest of June and all of July to Phase III. I have off-site clinics set up in Heart Butte and East Glacier, and I've recruited drivers to pick up anyone who needs transportation. The first scheduled session in East Glacier is Friday. But if the vaccine arrives early enough tomorrow, maybe I'll get a few vaccinations in ahead of time, at the clinic."

MacStirling chuckled.

"I'm anxious to get started too, but I'd prefer you wait until Friday. Since I didn't make Phase I or Phase II, I very much want to be there for the kick-off of Phase III, and that's the earliest I can make it. I'm leaving Portland at seven."

Isabel knew she should act pleased, but a visit from MacStirling was the last thing she needed with everything else going on right now.

If he noticed her failure to respond, he chose to ignore it.

"That portable refrigeration unit we shipped you working out okay?"

"Yes. It's just what I need for the off-site clinics."

"Lovely. Now for the really brilliant news. Pfister has signed on. Thanks to your success with the first two phases, we now have a corporate partnership with one of the strongest, most aggressive pharmaceutical companies in the world."

"Congratulations. I know that's good news for ImmuVac, but what does it mean for the HantaVac?"

"With the resources Pfister has—not just capital, but a staff of attorneys and regulatory people experienced in rushing a drug through approval—it's realistic to think the vaccine will be available commercially within a year."

"That's wonderful. Really."

"Hey," MacStirling said, "you don't sound quite yourself. Everything okay out there?"

Okay?

In addition to her own legal troubles, Isabel was falling in love with a man who just happened to be the focus of an intense manhunt. A man who was leaning more and more toward turning himself in, despite Isabel's fierce opposition and the knowledge that if he did, he would undoubtedly be charged with a murder he did not commit.

"Sure. Everything's great," she said. "Listen, I wanted you to know that I plan to be the first vaccinated with the new lot. I know you discouraged me before, but there's certainly plenty of vaccine now." She had argued with Monty about this the night before and wasn't in the mood to argue with MacStirling. "It's a matter of principle for me, Ken. If I encourage my patients to participate in this study, I have to be able to demonstrate my own faith in it."

"Tell you what," MacStirling replied. "Go ahead. But let's not include your name in the data we turn in to the FDA. They won't like the investigator participating in the trials. You know that."

"What if I experience adverse effects? You'd expect me not to report them?"

"You are one determined lady. How about this? If you experience adverse effects, we include your data. If not, we leave you out. Can you live with that?"

"I suppose."

Funny, Isabel thought after she hung up the phone, during their discussions about her immunizing herself with HantaVac, both Monty and MacStirling had called her a "determined lady," as though women who stood firm when it came to their beliefs were somehow unreasonable. With MacStirling, she didn't care enough to let it bother her. But last night, when she and Monty had argued about it, she'd used his similar comment to turn on him.

"*I'm* determined," she'd practically shouted at him. "What about you and this insane idea of turning yourself in? What's crazier? Me taking a vaccine that could save my life, or your turning yourself in and ending up spending the rest of your life in prison for a crime you didn't commit?"

"Far as I'm concerned," he'd answered hotly, "they amount to the same thing. Both of us could be throwing our lives away."

"Why are you so damn paranoid about this vaccine?" she'd cried. "We've vaccinated two hundred people now and there hasn't been a single serious reaction to the vaccine. But come next spring, those same two hundred people will be protected against the virus that killed Joe Winged Foot, Will Echohawk, and Dolores Birdsong."

"You're right. We lost three, three too many. But that doesn't warrant risking the lives of an entire tribe."

She'd turned on him fiercely and reflexively.

"How *dare* you accuse me of jeopardizing lives?"

Monty had reached out and grabbed her arm.

"I understand why you're so senstive about this study, Isabel. I know you believe in it. But do you actually think you can be objective about it?"

"What the hell does that mean?"

"Only that maybe this study means too much to you. You're so damn determined to undo what happened with your husband."

"I never wanted to get involved with this study in the first place," she'd snapped, filled with indignation. How dare Monty imply that this study had anything to do with Alistair? "I only did it because it was the only way ImmuVac was going to proceed with the vaccine."

"Listen, it doesn't really matter what made you take on this study. You can't know for certain that this vaccine is safe. No one will know for a long time if that's true. I just don't want you taking the HantaVac."

"You don't want me taking it?" Isabel's voice had risen. "What are you thinking?"

Monty had dropped the hold he had on her arm.

"I'm thinking that a lot rides on this clinical trial of yours," he'd answered, his mouth tight with anger. "For my people. And for you."

THE CLOCK TOWER in the chapel across the street had just struck twelve when Suzanne's ashen face appeared in the doorway of Isabel's office.

"What is it?" Isabel asked.

"It's Leroy. He's dead."

The gasp that escaped Isabel was more the sound of a wounded animal.

"How? What happened?"

"They killed him. Those bastards." At this Suzanne began sobbing. "They broke into his house again last night and murdered him."

Isabel's world began spinning out of control. She had to get to Monty. Had to be there when he learned this horrific news about his father.

She pushed back from her desk and grabbed her bag, all but oblivious to Suzanne, who still stood sobbing in her doorway.

"Where are you going?" Suzanne asked, clearly startled by the power of Isabel's reaction to her news.

"I don't know," Isabel said. "I just have to get out of here for a while. Have to get away."

Suzanne followed along at her side as Isabel half ran to her truck.

"You sure you're okay? What about the rest of your appointments?"

"Cancel them."

•   •   •

ISABEL DROVE WITHOUT caution, completely ignoring the yellow stripe that indicated a no-passing zone as she accelerated around a brown '72 Chevy laboring on its climb up one of the many hills leading to East Glacier. Morning clouds usually clung to Glacier's peaks and the surrounding foothills long after they'd burned off on the plains below. By the time Isabel approached the turn-off to her cabin, the sun had disappeared behind a veil of thick gray clouds.

Rounding the last bend to her cabin, she came within yards of hitting a cow meandering down the gravel road. Uncharacteristically, she laid on the horn, but the animal, unfazed, continued dead center down the road. She yanked the pickup's wheel hard to the right, relying on its four-wheel drive to maneuver her over the abrupt grassy shoulder, past the lazy Jersey.

Even from a distance she could tell that the figure sitting on the front steps of her cabin was not Monty. Drawing near, she saw that it was a Blackfeet woman. The woman barely moved when Isabel pulled into the driveway.

Isabel threw the truck into park and jumped out, rounding the pickup's front end to head for this unexpected visitor.

Who was she? And why had she shown up now, when all Isabel cared about was seeing Monty?

"Can I help you?"

Slowly, the woman got to her feet. Isabel had learned long ago that the age of Blackfeet women was a difficult thing to judge. Some looked far older than their years while with others, usually the stouter ones, like the woman before her, she'd often been surprised to learn they were years older than she'd guessed. This woman she would put in her late fifties. She was dressed in attire typical on the reservation—black stretch pants and an oversized, powder blue Coors T-shirt that, though generous, hugged rolls of flesh around her torso.

"Monty said that you might be able to give me a ride back home."

She had the same lyrical tone that typified Suzanne's speech. Her words—even this simple and surprising statement—seemed spoken to unwritten music.

"Monty? I don't understand."

Alarmed, Isabel stepped onto the porch and tried to look inside.

"He's gone," the woman said matter-of-factly. "I didn't think you'd want a stranger in your house, so I've been waitin' outside."

"What do you mean *gone*?" Isabel said. "Where? Where did he go? And who *are* you?"

"My name's Edna. Edna Northrup. I'm Leroy's neighbor. Leroy's dead." She delivered this news without expression. "I came out here to tell Monty."

"But how did you know where to find Monty?"

"Monty's been callin' me every coupla days, to check on Leroy. He wanted me to tell Leroy he's okay, so Leroy wouldn't be too worried about him." She shook her head slowly from side to side. "Now this."

"You mean Monty called you from here, from my house?"

"Coupla times. But I ain't told nobody. Monty told me to keep my mouth shut. And I have. He told me not to come out here ever, but I had to tell him . . ." Like Suzanne, the woman finally broke down as tears streamed down her cheeks. "I had to tell him about Leroy."

Isabel was usually a tremendously compassionate person, one who could not stand to see someone upset without trying to help, but her concern for Monty, her fear, now overpowered even her most deeply instilled instincts. Instead of trying to comfort Edna, she stooped to the other woman's height and pulled her hand away from her eyes.

"What happened?" she cried. "What did Monty say when you told him what had happened to Leroy?"

Edna sniffled loudly.

"He went after them. After the guys who killed Leroy. I gave him my car."

"You *what*?"

"I gave him my car. It might not get him very far, but it's better than nothin'."

"How long ago?"

"Oh, I dunno. Maybe two, two and a half hours."

Isabel collapsed onto the front steps. Stunned, she sat in silence. Shortly, Edna lowered herself next to her onto the step, and both women stared out at the peaks of East Glacier.

"You were Leroy's neighbor?" Isabel finally said, her voice softer now, as she thought about what Edna had been through.

"Yes. I been bringin' him meals since he got out of the hospital."

Isabel knew the Blackfeet did not like to discuss the dead. Nor did she want to hear the grisly details of how Leroy had died. But some questions needed to be asked.

"How would Monty know who did it? Was there a witness?"

"Those mining people are the only ones who woulda done that to Leroy."

"How can you be sure? How could Monty know that for sure?"

"Nobody on the rez would hurt Leroy. He's just an old man. A harmless old man."

"But how can Monty find who killed him? He can't possibly know who actually did it."

"I dunno. He seemed pretty sure 'bout it."

"Did he say who he was going after? Did he mention a name?"

"No." Edna grew quiet for a moment, her amazingly unlined brow furrowing. "He got awful upset. Punched his hand into your wall—don't think he hurt the wall none since it's logs, but his hand has to be hurtin' pretty bad. Then he asked me for my car. Said he couldn't take me home 'cause he was goin' the other way."

"Did he say anything about me? Did he want you to tell me anything?"

Edna squinted, thinking.

"Just that you might be willin' to give me a ride home."

CHAPTER

THIRTY-SIX

WHEN KEN MACSTIRLING realized that his schedule for Thursday was unusually light, he picked up the phone and called down to Frankie, ImmuVac's receptionist. He'd have Frankie change his reservations to Kalispell. Might as well go tomorrow instead of Friday morning. If she was free, maybe he could take Isabel to dinner. She'd sounded so strange when he talked to her. If they had some time together he might discover what was bothering her.

"Reception," an unfamiliar voice said.

"Hi. This is Ken MacStirling from research. I'm looking for Frankie."

"She's home sick today. I'm a temp filling in for her. Anything I can do to help you?"

MacStirling hesitated. He hated dealing with temps. They usually made a mess of things.

"I was just going to have her change an airline reservation she made for me earlier. But I might as well do it myself.

"Sure you don't want me to help?"

"Thanks, but I can handle it."

He picked up the phone and dialed directory assistance.

"The number for Rainy Day Travel," he asked the operator politely.

At the travel agency, a friendly voice, belonging to "Kim," answered.

"This is Dr. Ken MacStirling from ImmuVac. I believe you do all our corporate bookings for us. Our receptionist booked a flight for me, and I'd like to reschedule the outbound leg."

"What company did you say you're with?" the voice on the other end said. It was clear she hadn't been paying attention.

"ImmuVac."

"Janet usually handles those bookings, but she's at lunch right now. Let's see what I can find in the ImmuVac file . . ."

Batting oh for two—Frankie and now his regular travel agent—MacStirling waited patiently, picturing Kim on the other end running through computer screens to locate his reservation.

"Here we go. Did you say you're Dr. Kirov? A ticket for Leningrad?"

MacStirling couldn't help but laugh at the incompetency.

"You're a couple months off. Dr. Kirov's trip was this past spring."

"Not according to this entry. It says here he requested a ticket for Leningrad just two days ago."

"That can't be."

"Well, if you want to argue about it, you'll have to talk to Janet. Now, if you're not Dr. Kirov, what did you say your name is?"

"Dr. MacStirling. Ken MacStirling."

There was a pause.

"Okay, here we go. Now I've found you. Dr. Ken MacStirling. Round trip to Kalispell, leaving Friday at six A.M."

"That's more like it."

MacStirling made the change to Thursday, then hung up, thoroughly distracted by the information that Sergei Kirov had booked a trip to Russia. Lyons had told everyone at ImmuVac that the scientist returned to his homeland months ago.

It had to be some mistake—someone made an incorrect entry. That had to be it.

MacStirling had already put that thought out of mind when, later in the day, his own phone rang.

"Dr. MacStirling?" a female asked.

"Yes?"

"This is Hillary Gilbert calling from New York. I'm Pfister's director of quality control. I'm afraid I was out of the country last week when you and Dr. Lyons paid us a visit, so I missed the opportunity to meet both of you. I thought I'd call and introduce myself."

"How thoughtful of you," MacStirling said. "If I remember correctly, they told us you were in London."

"That's right. We're sponsoring a study at Cambridge. I try to get over there every three or four months."

"Well, I'm sorry we didn't get a chance to meet last week," MacStirling said, "but I'm sure we'll have another opportunity before long."

"Absolutely. I'll look forward to it. In the meantime, I wanted to check in with you on your hantavirus vaccine. It's my understanding that you're about to commence Phase III."

"That's right. In fact, the first lot was shipped yesterday. I'll be heading to Browning myself tomorrow to be there for the first of the Phase III vaccinations."

"Great. I'm glad to see you're a hands-on person. We encourage that at Pfister. You say you already shipped some of the Phase III vaccine. I'm assuming you kept a sampling for QC."

Who did she think she was dealing with? The question offended MacStirling, but he decided to keep his tone friendly.

"Of course," he said. "I keep a sample of each lot. We used the same lot for Phases I and II, but because of the size of the third phase—we expect to vaccinate up to seven thousand participants—of course we had to manufacture a new lot."

"You've run a YOYO dye on each lot then?"

MacStirling hoped Gilbert didn't notice his momentary hesitation.

"Yes," he lied. "The first lot was also tested by an independent laboratory, which verified its purity."

He did not offer the information that the third-party testing had been at the insistence of Isabel McLain.

"Did you have third-party testing of this most recent lot?"

"There was no need. I'm pretty much a one-man show. I prepared the lot. The formula didn't change."

"And the YOYOs? How do they compare for the two lots?"

"About as close to identical as possible."

"Great," Hillary Gilbert said. "I'll look forward to seeing the photos when I come to Portland."

"And will that be anytime soon?"

"You can count on it."

Damn. MacStirling hung up, the good mood occasioned by the start of Phase III and the prospect of dinner with Isabel dashed.

He hadn't expected to feel Pfister's heavy hand quite this soon. In his entire professional career, until now, he had never before lied to a colleague. But his pride, plus an earlier conversation with Lyons, caused him to this time.

ImmuVac had only acquired the new YOYO technology recently, and he knew that to admit as much to Gilbert would immediately label ImmuVac, in her eyes, as another minor-league biotech startup. A lightweight to be pushed around by its new, bigger, and more powerful partner.

MacStirling had, indeed, tested both lots for purity, but instead of using the newest technology, he'd run gels. For decades, scientists had used a method known as gel electrophoresis to determine the genetic fingerprint of DNA fragments. Gels were capable of detecting contaminants in vaccines and other medications. States linked by a national network of computers were able to share genetic profiles, derived from gels, of microbes causing outbreaks of food poisoning, which enabled epidemiologists to identify multistate outbreaks, trace their origin, and issue prompt public warnings.

But traditional gels were cumbersome. They could take as many as eleven steps, and several hours. More recent developments, such as YOYO dyes, saved scientists trouble and time.

YOYO dyes were state of the art, and standard equipment in research labs like those at Pfister. Solutions of DNA molecules were dyed with YOYO-1, then applied to a silicon-based mold lined with channels a few micrometers wide. Single dyed DNA molecules were drawn by capillary action into each of the channels, then illuminated with a laser. The flouresced dye revealed the size of the molecules. This process could be completed one hundred times faster than traditional gels, and remarkably, it used a million times less sample.

For months MacStirling had pleaded with Lyons to buy the new YOYO technology, to no avail. He'd run traditional gels on the single lot used for Phase I and Phase II of the hantavirus vaccine. Then, just before the trip to New York, when Lyons still had not acquiesced, he'd run a gel on the lot for Phase III. As he told Hillary Gilbert, the results from both lots were nearly identical.

Unbeknownst to him, however, Lyons had ordered a YOYO device earmarked specifically for him, in "celebration," as Lyons put it, of their new partnership. When they returned from New York, one had been waiting. Indeed, the ImmuVac CEO had splurged and purchased a multiplex device capable of sizing up to eight samples at once.

"If we want to hold our own with Pfister," Lyons had said, "we need to be cutting edge all the way. Gels are antiquated."

Since both techniques accomplished the same thing and he'd already gone to the trouble of running gels on both lots, MacStirling hadn't planned to use the YOYO device on the clinical trial lots of the hantavirus vaccine. But now that Hillary Gilbert expected to see them, he had no choice.

Glancing at his watch, he saw that he had exactly one hour before his four P.M. staff meeting. Just enough time to start the YOYOs. The staff meeting could be counted on to run late, after five. And he'd promised his wife he'd make it home before six for a dinner party she'd had planned for weeks. But he could start the dyes now, then come back later in the evening to check the results.

Maybe, with a little luck, he could still catch an afternoon flight tomorrow to Kalispell.

With a little luck.

THIRTY-SEVEN

H E FELT LIKE a time bomb, each beat of the windshield wipers the ticking of its clock. The wipers had become necessary just before Snoqualmie Pass. The brutal desert sun that had caused him to pull over twice, first at the top of Ryegrass and again leaving Cle Elum, was now nowhere to be seen. Just rain. Dark, gray, matching his mood.

He liked the analogy. That of a time bomb. Each second that passed, his fuse grew shorter, the inevitable, welcome violence at its end closer. For only violence could put an end to the anger and guilt that filled every pore, infected every fiber of Monty Four Bear's being.

Two stops to give Edna's old Impala a chance to cool down had set Monty back over an hour. He'd pushed the car to its limits coming over the mountains, and finally, climbing I-90 out of the Columbia River Gorge near Ryegrass, it had overheated. Adding water and letting it sit awhile had done the trick, and before long, he'd been on his way again. But it happened again at Easton, just east of the pass. A Colville brother named Bob had pulled over to offer assistance that time. Good-natured and obviously in no hurry, Bob had watched Monty add more water, then waited with him to be sure the Impala started again. He'd followed Monty to North Bend, where he rolled down the window of his turquoise Toyota pickup and gave Monty a thumbs-up before turning off Interstate 90.

Before leaving Montana, Monty had considered crossing the border into Canada just north of Whitefish, but he'd decided it was too close to home. Agents at the Montana and Idaho state lines would be much more likely to know about the explosion and be on the lookout for him. He was taking his chances here, too, but at this point in time there was no warrant for his arrest. Technically, he was only wanted for questioning. The number of individuals who fit that description heading north out of Seattle surely made keeping track of them unrealistic.

And the route he'd chosen—out of Missoula, I-90 all the way to I-5 in Seattle—also meant traveling high-speed interstates most of the way, which would save precious time. For every minute that Leroy's death went unavenged weighed like a boulder on Monty's grief-stricken heart.

Despite that fact, Monty welcomed the delay when he approached the Canadian border and saw the backup of vehicles beneath the Peace

Arch—a downsized replica of the French Arc de Triomphe that symbolized the friendship between the two neighboring countries. It might cost a few extra minutes, but the long line of cars and RVs waiting to enter Canada would limit the amount of attention paid to Monty.

"Are you a U.S. citizen?" the guard asked now from his booth. His elevated seat gave him a good view into the car's interior, but aside from a plastic bag filled with flattened beer cans that Edna collected weekly from several East Glacier campgrounds, there was not much to see.

"Yes," Monty replied. "Montana."

"Where you heading?"

"Vancouver."

"How long you plan to be in Vancouver?" the guard wanted to know.

"One night, maybe two," Monty replied.

"Business?"

"Yeah. Business."

"May I see your driver's license?"

Monty reached for his wallet, grateful that Edna had run after him waving it in the air as he commandeered her car.

"Don'tcha need some money?" she'd yelled after him.

Poor Edna. He hadn't even given her a ride back to her house.

The guard took a quick look and handed the wallet back through the window.

"Have a safe trip."

Monty nodded, then shifted the rumbling car into drive and crossed into Canada.

A highway sign declared the distance to Vancouver forty kilometers. If only he still had those files on ImmuVac. It was long past quitting time at WRI. If he had the files, he could find LeCoque's house. Without them, he would be forced to wait until tomorrow. Maybe, just maybe, LeCoque's residence was listed in the phone book.

As soon as he entered the city, Monty pulled over at a phone booth in the parking lot of a gas station. He rifled through the tattered directory hanging from a chain attached to the booth.

There was no listing for a Jon LeCoque. He dialed directory assistance and was told the number was unlisted.

Next he turned to the Ws, and there he found what he was looking for: the address of WRI's corporate headquarters.

1515 W. Georgia.

Flipping to the front of the book, he found a city map. He ripped the page out and, stuffing it inside his shirt to protect it from the rain, returned to the car.

As the Impala inched its way through the congested streets of Vancouver, Monty found himself somewhat surprised by the sights. He'd expected a carbon copy of Seattle, but crossing Granville Bridge into the heart of the city, instead of Seattle's brisk, yuppie-friendly feeling, the pedestrians and shops struck him as decidedly slower and more sophisticated. Less crassly commercial than its American counterpart. And there were more people out at night, on the streets.

Georgia looked easy to find on the map, but a series of one-way streets forced Monty to circle around several times before finding 1515.

When he finally did find it, the sight of a giant WRI logo etched in the glass above the front double door hit Monty hard. Shaken, he pulled over across the street from the building and sat staring, pulse pounding, at the supersized letters.

WRI.

The building gave the appearance of being made entirely of glass, city lights reflecting off its windows like dozens of mirrors. But its roofline set it apart from the others, sloping dramatically to the east, as if a giant hand had come along and lopped its top off at a forty-five degree angle.

It had taken a great deal of money to build such a monument to WRI's greed. How many people had paid the tab along the way?

DINNER WITH STELLA'S friends had been a long, drawn-out affair, made all the more grueling by MacStirling's impatience to get back to the lab and complete the YOYO dyes that evening.

When he'd finally made his escape, he'd found the ImmuVac building deserted. Carefully reading and rereading the instructions that came with the device, he'd added the YOYO dye to the DNA solution and, as directed, applied drops from each solution to adjoining grids, one for each lot.

Gels took hours, but since he'd already added the enzymes, which would slice the DNA molecules into small pieces, before leaving ImmuVac that afternoon, MacStirling only had to give the YOYO devices ten minutes to allow the capillary action to pull the dyed DNA molecules into the apparatus's channels.

Curious, but sure of what he would find—identical patterns in the side-by-side grids, indicating identical solutions for Lot One and Lot Two—MacStirling read through the material that had accompanied the device again, then he turned on the laser lights positioned above the grids and strode over to the light switch.

With gels, it took longer for larger pieces of DNA to travel the electric field of the gels than for the smaller pieces. Therefore, when the shortest molecules reached the end of the charged gel and the gel was illuminated under ultraviolet light, a pattern that looked somewhat like a bar code emerged, with shorter DNA pieces (having traveled farther) at the far end, and longer pieces closer to the starting point.

With the YOYO dye, single molecules of dyed DNA were pulled by capillary action into the grooved channels of the device. When the molecules were subsequently exposed to flourescent light, the larger molecules absorbed more and gave off more light. The size of the molecules could therefore be determined from the pattern of brightness.

Though MacStirling knew that the end result of the two processes would differ in appearance, he'd fully expected the pattern created in the two side-by-side grids of the YOYO multiplex device to be identical, just as the two gels he'd run on the solutions had been.

Flipping off the light switch, he'd hurried back to the counter where the equipment sat, his earlier irritation at having to run the tests suddenly replaced by an anticipation like that of a kid unwrapping a new toy. Ever since reading about the new technology, he'd been anxious to see firsthand how it worked.

The darkened room and laser light had heightened the sense of drama.

MacStirling leaned over to view the results of the YOYO tests.

"This can't be right."

Two very distinctive patterns glowed back at him in the dark.

His hands beginning to shake, MacStirling placed them on either side of the device and folded his long torso closer to the table for a better look.

Upon closer examination, he saw that the two patterns had more in common than he'd first realized. The grid on the left, which represented Lot One, the vaccine used for both Phase I and II, was virtually mirrored in the grid on the right. He hadn't realized that at first because there was more, much more to the right grid. On the right side, DNA not seen in the other grid glowed so brightly that at first it had obscured the similarities of the two.

A contaminant.

The realization took the breath out of MacStirling.

The additional DNA in the righthand grid indicated that Lot Two contained material not found in Lot One. Additional, unwanted material. A contaminant.

But how? How could it possibly have happened?

Trying with little success to fight back the panic, MacStirling's mind raced from one unpleasant thought to another. How would he tell Lyons? Phase III had already been scheduled. What would Pfister think if it now had to be delayed? And Isabel, how would she respond?

Would a new lot have to be manufactured?

Lyons had been calling him a hero, crediting him for the Pfister deal. What if they hadn't actually signed all the papers yet? Could Pfister still pull out of the partnership?

But despite the myriad other questions running through it, his mind kept returning to the first one.

How could this have happened?

He'd run the gel on Lot Two just before his trip to New York. It matched that of Lot One, confirming the purity and conformity of both lots.

Lot Two now contained an impurity. The contamination had to have occurred after he'd run the last gel.

But how?

CHAPTER

THIRTY-EIGHT

I HAVE TO have that address."

Ken MacStirling had waited in his car outside the Rainy Day Travel offices since seven A.M. At just past eight, a red Volvo finally pulled up. An attractive brunette slid out from behind the wheel and approached the office's front door. As she unlocked it, MacStirling had startled her.

"Kim?"

The woman had turned, reflexively pulling her purse into her body.

"No. I'm Janet. Kim comes in later. Around nine."

"Actually, you're the one I need to talk to," MacStirling said. "I'm Dr. MacStirling from ImmuVac."

Instinctively, this announcement caused the woman named Janet to relax. A smile finally broke her heavily made-up face.

"Oh, Dr. MacStirling. I'm sorry. You startled me. I'm always a little nervous about opening the office alone."

"I understand. And I'm sorry to surprise you like that. It's just that there's been a little emergency and I thought you might be able to help."

By now, Janet had unlocked the door. Holding it open, she said, "Please, come in. We can talk in here."

She directed him to her desk, where she deposited her bag on the floor and turned to give him her full attention.

"How can I help?"

"I need the address of another ImmuVac employee. His name is Sergei Kirov. You booked a flight for him recently to Leningrad." He did not tell her that he'd obtained that information from her coworker. "He's on vacation and there's been an accident in his lab. It's imperative that I reach him. I have to have that address."

Janet's brow scrunched in puzzlement.

"Surely your personnel department can give it to you."

"That's the problem. Kirov moved recently. We all knew it, but apparently no one ever thought to get his new address or telephone number. I'd just booked my own flight to Kalispell yesterday. When I did, Kim verified my home phone and address. So it occurred to me that you'd have that same information on file for Sergei. I'm just hoping it's the updated information."

Janet's expression told MacStirling she clearly did not know what to do.

"I have to have that address," MacStirling reiterated. "One of our lab workers may have been exposed to a dangerous disease. Time is critical. If I have to, I'll go to the police and you'll be forced to provide it to them. But please don't make me do that. As I said, time is critical if our lab technician has indeed been exposed."

The lab worker angle seemed to sway her.

"How awful." She flipped a switch on her computer to boot it up. "It *is* highly unusual, but let me see what I can do for you."

Ten minutes later, Ken MacStirling walked out with an address. It was a rural route, in Gaston.

AFTER THE SCIENTIST from ImmuVac left, it occurred to Janet McIntosh.

Why hadn't they thought of it?

She had Sergei Kirov's telephone number right here in his electronic file. It seemed odd that that doctor from ImmuVac—MacStirling, wasn't that his name?—hadn't even asked for it. Of course, she could see he was in a state of panic. That, as much as anything, had convinced her that the right thing to do was cooperate by giving him Dr. Kirov's address. It probably also explained why he hadn't even thought to ask for the phone number.

But since time was so critical, maybe she could help. Do her good deed for the day.

The phone only rang once before being picked up.

"Dr. Kirov?"

"Yes."

"This is Janet McIntosh from Rainy Day Travel. I just wanted to let you know that one of your colleagues was in here a few minutes ago asking for your address. A Dr. MacStirling, I believe. He said there'd been an accident at your lab and that he needed to contact you immediately. After he left I couldn't believe neither of us had thought of calling you. Anyway, he's on his way out there now. I thought my calling ahead could save time."

"How wise of you," the Russian said. He sounded truly appreciative. "I'll be on the lookout for Dr. MacStirling."

. . .

"THEY JUST DELIVERED the vaccine," Suzanne whispered to Isabel as she entered the examination room to help placate an uncooperative four-year-old whose ears Isabel suspected were infected.

Isabel made brief eye contact with Suzanne and nodded.

"That's great," she said, returning to the exam table with a rubber glove, which she handed to Suzanne. The child's already large eyes grew even bigger at the sight of this new person and the glove, but then, when Suzanne held the glove to her mouth and began blowing air into it, creating a grotesque version of a balloon, he erupted in giggles. Isabel used the opportunity to insert the otoscope in his left ear and have a good look. The inner surface of the outer ear bore multiple blisters.

In reality, the news that the vials of vaccine had arrived, the realization that Phase III would commence the day after next, failed to make any impression on Isabel whatsoever. She was simply going through the motions. She'd been on autopilot since yesterday when she heard about Leroy. The only thing keeping her going was the knowledge that her patients needed her.

Her first instinct had been to follow Monty. She was still thinking about it, but had been held back by several concerns. First and foremost was the fact that Monty would not want her to follow. Of that, she was certain. The likelihood of actually finding him, if she did, was small. And she worried that her sudden disappearance could end up exposing not only her involvement with Monty, but possibly Gus's as well.

Edna seemed to have read her mind. When she'd driven her home—to a dark, brown planked structure with a single window on each side and one long, thin stovepipe sticking out from the low, barely angled roof—Edna had turned to her before climbing out of the pickup.

"You done a good thing helping Monty," she said. "But you gotta be careful. Monty's always drawn trouble. You're a good girl. And the people need you. Don't be doin' somethin' stupid like goin' after him. Ahright now?"

The evening had passed with no word from Monty. Only a call from Gus, making sure she was okay. He'd heard about Leroy. He didn't even seem surprised to hear Monty had taken off.

"I figured as much," was all he said. Then he, too, had warned her. "Don't you lose your head over this. Want to come spend the night here with me and Grunt?"

"No," Isabel answered. "Maybe he'll try to call."

But the phone had not rung again and the night had crept along at a slug's pace, with Isabel laying sleepless in the bed she and Monty had shared.

She wanted to feel angry with him for taking off on this mission for which the only possible outcome could be tragedy. But the only anger she felt was directed at WRI. The murder of Monty's father was cruel and senseless. She shared Monty's rage. Combined with the guilt he also had to be feeling—knowing Leroy had been sacrificed to exact revenge upon Monty—it was no wonder Monty had, as Edna put it, "gone a little bit crazy."

Isabel had always been a take-charge person. But now, when she most cared, she felt helpless.

"You still need me here?" Suzanne asked after Isabel had examined both the child's ears.

"Go ahead. I can handle it from here. Have you refrigerated the vials yet?"

Suzanne nodded.

"First thing. There's sure a lot of them. Just lookin' at how many made me realize how big a thing this is. Enit?"

"Yes. It is a big thing."

"You don't seem very excited about it anymore."

Isabel had the distinct feeling that Suzanne knew about her and Monty. She'd been trying to act as though everything was fine, but Suzanne knew her too well to believe that. Still, Suzanne did not pry and Isabel appreciated that.

"That's not true. I couldn't be more pleased with how things have gone. Still, we've got a big job ahead of us."

"We'll get it done."

"Yes, we will."

After the boy and his aunt left, Isabel walked down the hall to Suzanne's desk.

"When's my next appointment? I want to run down to Ben Franklin's and pick up something to read."

"You've got almost half an hour," Suzanne said. "After that you're done for the day. Maybe a good book will get your mind off everything."

Isabel decided not to pursue that line of discussion.

"Can I bring you anything?" she said instead.

"No, thanks."

Isabel drove the three blocks to TeePee Village. At a newspaper box in front of the Ben Franklin store, she bought a Kalispell *Daily Interlake*. Suzanne had no new information on Leroy's case. Perhaps the newspaper would.

She climbed back in her truck and scanned every page. The paper contained no mention whatsoever of Leroy's death. Apparently the annual "Art on the Green," featured on the front page, rated higher in importance than the death of an Indian on the Blackfeet reservation. Frustrated, Isabel threw the paper down on the seat next to her and sat staring across Browning's main street.

Two of the dogs she frequently gave handouts at the clinic wandered down from one of the side streets. They stopped every few feet to pick up the scent of earlier dogs and sniff at litter strewn everywhere, then slowly meandered across the empty street.

Isabel sat like that for some time, just looking out. She watched as the wind picked up a Subway wrapper and rolled it across the street. It was the first time she'd noticed that the 'P' was missing on the NAPA Auto Parts sign across the street. An elderly man, bone thin and dressed in a torn down jacket despite the seventy degree weather, leaned heavily on his crutch as he slowly made his way out of the liquor store and down the sidewalk, brown paper bag in hand.

So engulfed was Isabel in her own thoughts that when something rapped tersely on her window, she let out a sharp, startled gasp.

She turned her head to see an elderly Blackfeet woman holding a cane to the glass. Strands of wiry gray hair had escaped her colorful flowered scarf and blew across a face etched with almost a century of hard living.

Isabel realized that she'd seen the woman before. The day of the mining protest. She had called Clyde Birdseye to task that day.

Hurriedly rolling her window down, Isabel managed a flustered smile.

"Can I help you?"

"You're the lady doctor."

"Yes. I am."

"I saw you sitting here."

Isabel did not know what to say in response, but it did not seem to faze her visitor.

"Monty's in a lotta trouble," the old woman said. "He might not be back."

Isabel drew up, tensing. She leaned toward the woman, grasping the upper edge of the rolled down window with both hands.

"What have you heard?"

"Nothin'," the old woman said. "But I know."

"If you haven't heard anything, how do you know?"

The woman simply stared at Isabel, into her eyes, as if she did not hear her. Her eyes were small and sharp, like the eyes of a wizened crow. Isabel felt pierced by them, but she could not look away.

"You're one of us, aren't you?"

Isabel did not answer.

"It's hard for a child to grow up when they belong to two worlds," the woman said.

"But I didn't know when I was growing up. I only . . ."

The woman waved a knobby hand, cutting her off.

"I don't mean you," she said impatiently. "I don't mean you. Even if Monty don't come back, you should stay. The child belongs here."

"What child?" Isabel said.

But the old woman had already turned, pivoting on her cane, and begun hobbling toward the sidewalk.

"Wait a minute," Isabel cried. "What do you mean?"

The woman did not answer.

"What's your name?" Isabel called after her.

The wind was strong and the woman's voice so low that Isabel barely heard her response.

"Sky," she said, over her shoulder. "Sky Thomas."

ISABEL RETURNED TO the clinic and her last appointment of the day.

Afterward, she stopped in the supply room and opened the refrigerator sent to her by Ken MacStirling. She hadn't realized Suzanne was just steps behind her.

"See what I mean?" Suzanne said from over her shoulder. "There must be a thousand doses there."

"I think that's exactly how many Dr. MacStirling said he'd be sending. We'll get a new shipment every couple weeks. Would you mind handing me a three-cc syringe?" Isabel said over her shoulder as she grabbed a tiny glass vial from the refrigerator's top shelf.

"You finally talk Dr. MacStirling into letting you vaccinate yourself?"

"I didn't exactly give him an option this time."

"You shoulda just vaccinated yourself back in Phase I," Suzanne said. "Want me to give it to you?"

Isabel turned to look at Suzanne. According to Suzanne, the former clinic doctor, Dr. Hammer, used to let her give shots all the time. Suzanne had been very unhappy when, during her first weeks at the clinic, Isabel made it clear that practice would have to end.

"Would you mind?" Isabel said.

" 'Course not. I like giving shots."

THIRTY-NINE

A T FIRST, KEN MacStirling passed right by the old redbrick building. Sergei Kirov had lived in an apartment building in Portland. MacStirling was looking for another multiplex or perhaps even a small house. The idea that Sergei could be inhabiting the old schoolhouse, which looked deserted, did not occur to him until he drove another two miles down the road and failed to find another building. Not even a turnoff.

Finally, he turned his Land Cruiser around and headed back down the two-lane road. He slowed at the old schoolhouse. The first time by he hadn't seen the numerals etched in the stone above the front door. He had to squint now to make them out. He looked at the numerals, then back to the piece of paper upon which Janet McIntosh had written Sergei Kirov's new address.

They matched.

MacStirling pulled into the gravel lot. He looked for a car, but found none. However, a narrow drive appeared to circle around the back of the building.

He approached the front door, hesitated, then knocked loudly three times. There was no answer.

He knocked again and waited.

Still, no answer.

If this was indeed where Sergei lived, he must not be home. Emboldened by his anger and panic at discovering the vaccine had been contaminated, MacStirling reached for the door knob and turned. It opened easily.

He pushed the door open and called inside.

"Hello?"

He was greeted by silence.

He stepped inside and found himself in what had obviously once been the lobby of a school building, but a television and chairs and a broken-down couch with several beer cans on the floor in front of it indicated someone now resided there.

MacStirling had left the front door open, perhaps subconsciously, as a safety precaution, and morning sun spilled in across the floor. The feathered inhabitants of the thickly forested area surrounding the building chat-

tered so noisily just outside that MacStirling wished he'd shut the door
so that he could better hear what, if anything, was going on inside. But
still, as he walked back by the door on his way to the staircase, he refrained from pushing it shut.

Scattered lines of sawdust and the smell of newly milled pine indicated the stairs had recently been rebuilt.

MacStirling climbed them slowly, stopping several times to listen. He
no longer felt comfortable calling out. He felt drawn upward, to the higher
levels of the building, yet at the same time an inner voice told him to get
out.

He continued up the stairs.

At the top, he could see where boards had been nailed across several
doors opening off the long hallway. Another door was partially closed. At
the very end, he could see what looked to be a kitchen. Slinking along,
hugging close to the walls, as if doing so made him less visible, he approached it.

He found the kitchen empty. Dirty dishes sat in a sink. A coffee cup
and partially eaten Hostess apple pie, its wrapper turned back like a
rolled-up sleeve, sat on the table.

An open door revealed another flight of stairs, leading to the third
floor.

MacStirling turned slowly around. Should he enter the stairwell? The
sign above indicated it had once been an emergency exit for schoolchil-
dren.

Tentatively, he placed a foot on the first step. The stairwell was not
lighted, and a door at its top was closed. He had to feel his way up,
running his hands along the wall for support. By the time he'd reached
the top, his eyes had adjusted somewhat to the absence of light. He could
see the door handle.

He reached for it and turned.

The door creaked open. MacStirling stepped through it, into a narrow
corridor. This floor was well lit from large paned-glass windows on each
end. Again, MacStirling saw no sign of life; however, a steady humming
sound came from the other side of the wall facing him.

MacStirling crept down the hall, toward the first door on his left, the
direction from which the sound of machinery seemed to emanate. Fifty-
and one-hundred-mile bike rides every weekend normally kept his pulse
in the low sixties, but he could feel it now, beating nearly out of control.

He could see the upper third of the door was dominated by a window.
Reaching it, he kept his body to one side, then slowly peeked inside.

What he saw stunned him.

Laboratory equipment—an autoclave, a magnetic resonance machine,
several microscopes, and a computer—filled one long table. In disbelief,
MacStirling stepped closer, craning his neck to see the rest of the room.

"Would you like the grand tour?" a voice said from behind him.

He knew the owner of the voice before he turned.

"Sergei," he said. "What are you doing here?"

He found himself face-to-face with the Russian, who was wearing a blue blazer and tan slacks. A red handkerchief stuck out of the blazer's top pocket. It was the first time MacStirling had ever seen his colleague in anything other than a lab coat.

"Here?" Sergei answered. "As in the United States? Or *here*, as in his laboratory?"

"Both."

The Russian smiled slowly. MacStirling couldn't remember ever seeing Sergei's teeth before. They were straight, but disproportionately small, exposing a great deal of gum. MacStirling reflexively stepped back.

"In answer to your question," Sergei said, "I'm back to continue the work I started in the Soviet Union."

"Your work in the Soviet Union? I thought you were involved in Russia's biowarfare research."

"That's right."

This was crazy.

"Who are you working for now?"

"ImmuVac, of course."

"You're doing biowarfare research for ImmuVac?"

"No, not exactly. I'm actually helping our beloved leader, Dr. Lyons, by developing a vaccine that will be quite valuable when biowarfare does, indeed, break out."

MacStirling did not know what to think. None of this made sense. Why had James Lyons secreted Sergei out here in Gaston, while telling the rest of the ImmuVac employees the Russian had returned home?

"What kind of vaccine?"

Kirov giggled. Almost like a woman. The sound sickened MacStirling.

"Smallpox."

MacStirling stared at Kirov. The Russian was playing with him. But what was the game?

"Now," Kirov said, "to what do I owe the pleasure of this most unexpected visit?"

MacStirling momentarily wondered if he was going mad. The discovery that the HantaVac was contaminated. Sergei's lab in Gaston. It all had taken on a sense of the surreal.

He shook his head.

"I don't know," he said. "I just found out you might be back yesterday. It was an accident, the girl at the travel agency said something about your buying a ticket to Leningrad."

"Yes. I will be returning home. Shortly. But enough about me, how is your study going? The HantaVac trials?"

"Brilliant. Great. At least they were, until late last night when I discovered that the most recent lot had been contaminated."

"Contaminated? How dreadful."

"Dreadful hardly describes it. Phase III is scheduled to begin tomorrow morning. The entire trial may be jeopardized."

"You can't mean that you've called off Phase III?"

Kirov's voice had risen now. His casual, almost teasing demeanor seemed to turn stiff as he stuck his hand into the pocket of his blazer.

"I haven't called it off yet. In fact, I haven't even told Lyons about the contamination. You know how he'll react. But you know as well as I do that we can't use a contaminated vaccine. Not until we identify the contaminant and establish it's harmless."

"Dr. Lyons doesn't know about this yet?"

"No." MacStirling studied Sergei. "I just told you I hadn't told him yet."

"Who *have* you told?"

"No one. I've told no one. I wanted to have some answers before I did. That's why I came here."

MacStirling didn't like the direction this conversation had taken. He'd come here to be the questioner, not the person being questioned.

It had occurred to him in the middle of the night. He'd returned from the lab in a state of near hysteria. Since Stella had locked him out of the bedroom, he'd literally paced the living room floor for hours, trying to imagine how a contamination could have occurred while he was out of town.

And then, at some point, after he'd worked through countless possibilities, none of which seemed even remotely possible, the words of the travel agent had come to him.

Here we go. Dr. Kirov? A ticket for Leningrad?

According to the travel agent, two days earlier Sergei Kirov had purchased a ticket to Leningrad. MacStirling had finally decided the girl was mistaken, that she was referring to the ticket purchased before Sergei took his long trip, the one that ended in Lyons's announcing Sergei had decided to stay in Russia. But as he paced the floor last night, MacStirling began to contemplate the possibility that Sergei had returned to Portland. That he had, indeed, purchased another ticket out of the country.

His going to Rainy Day Travel had been a shot in the dark. He hadn't really expected any cooperation, and even if anyone at the travel agency did agree to help, he'd expected to learn that the ticket had been purchased before Sergei disappeared.

But the new address given him for Sergei changed all that.

After the seed regarding Sergei had been planted last night, he'd come up with other damning evidence.

The only other person who ever seemed comfortable working in the maximum-containment annex at ImmuVac had been Sergei Kirov.

Sergei had shown clear resentment at having funds channeled into the hantavirus vaccine instead of to his own work.

If, indeed, the contamination was deliberate, Kirov would have been a logical suspect—if it weren't for the fact that he'd returned to Russia.

But now MacStirling knew that Kirov hadn't returned to Russia. He'd instead been set up in a lab that no one knew about, twenty miles outside Portland.

On his drive out to Gaston, MacStirling had tried to make sense of it all. He'd been furious. Furious to know Kirov still resided in the area. More furious still to think he may have been the one to contaminate Lot Two.

He'd planned to let Kirov have it with both barrels, but the eerie setting and discovery of the third floor lab had unsettled him.

And now he'd allowed Kirov to turn the tables on him and become the interrogator.

"Listen here, Sergei," MacStirling said, stepping forward again, into Kirov's face. "I came here to find out if you'd been in the maximum-containment facility."

Kirov's eyebrows rose.

"You think I am the one who contaminated your vaccine?"

"Right about now, I don't know what to think. But I know that I need answers. Preferably before I go to James Lyons."

This time it was Sergei who stepped back. When he did, he simultaneously withdrew his hand from the pocket of his blazer. It held a small handgun.

"You won't be going to Lyons with anything," he said.

MacStirling's eyes darted from the gun to Sergei Kirov's expressionless face, his worst fears confirmed.

"It was you. You contaminated the vaccine, didn't you?"

Kirov displayed his gums once more.

"Of course it was me. No one else at ImmuVac is smart enough, or courageous enough, to do it."

"But why? Why would you do it?"

"Technically, I did it for money. I was paid to contaminate the vaccine. But the truth is, I've been wanting to destroy your precious trial ever since it started." He laughed then. "At first, I'd hoped to talk Lyons into calling it off. But now, now you see, I find myself in a position where I cannot allow that. Phase III must go forward. It's the only way I'll receive the money I've been promised. And then I will leave this godless country."

"Sergei, listen to me. You don't realize what you're doing. We can't allow a contaminated vaccine to be used. It could be dangerous. This is bigger than a petty rivalry between two scientists. People could be harmed by it."

"You are very correct about that," Sergei said. "There's no doubt. Most will die."

"What?"

"Most will die. I predict approximately ninety percent."

"What is it?" MacStirling shouted, ignoring the gun now as he grabbed Sergei by the collar. "What did you contaminate the vaccine with?"

Turning, he followed Sergei's smiling eyes through the window into the lab.

"No, God, please, tell me. Not smallpox. You didn't use smallpox, did you?"

He heard the click then and turned back to Kirov.

Only two inches separated his forehead from the barrel of the gun.

"You can't get away with this," MacStirling said, sweat running down his face and beading on the point of his chin. "Isabel's expecting me there tomorrow, at the start of Phase III. She won't begin it without me. Don't you see? You can't kill me."

Kirov hesitated just long enough to be sure MacStirling registered the last words he would ever hear.

"Oh, can't I?"

And then he pulled the trigger.

CHAPTER

FORTY

AFTER A SLEEPLESS night in Edna's Impala, Monty had used a gas station rest room to wash up and then, a little after nine, he'd strolled into the WRI building, his hand in the pocket of the hooded sweatshirt he'd taken from Isabel's closet, over the pistol Gus had given her.

The directory in the lobby listed the sixth floor for the executive offices. Never removing his hand from the pocket, he'd stepped onto the elevator with two well-dressed women, both of whom got off before six. When the doors opened on six, he'd stepped into a marble-floored reception area. A heavily made-up Asian woman drew back at the sight of him.

When he'd asked for LeCoque, she'd told him WRI's CEO was out of town.

"When's he due back?"

"I'm not sure," she'd answered, though Monty knew that she was sure. He saw her hand going for the phone, no doubt to call security.

Not wanting to wait around for security, Monty had turned and stepped back onto the elevator, which hadn't yet left the sixth floor. This time he pressed the button for four, which is where the directory said Wilderman's office was located.

The receptionist on four, more accustomed to crewmen visiting the office, was far more relaxed.

"Can I help you?" she'd said with a smile that indicated Monty's good looks were not wasted on her.

"I'm looking for Tony Wilderman," Monty said. "I'm a friend of his."

"Tony's out of town today, with Mr. LeCoque. He'll be in the office again first thing in the morning. Who should I tell him stopped by?"

"Thomas Rose," Monty answered.

"Well, you're welcome to come back tomorrow, Mr. Rose."

"Thanks. I'll do that."

Patience had never been Monty's strong suit and the idea of having to wait another day to confront LeCoque and Wilderman made him half crazy. Another night of sleeping in the car, counting the hours until he would avenge Leroy's death.

If only he had that file . . .

Suddenly a visual image of the Intelligence Gathering Unit sheet on Lyons came to him. It had stated his address, but there was something else. Something about a boat. A yacht that he kept harbored nearby, so close that he could see it from his office window. Monty had thought it silly and useless information when he'd first read it. He'd questioned IGU's use of time. But now it stood to be very valuable, and he had AIM's IGU to thank.

Finding itself all too often the target of government-backed intelligence investigations, years earlier AIM decided that its survival depended upon developing its own spies. The IGU had proven itself indispensable in alerting members to pending anti-AIM activities by the FBI and other governmental agencies.

Reports from IGU had also proven a valuable tool in the organization's many crusades. More and more of the report on Lyons came back to Monty now. LeCoque often slept aboard the vessel and he *liked to brag about being able to keep an eye on it from his high-rise office.*

Bingo.

•   •   •

JON LECOQUE HAD asked Tony Wilderman along for his meeting with Walt Lundgren of Global Finance. He and Wilderman had just returned from a trip to southeastern Oregon, where they'd been informed that Hudson Bay Mining had already secured rights to the Grassy Mountain deposit Wilderman had investigated earlier, on the same trip when he'd discovered the Blackfeet deposit. LeCoque wanted Lundgren to meet Wilderman. He felt that the geologist's assurances that WRI had several promising deposits under exploration could help convince Lundgren to provide the bridge financing WRI needed to survive.

They'd driven straight to the restaurant from the airport.

LeCoque and Lundgren had a history together. They'd both grown up dirt poor in a small town outside of Calgary, where they'd attended the same school. Both ended up heading large corporations in Vancouver and had been deemed "mavericks" by the press for their willingness to take risks. And, perhaps their greatest bond, they both understood the desperation occasioned by the prospect of losing the respect and power they'd fought so hard to obtain.

"Tell you what, Jon," Lundgren had told him over dinner at Rudy's Grill, "I told you I'd consider the loan if in the next six months you could show me where you'd have an active, productive mine by the year 2002. Based on our friendship and your excellent record with Global, I might just be willing to extend that time frame another year. You provide me with a solid lease on a solid deposit in the next eighteen months, and my original offer stands."

"You know I appreciate that, Walt," LeCoque had answered. "As you heard tonight from Tony, we're confident we can do just that. All we need is a little extra time."

One of Lundgren's bushy black eyebrows shot up.

"You got something up your sleeve?"

"Hell no. But Wilderman's the best damn exploratory geologist in the business. And we've still got the right of first refusal on that Blackfeet deposit."

"Too bad about that Blackfeet business. Good deposit, close to home. With that kind of P-and-L, it could've been a bonanza for WRI."

"Who knows? Still could be."

"You never know," Lundgren conceded. Then he broke into a grin. "Hey, remember that time we snuck that truckload of beer over the border and sold it on the reservation?" He turned his toothy grin on Wilderman. "We made about as much money in one trip as Ike Newman paid us the entire summer working at his Dairy Queen."

"I remember." LeCoque forced a laugh. He hated Lundgren's trips down memory lane. He'd spent a lifetime trying to forget where he came from. Lundgren, however, suffered from no such compunction and loved to dredge up their youths, which is why LeCoque avoided including other business associates in their meetings whenever possible.

"Listen, Walt," he'd finally said. "We'd better call it a night. I'm leaving for Ontario in the morning."

In the car, he invited Wilderman back to *Chesire* for an after-dinner drink.

"I've got Rod Sokaski meeting me there," he explained. "I thought the three of us might have a little chat. After finding out Hudson Bay's tied up rights to Grassy Mountain, I think it's even more important that we see if there's anything else we can do to salvage that Blackfeet deposit."

Wilderman had been glum all day, ever since learning Hudson Bay had beat them to the Oregon deposit, but he brightened a bit at the suggestion.

"Can't hurt anything," he'd mused.

ARRIVING AT THE yacht club, LeCoque parked in his reserved stall, then the two men picked their way carefully down the rain-slickened walkway to the gated pier. A wrought iron gate prevented unwelcome visitors from proceeding further. LeCoque punched in the three-digit code and the gate swung open.

As a charter member of the yacht club, LeCoque had been given his choice of moorage. He'd chosen the end of the pier for its unobstructed view of the mountains and city. Approaching *Chesire*, LeCoque noticed that her cabin was cloaked in darkness. An automatic timer had been set to turn on a cabin light each evening at dusk. The bulb, he observed out loud to Wilderman, must have burned out.

LeCoque fumbled momentarily with the key to the cabin door, then stepped inside. Clutching the railing tightly, he descended the four stairs to the cabin, with Wilderman following on his heels.

"Blasted dark in here with that light burned out outside."

He placed his palm flat against the cabin wall and inched toward the light switch, irritated at the discomfort and sense of vulnerability caused by something so minor as a burned-out light bulb.

His hand finally made contact with the light switch, and as he flipped it, an inexplicable sense of foreboding raced through him. Simultaneous with the light flooding the room, LeCoque sensed the presence of someone besides Wilderman.

As he turned, he heard a distinctive click.

Above the barrel of a .38-caliber handgun, the wild eyes of a disheveled, dark-skinned man—unmistakably Indian, whether American or Canadian, it took LeCoque just seconds to learn—met his.

Expressionless, except for the glint in his black eyes, his visitor looked at home in LeCoque's favorite captain's chair, his feet planted squarely, legs splayed. He clutched his right arm close to the chest of his soggy flannel shirt.

"Monty Four Bear," Wilderman sputtered.

Four Bear simply stared at them. The sense of danger he exuded—his silence and steely demeanor—utterly terrified LeCoque. From the absence of sound or movement next to him, he knew that Wilderman was experiencing the same fear.

"*What is it you want?*" Wilderman asked. "You won already. Didn't you? Your tribal council kicked us out. What more could you want?"

Rising from the chair, the gun's aim never wavering, Four Bear took one step toward LeCoque and Wilderman.

"Who did it?" he said, his eyes trained now on Wilderman.

"Did what?" Wilderman cried.

"Who killed my father?" With each word, LeCoque's sense of dread grew. He was grateful, however, that Four Bear seemed more focused on Wilderman. "Who did you pay to pull the trigger?"

"I don't know what you're talking about."

Four Bear crossed the distance separating them in an instant. Backhanding Wilderman across the face with the gun, he exploded.

"Don't fuck with me!" he screamed. "Just tell me. I want a name. Who did it? Who killed my father?"

The blow threw Wilderman to the floor of the cabin. With Wilderman down, groaning in pain as he held his shattered jaw, Four Bear turned on LeCoque, the gun still raised threateningly.

"Please," LeCoque begged, "There's no need for that. I'll tell you. We had Sokaski beat him up . . ."

"Jon, *shut up*," Wilderman screamed from the floor.

"He's going to kill me," LeCoque snapped back. "Kill both of us." He turned pleading eyes on Monty. "Sokaski did it. He beat him up. It was his," he nodded his head toward Wilderman, on the floor, "*his* idea."

Another low groan, this one of dread, could be heard from the floor.

"Who killed him?"

LeCoque shook his head.

"We didn't have him killed. We just wanted to scare you, make you back down. I swear, we didn't kill him."

Just then, LeCoque's peripheral vision picked up movement behind Four Bear. The cabin door had opened and muddy brown construction boots silently began their descent of the stairs.

Thank God, Sokaski had arrived.

•   •   •

MONTY FELT HIS presence before he saw it.

Gun first, he spun around and recognized the man descending the stairs as the big-mouthed miner who'd been involved in the fight at the protest. Now he looked considerably milder, picking his way down carefully, both arms held high in the air. Behind the big miner, an even bigger man also descended slowly.

Bud Wolfkill. He held a gun to the miner's back.

"What are you doing here?" Monty asked.

Wolfkill's eyes quickly assessed the situation.

"Saving your ass, what else?" he answered. "Drop that, Monty. Do you know what a jurisdictional nightmare it would be if someone got hurt here?"

"Sorry, Bud, but you shouldn't have followed me. If you think I'm gonna let them go, you wasted your time. I'll die before I let that happen."

"You don't know who killed Leroy, Monty. But we'll find out. The legal way. Now drop that gun."

Ignoring him, Monty raised it instead, level with Sokaski's face.

"Drop the fuckin' gun, man," Sokaski said, sweat beginning to bead along his hairline and the stubble on his upper lip.

"You did it," Monty cursed. "You killed Leroy."

"I don't know what you're talking about."

"Play games with me and I'll blow that ugly face off."

Bud did not move from his position behind Sokaski, where his eyes roamed from one WRI man to another.

"They admitted you were the one who beat Leroy up," Monty said, closing the gap between him and Sokaski. "You killed him too."

Sokaski eyes went from LeCoque to Wilderman.

"You sons of bitches. You told him."

A new level of panic seized his features.

"Okay. I admit it. I beat him up. They paid me to." He hesitated. "But I'm not the one who killed your old man."

"You expect me to believe that?"

Deftly, with amazing quickness, Monty backhanded Sokaski across the face.

Reflexively, Sokaski's hands dropped to protect himself.

"Put 'em back up," Wolfkill ordered.

Slowly, the arms rose again.

"Okay. Okay," Sokaski said. "I told you. I just roughed the old guy up. I didn't kill him. But I can tell you who did."

Every eye in the room turned on Sokaski.

"It was this guy with this Southern accent," he declared, his eyes clearing of some of their panic. "That's who killed him. He called me. He wanted to hire me to kill some Russian dude outside Portland. *He's* the one who killed the old man. He told me he slit his throat while he was sleeping."

Monty had assumed Leroy was shot. The idea of someone using a knife . . .

Enraged, he lunged forward with a deep growl, tackling Sokaski.

"No one makes a move," he heard Wolfkill say from where he stood over Monty and Sokaski.

Seconds later, a sharp boot landed in Monty's back.

"Monty," Wolfkill bellowed, "in about two minutes the Canadian police are gonna be showing up. Do you want to hear what this asshole has to say about Leroy's killer, or do you want to leave the whole thing to the Canadians?"

Monty released his lopsided hold on Sokaski. He grabbed him by the collar and pulled him to a sitting position on the floor.

"Who is he?" he demanded. "The guy who called you."

Sokaski shook his big head.

"I dunno. He wouldn't give me his name. Only a phone number. It was from Seattle."

"Why did he want to kill the Russian?" Wolfkill broke in.

"Forget that," Monty snapped. "We're here about Leroy."

But Sokaski ignored Monty and looked up at Wolfkill.

"He said he wouldn't need the Russian after tomorrow. He wanted me to kill him to make certain he wouldn't talk."

"Talk about what?"

"Goddamn it, Bud," Monty barked, "let someone else deal with this fucking Russian. I want to know who this Southern guy is."

"I told you," Sokaski said, "I don't know. He never gave me his name. But he said he hated all you Blackfeet. Something about his wife being a traitor."

"I might be able to help," Wilderman offered from the floor.

"I think I know who he's talking about," he continued. "He's a doctor. I ran into him a couple times in East Glacier. A strange bird, really interested in the mine on the reservation. Beating Four Bear's father up was his idea. He's the one who suggested that it would scare you into backing down."

"You know where we can find this guy?" Wolfkill asked. "What his name is?"

Wilderman reached for his back pocket, then seeing Bud take aim on him, explained, "I've got his card in my wallet."

When Wilderman finally produced the business card, Wolfkill scanned it first, then passed it to Monty. But by then, Monty already knew what he'd see.

ALISTAIR BOTT, M.D. Isabel's ex-husband.

Monty's gut twisted at the sight. He snatched the card from Wilderman and turned a wary eye on Sokaski.

"Why would Bott want to kill Leroy?"

"I told you. He hates you Blackfeet. He said he was gonna take care of all of you once and for all. That he hired the Russian dude to do it for him. He wanted me to kill the Russian after tomorrow. Said he wouldn't need him after that. Told me I'd find fifty-thousand dollars on him. That was supposed to be my payment. But I told him I had to have money up front and he never sent it."

"Tomorrow's the big vaccination clinic on the rez," Bud Wolfkill said softly.

Monty's head jerked up to catch Wolfkill's eye.

"Could there be a connection?"

Wolfkill's expression was somber.

"We better find out." He turned back to Sokaski.

"What more can you tell us about this Russian?"

"Just that he lives in an old schoolhouse. In a town called Gaston."

WOLFKILL HAD CALLED the Royal Canadian Mounted Police before surprising Rod Sokaski outside the *Chesire*. When they showed up minutes later, they took Sokaski, Wilderman, and LeCoque into custody.

Monty and Bud sped to the airport, where Bud had landed only five hours earlier—after following his hunch that Monty could be found near LeCoque.

At the airport, they learned they would have to fly from Vancouver to Seattle, before changing planes for Kalispell. While they waited, Wolfkill placed three calls.

The first was to the station in Browning, telling them to be on the lookout for Alistair Bott. The second, with identical instructions, was to the Seattle police.

The final call was to the local police in Gaston, Oregon.

"All I know," Bud stated into the phone, "is that this Russian lives in some old schoolhouse in your town. We need this man detained. It's urgent."

The officer on the other end knew right away what he was talking about.

"Must be the old elementary out on Ridge Road. Someone's living there now. I'll send an officer right out."

Before they boarded, Bud pulled out a pair of handcuffs and fastened first Monty's good arm, then the bad.

"Sorry about this, pal," he said. "But in the frame of mind you're in, you wouldn't think twice about makin' a fool outta me."

Monty glared at him. Neither man said a word to the other on either flight.

When Bud went to the pay phone at the Kalispell airport, his order that Monty stay at his side was unnecessary. Monty stood close enough to smell the gum on Wolfkill's breath, his eyes focused intensely on Bud, while Bud listened to a wild tale told by the chief of police in Gaston, who'd been called in to handle the city's first homicide in two decades.

"You mean to tell me it's too late? The Russian's already dead?" Wolfkill asked.

"The guy who died was British or Scottish," the Gaston chief of police reported, "not Russian. He was a scientist at a company nearby, in Portland. An outfit called ImmuVac."

Bud visibly stiffened at the familiar name. ImmuVac was the company sponsoring the HantaVac study on the reservation.

"What about the Russian? Where's he?"

"We don't know. Apparently he shot the guy we found out there at the old schoolhouse. The poor fella was near death, medevacs couldn't save him. But he could talk a little. I'm not sure he was all there though, if you know what I mean. Said some pretty bizarre things."

"Like what?"

"My officer said he was pretty hard to understand, but before he died, he kept mumbling something about 'phase three.' "

"*What?*" Wolfkill pressed. "What was it he said?"

"Something about a contamination. That the Russian who shot him had contaminated phase three—whatever *that* is."

Wolfkill's face had drained of color.

"Did he say what, what he'd contaminated it with?"

"My man swore he said it was smallpox."

BUD WOLFKILL LOOKED at the clock above the gate where they'd just disembarked. Nine A.M. One hour until the vaccinations were to start.

He went to the telephone and called the Browning clinic. A recording. They'd already left for East Glacier.

He couldn't waste any more time. He could make it to East Glacier in an hour. And he would radio ahead for reinforcements from the car.

He started to jog through Kalispell's sleepy airport. Monty kept pace with him, silent. When they reached the squad car, in the parking lot where Bud had left it the day before, Wolfkill climbed in and slid the key into the ignition.

Monty did not follow suit.

Wolfkill reached across the seat and opened the door.

"Get in, dammit," he said. "We can't afford to waste time."

Monty bent to look Wolfkill in the eye.

"I'm going after him, Bud. After Bott."

"Goddammit, Monty. You're under arrest. Get your ass in here, now."

"It only takes one of us to stop the clinical trial. You go to East Glacier. I have to do this, Bud. Can't you see? I have to be the one who brings the bastard in. If I go back with you now, I'll be taken into custody and he could go free."

Bud had never known Monty Four Bear to plead, but he was pleading now.

"He killed Leroy, Bud. And look what he's done to Isabel, and to our people. I give you my word. I'll be back. But first let me do what I have to do."

Wolfkill's fist came down hard on the steering wheel.

"Jesus Christ, Four Bear," he growled. He stared out at the cloudless sky for several seconds, then punched the steering wheel once again.

Finally he turned troubled eyes to Monty. "Nobody knew how Leroy died. We kept that quiet. Nobody knew. Except the murderer. The way I see it, that could still be Sokaski," he said. "Or it could be Bott."

He pulled the keys out of the ignition.

"Put your hands out."

Monty struggled to extend both hands, his injured shoulder not allowing full extension of the right arm.

Wolfkill stretched across the vehicle's front seat and inserted the key. The metal links dropped noisily to the seat.

"Now get out of here," he ordered.

CHAPTER

FORTY-ONE

WHILE SHE NO longer felt much of anything besides a gnawing grief and worry related to Monty's disappearance, Isabel could not help but feel grateful to see the sun shining this day.

The former shoe repair shop on the edge of the town of East Glacier, which had been offered as a site for the kickoff of Phase III, had a depressing air about it. Isabel had learned from Phases I and II that participants were jumpy enough about taking part in the clinical trial. They didn't need their sense of dread heightened by a damp, musky setting.

The sky had turned a soft, silky blue just before sunset the previous night, and Isabel had awakened this morning to near-blinding sunlight streaming through her windows. She'd closed her eyes, pressing the back of her hands to them, as if she could keep the tears away with sheer physical force.

Now, just after nine A.M., the temperature had climbed into the mid-seventies. A soft breeze promised to keep the day comfortable. She'd asked Suzanne to help her set up a table for the vaccinations outside, on the wooden porch.

A young Blackfeet mother with her two children in tow had arrived while they were setting up the table. She did not introduce herself to either Isabel or Suzanne, but instead went to sit on the edge of the long wood-planked boardwalk that ran the length of what was officially down-town East Glacier, watching as her children played in the weedy area between the abandoned shoe repair shop and a gas station that had closed years earlier.

"Good morning," Isabel said, approaching her.

"Mornin'," the woman returned softly.

"Are you here for the clinical trial?"

The young woman nodded.

"I'm Dr. McLain."

"I'm Lucy Freeman."

"Nice to meet you, Lucy. Since you're the first here, you'll be lucky enough to be the first done. I'll have Suzanne come over and talk to you about what to expect today." She looked at her watch. Nine-fifteen. She'd told MacStirling the trial was to begin at ten, but she could tell by how nervous Lucy appeared that that long a wait would be difficult for her and her children.

"The vaccinations aren't supposed to begin until ten."

"Ten? I heard nine." Isabel could see Lucy's anxiety level rising with the news that she and her children would have to wait.

"We're expecting Dr. MacStirling from ImmuVac to arrive any minute. Maybe we can get started a little early."

"I hope so," Lucy said softly.

More study participants, Isabel knew, would come straggling in over the next couple of hours, regardless of the appointment time that had been given them. Isabel had learned early on not to be a clock-watcher when it came to her Blackfeet patients. If they had an appointment, she could usually count on them eventually showing up.

Knowing Ken MacStirling, he would arrive early and they could send Lucy and her kids on their way. Just as that thought entered her mind, Isabel caught sight of a gold vehicle approaching from the west, on High-way 2. She stood watching, then as it slowed upon entering the town of East Glacier, she recognized Ken MacStirling's Land Cruiser and began waving.

But MacStirling cruised right on by, as if he didn't see her.

Isabel watched as the Land Cruiser slowed to a crawl, then pulled over at the sign she and Suzanne had made just that morning.

EAST GLACIER CLINICAL TRIAL SITE.

By the time she reached MacStirling's vehicle, the door on the driver's side had opened. Isabel stepped down off the sidewalk to greet him.

But the man who emerged was not Ken MacStirling.

Isabel took a step backward and looked at the license plate on the front of the Land Cruiser.

Oregon. She hadn't been mistaken. It was Ken MacStirling's vehicle.

By now, its driver had honed in on her and approached, right hand extended.

"Dr. McLain?" He spoke in a thick accent and looked woefully out of place in his blue blazer, with a silly red hankie poking out of the upper pocket.

Confused, Isabel nonetheless extended her hand and grasped his.

"Yes. Where's Dr. MacStirling?"

"I'm Dr. Kirov, an associate of Dr. MacStirling's. I'm afraid he's fallen ill. He asked me to take his place today."

"I hope it's nothing serious."

"Not at all. Just a touch of the flu. But it was important to him, to all of us, that a representative from ImmuVac be here on this important day. In fact, as you can see, Dr. MacStirling even loaned me his car."

"I'm surprised Dr. MacStirling didn't call me," Isabel said. After all, if Dr. Kirov had enough time to drive all the way to East Glacier from Portland, MacStirling had plenty of time to call Isabel and tell her he'd sent a substitute.

The comment seemed to throw Kirov off. He hesitated before responding.

"He can barely speak." Maybe she'd imagined it. "Laryngitis. I'm afraid it's my fault no one called you. Dr. MacStirling asked me to and I simply forgot."

Something about Dr. Kirov bothered Isabel. His formal attire and manner of speech were entirely out of place there, on the reservation. But it was more than that.

ImmuVac had every right to have a representative present at the start of Phase III; still, Isabel resented Kirov's presence, when she had so much to do. She'd understood MacStirling's desire to be there; but, technically, he had no role in the actual administration of the vaccine. Sending Dr. Kirov in his place was nonsense. She had enough on her mind without having to play host to some figurehead sent there as a symbolic gesture.

"I'm most eager to get started," Kirov said then, further annoying her.

"Well, we're not scheduled to begin for another forty-five minutes, but as you can see, people have already begun arriving." Two more cars had pulled up, alongside the Land Cruiser. "I was thinking we may actually want to begin a little early. Lucy Freeman, the young woman over there with the two cute kids, thought we started at nine. I'm afraid she may change her mind if we keep her waiting much longer."

"Then by all means, we should accommodate her."

Isabel looked around. There was no real harm in starting a little early. She should just be pleased to see the turnout they already had. It would be a shame to lose anyone who got nervous during their wait.

"Okay," she said. "Let's. Listen, you might as well take off your jacket. It's warming up and it's going to be a long day. I'll just have Suzanne help me set up, then after we introduce you, we can get started."

"There's no need to introduce me," Dr. Kirov said briskly. He made no move to take off his blazer, but stood stiffly, appearing overly anxious, even irritated, at any possible delay, however insignificant.

The arriving participants had begun shooting curious glances Kirov's way.

This is just what we need, thought Isabel. Many of her patients had grown used to seeing MacStirling around. And to give him credit, Ken did have a low-key manner about him. This Dr. Kirov, however, was another matter entirely. Isabel could see his presence made many of those gathering around the table uneasy.

She stepped closer to him and lowered her voice.

"Listen, Dr. Kirov, these people are somewhat uncomfortable with outsiders. Especially when it's related to this trial. I think it would be a good idea for you to either stand back some distance, where you'd be less visible, or take off your jacket, roll up your sleeves, and get busy. Would you like to assist me by drawing the vaccine while Suzanne does the paperwork?"

"I prefer to keep my jacket on. But of course I can help you with the vaccine."

Isabel decided to dispense with any formalities and get started, before Kirov's presence did too much harm. Besides, why bother introducing this pompous jerk?

She picked up the clipboard that had been sitting on the table. She and Suzanne had worked out a procedure for the large-scale Phase III clinics. Suzanne would have participants sign in as they arrived, then, once she verified that the signed application and consent forms were on file— they'd brought two portable filing boxes full of documents with them— she placed a red check mark after each name.

Isabel looked at the top of the list.

Lucy Freeman, then the names of her two children, Marcus and Nancy. A red check mark followed all three names.

"Mrs. Freeman?" Isabel called out.

Lucy Freeman approached slowly from her spot on the end of the sidewalk. On either side, a young, reluctant child held tight to her hand.

"Now," Isabel said with a reassuring smile, "who would like to be the first one vaccinated?"

Lucy Freeman bent at the waist to consult with her children. Isabel could just hear her.

"Would you guys like me to go first, or do you want to get your shots over with first?"

"You go first, Mama," the little girl said, still clutching Lucy's hand.

"No, I'll go first."

The boy stepped forward, toward Isabel.

Isabel looked to Lucy Freeman for a definitive answer.

"Let Marcus," Lucy said.

"Okay, Marcus," Isabel said, "let's go right over to the table. See that chair? All you have to do is take a seat there and roll up your left sleeve."

The crowd parted as all eyes followed Marcus, who marched bravely to the chair. Isabel nodded at Dr. Kirov. He reached into a box labeled MONOJECT SYRINGES, then into a small cooler sitting next to it.

As Isabel helped Marcus roll up his sleeve, Kirov inserted the hypodermic needle he'd withdrawn from the box through the rubber seal of a vial he'd taken from the cooler. The vial contained two and a half cc's of clear liquid—the HantaVac vaccine. Pulling back on the syringe's stopper, Kirov drew the fluid into the syringe.

Then he handed it to Isabel. Isabel dabbed Marcus's upper arm with alcohol. Then, as Marcus winced, she inserted the needle and emptied the syringe's contents.

LUCY FREEMAN WAS next. But when it was her little girl's turn, the child began screaming and crying, her howls filling East Glacier's main street.

"Ms. Freeman," Isabel said, "maybe you should take Nancy on a little walk. See if she calms down a bit, and then you can come back."

Isabel could tell the child's howls were beginning to unnerve some of the dozen or more people who had arrived in the past few minutes.

"No," Kirov said, "we must vaccinate her now."

"Dr. Kirov," Isabel said, making a great effort to conceal her anger. "May I speak to you in private?"

When they'd stepped inside the former shoe repair shop, she let him have it.

"Do not contradict me in front of my patients. You are here as an observer. Nothing more."

Isabel was startled to see Kirov smile.

"Let me ask you, Dr. McLain. Have you received the vaccine yet?"

"Yes. Just yesterday."

"You did not participate in Phase I or Phase II?"

"No. Ken MacStirling asked me not to. But I insisted on being vaccinated now."

"A very wise decision," Kirov said. "I will behave myself, Dr. McLain. Please, let's proceed."

Back out on the sidewalk, things had calmed down. Isabel looked at her watch. Almost ten A.M.

"Okay," she said to Suzanne. "Who's next?"

"My aunt Mary," Suzanne answered, nodding toward the frail woman standing next to her.

"Hello, Mary," she said. "Why don't you make yourself comfortable over here, in this chair?"

The syringe containing the dose of HantaVac drawn for Nancy Freeman still lay on the table. Isabel reached for it as she swabbed Mary's bony upper arm.

As she raised the syringe, a sudden squeal of brakes, followed by the sound of gravel flying drew everyone's attention toward the road.

A Tribal Police car shuddered to a stop and the door flew open.

Why would Bud Wolfkill be here?

"Don't do it," Bud yelled to her. "Don't give her the shot."

Isabel hadn't realized that she still held the needle, poised above Mary's shoulder.

Bud Wolfkill had started forward, toward her.

"Don't come any closer," a voice from behind Isabel ordered.

She turned. Dr. Kirov no longer stood behind the table, where she'd last seen him. Instead, he had moved to Suzanne's side. A wash of adrenaline seized Isabel when she saw the gun he held to Suzanne's temple.

"Immunize her," Kirov said calmly. "Now."

"Don't do it, Isabel." It was Wolfkill again. "He contaminated the vaccine with smallpox."

Most of the crowd had scrambled upon seeing the guns, but the word "smallpox" brought gasps from several directions. Out of the corner of her eye, Isabel saw two men restraining Lucy Freeman. She could hear the young woman's sobs, mixed with the cries of her children.

Kirov's eyes jerked back and forth between Isabel and Wolfkill, who had frozen in his tracks. Wolfkill had pulled his gun and now held it in both hands, arms outstretched and directed at Kirov.

"Don't you move," Sergei Kirov ordered Mary Talking Horse.

Isabel placed a reassuring hand on Mary's shoulder and squeezed. She could push the woman to safety, then try to position herself in the line of fire between Kirov and her. But with Kirov holding the gun to Suzanne's head, any movement could have deadly repercussions.

"Immunize her," Kirov repeated. "Now."

"Don't do it," Suzanne said weakly.

"Dr. Kirov," Isabel said. "*Please,* lower your gun." She couldn't help herself. "It isn't true, is it?"

The sound that issued from Kirov's throat—laughter—could not possibly be human.

"Oh, but it is true," he said.

"But Dr. MacStirling . . ."

"Dr. MacStirling had nothing to do with it. In a way, it's a shame that he could not be here . . ."

It all suddenly made sense for Isabel. Nothing could keep Ken MacStirling away on this day.

"Oh my God. What did you do to him?"

Kirov's eyes were devoid of emotion.

"Vaccinate the woman. Or this one dies."

Suzanne closed her eyes as he touched the gun's barrel to her temple.

"Why?" Isabel was stalling for time. "Can you tell me that? Why does it matter if she's vaccinated?"

"Before I die, I want to see my life's work realized. I want the world to remember Sergei Kirov."

"But *I've* already received the vaccine," Isabel said. "I told you. So has Lucy Freeman, and Marcus. So you see, you *will* be remembered."

When Kirov did not respond, desperate, she kept trying.

"Why do you think you have to die, Dr. Kirov?"

"I would die before I would live with the scum your society puts in its prisons."

"Listen to me," Isabel said. "You can run. Take me as a hostage. Let Suzanne and Mary go. I'll go with you. To Canada. The border's less than fifty miles from here."

"Don't do it, Dr. McLain," Bud Wolfkill ordered.

"Let's go, Dr. Kirov. Take me with you."

"Dr. McLain," Bud Wolfkill called out, "leave this to the police."

"Mary doesn't need to receive the vaccine," Isabel said, locking eyes with Kirov. "Marcus and Lucy already have. And *I* have."

"How do I know you're telling me the truth?"

"Why do you think I'm willing to go with you now? It's because I have nothing to lose, do I? Not if that vaccine is contaminated with smallpox."

This reasoning seemed to make an impression on Kirov.

"Come here," he said.

Dropping the syringe, Isabel gave Mary a shove.

Quickly, as Mary scrambled to safety, Isabel moved toward Kirov. When she was within reach, he lifted the gun from Suzanne and redirected it to Isabel.

"Let's go," he said, reaching out and grabbing her roughly by the elbow.

"You're not taking her anywhere," Wolfkill protested, but Kirov seemed to know that he would not risk trying to stop them.

Sergei began maneuvering Isabel toward the Land Cruiser, the gun poking sharply against her spine.

"Drop your gun," he barked at Wolfkill.

Wolfkill did not move.

"Do as he says, Bud," Isabel pleaded.

"I can't do that. He's already killed Dr. MacStirling. If we let him go, he'll kill you too. And who knows how many others?"

Ever the man of reason, Kirov paused.

"I will make you a deal," he said. "You will allow us to leave now. And you will not alert the border patrol. If we make it safely inside Canada, I will release Dr. McLain and tell her where to find my smallpox vaccine. It's the only chance she has to survive the contaminated vaccine she received. But everything must go as I say. If not, one way or another, she will die."

"Let us go, Bud," Isabel coaxed. "That vaccine's our only chance."

As Bud lowered his weapon, Kirov smirked at Wolfkill and pushed Isabel forward. She stumbled, and in that instant, a shot rang out.

Without another sound, Sergei Kirov fell to the ground.

ALL HEADS TURNED in the direction of the gunfire.

Across the street, rifle poised across the bed of his green pickup, Gus Dearing straightened his old arthritic form.

Wolfkill dropped to the dirt, next to Sergei's lifeless form, and began shaking him.

"Don't die on me, you son of a bitch."

A pool of blood had already formed under Kirov's head. Wolfkill rolled him over and saw that the left side of his face no longer existed.

Isabel searched in vain for a pulse.

"He's dead," she said.

Dead. And their chances gone with him.

"Are you okay?"

The voice, clearly shaken, came from above where Wolfkill and Isabel knelt. Simultaneously, they looked up.

"Gus."

In his misguided attempt to save Isabel, Gus had robbed her of the chance to live.

FORTY-TWO

MONTY SPENT A cold, damp night in the Toyota he'd rented at Kalispell Airport before moving into the house that Isabel had once occupied. He was waiting for Alistair Bott to return to his home in the Magnolia neighborhood Isabel had described so well. Ridiculously large houses, landscaped yards. Just the right cars parked out front. Sidewalks, as if pedestrians were welcome, yet he had to wonder how many friendly *hellos* a long-haired Indian might expect.

That first night, he had parked the Toyota at a remote corner of a lot that serviced the local marina and an assortment of restaurants, the smells from which tormented his empty stomach. The next day he broke into Bott's house and helped himself to the contents of the refrigerator. The food was fresh, indicating Bott had been there recently.

At night, under cover of darkness, he'd left his car and hiked up the steep hillside, to the top of the bluff overlooking Elliott Bay. After driving by it half a dozen times, he'd been able to recognize Bott's house—the house that Isabel had once lived in—from the back. It was just three-fourths of a mile and a dozen or so houses along the bluff. Keeping low, he skirted each yard and used the beef jerky he'd bought at a nearby 7-Eleven to buy passage from a couple of menacing dogs.

When Monty broke into the house, it immediately became clear that Alistair had skipped town suddenly. Clothes strewn everywhere in the bedroom, food left on the kitchen table, and the computer still on in an upstairs office. Monty jiggled the mouse to get rid of the screen saver—a picture of Isabel in hiking shorts, boots, a backpack, and a smile that stung Monty. A message box in the middle of the screen, overlaid across an adult Web site entitled "Candy Girl," indicated the Internet connection had been terminated due to inactivity, but Bott had clearly been enjoying the buxom blond's photo gallery until something pulled him away.

RECONNECT? a second box flashed.

Monty had hoped Bott would return—that in his haste he might have forgotten something important, important enough to risk coming back. But now, after two days, that seemed unlikely, and the waiting game was threatening to drive Monty mad. The downtime agreed with him physically—his shoulder was healing and he was regaining the strength he'd lost—but mentally, he was close to going over the edge.

He had absolutely no sense of where Bott had fled.

Returning to the reservation without him was not an option.

One person might be able to provide some answers, a lead. At least once each day, Monty would find himself staring at the telephone. Isabel might be able to help. But as hungry as he was for her voice, as desperate as he was to find Bott, he could not draw her into this. His plan for revenge. And who knows, by now her phone could be tapped. Even Bud Wolfkill had his limits. A call like that could bring Monty down.

He'd gone through every drawer in the house, hoping to find something that might indicate where Alistair had fled. Even a letter, perhaps from family or a friend, would have given him something, some kind of lead. But if Alistair Bott had friends or family with whom he maintained close ties, their existence was not in evidence in his home.

The night before, long after the lights in neighboring houses had gone out, Monty had stolen outside, moving soundlessly along the cement wall that separated Bott from his neighbor to the west. There was a street lamp that made some exposure absolutely unavoidable, but Monty darted in and out of the lamp's arc like a light breeze. Within seconds, he'd removed the contents of the mailbox and returned to the shadows.

Back inside, a quick search through the mail provided some information, but ultimately proved disappointing. It appeared to have been sitting in the box for three or four days, which meant Alistair had skipped town the day before Monty showed up—the same day that Ken Mac-Stirling's body had been discovered.

Monty pocketed a replacement MasterCard in Bott's name. He was running low on money.

Aside from bills and a copy of a final decree of divorce between Bott and Isabel, Monty found nothing. He soon came to realize that it was an impossible task, finding a man he knew so little about, who appeared to have so few ties to the rest of the world. He had to have help.

His search always returned to the third floor office, where, despite Alistair's absence, faxes came in daily. There was a stack of them. Monty had never seen anything like it. All solicitations from drug companies, trying to get Bott to either head up this study or that, or refer patients to an ongoing study.

Three thousand dollars per patient!
Enroll fourteen patients by September 1st and earn an additional
   $2,000.
Authorship of drug study (we hire the medical writer!)
Too busy to conduct a study? How about a $500 finder's fee?

Monty passed time on the computer. Accessing Bott's e-mail account could prove invaluable in providing some kind of clues. He spent hours making up passwords. But the task proved impossible. Time after time, after trying everything from the name of the street he lived on to Bott's middle name—Arnold, according to the divorce decree—he failed. It was while he was playing around with passwords that the hum of the fax machine kicked in, signaling a new arrival. It had become a diversion for him—almost a form of entertainment—to read the fucking things, though with each new scheme, Monty's contempt mounted.

Out of the corner of his eye, Monty watched another drug company logo make its appearance on the other side of the machine as he finished reading the online edition of the *Daily Interlake*'s account of the investigation into the death of a WRI guard in an explosion at the drill site on the Blackfeet reservation. Monty's name was not mentioned, but the article reported that "two men, one Blackfeet, one Cheyenne, with known ties to the AIM, are being sought. They are considered armed and dangerous."

Disgusted, Monty clicked off the article. He was surprised to see the fax still coming. All the previous solicitations were short and to the point—*Want money? We can help*—but this one apparently consisted of two pages.

As the second page inched its way onto a tray so full its contents had become level with the incoming transmission, it had begun pushing the preceding page forward, out of its way. With a soft swoosh, the first page disappeared.

Monty rose from the chair and went to explore. The fax had fallen into the small space between the end of the desk, where the fax machine was situated, and the filing cabinet.

He dropped to his knees. He could see the white page, within reach. He tried poking a finger into the space but there wasn't enough room. He reached for a pencil on top of the desk and used it to poke at the page, teasing it his way, until a corner protruded from between the two pieces of furniture. Grasping it between thumb and forefinger, Monty also grabbed the sheet that had just arrived and took both back to his desk.

He noticed immediately that the two sheets did not belong together.

The fax that had just come in was from a company named GenSearch. The last sentence at the bottom of the page was incomplete, confirming the fact that a second page would follow.

The page he'd just retrieved from between the desk and filing cabinet was from a company named VacRx. The date on the top indicated it had been sent months ago, some time in February.

Monty stood again and went back to the filing cabinet. Allowing his good arm to do most the work, he wrestled the heavy cabinet away from the desk.

What he discovered gave him some degree of pleasure. Several sheets of paper lay nested between the two pieces of furniture.

Perhaps one would provide a clue as to Bott's whereabouts.

If nothing else, at least he had some new reading material.

NEVER IN HER life had Isabel seen a face so full of grief and remorse as that of Gus Dearing.

Despite her admonitions, he came each day, roaring up the road to her cabin as if the place were on fire, Grunt's head hanging out the passenger window of the truck, tail wagging to beat the band.

Today, as she had the two days before, Isabel jumped up and closed the windows at which she'd taken to sitting for most of each day. Summer had finally arrived, and Isabel spent hours at a time coming to know the sparrows, barn swallows, and squirrels that visited the birdbath Gus had made for her. She had never known idle time before, not in her entire life, and despite the circumstances—or perhaps because of them—the summer breeze, carrying hints of fields of mountain flowers and songs of swallows and whippoorwills, soothed and comforted her.

Like Suzanne, she had already decided that if she were to die, she wanted to go right there, in her little cabin in the woods.

The recent change in weather had had a healing effect on Gus's old, arthritic body, and watching him now, walking toward her with just the slightest of limps, clad in denim head to toe, that fact pleased Isabel. She picked up the cordless telephone that he had brought her the first day and sat in her rocker, still now, waiting as the old-timer fumbled with the cell phone he'd purchased for himself at the same time.

It took a full two minutes, but finally the phone in her hand rang.

"Damned contraption," Gus growled.

"You know you shouldn't be here," she told Gus, their eyes meeting through the window and across the patch of wild grass that separated them. "You have to take this quarantine seriously, Gus. It's dangerous for you to come."

As usual, Gus ignored her scolding and launched right into his interrogation.

"Any temperature?" he asked.

"None."

"Rash? Any sign of a rash?"

On down his list.

To each Isabel answered the same: "No."

Finally, he paused, shaking a head of hair that overnight seemed to have grown more shockingly white.

"Damn, Iz. What have I done?"

"Stop that, Gus. You saved my life, that's what you did."

"But I killed the son of a bitch. And he had the only thing that could save you now."

She would smile when he made comments like that, and stand for him to see her.

"Look at me, Gus. I'm fine. Can't you see that? Who's to say I've contracted smallpox?"

Isabel did not dare tell him that a CDC immunologist had telephoned just yesterday, confirming Isabel's worst fear—that Lot Two of the Hanta-Vac was, indeed, contaminated with live smallpox virus. Without emotion, he had informed her that the likelihood of her contracting the deadly disease was considerable. In his words, "greater than seventy percent." And that the onset of symptoms could be expected within ten days of exposure. He had strongly advised her to check herself in to the hospital in Missoula or Cutbank, and then, when she refused to discuss the matter, become threatening.

But K. T. had assured Isabel that she had the right to refuse, so long as she did not endanger others in the process.

Isabel did not think she could bear to see the pain in Gus's eyes if she told him about that call.

"How are Marcus and Lucy?" she asked instead, as she did each day. Marcus and Lucy Freeman had been taken to Cutbank Hospital's isolation unit. "Have you heard anything?"

Grunt had returned from his customary exploration with a thick branch protruding from either side of his mouth, which he dropped at Gus's feet. His eyes jumped eagerly from master to stick. Gus bent down, picked it up, and tossed it into the air.

"They're doing okay. So far anyway." The guilt was clearly there too. Sergei Kirov's smallpox vaccine might have saved Lucy and Marcus as well.

"Is there anything I can do for you, Iz?" Gus pleaded. "Anything at all?"

Isabel had thought about that, long and hard, these past couple of days.

"Yes, Gus. There is."

Gus's eyes brightened.

"What? You name it."

"You can tell me about Hattie."

THE COMPUTER HAD, in the end, been his salvation. Since arriving in Seattle, Monty had several times tried telephoning mutual friends of his and Clyde's on the Wind River reservation, hoping to find Clyde. But the numbers he had for them had been disconnected—a tactic often used by AIM members, who changed phone numbers regularly.

Then it had occurred to him—he remembered the e-mail address of one of them,

Richie Greyhorse: *runningpony@aol.com*.

Since his ongoing efforts to break into Bott's e-mail account had been fruitless, this recollection proved of little value until, on the third day, a banner at the top of the Yahoo Web site drew his attention.

Free e-mail, it flashed.

Monty clicked on the banner and opened an account in the name of Alistair Bott, using the address from one of Bott's bills. He typed with trembling fingers.

Runningpony:

Trouble, need to locate lost cousin. Do you have any information?

Blackfeet brother

The response had come quickly.

Dear Blackfeet brother,

Cousin is safe; how can we help?

Running Pony

Monty knew that AIM members' e-mails were sometimes monitored by the FBI and that the simple correspondence between them might already have put Richie, and perhaps Clyde, at risk. He thought long and hard about how to respond.

If my cousin remembers where the arrow pierced his heart, I will call you there.

Less than one minute later, the response:

He remembers. Call in one hour.

Monty's smile was his first since learning of Leroy's death.

When Monty and Clyde had worked together on the Wind River reservation, they frequented a hamburger joint. The Full Moon was owned by an old Arapahoe woman named June. Clyde had fallen in love with Lizzie, a pretty young Arapahoe waitress at Full Moon. They'd dated several times, but Lizzie disapproved of what she called the "trouble-making" side of Clyde and eventually, much to Clyde's anguish, ended their relationship. To Monty's knowledge, Clyde had never fallen for another woman as hard as he'd fallen for lovely, gentle Lizzie.

Now Monty was faced with a problem. His car was parked at the marina and it was broad daylight. Apparently on alert from Bud Wolfkill, the police were cruising by Bott's house regularly. Twice they had stopped and, to Monty's considerable amusement, pressed the doorbell. On the reservation, Bud would simply have broken in to see if Alistair was inside. In the end, Monty decided that walking to his car, in order to drive to a pay phone, would present more risk than using Bott's phone to place the call to the Full Moon.

He waited until fifty-five minutes had passed, then called directory assistance for Fort Washakie. There was a moment of panic when the operator claimed not to be able to find the restaurant's listing, but then, sounding irritated at having succeeded, she announced she had it.

Monty waited five more minutes, then dialed.

"H'lo?" It was a woman's voice.

"Is this June?" Monty asked.

"Yeah, it's June. Who's this?"

"An old friend. I'm looking for someone, a tall Cheyenne. He's supposed to be there with an Arapahoe named Richie Greyhorse."

"You mean Clyde?"

"Yes. Clyde."

"Hold on then."

Monty had been so void of any emotion besides unrelenting anger that the effect of hearing Clyde's voice left him momentarily speechless.

"Is that you?" Clyde said. "Hello?"

"Yeah, it's me. It's good to hear your voice, bro."

"Damn, it's good to hear yours. I hear you're off on some wild goose chase."

"You've talked to someone back home? Have you heard anything about Isabel?"

"You mean the lady doc?"

"Yes."

There was a pause.

"So that's what I get for leaving you there."

"Tell me, is she okay?"

"I don't really know, brother. I heard she was in isolation. That she took that vaccine."

No, God no.

"Hey, you still there?"

Monty drew in a breath.

"Yeah, I'm here," he said softly.

"Sorry 'bout that, man. Maybe she won't come down with it."

Monty would not have believed he was capable of more anger than that he'd already been feeling, but Clyde's words gave rise to an entirely new anger in him, one even more intense and violent. Any caution about whether it was safe to have this discussion on Bott's phone simply disappeared.

"You have to help me find the guy who did this to her. I'm sure he killed Leroy, too. His name is Alistair Bott."

"That's the name that was on that e-mail you sent Richie."

"Yeah. I'm using his computer."

"Let me talk to Richie. We'll contact the IGU. Call us back tomorrow, same time. Okay?"

"I don't want to wait that long," Monty snapped.

"Listen, brother, you gotta give us a little time. Hang tight, okay?"

FORTY-THREE

GUS'S EYES SEARCHED for Isabel's, but they were too old, too farsighted to give him the answer he needed. He stepped closer, onto the porch and out of the glare.

"You know about Hattie?" he asked, his disbelief coming through loud and clear despite the crackle of his cell phone.

"Yes." Isabel nodded. "I know."

Gus stared at Isabel through the window, silent, for a good long while. Then, slowly, as if the arthritis had just returned, he took several short steps to the stack of firewood and lowered himself to the dusty porch, his back propped against the woodpile and his face to Isabel, his free arm slung over both bony, bent knees. But when Grunt ran up enthusiastically and dropped onto the porch beside him, Gus reflexively straightened one long leg out in front of him and Grunt's heavy head plopped down on the old man's thigh.

It was an odd sight. That cranky old man sitting there on the porch, stroking his sleeping dog's head as he spoke into the cell phone pressed to his ear.

"My wife Marian and Hattie Day were best friends," Gus started, "back at a time that nice white girls like my Marian weren't supposed to be runnin' around with Indian girls."

He looked up at Isabel to monitor her response, then continued.

"Hattie's father was a Cheyenne. Her mother was Salish. She never did know her father, but Marian always said her mother did a real good job of raising Hattie alone."

"What was her name?" Isabel asked.

"Whose?"

"Hattie's mother."

The hand on Grunt's back went still as Gus tried to remember.

"I don't rightly recall. She'd already died by the time I met Hattie. I think Marian said it was from polio."

"When was that? That you met Marian?"

"Back in 1943. That's when I fell in love. I'd just come home from the war and took over my grandfather's ranch here. We had an awful drought that year, none of the timothy was worth a damn and the cattle were near to starvin' to death. Marian's family ran a big spread down near Pablo, where the drought hadn't been so bad. I bought hay from them that summer to keep from losing any more cattle. Marian was about eighteen then. She helped her brothers load my truck. I'll always remember that, the first time I saw her. She did just as good a job as they did, only she was a helluva lot prettier."

Gus's initial wariness had faded.

"I started going down to Pablo on weekends after that, and during the week, if I could come up with a good excuse. That's when I met Hattie. Since she and Marian had always been schoolmates, Marian's family kind of took her under their wing when Hattie's mother died. She lived in the same little house in Pablo that she'd grown up in, but she was around the ranch a lot."

Isabel's breath seemed to leave her. They were discussing the young woman whose name she'd found in the trunk in Nada's house.

On her birth certificate.

"What was she like, Gus?" She struggled getting the words out.

Gus seemed to sense the emotional impact his recollections were having on Isabel, but intuitively, he knew he could no longer keep anything from her. She had come this far, she had to know everything now.

His face creased in a tender smile.

"She was a real nice young lady," he said. "Like you. She was quiet, but you always knew there was a lot goin' on inside her head." He was watching Isabel for her reaction. "And she was a real beauty. You have her eyes. And her nose."

Isabel did not know whether to laugh or cry. Her entire life, a piece of herself, of her very being, had been missing. She'd known it, felt it, always. And now, Gus was giving her that single, magical piece that enabled her, for the first time in her entire life, to truly know and understand who she was.

But the joy that this gift might once have given her was tainted now. She had so recently buried her own mother. The only mother she had ever known. The woman who had loved her so dearly. Obviously much more dearly than Hattie Day, who had given Isabel up.

"Marian and me got married in 'forty-six," he continued. "She moved up here on to the ranch, and after that, we'd see Hattie from time to time, but she and Marian both had busy lives. Hattie married an Indian fella— Kootenai I believe—and it seemed they were doin' pretty well with a garage he owned there in town. But then he died in a car wreck. And a little after that, your father arrived in Pablo to run the clinic there."

Again, a quick glance at Isabel.

"Go on," she urged.

"Well, Hattie was no mechanic, so she took to cleaning houses, and that's how she met your father. She cleaned house for him. The way

Hattie told it to Marian—'cause this wasn't anything she was gonna share with me or anybody but her closest friend—the two of them just fell in love. Hattie knew he was married and she told Marian he tried to do the right thing, but neither one of 'em could help themselves. Your dad, he was only gonna be there a year, and the end of that year was comin' and Hattie turned up pregnant. According to Marian, your dad wanted to marry her. But Hattie was a good Christian and she wouldn't have any part of breaking up a marriage, so she sent him on his way. 'Bout near broke her heart, but she figured she'd always have the baby, even if she didn't have him.

"From all Marian could piece together, 'cause this wasn't stuff that anyone talked about in the open, your father went back home and told his wife that he'd fallen in love with an Indian girl. He told her he wanted to go back and live there with her, marry her. That him and Hattie were about to have a baby."

Even Gus seemed to find the discussion too painful now to meet Isabel's eyes. Instead he kept his gaze on Grunt, stroking him all the while he told his tale.

"You came early, Isabel. Your father hadn't returned to Hattie yet. He was still trying to smooth things over with your mother, I guess. Trying to make things right for her. They kept you in the hospital 'cause you were so tiny. And that's when it happened . . ."

His wrinkled hand grew still once more and his strikingly blue eyes finally came up to meet Isabel's.

"Hattie got herself killed drivin' out to Marian's family's place. She was gonna borrow the camera to take pictures of her new baby. Of you, Izzie. It wasn't her fault. Some drunken Indian crossed right into her lane and hit her head on."

Isabel's gasp shattered the stillness that had taken hold.

"You okay?"

Biting her lower lip, she nodded.

"Want me to stop?" Gus asked, his voice plaintive.

"No. Tell me everything."

"Well, there's not a whole lot more after that. When your father found out about Hattie, he showed up in Pablo right quick and took you back to Seattle with him." Gus's kind eyes fixed now on her face. "And we never knew what happened to you. Until now. It appears your mother was another good woman. She took you in and raised you as her own child. She did right by you, didn't she, Izzie?"

Isabel could only nod her head, so overcome was she by this tale, a tale she somehow always knew existed. A tale kept hidden from her her entire life.

And now, finally, she understood why.

"Gus?" she said, after several minutes of silence had passed between them.

"Yeah?"

"Do you know someone named Sky Thomas?"

"Sure. She's the oldest living Blackfeet. Has been for a long time. A lotta Blackfeet think Sky can tell the future."

A queasy, uneasy feeling moved lightly across Isabel's belly.

"Would she have known Hattie? Or my father?"

Gus scratched his head.

"Don't see how," he answered. "Never heard of Sky leaving the rez."

Just then, Grunt sprung up and bounded off the porch with a loud *arrff*, heading toward the road.

Both still reeling from their discussion, Isabel and Gus turned to see what had caught the dog's eye. At first, all they saw was a cloud of dust, but soon they could make out a patrol car, approaching at an even faster clip than Gus usually did.

What now? Isabel wondered. Could K. T. have been wrong? Were they coming to force her into the hospital? Or—worse yet, far worse—could something have happened to Monty?

The car came to a gravel-spraying halt behind Gus's truck. One second later, Bud Wolfkill emerged and came toward them with long, fast strides. His large brown hands carried a thick black binder.

A sense of foreboding paralyzed Isabel as she watched Bud approach.

"YOU KNOW YOU'RE not supposed to be here," Bud said curtly to Gus. Then he surprised Isabel by following with, "But I'm glad you are."

The heels of his black boots thudded noisily as he stepped up onto the wooden porch.

"Give me that thing, will you?" he said, nodding toward the cell phone Gus still grasped.

Gus handed it over.

Bud Wolfkill cleared his throat, removed his sunglasses, and, finally, met Isabel's frightened eyes.

She picked up her own phone and pressed it to her ear.

"What?" she asked. "Is it Monty? Has something happened to Monty?"

"Still no word from him," Bud said. "I don't imagine there will be until he finishes what he set out to do. This is about you. I brought something for you." He raised the hand holding the binder. "I'm gonna put this up against your door, then Gus and me are gonna step back a ways while you pick it up. You only have a few minutes to read it and make a decision. I'm afraid that's all I can give you."

"I don't understand," Isabel said.

"You will when you see it."

Bud had already stepped toward the front door, where he gingerly placed the binder, leaning it against the frame.

"Come on now, Gus," he ordered. "Back away."

Turning to shoot Isabel a troubled glance over his shoulder, Gus complied, stepping down from the porch.

When Isabel opened the door, Grunt's wet nose poked through.

"Go away, Grunt," Isabel said, pushing him back.

The dog whined as she reached for the binder.

There were no markings on its cover. None. She took it inside, to her seat by the window, and with trembling hands, opened it.

The first page was written in Russian.

She turned to page two. It read:

PROTOCOL

VAREOLA VACCINE

STRAIN X

She began flipping through the following pages. Data, results, earlier research papers. Returning to the first page, it suddenly hit her. Sergei Kirov had been Russian.

Incredulous, she lifted her eyes to where Gus and Bud stood, leaning against Gus's truck.

Bud Wolfkill still had the phone pressed to his ear.

She lifted her phone again.

"It's the protocol for Kirov's smallpox vaccine," she said. "Isn't it?"

Bud nodded. Even from this distance, his posture, the tilt of his head, declared his excitement.

"That's right."

"How did you get this?"

"I found it. Hidden in the spare tire on the Land Cruiser Kirov was driving. He'd been planning to leave the country. There was fifty-thousand dollars in cash too. And his passport."

"The CDC must want this," Isabel said, confused.

"They certainly would, but they don't know it exists," Wolfkill said. "I haven't told them yet. I wanted you to see it first."

Isabel tried to read Bud's eyes, but from this distance, it was impossible.

"I don't understand," she said. "Why would you want me to see it?"

"So that you could decide whether it looked like the real thing."

Isabel stared at Bud, trying to make sense of it all.

"Yes. It does. It's just what I would expect from a scientist like Dr. Kirov."

Bud Wolfkill looked from Isabel to Gus, then back to Isabel.

"Then would you be willing to bet your life on it?" he finally asked.

SUDDENLY, WITH A terrible sense of disappointment—for without even realizing it, she had allowed the excitement in Bud's eyes to give her hope—Isabel realized what Bud was thinking.

"You don't understand, Bud," she said. "No one could duplicate this work in the amount of time left before . . ."

"Before you come down with smallpox?"

"Yes. It's a wonderful discovery, it could save lives. But not mine. Not Lucy or Marcus."

Bud seemed to falter at the mention of the Freemans.

"I don't know about Lucy and Marcus," he said, dropping his head momentarily in despair. Then he raised it again.

"But it might not be too late for you."

Isabel was getting angry.

"It's too late, Bud. Believe me."

Shaking his head, Wolfkill turned on his heel and headed back to his car. This time he went to the trunk, where he removed a small silver thermos.

As he returned to the porch, thermos carried like a communion chalice in front of him, Isabel could see the Starbucks logo on it.

Bud came directly to the window, so close that he could reach out and touch Isabel if the glass did not separate them. He held the thermos within fifteen inches of where she sat. Then, slowly, he rotated it. As the logo disappeared, a label on the opposite side rotated into view.

Confused, impatient, Isabel did not like this game Bud was playing with her.

The sharp cry she let out when Bud stopped rotating the thermos and pressed it up against the window for her to read the handwritten label did not require a telephone to be heard outside.

VAREOLA VACCINE

STRAIN X

Gus had followed Bud up to the porch.

"What, what is it?" he demanded to know when he heard Isabel cry out.

Ignoring Gus, Isabel lifted the telephone to her ear. Bud did likewise.

"Is it . . . ?" she stammered, her eyes searching his. "Is it really Dr. Kirov's vaccine?"

Bud Wolfkill didn't smile often, but the one he flashed now made up for that.

"It sure as hell appears to be," he said. "I found it in the wheel well, with the notebook. Now, the question is—and you don't have much time to decide—are you willing to take the chance that it is?"

CHAPTER

FORTY-FOUR

DID YOU KNOW your man has ties to antigovernment, survivalist-type groups?"

The next day when Monty called the Full Moon, Clyde had picked up on the first ring.

Monty's grasp on the receiver tightened. Finally, a lead.

"No."

"You know that e-mail you sent us from this dude's computer? Well IGU used it to trace his movements on the Internet."

"They can do that?" Monty asked.

"Something about cookies. They're like these little markers that they can trace to see what Web sites you're surfing. Seems your man was spending an awful lot of time at porn sites and in survivalist chat rooms. You know the kind—antitax, antigovernment, racist, preparing for Armageddon."

Monty had already discovered Bott's prurient side. But his interest in survivalist groups came as a surprise.

"Like the Freemen?"

"Exactly. In fact, one site he kept hitting time and again is this group up there in Byrd, Montana. You might want to check out their Web site. Pretty ugly stuff."

"Tell me about them."

"Well, IGU's investigated them before 'cause they've caused some trouble up in that area for some of the Kootenai from Bonners Ferry. They're heavily armed. In fact, IGU believes they actually use a gun shop there for a front. A place called Powder Keg. Could be your guy headed that way. They're no strangers to fugitives. But these aren't people you want to mess with, ya know?"

Monty had thanked Clyde and departed Seattle within minutes, using Bott's MasterCard to buy gas on the way to Montana.

Climbing the interstate after crossing the Columbia River, Monty had thrilled momentarily at the sight of a herd of wild horses before realizing they stood motionless, the lead horse rearing on hind legs made of brass. Metal sculptures.

At one time Monty might have felt disdain for the trickery, but today he took it as a sign from the spirits, encouraging him in his pursuit.

The summer sun beat mercilessly into the back window as he drove east, crossing 250 miles of farmland, but by the time he pulled off Interstate 90 in Coeur d'Alene, Idaho, shadows had begun creeping across the rolling, lush green landscape.

He headed north on Interstate 95. The terrain felt more familiar to him now. The mountains in the distance did not compare to Montana's peaks, but there was more open space than in Seattle. He felt less confined by the dense growth everywhere, less claustrophobic. The closer to his native soil he came, the stronger, more confident he grew.

In Sandpoint, he stopped at a souvenir shop and bought a ball cap. He'd driven through Byrd before. An Indian with long hair would draw attention.

Driving further north, through Bonners Ferry, the sun finally disappeared into the foothills, which were becoming bigger and more spectacular the closer he got to the Canadian border. Two miles north of Bonners Ferry, Monty turned east, onto Highway 2.

In the dark, Monty negotiated the narrow highway with great care. It twisted and turned in corkscrews as it followed the course of the Kootenai River. The small white crosses on red poles that marked traffic fatalities and seemed every bit as abundant as the purple lupine lining the road sides kept Monty at a moderate speed. By the time he arrived, all the shops in Byrd would be closed. It would be another wasted night, spent in the car. No need to hurry, despite the sense of urgency that was eating him alive.

At Yaak Lookout, a sign announced Byrd was just four miles ahead. Ten minutes later, another sign welcomed him to Byrd, Montana, population 953.

Had that number recently increased by one?

As he'd expected, the shops had closed for the night. Most were completely darkened, while a few—the local mercantile and a drugstore— left lights burning inside.

The Powder Keg was easy to find. A two-story frame structure on Byrd's main street, with a wood-planked porch, much like shops in Browning. No lights illuminated the shop's interior, but above the structure, a single bulb glowed in a room with an open, curtainless window.

Monty cruised through town twice. On the second go-round, a Byrd police car coming from the other direction slowed to take note of the Toyota.

It would not be wise to stay in town. He did not want to draw attention to himself.

Monty remembered seeing a sign for a snowmobile trail at Yaak Lookout. Turning the car around, he headed back the way he'd come, on Highway 2. At the side road marked snowmobile trail, he exited and parked in the forest service lot, where he rolled down one of the Toyota's front windows, climbed in the backseat. The familiar night sounds soothed him into a deep sleep.

At dawn, Monty climbed the steep trail up to Yaak Mountain Lookout, where the panoramas of gently rolling mountains, the smell of mossy branches of the old growth forest, revitalized him. He prayed to the Great Spirit for the survival of his people and gave thanks for his sacred bond with Mother Earth. He prayed that Leroy's spirit be at peace.

And then, slowly and with renewed strength and purpose, he descended the mountain.

BUD AND GUS watched helplessly from the front porch as Isabel administered the vaccine to herself, her hands trembling so wildly that it took two tries.

Was this really happening? Was the liquid in the thermos what its label claimed? Even if it were, Sergei Kirov's protocol was the work of only one man, manufactured illegally, without FDA oversight. Was it safe? Did it contain live virus that might actually increase Isabel's smallpox exposure?

Even if it were the smallpox vaccine that Sergei Kirov claimed to have developed, even if it proved effective in protecting unexposed subjects against smallpox, could it do Isabel any good? Or was it too late now, three days after exposure?

All of those questions ran through Isabel's mind in the short window of time that she had to make her decision and act upon it. And in the end, none of the doubts mattered. What mattered is that Bud had just tossed her a possible lifeline. A reed-thin lifeline, but she grabbed hold of it with both hands.

"We have to get the vaccine to Marcus and Lucy," Isabel said. "The longer we wait, the less likely any vaccine will protect them."

A haunted look returned to Bud's eyes.

"I wish now that Lucy had been as stubborn as you about going to the hospital. You know as well as I do that none of those doctors are gonna take a chance on something I found in a car. Not with the CDC looking over their shoulders. That's why I brought it out here before I reported it. I figured I'd let you make your own mind up. 'Cause once I turn this stuff in, who knows what's gonna happen?"

With a sinking feeling, Isabel realized that Bud was right.

"I have to leave now, to turn these in," Bud said, nodding at the black plastic bundle in his hands. He'd brought along heavy-duty garbage bags, which he'd doubled over the thermos and notebook to retrieve them from Isabel's porch. "Maybe if I hurry there's still a chance."

Bud handed the phone over to Gus and turned away.

"Gus, please, put Bud back on," Isabel cried.

When Wolfkill pressed the phone to his ear again, he seemed reluctant to meet Isabel's gaze.

"How can I ever thank you?" Isabel asked.

A wisp of a smile returned to Bud Wolfkill's somber face.

"By staying alive," he answered. Then he turned and walked away.

CHAPTER

FORTY-FIVE

GUS HAD DEPARTED close on Bud's heels, leaving Isabel to ponder what had just taken place. The initial elation of Bud's discovery ebbed quickly as reality set in.

She had just injected a foreign substance, created by an obviously deranged man—a scientist who once headed a Russian biowarfare program—into her body.

Was she out of her mind? Or simply that desperate?

Time would tell.

Time. She was literally a prisoner of the passage of time right now. The waiting was growing intolerable. Days of waiting to see if she, Lucy, or Marcus developed a fever or rash, the first symptoms of smallpox.

Days, minutes, *seconds* waiting for word of Monty.

The seemingly endless wait for word regarding the FDA investigation into her involvement in Alistair's misdoings.

And now she could add another cliff-hanger to the list. Would the strain X vaccine she'd just bet her life on *save* her—or perhaps, if it wasn't what it seemed, kill her?

Her life had been put on hold, and Isabel had no idea whatsoever what it would be like when it was given back to her—if she was lucky enough to even survive.

Would Monty ever be part of it again? Would her license to practice medicine be revoked?

Was the life ahead of her one worth fighting for, or would it be stripped of everything that mattered to her?

She did not know if she could bear the guilt if Lucy or Marcus Freeman died. Lucy had entrusted Isabel not only with her own life but with those of her children. So many of the Blackfeet had trusted her. They had put aside their well-founded fears and distrust and voluntarily come forward to participate in the HantaVac clinical trial *because they trusted Isabel*.

And, as surely as if she'd been the one to come up with the hideous plot, as surely as if it had been her, and not Kirov, who actually tainted the vaccine, Isabel was now responsible for the fact that two of those who had trusted their lives to her could die.

For there was no escaping the cold, hard facts. Contaminating the HantaVac was Alistair's way to get back at Isabel. His ultimate revenge.

She was responsible. She was responsible.

When Gus's truck appeared later that evening, for the first time Isabel wished that her well-intentioned friend would just leave her alone. But the lopsided grin he emerged from the truck wearing managed to intrigue her.

Gus carried a large brown paper bag, which he plopped down on the porch while he fussed with the phone.

"Got a little present for you," he finally announced, reaching inside the bag for what turned out to be a binder. This one was a soft blue.

"What is it, Gus?"

"I thought you might want more time to look over those scientific documents that Bud found," he explained. "Bud had Suzanne meet us at the clinic so that we could sterilize the binder in that contraption . . ."

"The autoclave?"

"Yeah, the autoclave. Then I talked Bud into letting me borrow it while he called all the folks he had to call. Them gals at the Ben Franklin got an eyeful, tryin' to help me figure out that fancy Xerox machine they got there."

Gus looked like a new man now that there was reason to hope Isabel would survive the tainted HantaVac.

"You made a copy of Kirov's protocol?"

"Yup."

"Gus, you're brilliant."

He left the binder up against the door. Isabel was already reaching for it by the time the old green pickup disappeared down the road.

She must not give in to despair. For Gus's sake. For the sake of Lucy and Marcus Freeman.

Isabel settled back into her chair and began reading.

She read through the night. So much of the material was new to her. She had to go back over some sections several times to make certain she understood them.

Much of what she read horrified and repulsed her.

The strain of smallpox that had been used to contaminate Lot Two was no ordinary strain of smallpox. No, Sergei Kirov and his comrades had created a new strain of smallpox, one with a delayed onset.

It was right in the protocol, on page thirteen, the rationale behind developing a form of the disease whose onset was expected to be at least twice, perhaps even three times, as late as the natural strains of vareola:

> Delayed onset considered desirable in that it allows a greater degree of inadvertent exposure during that period of incubation in which the patient is asymptomatic.

Isabel had reread that portion of the developmental history of Kirov's vaccine over and over again, for it took time for her to accept the truth behind the cryptic words: that Sergei and his comrades deliberately engineered a new strain of smallpox whose onset was delayed *so that a greater number of innocent victims could be infected.*

Since smallpox spread readily through the air, in a single day a person who didn't realize she was infected could unknowingly expose dozens more while she went about her daily activities. The first symptom, fever, was not expected to appear for at least two weeks after exposure. Whereas the vaccinea strain the world had always known caused an eruption of telltale sores just two days after the onset of fever, with strain X, it could be another week to ten days before the sores allowed a definitive diagnosis. Thousands—perhaps tens of thousands—more victims could die, be disfigured, or be blinded, due to the delayed onset of symptoms.

It was a rationale so hideous and twisted that Isabel bolted to the bathroom sink. She stood there, hanging over it, sweat dripping from her chin to the white porcelain. She tried to will herself to throw up, to rid herself of the poisonous information she'd just acquired, but as foul and poisoned as she now felt, her body would not cooperate. She stood there, hands shaking, holding tight to the cool, smooth surface.

But when she returned to her reading, Isabel soon learned that the same subject matter that had just caused her such distress might have a silver lining. As she read on, she realized that as depraved as the genesis of the delayed-onset strain might be, that very characteristic of strain X stood to give Isabel, Marcus and Lucy a better chance of surviving. *If* the liquid in the thermos turned out to be Kirov's strain X vaccine.

Isabel read on with renewed intensity.

Most vaccines were intended to be given before exposure to a disease. However, with infectious organisms that multiplied slowly enough, such as rabies, post-exposure vaccination was known to succeed. The shorter the period between exposure and the development of severe symptoms, the less likely that a vaccine given after a person was exposed to a disease would work. Dengue fever, ebola, and smallpox, with its seven to seventeen day incubation, were typically considered not susceptible to post-exposure immunization.

Kirov's notes painstakingly explained that this was because immunizations produced two types of immune response: humoral immunity (the production of antibodies) and cellular immunity due to activation of killer T lymphocytes. Antibodies generated in the humoral response often provided the needed immune response for an infectious organism free in the blood plasma. However, once an infectious organism made its way into a target cell—an essential step in order for viruses to multiply—the only effective immune response became a cellular one.

Achieving a therapeutic level of cellular immunity took longer than the humoral response. Therefore, in the event the smallpox contaminant in the Hanta Vac vaccine managed to penetrate Isabel's target cells, the delayed onset engineered into strain X would give the cellular immunity produced by Kirov's vaccine time to build, hopefully producing a level high enough to save Isabel's life.

Isabel threw down the binder and reached for the phone.

There was still time to save Marcus and Lucy Freeman.

If they acted fast enough.

The sky behind Little Chief's peaks had just begun to show the first pink trace of daylight when Lehman Morris's rich baritone came on the line.

"Thank God you're there." Isabel sighed. "I need your help."

THE CAMPGROUND EAST of Byrd had become a home of sorts to Monty. He'd been hanging around the area for six days now but still had not caught sight of Bott. Down to his last twenty dollars and a stolen credit card, he was living in large part off the land, which didn't create that big a problem as he'd been able to devise a fishing pole. It was a pathetic attempt, whittled from a branch of white birch, but the Kootenai's pure, cold water was home to an abundance of rainbow, brown, and cutthroat trout, so Monty ate well each evening over a campfire.

The credit card enabled him to buy gas, and he'd found a Mini-Mart with a quick-swipe checkout. He'd used cash on his first visit and tipped the clerk, a pimply faced kid, two bucks—almost the amount of his purchase. It was money Monty could not spare, but it paid off. On several occasions after that, he used Bott's MasterCard for toiletries, beverages, and a daily newspaper. The kid, who worked afternoons, never asked to see an ID.

The biggest problem caused by the shortage of cash was the fact that without spending money Monty dared not hang around Byrd for long periods. He was pushing his luck already. He could feel Byrd's police eyeing him, but he took great pains to avoid giving them anything to hassle him about—no loitering, no speeding. Always polite to the locals. Yes, sir. No, sir. Thank you, ma'am.

The perfect visitor, only he knew that they suspected he wasn't another tourist.

Monty may not have seen Bott yet, but he'd become convinced he was there, in Byrd. And he was pretty certain he knew where.

Every night the light in the window above the Powder Keg went on at about the same time. It was always after the store had closed, after the redneck who Monty had pegged as the shop's owner left for the night.

Someone was living up there, no doubt about it. A man, slight of build. Monty had seen his back, just once, as he drove slowly down main street.

His frustration at not being able to stake out the place until he discovered whether the shadowy figure was indeed Bott led him to consider breaking in. He could wait until the shop closed and take his chances. But in reality he only had one chance at this. Monty knew that if it turned out not to be Bott up there, he'd have blown it. And the man who killed his father, the man who had put Isabel's life at risk, would go free.

He had to be patient. He had to be certain before he acted.

Besides, living outside sure as hell beat the jail cell he'd be going home to. He could take his time.

On the morning of the seventh day, Monty awoke to the sound of a visitor. He'd removed the backseat from the Toyota—which he'd been parking on a remote, no longer used logging road—and taken to sleeping on it on the ground in a stand of old growth cedars. Someone might be able to sneak up to the car with him sleeping inside, but no one could ambush Monty Four Bear out in the open.

But this morning, a white-tailed deer had done just that. This time of year most does her size were accompanied by a fawn or two, but this one foraged alone, just yards from where Monty lay. He watched the long-legged creature with no less appreciation, no less sense of awe than that he'd felt as a child on hunting trips with Leroy.

The day before, he'd hiked up above Kootenai Falls, then sat watching a herd of bighorn sheep, picking their way across the ledges and rocks high above the river. He'd also seen an eagle and several osprey along the river. All good signs.

Suddenly the deer sensed his presence. She stood, frozen, for several seconds, her nose high, picking up his scent. Then calmly, as if she knew that there was nothing to fear, she turned the cottony underside of her tail toward him and slowly disappeared into the dense underbrush.

That was when Monty knew.

Today would be the day.

•   •   •

HAIR TUCKED INTO the ball cap he'd purchased in Sandpoint, Monty entered the Three Rivers Diner and found an empty seat facing the window, with a good view of the Powder Keg, across the street and several storefronts down.

Heads turned, but after that the breakfast crowd showed only mild interest in the Indian, who did not seem to be a troublemaker. Down to his last three dollars, but clean-shaven from his morning bath on the shores of the swollen Kootenai, Monty ordered coffee and toast.

Across the street, shop owners and workers began arriving to open up. The same yellow Dodge pickup that sat outside the Powder Keg all day each day pulled up. A husky blond man dressed in black T-shirt, camouflage pants, and army boots emerged and went to the shop's door, where, with the use of a key, he entered and flipped the cardboard sign hanging on the window from CLOSED to OPEN. Several other vehicles pulled up in the time Monty sat there observing, but as had been true all week, none of the occupants resembled the portrait back in Seattle.

Monty dragged out his coffee and toast until the red-haired waitress, squeezed into a pink uniform two sizes too small, returned for the fourth time and asked, "Maybe you want to order something else? If not, I got some customers waiting for a table."

Monty could not see anyone waiting, but it would serve no purpose to make a scene. Tossing his three dollars on the table, he detoured into the restroom before leaving the restaurant.

He'd parked at the end of town, on a side street, where he hoped his car wouldn't draw attention. He crossed the street and walked down the sidewalk in the direction of the Powder Keg.

As he approached, the door opened and a tall, slender figure emerged. Monty recognized him instantly.

Alistair.

The silk shirt and slacks from the portrait in Bott's living room had been replaced by garb similar to that worn by the man who opened the shop. The only thing that kept him from fitting in with the other customers Monty had seen coming and going all week was the hair—too neatly styled for these parts.

It took all of Monty's resolve to keep walking. He could not, however, stop himself from glancing into the eyes of the man he believed to be Leroy's killer. The man who, in some twisted way that Monty did not yet fully understand, had put Isabel in harm's way.

They were cold, disinterested eyes that looked right through Monty as they passed one another on the sidewalk. The restraint that it took to continue on was made possible only by Monty's resolve to do this right.

He had been patient this long; now that he'd found Bott, that patience would soon pay off. Monty picked up his pace. When he got to the Toyota, he drove up Main Street and back down again looking for him, but Bott had vanished.

Not for long, however.

As the day progressed and town filled with traffic, both pedestrian and vehicle—folks coming in from the country and neighboring towns even smaller than Byrd—Monty felt safe parking the Toyota on the street, where he could keep track of the comings and goings at the Powder Keg.

Bott returned in midafternoon, in the company of a straggly looking redhead and a military type with shaved head. The threesome stayed inside for two hours, until closing at 5:30. Then the two who had accompanied Bott emerged, along with the driver of the yellow pickup. Reversing his routine of the morning, he reached in the shop, flipped the sign back to CLOSED, and, after several minutes' discussion on the sidewalk, bid the other two good-bye and climbed in the truck.

The remaining two sauntered down the street and entered the Three Rivers Diner. Bott, however, never reappeared.

As nightfall approached and the streets of Byrd emptied, Monty moved the Toyota to a residential side street that ran perpendicular to the back of the Power Keg. On foot now, he stationed himself in the grassy alley between the pharmacy and a Western-wear shop.

Just before nine, he watched as the two men emerged from the diner. They strode back toward the gun shop. Their clumsy, lumbering gate indicated they'd been drinking. Both men climbed into a green Blazer with Montana plates, which cruised away, to the east, without headlights.

Monty watched as the same light he'd observed each night went on in the room directly above the shop.

CHAPTER

FORTY-SIX

DAY NUMBER NINE.
Still no temperature.

Still no news about Monty. Each day, Isabel spent hours poring over the trio of newspapers Gus brought her regularly—the Kalispell *Daily Interlake*, *USA Today*, and the *Seattle Times*, always a day old—searching for news connected to Leroy's or MacStirling's death, or the explosion at the mine site. Anything that might hint at Monty's whereabouts or fate. Aside from one sentence in *USA Today*'s "Across the Nation" section— "two Native Americans, believed to belong to the American Indian Movement, are being sought in connection with an explosion at the site of a proposed gold mine"—she'd found nothing. But this morning an article that she'd overlooked the day before had caught her eye.

ONTARIO COURTS ALLOW MINING SUIT
In a precedent-setting decision, a lawsuit filed against World Resources, Inc., a Canadian mining company, over the death of a Kyrgyzstan woman is to be heard in Canadian courts.

At first Isabel failed to make the connection. World Resources, Inc. *WRI.* According to the article, a young mother had died after drinking from a lake poisoned by an accident at WRI's Kyrgyzstn mining operation. An entire village's water supply had been contaminated and several other villagers had ended up hospitalized. WRI steadfastly refused responsibility, but the Ontario courts had decided the multimillion-dollar lawsuit against WRI had merit. They would allow the suit to be brought in Canada.

Isabel didn't know whether to attribute the dull ache in her chest to thoughts of the young woman and her baby, or to another day without word of Monty.

But Gus had called her last night, telling her that Bud wanted to talk to him. Maybe today she would finally hear something.

By the time Gus's pickup roared to a standstill outside her cabin, Isabel was already dialing.

Climbing out of the cab, Gus looked startled when the ring of the cell phone in his chest pocket pierced the balmy morning air.

"For Pete's sake, Izzie, what's the hurry?"

"Did you see Bud?"

Gus cleared his throat.

"I just came from there."

"You said you'd call me right away," she charged. They'd discussed it last night. Gus had promised to call her from town, right after he saw Bud.

"I thought I should tell you in person. It's not good news, Izzie."

"Tell me."

"Dammit to hell, Isabel, can't we just be happy you got that vaccine? And that your Dr. Morris talked them folks at the CDC into giving it to Marcus and Lucy too? Can't we just be happy about that for a while?"

All the joy, all the hope, suddenly drained from Isabel.

Gus's blue eyes finally came up to meet hers.

"Bud says the FBI's brought murder charges against Monty and Clyde."

"*No,*" Isabel cried. "How could they do that after all they've learned? Monty and Clyde didn't mean to hurt anyone. They only went out there to destroy the equipment, to get back at WRI for what they did to Leroy. My God, Gus, he was beaten. Then murdered."

Gus's thin lips tightened in a grimace.

"According to Bud, WRI admitted to having Leroy beaten up, but they swear they didn't kill him. Bud's told those FBI agents all that. He told them everything that happened that night he followed Monty to Vancouver, all the stuff they learned from those hooligans. But I guess the FBI doesn't think that changes what happened out at the drill site that night."

"*Where are the charges against WRI?* And if the FBI believes WRI didn't kill Leroy, what are they doing to find who did?" Isabel ranted. "Why, Gus? Why are they willing to believe someone who comes right out and admits to beating an old man, but not Monty and Clyde?"

Gus's eyes locked with hers.

"You know the answer to the question, Isabel. We both do."

THEY'D CRUISED THROUGH Byrd twice now, but no sign of Monty.

"It'd help if we knew what he was drivin'," Richie Greyhorse said.

Clyde had driven all the way from Fort Washakie to Missoula, then he'd turned the wheel of the Ford pickup over to Greyhorse.

Clyde had been scanning the sidewalks and streets for Monty, but now he glanced sideways at Greyhorse's striking profile. Richie Greyhorse's noble and perfectly formed features—high cheekbones, chiseled nose, and strong jaw—had earned him cameos in *Dances with Wolves* and a TNT epic on the history of the West. Richie had been told that if he'd moved to Hollywood, he could have a lucrative career. But Greyhorse only used his occasional acting jobs—if they could be called that—to fund another kind of life. That of an activist bent on helping his people.

"He left Browning in Edna's car," Clyde answered. "But he wouldn't be driving it now. Too bad. Edna's car'd be easy to spot."

"It's been what? Six days since you talked to him? I bet he's long gone by now."

"Probably," Birdseye answered. "But I figured Byrd was just about on our way to Calgary anyway. I gotta at least try to find him. Talk him into coming with us."

"You're right. Monty's gotta get out," Greyhorse concurred. "Fuckin' feds."

They continued down to the end of Byrd's main street in silence.

"Pull into that Mini-Mart," Clyde ordered. "I've gotta take a piss. And I'm hungry as hell."

The smell of burned popcorn greeted them as they stepped inside. A towheaded teenager sat at the counter, head buried in an old issue of *Snowboarding* magazine. He did not look up.

Clyde left Greyhorse to wander around while he went to the men's room. It stunk of urine. Wadded paper toweling littered the floor.

When he emerged, Greyhorse was standing at the counter, watching the kid scoop popcorn into a paper bag.

"That stuff's burnt," Clyde said. "Can't you smell it?"

"Smells good enough to me," Greyhorse answered, smiling.

"Anything else?" the kid asked, turning to hand the bag to Richie. Poor bastard, thought Clyde. At least Indian kids didn't get such bad acne.

"Yeah. I'll take one of those hot dogs. And a large Coke."

He reached over into Richie's bag and threw some popcorn into his mouth.

"We're looking for a buddy of ours," he said between crunches. "An Indian. He would've been here sometime this past week. Seen anyone like that?"

In one hand, the kid had a hot dog pinched between a pair of tongs. With the other he was reaching for a bun. He turned and looked over his shoulder.

"Some guy's been comin' in here every day this past week or so."

Simultaneously, Clyde and Greyhorse stopped crunching.

"Yeah?"

"Yeah," the kid said, returning to where they stood, clutching a hot dog wrapped in waxed paper.

"What's this guy look like?" Greyhorse asked.

"Black hair. Braids. Thin."

"Know where we can find him?"

"He's camping in one of the campgrounds. I'm not sure which one. But he usually comes in here right about now. Buys some food, then takes off. Bet if you hang around, you'll see him."

Clyde paid for the food, then dropped a five-dollar bill in the prominently displayed tip jar.

The kids blue-green eyes lit up.

"Want me to tell him anything if he comes in?"

"Yeah," Clyde answered. "Tell him his cousin's looking for him."

THE NIGHT HAD always been Monty's friend. Even as a small child. Often, when Leroy had fallen asleep from too much wine, he'd sneak out of the house. He'd loved to roam the fields and woods surrounding the small frame house he grew up in, guided only by the stars, keenly aware of the other creatures keeping track of him.

Tonight's sky reminded him of those days. Those times—some good, many bad—with Leroy.

He'd left the .38 he'd taken from Isabel's cabin in the car. If he were stopped by police, carrying a gun would mean the difference between being arrested or merely sent on his way. But he did carry his knife, and before he headed for the back of the Powder Keg, he detoured to the city park. He'd formulated his plan days ago. An Indian from out of town couldn't walk into a hardware store and buy enough rope to commit a proper hanging, especially if all he had to make the purchase was a stolen credit card. Over the next few days, he'd scouted town for other options.

The children's play area in the park included climbing toys, a seesaw, and two swing sets, each housing three swings. Each rubber swing seat was suspended by a single length of rope that was threaded through the bottom of the seat and fixed on either end to the top of the swing set. Monty pulled out his knife, and with the speed of lightning, one swing fell. Then another. Then another.

Tying the ropes end to end, Monty headed back to Main Street. Hiding in the same alley, he coiled the final length of almost thirty feet over his shoulder, then, when no cars or pedestrians were in sight, he sprinted across the street and disappeared between the building that housed a row of shops, including the Powder Keg, and a barbershop that stood alone.

Back behind the building, the light from the room at the front of the second story filtered softly through the unlit room at the building's rear. It was warm tonight, and still. Like the one in front, the double-hung window stood open wide.

While the architecture and even the building materials varied from one to the next, the shops formed one continuous structure, all one story, with the exception of the gun shop. Scaling a giant oak tree whose branches brushed the far end of the single story roofline was child's play for Monty. He dropped onto the roof with little more than a dull thud, then moved with quiet grace toward the gun shop.

The night was still and quiet, with the exception of an occasional vehicle—mostly trucks—and intermittent blasts of raucousness when the doors to the diner were flung open. Monty took one long look skyward, then he stretched his arms high, reaching for the stars. For Leroy. At that moment, he could feel his father's presence, as real and powerful and comforting as the night sky. The glitter of Orion became Leroy's mischievous eyes, urging Monty on.

The gap between the single-story roofline and that of the two-story Powder Keg presented his first real challenge. Approaching the lower roof's edge, he dropped to his haunches and, cranelike, peered around

the corner of the two-story section. The window he'd seen from the
ground was beyond reach—perhaps twelve feet away. Through it, Monty
heard welcome sounds—those of a television, coming from the room at
the front.

He moved quickly, assessing his options. A rainspout ran from the
roofline of the second floor to the first with thick dark cables, most likely
telephone, running alongside it. Monty grabbed hold of the spout, testing
it for stability. It gave some, but in combination with the cables, which
were affixed to the building's siding with heavy-duty staples, it might just
do. With the rope still slung over his shoulder, he grabbed hold of the
rainspout and cables with his good hand and raised himself off the lower
roof. Pain shot through him as his right arm reached up and grabbed,
following suit. Slowly, lopsidedly, like an injured runner, he worked his
way up, the rubber bottoms of his running shoes against the horizontally
oriented siding making black tracks as he slid back down time and again.

Finally he reached the second-story roof and hoisted himself up and
over its edge, landing softly on his belly.

Jumping to his feet, Monty tied one end of the rope around the building's chimney. Then he threw the remainder of the coil over the roof's
edge and rappelled down its length, dangling over the side of the building,
until his foot found the ledge of the open window.

The moment he lowered himself inside, the smell of gunpowder—
thick and acidic—assaulted his nostrils.

The room had been filled with row upon row of boxes, stacked four
and five high. Ammunition, guns, and survival gear. 3-D, Smith & Wesson,
Colt. Handguns, rifles, night-vision goggles, and an open box of gas masks.

One corner of an NRA poster that had been taped to the wall flapped
loose, doubling over on itself and partially obscuring the message:

Preserve Our Freedom

On a metal folding chair next to the door sat an ashtray overflowing
with cigarette butts, and a spool of brown packaging twine. Empty or half-
full beer bottles lay everywhere. Several well-used guns and rifles lay
propped against walls and on top of boxes. It was clear the room housed
meetings, as well as inventory.

Enough firepower, thought Monty, to stage an uprising. Far more than
a shop that size needed.

Monty stole to the door and glanced across the narrow corridor.

After having seen Bott's portrait above the fireplace in his Magnolia
home, and then the real thing that afternoon on the sidewalk, Monty
recognized him instantly. Alistair Bott half reclined, half sat on a worn red
couch, its upholstery torn and frayed, with filthy, once-white stuffing protruding everywhere. Propped against one arm of the couch, with his right

leg extended to its other arm and the left resting on the floor, Bott faced the television, his back to the door. On the floor, next to his bare foot, lay a Glock automatic.

A sudden calm descended upon Monty as he crept forward, a length of twine stretched taut between his hands. He was completely unaware of his throbbing shoulder.

There was no fear in Monty at that moment. Only anticipation. And relief.

He stopped just inches from where Alistair sat, almost willing the other man to feel his presence.

And then, as if on cue, Bott's spine stiffened. Without turning to look, his arm shot out toward the floor, but Monty's hands had already swept down over the other man's face. They jerked back now, the twine cutting into Bott's neck as he gasped and struggled, clawing frantically at his throat and his attacker.

Monty kicked the gun, sending it spinning across the room. Expressionless, he watched Bott's terror. He took Bott just to the brink of passing out, then as his grasp on Monty's hands loosened and his head began to fall back, he let up just enough to keep his prey conscious.

Bott's head jerked sideways. At the sight of Monty, he tried to talk while gulping precious oxygen.

"My . . . wallet's . . . on . . . the . . . table."

"I don't want your fucking wallet."

The eyes grew wider, more confused. Breathing had become easier.

"Then the cash register . . . ah can open it. Ah know where Randy keeps the key."

A rage seized Monty. He jerked his hands back even more roughly this time.

Bott's fingers flew up again, wildly clutching at his neck, trying to work their way between the hemp and his flesh.

"Who are you?" he gasped. "What do you want?"

"A full confession. Nothing less. Do you hear?"

Nodding his head frantically, Bott mouthed through his spittle, "Yes, yes."

"I will kill you if you don't cooperate, do you understand?"

Again, a nod of blond curls.

And then, just as Monty relaxed his grip on the twine, the cold, unforgiving barrel of a gun dug in to the back of his skull.

"My, my," a hearty, nameless voice chortled from behind him. "It looks like we got ourselves a little war party."

THE FAIR-HAIRED GOOD looks were grossly misleading. Monty knew immediately that with the arrival of the husky blond—the shop owner he'd seen closing up earlier that evening—he was up against one ugly soul.

Bott rolled off the couch onto his knees, still clutching his throat, then rose from the floor slowly.

"This fucker about killed me, Randy," he said, his eyes wild with disbelief.

The shopowner let out another hearty laugh.

"Hell, Alistair, he was only toyin' with you. You been leadin' the soft life a little too long."

"Toying with me? The son of a bitch was strangling me."

Gun still trained on Monty, the shop owner reached out and gave him a powerful push into the center of the room.

"What do you have to say for yourself, Indian boy?"

"Fuck you." Monty glared, turning to face his captors.

"Well, well. An Indian with an attitude. We don't take too kindly to *Injuns* with attitudes up here in this neck of the woods, do we, Alistair?"

Bott had fallen back on to the couch where he continued to massage his neck, all the while glowering at Monty.

" 'Course Alistair here is new to our fair town too." The shop owner went on, clearly used to being center stage and always wearing a big, mean grin. "But it wasn't much different back where we came from, was it, Alistair?"

"No," Bott answered. "It wasn't."

"Just what do you suppose our daddies and their buddies would've done back then if an Indian with an attitude showed up in southeast Lousiana?"

Bott did not answer.

"You know, that just gave me an idea." The blue-green eyes lit up like a Christmas tree. "I think we oughta just have ourselves a little party. How's about I go make a call to a couple of the guys, have them meet us out at Turner Road, where we can do this up right?" He handed his gun— an antique Colt .45—butt first to Bott. "I hope you haven't become too citified to use this. Keep him quiet 'til I get back."

Bott nodded and took the gun. He turned it around, training it on Monty.

Monty remained standing in the middle of the room. He might be able to wrestle the gun away from Bott if he dove at him. But there was probably just as good a chance Bott would get a shot off. Either way, the shop owner would hear the scuffle downstairs and be on him in no time.

And either way, it wouldn't get Monty what he'd come for. Answers.

"Why'd you kill my father?"

The question seemed to startle Bott. After a moment, recognition lit his green, catlike eyes.

"You're Four Bear."

"Why did you kill my father?"

Bott snickered.

"So that's what this is about."

"That and other things."

"Such as?"

"The contaminated hantavirus vaccine."

"Whew, you're good. You know that?" Bott studied Monty. "Didn't I hear you're an attorney? And some kind of professor?"

"Why?" Monty pressed. "Why did you kill my father?"

"I didn't."

This had obviously become more of Bott's kind of game. A contest more mental than physical. A challenge of sorts.

"Then who did?"

"Some anvil-headed hockey player. He works for the minin' company."

Rod Sokaski.

"He said *you* killed Leroy."

Bott shook his head, grinning now.

"Maybe he's not such an anvil-head after all. No, I didn't do it. Other than the pleasure of knowing there's one less of your kind, why would I?"

"That's what I've been trying to figure out," Monty said. His eyes narrowed on Bott. "Maybe because of Isabel and me."

Bott's eyebrows shot up.

"My wife? *You* and my wife?"

"She's not your wife. Not anymore."

The attitude of detached reason had evaporated. Bott rose from the couch, an expression of disbelief and rage distorting his already sharp features.

"Are you fucking her?"

Monty did not answer. As Bott closed the distance between them, he raised the gun even with Monty's face.

"You're fucking Isabel, aren't you?"

Without waiting for an answer, he pulled back on the hammer, cocking it. He was so close Monty could see the thin line of dirt under the otherwise perfectly manicured nail on his index finger. The hand shook with Bott's fury.

"Hold on there, Alistair." The shop owner had returned. His smile indicated great amusement at what he'd just overheard. "We'll save that for the little party the boys are putting together. We leave here in half an hour."

Grabbing the gun back from Bott, he said, "Give me that. So that fancy doctor wife of yours has been sleeping with an Indian, huh? Don't that beat all? Here you went and made somethin' of yourself, got a doctor's diploma, some big house in the city, a trophy wife, and she ends up taking up with scum like him. Go figure."

Bott had begun pacing back and forth, clasping and unclasping the fingers of both hands.

"Sounds to me like you need to teach that wife of yours a lesson," Randy's goading continued. "I mean the woman's obviously a conniving slut. First she tries to destroy your career, then this. I know what I'd do if a woman of mine betrayed me like that."

The silence in the room was thick and filled with tension.

"He's already done that," Monty ventured, eyes still trained on Bott. "Haven't you? Isn't that why you contaminated the vaccine?"

Bott stopped his restless pacing and stepped face-to-face with Monty. For a moment he looked ready to throw a punch, but then, his eyes glimmering with a more powerful weapon, he began to speak.

"You want answers, do you? Why not? After all, you won't be doing much talkin' after tonight. Not after the party Randy has in mind. The same kind of parties our daddies used to throw when scum like you came through the town where we grew up. Randy's daddy here, he was an imperial wizard. Surely a liberal, educated fella like you knows what that means."

Bott's voice had slipped into a slow, backwoods drawl.

"You're right about the vaccine," he went on. "In fact, as a true gentleman, ah must give credit where credit is due. It was you who actually gave me the idea. All that material you had in your files, about how dangerous vaccines could be . . ."

"You're the one who broke into my house."

Bott chuckled now, almost a giggle.

"You thought it was WRI, didn't you? It was so perfect. Everything I did, including contaminating the vaccine with smallpox, would have been blamed on WRI. Who had a better reason to strike out at you, to want to kill all you people? They had a first right of refusal on that deposit. Kill off enough Blackfeet and it would have been theirs. If they were smart, they would have thought of it themselves.

"I'd been trying to decide how to get back at Isabel," he continued, clearly enjoying himself, "how to make her pay for what she did to me. And there it was, right in front of my eyes, in those files of yours. ImmuVac's hantavirus vaccine. What better way to make her suffer? Kill her beloved patients, and maybe, if I'm really lucky, her too."

His twisted smile indicated he knew the effect his words had on Monty, who fought to keep his expression neutral.

"It was brilliant, really. Surely you see the beauty of it. I mean, using a clinical trial to destroy her, bring her down, just like she brought me down. And wipe out you fucking redskins at the same time. And from what we've been hearing the past few days, it worked. Some of Randy's friends that live up that way say the word is that Isabel has come down with smallpox. She's dying, all alone, out in that disgusting little cabin of hers. And I have you to thank."

Something in Monty broke at that moment, but he did not flinch, did not look away. He would not give Bott the satisfaction.

"You're even sicker than she said you were," he said calmly. "I can see why you disgusted her. She told me she was repulsed by you."

"Shut the fuck up!" Bott screamed, suddenly lunging at Monty.

Monty let Bott wrestle him to the floor. It was almost like child's play. Bott knew how to use words as weapons, but he had no idea how to fight with his hands. His fists pummeled Monty without doing any damage, while above them, the smiling face of the shop owner hooted and chortled wildly.

Finally, a big, thick-wristed hand reached down and grabbed hold of Monty's hair, pulling his head sharply back. Before Monty knew what was coming, the barrel of Randy's antique gun had been shoved in his open mouth.

"I guess mebbe we don't actually have to wait for all the other fellas to start havin' ourselves a little fun," the shop owner said eagerly.

Monty saw them first, out of the corner of his eye. But Bott and his buddy were too wrapped up in their perverted game. They were caught totally off guard.

"Make one move and we'll blow both your fucking heads off."

The grip on Monty's hair loosened as Randy swiveled toward the doorway.

In it stood Clyde Birdseye and Richie Greyhorse. They were armed to the teeth.

ALISTAIR BOTT ROSE from the floor with both hands held high.

"Don't shoot," he cried.

With Randy momentarily distracted, Monty fell back, one leg twisted under him, The gun, however, was still trained on him and when Randy turned his attention back to Monty, he lifted it dead even with Monty's forehead.

"Your buddy dies with me," he declared.

Birdseye and Greyhorse froze momentarily, but Monty's bent leg shot forward, connecting with Randy's knee. There was a loud grunt, simultaneous with a shot that rang out, nicking the skin on the upper edge of Monty's ear. And then the big form of the shop owner came crashing down under the weight of Birdseye's tackle.

The tackle had stunned Randy. Monty watched as Clyde lifted the other man's head in both hands and slammed it into the hardwood floor.

Clyde was just as tall, but at least twenty pounds lighter. Still, he had one big advantage: a lifetime of anger to unleash. Randy put up a struggle, but Birdseye had more endurance, and more at stake. When the two rolled within reach of the Glock, Birdseye reached out and brought it down hard on the shop owner's skull. Instantly, the big man fell limp, lifeless.

"What the hell are you two doing here?" Monty finally asked as he watched Greyhorse grab hold of the bottom of the shop owner's boots and flip him onto his stomach.

Sitting on the floor, Clyde flashed a grin.

"Just passin' through."

"What do you mean, passing through?"

"On our way to Canada. I didn't know if you'd still be hanging around, but Troy was practically on the way, so we figured we'd try. Looks like a good thing we did."

"You can say that again. But how'd you find me? I mean, here? tonight?"

"We got here this afternoon and started askin' around. Kid down at the convenience store said you were living out of your car somewhere but you came into town just about every afternoon. We hung around there all afternoon, but you never showed up, so we checked out all the campgrounds. Found your fire pit out there near the falls. Then we headed back into town. We knew that eventually you'd show up around the gun shop. When we went around back tonight and saw the rope hanging from the roof, we figured you were probably doing something stupid, like trying to take on an armed militia singlehanded."

Monty shook his head in wonder.

"Why do you suppose I'm always getting rescued by some big ugly Indian?"

Both Clyde and Richie Greyhorse looked at each other and grinned.

"Which one of us you callin' ugly?" Greyhorse asked.

They used the rope from the playground to hogtie the shop owner and a wild-eyed Bott, who maintained a frightened silence.

"We better get them out of here. Fast," Monty said. "They've got friends waiting for them outside of town. When they don't show up, they're sure to come looking."

"What're you gonna do?" Clyde asked, turning serious brown eyes on his friend.

"Take him back to Browning," Monty said, nodding toward where Bott lay.

"Come with me, bro, to Canada. We can drop them both somewhere, leave them in the trunk of the car you're driving and call Bud to tell him where to find them."

"Nope," Monty said. "I'm taking him back home with me. I gave Bud my word."

"Don't do it, man. The feds have filed murder charges against us. Did you know that? That's why I'm going over the border. You can't go back, Monty. Come with us. You've found your man now. Bud'll make sure he pays."

"But that's it," Monty said, shaking his head. "I still don't know who killed Leroy. I don't know if he's the one."

Clyde looked long and hard at his friend.

"If you haven't got the right man now, you never will. You go back and they'll put you behind bars." He turned away, clearly anguished, then once again drilled those big, dark eyes into Monty's. "It's her, isn't it? She's the reason you're willing to take that chance."

Monty looked around him. Two bound bodies. Two of his best friends on the run to Canada.

And back home, Isabel was dying.

Clyde was right. What was there to return to?

"Isabel's a big part of it. But not all. I *have* to go back. It's my home, man. My land. My people." His eyes searched Clyde's, and then Greyhorse's, for understanding. "It's all I really have."

CHAPTER

FORTY-SEVEN

T HE BEST PART of Isabel's isolation took place while she slept.

The night Gus told her about the murder charges, she'd awakened in a sweat, thinking of Monty facing a future locked up in a cold, sterile jail cell. How could someone whose connection with the earth so defined his very being survive prison? She feared the answer to that question.

But ever since that night that she felt such deep despair, a miraculous thing had been happening. Isabel did not know where Monty's physical being might be, but when she was asleep, his spirit came to lie with her.

It had happened several times. He would stay with her while she drifted in and out of a dreamlike state. Don't leave me, she'd plead silently. But by morning, he'd be gone.

During her more conscious moments of the first night it happened, Isabel became frantic, thinking she'd developed a fever that had made her delirious. But the next morning she felt well, better than she had since going into quarantine, and she'd realized the visits were not her imagination, nor caused by febrile hallucinations.

After that she no longer feared the visits. In fact, her fear now focused on going a night without them.

This evening, Isabel finally drifted off, after watching the embers of the fire burn out, one by one.

Hours later, a wild chorus of yips and howls tugged at her consciousness, pulling her reluctantly from her sleep. Coyotes announcing a kill, calling their friends to a meal.

She hoped it wasn't the gimpy wild turkey she'd seen hopping across the meadow behind the cabin on one leg, the other dangling useless. Or a young fawn. She'd enjoyed watching several foraging in the meadow with their mothers, in the half light of each evening.

The sound, and the thoughts it evoked, made her feel terribly lonely and heartsick. She turned into her pillow, wanting to retreat back into sleep, wondering if she would ever look forward to awakening again.

"It's the full moon."

Isabel's eyes sprang open. She'd only *felt* Monty's presence during his previous nightly visits. She had never actually heard him. Or seen him. But now, the room washed by the light of the moon, she did. He was sitting on the side of her bed, smiling down at her, his hair long and loose, his face all planes and angles in the light.

"It's just the full moon," he repeated. "They're just celebrating. Don't let it make you sad."

Isabel issued a single, heart-wrenching sob and reached for him. Half expecting to find nothing but air, another sob followed when she felt Monty's cool, rough hand cup the side of her face. She turned into it hungrily, pressing it to her lips and inhaling his familiar scent of trees and wind and dried sweat.

This was no dream.

"You're all right," Monty whispered over and over as he stroked her skin. "He told me you were dying. That you'd come down with . . ."

"Oh my God," Isabel cried suddenly, interrupting him. She bolted upright. "You can't be here. I'm quarantined."

Monty tried to pull her back.

"You don't have to worry."

"Of course I do. You have to leave, Monty. Now."

"It's okay, Izzie. I've been vaccinated."

"What?"

"Bud gave me the vaccine."

"How could he? He turned it over to the CDC."

"He didn't turn it all over. He kept some, in case they refused to give it to Lucy and Marcus Freeman. He was planning to sneak it in to them at the hospital. But the doctors approved giving them the vaccine, so Bud still had some. I vaccinated myself. Just before I came out here."

"But you . . . you've always said . . ."

Monty finally succeeded in pulling her down beside him. He lifted himself onto his elbow to see her better.

"I've said and done a lot of stupid things. Nothing would have kept me away from you tonight. Vaccine or no vaccine. But I knew you wouldn't let me stay if I didn't take the shot." He smiled. He looked stronger, healthier. And peaceful. "It was a small price to pay."

"But we still don't know whether the vaccine will work."

"You haven't gotten sick yet, have you? Or Marcus and Lucy?"

"I hope you're right, but I don't want you exposed. You have to leave, Monty. We can't be certain that the vaccine protected me for another two weeks. I'll be quarantined that long."

"*We'll* be quarantined that long."

"They'll find you, Monty. The FBI will find you here. They've been here several times already, asking questions."

Monty laughed. A sound so pure and musical that Isabel's heart momentarily forgot its pain.

"They've dropped the charges, Is. Apparently WRI already has their hands full with another legal matter. A lawsuit over a cyanide spill. When they learned that their man killed Leroy, they did an about-face."

"Wait a minute. Someone from WRI killed Leroy? Bud said you went after Alistair because you thought *he* killed Leroy."

"Rod Sokaski killed him. It turned out the guard who died at the drill site that night was a good friend of Rod's. He killed Leroy to get back at me. Then he tried to make us believe Bott did it. When WRI learned the truth, they said they wanted to do the right thing. They urged the Feds not to bring charges. With all the attention their lawsuit's getting, I'm sure they decided they didn't need any more bad publicity. The guard's death and the explosion will be left to the tribal courts, Is."

"Alistair . . . ?"

"I found him."

"Is he . . . ?"

"He's in Bud's custody."

"Thank God."

Isabel had thought about it long and hard. She wanted Alistair brought to justice but she did not want him harmed. She would rather he live each day with the knowledge that he would never get his life back. That he would pay, each and every moment of each day, for the lives he had endangered. And those, like Bernice Hougham, who had died. She wanted him to pay for the fact that Isabel might be deprived of the one thing she believed she'd been born to do. Like her father before her.

Practice medicine. Here, with the people she loved. A people she now belonged to.

If she was to lose that, she wanted Alistair to pay for it dearly.

Monty reached into the back pocket of his jeans.

"I have something for you," he said, producing a folded piece of paper. "A present."

Isabel took it and slowly unfolded it. The moonlight allowed her to see that it contained a list of some sort, but she could not read it. She reached for the lamp on the table next to the bed.

The light brought the document to life.

It was printed on Harborview Medical Center stationery. Isabel's first impression proved correct. It was a list.

Still squinting from the harshness of the light in the middle of the night, she pulled the paper closer.

At the top left, the column heading read: *Dr. McLain's ER patients.*

THE LIST WAS arranged in two columns. The first listed the name and date of birth of patients. Many of the names, including that of Bernice Hougham, looked familiar to Isabel. Underneath each name was an address and telephone number.

The second column contained notes.

Isabel clamped hold of it as she read the comments addressing each patient on the list.

After the name of one, a forty-eight-year-old man whom Isabel remembered treating for a severe asthma attack, it read: *Smoker, but otherwise fits profile for asthma inhaler study.*

The next patient's name was followed by a star: *No insurance. Good candidate for cholesterol lowering.*

Her eyes scanned downward. Many stars, always noting patients who'd come to the ER uninsured.

"My God," she whispered.

"What?"

"They deliberately went after patients without insurance."

"Why would they do that?"

"Because they're the most desperate, the ones who would be the most eager to participate in a study that promises free treatment."

"Even if the drug hasn't been shown to be safe." Monty scowled. "Or even effective."

"Exactly. From what I read in that affidavit the FDA investigators showed me, Alistair downplayed any risk and exaggerated any potential benefits. And look here, look at this one. It's Bernice Hougham, the woman who died of heart failure after they'd bombarded her body with anti-hypertensive drugs."

The comments after Bernice Hougham's name read: *Already on anti-hypertensive meds and bp too high, but Ms. Hougham would be easy to recruit.*

Isabel pressed her hand to her mouth.

"Do you know why that is?" she asked Monty. "Why someone wrote that? Because she was just such a sweet, trusting soul."

They were sitting on the side of the bed. Monty wrapped both arms around her and pressed his face up against hers.

"You did nothing wrong, Isabel. Don't you see? This proves it."

Isabel turned to him.

"It does, doesn't it?"

"Look at the bottom."

Isabel hadn't even noticed yet the words at the very bottom of the page. They were so faint and difficult to read. They'd been written by hand, a note from the sender. She raised the paper to the light, but Monty took it from her.

He did not have to strain to make out what it said. He'd already done that. Many times.

Dr. Bott, he read, *I've still not received payment for the last list. AP.*

"AP," Isabel mused. "AP . . . Ariana Pitts! She worked in admissions. I saw Alistair talking to her the night Mrs. Hougham came in. Ariana would have had access to all the records."

"There's your connection. The reason so many of your ER patients ended up in Bott's studies."

Isabel sat stunned.

"This is proof. Proof I had nothing to do with it. Proof that Alistair knew he was recruiting patients who didn't belong in the studies."

A slow smile spread across her face, half joyous, but equally sad.

"I won't lose my license," she said softly. "I'll be able to clear my name . . ."

"And complete Phase III of the HantaVac study," Monty finished.

Isabel turned to stare at him, at this man who had risen like a phoenix from the ashes, bringing with him everything she cherished. The life she'd thought she lost.

He looked so incredibly noble and handsome. Like one of those chiefs her father used to show her in history books. Books about Native Americans. *Her* people.

Letting the paper fall to the floor, she pulled his lips to hers. Their kiss was sweet and tentative. The kiss of two people afraid to believe the moment was real.

"Thank you," she whispered, moving her mouth to his ear, then down his sinewy neck. Monty uttered a low groan and pulled her down on to the bed.

Isabel reached for the light, to turn it out, but his hand caught hers.

"Don't. *Please.* I need to see you."

.   .   .

THEY SLEPT WELL beyond sunrise, beyond the hour that Gus usually arrived to check in on Isabel. For some reason he hadn't come this day. Isabel suspected the moccasin telegraph had been on fire since Monty showed up at the police station, and that word of his return had reached Gus.

"Does the fact that the FBI dropped charges mean you'll go free?"

She had been perched on her elbow, watching Monty sleep, waiting for his eyes to open. Waiting to ask the question foremost on her mind.

Monty brushed the back of his hand across his dry mouth and squinted against the bright morning sun filtering through the cabin's curtains.

"No matter how you look at it," he said somberly, "I killed a man."

"But it was self-defense."

"I was in the act of committing a felony, Isabel. Self-defense may not cut it. Even in tribal courts."

"But they'll understand. They'll know that you were set up. They know what happened to Leroy and . . ."

He pressed a finger to her lips, silencing her.

"I'll accept whatever the tribal courts decide. You have to too. The whole world will be watching. The tribal court must issue a fair ruling. And that may mean I end up in prison."

Stifling a sob, Isabel pressed a hand against the fluttering that had become so familiar in her abdomen. Slowly, eyes wide, Monty reached out and placed his large hand on top of hers.

"I'll wait for you as long as I have to," she whispered through tears.

Monty drew in a deep breath of morning air. Regardless of his fate in tribal court, his eyes mirrored a peace, even joy. He studied Isabel for a good long while before speaking.

"Did I ever tell you where we got the name Four Bear?"

Even through her tears, Isabel couldn't help but laugh.

"Where did that come from?" she asked. Then she saw the serious expression on Monty's face and said, "No, you haven't."

"My grandfather," Monty began, "Leroy's father, went by the name Spoonhunter most his life. He was an amazing man, a spiritual leader for my people. He'd go up on the mountain and fast for days. This one time he was up there and he saw this grizzly mama. She comes up to him where he's sitting on this rock, and pretty soon her three little cubs come along. Three cubs. That's almost unheard of. Grandfather used to tell how they sat there with him all that night. That he spoke to them and learned from them. That they had entered his spirit and he theirs. They started calling him Four Bear after that."

Isabel searched Monty's somber eyes, trying to understand.

"Why are you telling me this now?"

"Because I was hoping you'd consider taking my name," he answered. He reached out and ran his finger along the angle of her jaw. "And I thought you might like to know."